Nights

in the Gardens

of Spain

Also by Witi Ihimaera:

NOVELS

Tangi
Whanau
The Matriarch
The Whale Rider
Bulibasha, King of the Gypsies

SHORT STORY COLLECTIONS

Pounamu Pounamu
The New Net Goes Fishing
Dear Miss Mansfield

OTHER COLLECTIONS (editor)

Into the World of Light
Te Ao Marama (Vols. 1—4)
Vision Aotearoa

NON-FICTION

The Legendary Land
Land, Sea, Sky
Masks and Mirror
Maori

WITI IHIMAERA

Nights in the Gardens of Spain

Secker &
Warburg
New Zealand

For Jessica, Olivia,
Murray
and Jane

~

First published 1995 by Secker & Warburg, an imprint of Reed Publishing
(NZ) Ltd, 39 Rawene Road, Birkenhead, Auckland 10. Associated
companies, branches and representatives throughout the world.

First published in paperback 1995

Cover and text design by Susan Johnson

Quotations in this book are from *Peter Pan* by J.M. Barrie.

ISBN 0 7900 0406 2

Printed in Australia

Contents

Nights in the Gardens of Spain takes place in Auckland in the 1990s, but some details of setting and events, in particular an account of a visit by a nuclear-powered ship, are fictional. Although some of the characters parallel people in my own life, they too are fictional.

Prologue

THE STEAM PARLOUR

1

NIGHT AND RAIN. The street is busy with buses and traffic streaming up from Queen Street. I pull the car out of the flow and across the intersection. Headlights dazzle like golden showers.

Ten minutes later, I park the car down a side alley. Get out and lock. Quick steps take me away from the rain and along the pavement, following the curved wall of glass frontages. Each window is a mirror of desire. The headlights pinion me, popping flashbulbs like a photographer leaping out of the darkness, Gotcha.

The anonymous black door to The Steam Parlour is a street-level entrance set back from the glass wall. On one side, appropriately, a pharmacy sells late-night supplies. On the other side is a menswear shop. Opposite, a twenty-four hour video rental joint. Car doors slam as young guys, whistling nonchalantly, hands in pockets, saunter in to rent the latest X-rated epic.

There is no sign on the door. Only logos which indicate that Bankcard or American Express are accepted. You have to know the door is there. Nobody goes in by accident. You go in because you want what's inside.

I push open the door. Get away from the searchlights of the traffic. Leave that other world behind.

The warmth envelops like an old friend. A brightly lit stairway leads up to a closed window hatch. There is a sign above it:

LET US STEAM CLEAN YOR BODY.

The words are large black ejaculate, and the 'u' in the 'your' is missing.

The hatch slides open. The Spaniard's face appears. He watches as I ascend. Grinning. Gold tooth flashing. Earring glittering in dyed black hair.

Waiting.

None of us who are regulars has yet worked out how The Spaniard knows when clients are coming up the stairs.

'There must be a beam when you come through the door,' The Bald One offers. The steam turbans his head. He always avoids the single red bulb in the steam room. If he sits beneath the light his pate will glow like a red beacon and put off the young hunks. First impressions are everything and baldness is not attractive currency in this world of hair, curls, moustache, chest, armpit and pubic thatch.

'Nah,' Wet Dream Walking disagrees. 'I reckon he has a sensor on the stairs.' He hunches forward, the red light limning his chest and washboard stomach. His pectorals pop like mountains in the steam. He needs no darkness to obscure any physical deficiencies, for he has none. He is an athlete of smouldering proportions, the stuff of adolescent desires, and wherever he goes both men and women follow.

Then Hope Springs Eternal says, 'Oh, chaps, we all know he does it with mirrors.'

That cracks us up. Not just because of Hope Springs Eternal's upper-class delivery but also because it could well be true. The Spaniard is suspected to be a voyeur, but aren't we all? We are fairly sure he has two-way mirrors in the cubicles, where the one on one action takes place, and in the bunk room at the back. At least, that's what we think or like to think. In this place imagination is as potent an aphrodisiac as the reality. Imagining someone looking turns us all into performers. Turns us on. Cranks up the exhibitionist nature. Makes us strut and spout.

Poor Hope Springs Eternal starts to remonstrate against our laughter. Then, good-naturedly, he flaps his hands.

'Okay, okay, you fellows know better.'

Although Hope Springs Eternal is around my age, thirty-one, he somehow seems at least ten years older. Jester to our court, he is a blind albino bat peering out from the darkest corner. Never approached for sex, he has accepted a role as onlooker. But if he takes his glasses off he won't see anything and if he leaves them on they steam up. Windscreen wipers are no solution. The onlooker who needs glasses in the steam room must be the most frustrated man in the world.

We are still laughing when, outside the door, there are sounds of footfall. Then the muted spraying sound of someone in the shower.

Of all the times at The Steam Parlour, this is the one filled with expectancy.

Who knows who will come through the door? Someone youthful, bringing hope. Someone strong, bringing power and domination. Someone handsome, someone to worship. Someone pliant, bringing succulence. Someone smiling, bringing love. Someone shining, bringing destiny.

Someone.

Anyone.

A hiss. An eddy of steam.

The door opens.

The Spaniard may grin but he never smiles. Although he knows who I am, he still checks my membership card. It is as if he has never really looked at me, looked at us. He grunts and hands me a key to a locker.

I am puzzled at the spelling error in YOR. It is totally out of character for The Spaniard. When I telephoned him, five years ago, to ask if the establishment was exclusively a steam parlour or steam parlour combined with sauna, he had replied, 'The former.'

I had almost gone somewhere else. One never expects such formality in places like this, where machismo reigns.

'I know what you're thinking,' The Spaniard says as he hands me a towel. 'Schools teach kids nothing these days.'

He jerks his head and, behind him, I see a new Young Thing. Who knows how The Spaniard finds them, these young men to hand out towels, keep the place clean and, by being decorative, titillate and titivate?

The Young Thing pretends indifference. He is wearing a cap back to front and a tee-shirt which has been carefully ripped. His jeans look as if they've been bashed to death to get the right torn and weathered look. His body language is defensive and he refuses to look me in the eye. His petulant silence says more potently than words that he is above all this. He is only doing it because it's a job. Fuck, do you think he really wants to be here? He only came because the advertisement promised good money.

His look of innocence is refreshing. Even so, there is a sensuality that marks him as being one of us.

I try to put him at ease.

'Hi,' I call.

But he ignores me. Frozen, my greeting snaps in mid-air.

'So,' I ask The Spaniard, 'what's his name?'

The Spaniard looks to heaven.

'Three guesses.'

Another Mark. Jesus.

The Spaniard presses a button. There is a buzz, the door to the right of the hatch opens and I am in.

Journeys into places like The Steam Parlour are always accompanied by diminishing light. Nothing blazes, nothing glares or explodes. Light dies here, becomes ambient. The discreet darkness hides who we are. Hides what we do. Gives us anonymity and glosses us with glamour. In the netherworlds the wattage is always way down low.

Not even low lighting, however, could ever transform the vestibule of The Steam Parlour. Like others of its kind, it exhibits wall-to-wall tackiness. On the left is a mural, presumably of a Spanish hacienda, complete with lurid red flowers suggestive of sex. On the right, a giant plastic cactus. In the middle is a bar selling watered-down beer, Coca Cola and stale potato chips. Four stools next to it are where you can catch your breath or use the telephone, and on the bar are bowls of plastic-wrapped condoms. Be careful you don't eat them with your chips.

But the vestibule at least serves its purpose. It provides a moment to get ready, to check out the scene, to pose and breathe in the heady sweet-sour smell that only places like this have. To acclimatise before moving on to the locker room. Extend your tongue and you can lick the warm sweat off the air.

Through the door to the locker room.

'Hey, man,' a voice greets me. Snake Charmer is climbing into his sweat pants. 'How ya doing?'

'Pretty good,' I answer. I look around. There are just the two of us.

'Things are slow,' Snake Charmer says.

Some nights are like this. But you can never tell. The potency of The Steam Parlour lies in its promises, the infinite possibilities. I shrug my shoulders. Begin taking off my clothes. We got it on together once, Snake Charmer and I. Now we no longer interest each other.

With some men once is enough to tell you all you need to know. There's nothing to boost you beyond the climax, as stunning as that might be, to wanting to know more — where they live, what they do, what animates them — all those curiosities which hook us into each other, which take us from anonymity to having names. After it's done, may as well shake hands.

That's not Snake Charmer's fault, nor mine. The chemistry just isn't there. Despite the intrigue and glamour of his Indian ancestry and the aromatic scent of curry in his sweat, nothing. Just skin, bone, being given sex and giving sex, and five minutes of his life and mine. That's all.

'Well,' Snake Charmer says, slamming the locker. 'See you around.'

And is gone.

Snake Charmer is right. Exit the locker room and there is hardly anyone in the space euphemistically known as the lounge, which connects to the showers and the steam room itself.

Hardly anyone except, of course, for Always A Bridesmaid and Fat Forty And A Fairy. There they languish, carefully draped in towels, staring at a dead television screen. Obviously The Spaniard hasn't hooked the latest Cadinot sexpic into the video yet. Do they ever go home? Do they ever move from this place of flickering magic?

I wave to them. We have only exchanged a few words, ever,

but I know their wit to be devastating. Once, Fat Forty And A Fairy, after a playful bout with a partner, called out, 'Thank you very much. Have a nice day. Next please.' His voice cut through the entire establishment and filled it with mirth.

I am ashamed of my attitude to them but add another prayer to my list: Thank you, Lord, for the equipment I have, but when I reach forty cut it off so it doesn't control my life.

Always A Bridesmaid smiles across the room. Like two boatmen at the River Styx, he and Fat Forty And A Fairy wave me through into the passage leading to the shower room.

There but for God go I.

The shower room is small and octagonal. In total contrast to the preceding dimness, the light is bright here, razor-like, flashing off the eight enclosing steel walls and white ceramic floor. The showers are silver stalks attached to a central pillar in the middle of the room. Each stalk is topped with a shower nozzle. A bouquet of metallic roses. Beyond is the closed wooden door unnecessarily labelled 'Steam Room'. To the left is the corridor leading to the cubicles and bunk room beyond.

Nobody is showering. I take off my towel and put it on the hanger. There are two other towels. The Spaniard hasn't done his round yet.

When I first came here and was exiting the showers, I saw that my towel was gone. I thought someone had taken it until, on subsequent visits, I caught The Spaniard removing all of them.

'The house custom,' he winked.

There is no room for coyness or embarrassment here. Seeing guys either striding or sidling back to the front desk, either swinging it left and right or cupping it in protective hands, adds to the titillation.

'Uh, you got another towel?'

You learn a lot about the guy that way. How easy he is, how comfortable or uncomfortable he is with his nudity. It's all part of the fun. And The Spaniard makes a buck fifty on every fresh towel.

Once you're in the know, however, and if you're still coy, you stash your towel in the empty rack just outside the shower room.

Move over, guys.

I step up to the shower and my reflection flashes around the entire room. Suddenly I feel alone and yearn to fill the room with other men. I try to will them to appear, all those wonderful men, laughing and shining in the glory of their years.

Most are dead now. Or dying.

Quickly, I turn on the shower, close my eyes and try to forget. Reach for the soap. There is always just the one bar of soap in the shower room. It is meant to be shared, passed from one man to another, to help start up conversation between strangers.

'Hey, have you got the soap? Great! Do you come here often?'

In all my times here I have never found the soap missing. It belongs here. To take it would be an act of selfishness. Of unsharing.

The Spaniard shows impeccable taste. The soap is fragrant, blossoming into rich lather. It is talismanic. Its magic is collected from all the bodies that have slipped it around the curve of buttock, beneath and around and along the sweetmeats of our thighs. Sharing this intimacy makes the soap sacramental. So slide it everywhere, spread the potency and add to it.

The water streams in rivulets down my face, rushing over the planes of my chest, down through the matt of pubic hair, around the tube of my cock to the testicles beneath, pouring between my thighs.

When I open my eyes again the light dazzles. And suddenly I see my naked reflection shooting off the glistening octagonal walls like a steel honeycomb. The uneven planes make my face sphinx-like, shimmering, remote. On each face is the question: What is it that walks on four legs in the morning, two legs in the heat of the noonday sun and three legs in the evening?

The shower room is the place to respond to the sphinx's age-old riddle. To say either 'Yea' or 'Nay' to desire. The creature who crawls, then strides on two legs and then on three is not only a man in his infancy, maturity and old age with walking stick. He is also man driven by sex from crawl to walk to full erection.

But one might not need to respond to desire tonight. Don't predict the auguries. They will, after all, depend on who comes bearing them.

And it is already too late to say 'No.' Muted laughter comes from behind the door of the steam room and, somewhere else, the sounds of soft sighs in the humid night. They quicken my desire to be part of the action.

So. Quickly. Five in the steam room, huh?

Turn the shower off. Nostrils flaring.

Two strides. Already, tumescence.

Into the steam room.

After midnight, and I am driving back to my flat from The Steam Parlour. But first, turn off at the motorway and travel the rain-slicked streets through Parnell to the two-storeyed house at the top of the rise. Around the corner, the wheels slipping on the steep incline, and there it is.

Silhouetted against the sky, the house is a Ship of Dreams, a galleon set full sail toward the shining star second from the right. The forward sails are luminous with the moon. The mainsails are unfurling, sprinkling stardust as they billow and swirl.

I turn off the engine and freewheel into the accustomed watching place, beneath the trees on the other side of the street.

All the lights are out.

My two princesses are asleep.

Suddenly there is a menacing movement. Adrenalin pumps my body with alarm and I am ready to leap out of the car and —

But the movement is only the wind gusting against the shutters.

Has Annabelle remembered to check the doors and windows? Has she put the safety locks on? For something wicked may come this way. Something with slavering jaws to huff and puff and blow the house in. Or something bearing a red apple poisoned to send my princesses to eternal sleep. Or something with a needle to prick their fingers. Something.

The wind comes up, swirling the midnight tides of the night universe. The sails snap and bell into fullness. The house is like a shining fairy galleon, spun of dreams and laughter, tugging at the moorings and ready to weigh anchor.

Turn the key. Start the motor.

Dear Lord protect my little ones. Always.

I close my ears to the filigree of silver laughter. As I leave, the sound of tiny bells tinkles in the wind.

Away from that Ship of Dreams.

Part One

ONE'S REAL LIFE IS OFTEN THE LIFE ONE DOES NOT LEAD

2

THE MORNING AFTER the night before and the alarm begins to ring, jangling through my dreams. It can't be six-thirty already. I open one eye and, Jesus, it's still dark outside. Maybe I'll sleep in and give the gym a miss this morning.

Yes? No. Yes? Yes?

But just as I am turning off the alarm, I catch the stern glance of Rebecca, glancing out from a photograph she gave me last week. There she watches, from the bedside table, in her school uniform, arms folded.

'No, Daddy. Get up. Even if you don't go to the gym, you still have to prepare for your ten o'clock class.'

Nine years old and already a disciplinarian. Not like the seven-year-old Miranda, in a companion photograph, dressed up as a fairy with a wand.

'You don't have to go to the gym, Daddy. I'll wave my wand and you'll be fit without any need to exercise.'

Rebecca, however, applies withering scorn. When she speaks again, it is in the voice of her mother.

'You know very well, sport, that magic doesn't work against flab. If you want to keep it off, go to the gym.'

Flab? That does it. I throw off the duvet and get out of bed. A yawn and stretch and vigorous shake of head and I am feeling a

15

little more alive. My penis is half tumid against my thigh, sleepy like I am. Wakey, wakey. A scratch, another yawn, a fondle and pat and now off to the bathroom. Splash my face with cold water.

Now, wide-eyed, I see myself in the mirror.

This Roman face, so people tell me, is strong, kind and open. I well know it can fool all of the people all of the time. Its structure takes to the camera and does not show its thirty-one years, or the person inside. Taken from the left side, it photographs as strong and chiselled. But a centimetre to the right and the chiselling is gone, replaced by flaws in the planes and a mouth that is too pronounced. That is the real me.

I suspect that if I ever met myself there would be no recognition. Sure I would find something familiar about the springing hair, the aquiline nose inherited from my father, the bits and pieces of features that together make my appearance what it is. But otherwise I would probably smile, nod and pass by, wondering where I had seen me before. Nor would I recognise what it is in me that is attractive to people. Annabelle used to say that apart from a well-put-together body, it was my sense of unbounded confidence. And sexually, I am equipped no better and no worse than most. But as I have learnt, it is not what you have but what you do with it that matters. Perhaps that is where my success lies, for as far as sex is concerned, I am unashamed.

But this I do not see in the mirror. All I see is how I present myself to my world. A tilt of face, a mask of light, a lift of eyes here, a smile of shyness there. We are people of many lives and of many faces. Compartmentalised, we allow the people in each of our lives to see only what we want them to see.

Now get outta here.

It is not yet seven, but the gym carpark is crowded. Ahead I see The Noble Savage pulling out.

'Yo, David.'

The Noble Savage is a Maori. His black hair is long and still wet from showering. Today he looks brand new, as if he has just stepped out of a Gauguin painting, straight out of Eden. Sometimes, as this morning, he wears a red flower behind his ear in unaffected delight.

My heart always leaps to see him. Activist, outspoken and out front, he commands admiration and respect for the gay Maori and Polynesians of our city. Head of a new gay tribe, his is a strong voice working with the Aids clinic, health authorities, city fathers, Prostitutes' Collective and whoever else will listen.

'We're having a meeting tonight,' he calls. 'To raise money for a Polynesian centre for young gays. Come if you can.' He zooms off.

We have always been friends but never lovers. He is out of reach. His politics make him unavailable to whites. It is bad enough to be gay in his cultural milieu, but it is doubly disempowering to have a white lover of either sex. He cannot afford an ambiguous credibility. His people have already been fucked by whites. First as imperialists. Then as second-class gays within our own white-driven gay networks. He has accepted his destiny as gay icon of Polynesia.

Into the gym. Down the hall to the men's dressing rooms. Flash my ID. Stash my towel, soap, shampoo, conditioner, hair gloss, comb, toothbrush, shaver, shaving cream and deodorant in a locker. All the cosmetic appurtenances of the modern man.

'Hi there.' Left Dress, one of the regulars.

'Hi,' I answer. 'How's life?'

Left Dress is a friendly guy with a young earnest face and clear complexion. Short, skinny and squeaky clean, he looks as if he has just walked off the set of a prime-time American sitcom.

'Fine. And yours?'

'Fine.'

At seven, conversation is absolutely minimal. Other guys at other lockers are springing out and up to the aerobics class or the circuit. Jockstraps snap, crackle and pop. We are all conserving our strength for the workout.

'Okay,' he answers. 'Hope I don't see ya.'

Left Dress works as a counsellor at the Aids clinic. Just a kid, Lord, just a kid.

Up the stairs I go to the first floor. The instructor sees me, nods, takes out my progress card and asks, 'You doing a full workout today?'

'I guess so.'

He laughs, sensing the reluctance in my voice. An hour and a half of sheer agony. The bike first. Then the rowing machine. Ten minutes on the treadmill. After that the weights and the Nautilus equipment.

'Okay, but —' He shadow-boxes around me. 'No cheating. And no shortcuts.'

I give him a look of wide-eyed innocence and touch my heart as if mortally offended. I hop onto one of the bikes.

There are two people ahead of me on the circuit. Mister Gargantua is pulling at the oars of the rowing machine. Miss Cellulite pedals in vain, dreaming of the slim girl she knows is inside her. Far beyond are the gods of the gym. The weightlifters and bodybuilders, apparitions from another planet.

Ah well. Time to pedal.

Idly at first, the pedals rotate. Then faster and faster. The body starts to heat up. The blood rushing. Yes, that's the way. Pump oxygen through all those arteries and form an army against any foreign invasion.

Down below, the aerobics class is beginning. Men and women in fluorescent leotards and tights rush through into the main gymnasium. The fluorescence moulds itself to every contour, flowing over buttocks, thighs, curve of belly in case of women and bulge of groin in case of men.

This morning the session is taken by The Black, a solo champion on the aerobics circuit and a great hit with the women.

'Are all you kids ready to sweat?' he sneers.

'Readyo yo yo yo.'

'You really want it, dontcha?' Simulating sex.

'Readyo go go go.'

'You want it fast or slow?' Grinning.

'Readyo no slow no.'

'Then start *mooovinnn*, fuckers, before I *kick ass*.'

The loudspeakers boom with a pulsating beat. The class gives a roar and, taking their lead from The Black, begins to stretch, kick, bend and lift.

'Push it, lover, push it,' The Black calls.

The pelvic thrusts are timed to the beat of the music.

'Work it, honey, work it.'

Bubble bubble, toil and trouble, bump and grind. They are all loving it. Moved by the funk. By The Black. Needing his cracks and sneers. Taking it. Faking it.

Making it.

After the workout, and now it's time for a shower. The extra half hour has made me late and I run into the guys coming down after the aerobics class. Not that I'm complaining. Being surrounded by nude males has its moments, and there is a camaraderie about having achieved a level of physical fitness. The intoxicant of the gym is that it fools us into believing it is a fountain of youth. We drink deep. We stay young. We celebrate this excitement in the steam of the shower room with elation, good humour and fun.

Somebody bumps past me with a friend. Bright Eyes. One of my students, blond curls and eyes as blue as the sky.

'Oh,' he crimsons.

I laugh and shrug my shoulders. He carries on down to the shower room. At the bottom he gives me a backward glance of surprise and grins.

Unlike The Steam Parlour the shower room at the gym has an innocent beauty. It is filled with men and boys soaping up and sluicing off, entering into or emerging out of the chrysalis of water. They bring back adolescent memories of towels flicking at bums, wet revenging wrestles over some sporting defeat, games of domination and laughter.

Not that the shower room at the gym is always entirely innocent. Although the regulars are predominantly heterosexual, some of the straight guys are outrageous. Aware of the homosexuals among them, they pout, stretch, preen, arch, pose, sulk, flash, spin, wiggle and strut through an artificial waterfall. Each one has his own technique. Like All American, for instance, who loves to hold both arms high as if doing chin-ups, the water slashing at the diadem of his groin. Or The Hulk, who likes to flex his biceps fast so that the water shoots off them like bullets. That Boy's Deformed appears simply to prefer to stand in profile so that his disproportionate penis can create maximum havoc and consternation. Big Balls habitually hunches over with buttocks upthrust, forever soaping at the dual weights between his legs, riding the froth like surf. Then there is Bionic Cock, reputed to have had a penile implant. He likes to stand feet apart, twisting his nipples, directing the flow of water onto the silicon so that it shines and expands.

Such playfulness and flirtation provoke the occasional tumescence from the helpless onlooker. But the phenomenon is accepted good-naturedly by the dudes, the pretty boys, the sportsmen and the flirts as evidence of their obvious attractiveness. As their due. All innocent fun.

Then Bright Eyes walks past. He takes off his towel. No striptease can compete with the sight of the unconscious beauty of a man who is comfortable in his skin. The shower wraps him in aquatic silk.

Above all else, the shower room is the place which provides the definitive proof that all men are *not* created equal. Clothed, you can never tell what you're getting. Unclothed, you see all. Here, silvered by falling water, you see men in all their pride, their beauty and ugliness, their variety, their collective manhood, ashamed or shameless. The family of Man in all his perfection and imperfection.

If all the sons of Adam were gathered together they would look just like they do in the shower room at the gym.

Back at home Rebecca's photo has assumed a look of smugness.

'See? Wasn't I right, Daddy?'

I blow her and Miranda a kiss. Look at my watch. If I ring I might just be able to catch them before Annabelle takes them to school. No, too late. Ah well, change into slacks, shirt and jacket. Grab at a cup of coffee and eat the leftover chicken sandwich in the refrigerator. Pick up the briefcase and head for the door. Twenty minutes drive, say, to the university, ten minutes trying to find a park. I'll just make the staff meeting.

At the last minute, I notice that the light is flashing on the answer machine:

'*Beep*. Hi —' Chris. Since I left Annabelle, Chris has become the main contender for my life. Just thinking about him makes my blood rush. He is a striking six-footer with eyes as dark green as the sea. 'I called by last night but you weren't in. Don't forget that

Petrushka opens this Friday. The performance starts at eight sharp. Your ticket will be at the box office. Come backstage afterwards. Say hello to your fat friend.'

Click.

When Beau Brummell met up with his patron, the Prince Regent, from whom he had become estranged, he scandalised the court by ignoring the royal presence. Instead, he turned to the Prince Regent's companion and asked, 'Who is your fat friend?'

Chris had cheekily asked me the same question when I undressed the first time we made love.

There is another message.

'*Beep*. When are we going to see each other again, buddy?' The Slut's voice comes laughing down the line. At the sound my palms start to sweat. 'You name the place, date and time.'

He imitates the sound of revolver shots.

'Bang, bang.'

Click.

3

AHEAD, THE HUMANITIES Department of the university. Although I leap the stairs two at a time, that still doesn't help. The staff meeting has started and, as I take a seat next to Spinster, she pinches me and hisses, 'David, you were supposed to be here to support my proposal.'

The department is restructuring and Spinster, who teaches classes in Third World writers, is trying to head off God's Gift To Woman. He is attempting a takeover of her allocated office space, arguing that an increase in the first-year rolls for American literature, his discipline, necessitates his taking over her tutorial rooms.

'So how did it go?' I ask her.

'We voted in your absence,' she answers spitefully, 'for him to have the Film Studies theatrette whenever you are not using it. Brenda has been assigned to work out an appropriate usage timetable.'

I go to remonstrate and then see the twinkle in her eye.

'Don't get your knickers in a twist. The takeover was headed off by Brian.'

'Brian?'

Head of Theatre Studies, the obvious ally, but no friend of mine. He has been trying to take Film Studies from my bailliwick for years, considering my methodology and theory highly suspect. In his estimation, the study of Bad 'B' Movies of the 1950s is not an appropriate paper for MA students. Nor the Politics of Indigenous Movie-Making.

'Brian has suggested that the department set up a subcommittee to look at the question.'

Ah yes. The subcommittee. The ever-handy academic answer to any difficult issue. Set up a group of people who hate a proposal and let them kill it by calling for studies, statistics and working parties. If you're lucky you can stonewall the proposal until way past the end of the academic year.

'I didn't realise that you and Brian had buried the hatchet,' Spinster muses.

'We haven't,' I answer. 'But when there is a threat from outside, better the devil you know.'

Not only that, but Brian's aversion to God's Gift To Woman is total. Why is it that some heterosexual men have no qualms about placing their sexual lives in the public province? Not only is God's Gift To Woman boastful, but his sexual habits leave much to be desired. I am not the only one among the staff wary of accepting any of the cakes or buns offered from his fingers at our dreadful morning teas.

The staff meeting is winding up. I must prepare for my first class in an hour: Shakespeare and Film. Across the room I see Predator, smoothing her dress and giving me the eye. She is wearing her red Fuck Me shoes.

Not today.

I edge out of my chair, ready to exit.

'Well,' I say to Spinster. 'Congratulations.'

'That's okay, David dear,' she answers. 'I'll do the same for you one day.' The smirk on her face reminds me of her acidity. If she was Cleopatra bitten by an asp, she would kill it.

No sooner am I through the door of Film Studies than Brenda, my secretary and a platinum blonde at sixty, wants a piece of me too.

'In a moment,' I tell her.

'But —'

I shut the door. I need five minutes alone.

This is my office at Film Studies. Here, five days a week, I practise my career. I am director of my own department and this is my life. I have successfully scaled the pinnacles of academia and reached the hallowed towers that spike the hills of this city. From my window, behold, there below are the commerce and port that mark the town. I guess I should be grateful that the city is prosperous but it is also streaked through with puritanism and all the meanness that marks the mercantile classes. Although it is our customer and custodian, it is also our cross. Every academic year it sends the flotsam and jetsam of its youth, those who have risen to the surface of its mediocrity, for us to temper from base metal into intellectual steel. It should have gone in for real smelting, an industry with which the city would have had more success. Yes, mercantile endeavour is what keeps the city in cash, folks. And just to make sure we remember it, the local newspaper applauds the barons of commerce, extols profitability, and who gives a damn about how it was acquired?

Mind you, the university is not exactly a model of morality. As an academic institution, our success has been based on always taking an equivocal position. The university fathers are not beyond persuasion, especially if the city fathers come across with an increased percentage of their coffers for university studies. Our cross is that we have succeeded spectacularly by adopting the lowest possible standards, sufficient to enable the children of the citizenry to succeed. The pursuit of excellence has been replaced by the exigencies of matching the pass of the student to the purse of the parent.

So don't be fooled by the ancient brick and mortar heart, the Victorian clock tower and ivy-clad historical wing. Look instead to the awful additions, the donor bequests which prove time and time again that the university fathers have given in to city goals. Thus the Sir Always Boasting About Himself commerce wing is a three-storey construction of up-to-date technology, mediocre standards but high pass rates. The Lady Wouldn't Know A Bunsen Burner If She Saw One building is a handsome science wing donated by a woman who, with its donation, bought her idiot son a professorship on the science faculty. The Lord Mayor Whose Term Was An Absolute Disaster bequest has funded an architectural school which determinedly teaches that the said Lord Mayor's town planning skills and black monolithic multi-storeyed office blocks mark him as an astounding visionary years before his time.

Among all this finery, the buildings for the Humanities — History, Geography, English, Film Studies and poor old Religious Studies and Anthropology — are not so morally dubious. Our bequests have come from the more charitable, high-minded or philanthropical institutions, like the Daughters Of Missionaries Association or the Freda Nonentity Poetry Society. Or the dreary personages who give their names to lecture series attended by the old, the gummy and the decrepit. But from the fathers of commerce? Never. The city sees little of value in that dreaded bastion of up-themselves arty farties who inhabit the Humanities, preach revolution and hand out condoms to the students.

Be that as it may, we in the Humanities continue to wear our threadbare garments with dignity.

Not that there is much dignified about Film Studies and the theatrette. We are an afterthought, an annexe to the Humanities, a large box of five rooms and the theatrette itself. I doubt that we would exist at all were it not for the bequest from the estate of a Betty Grable fan that set us up and keeps us going.

Then, all due credit to Ronald, my assistant, who has scrounged the decaying theatres of the north for screen, chairs, posters, memorabilia and, from time to time, precious copies of film from the silent era to the present. His continuing success in finding films nobody else has heard of brings a constant stream of researchers of cinema. They in turn write learned papers acknowledging us as their primary source. This in its turn has given us a reputation and access to further research funds from American sources. The occasional premiere of a newly rehabilitated print of some Laurel and Hardy film, attracting aging cinema luminaries, has not harmed our status either. Ergo, a public success which nobody in academia or the city can deny.

In all this my tenure as director has been secured by the ability to write and lecture about film in an obscure and thoroughly confusing manner. Ronald and I have a great respect for each other, as long as each of us leaves the other to his own devices.

There are only two others on the Film Studies team. Our young tutor, Stephen, and Brenda, who pounces on me again as I go to my ten o'clock class. Although the years have rolled on, Brenda still thinks she's in the 1950s. It's all Marilyn Monroe's fault. A natural brunette, Brenda changed to blonde after seeing *How To Marry a Millionaire* and has been the same ever since.

'Do you want your messages or don't you?'

Brenda affects a squeaky little girl voice, pouts and thrusts memos in my hands. I pause, taking them in. The usual inter-departmental communications, notes from hysterical students pleading for extensions on assignments, a reminder that a visiting American academic wants to look at our files on Rudall Hayward's *Rewi's Last Stand* and —

Please remind David that he is to pick up Miranda and Rebecca from his mother's today at four. He is not repeat not to take them out for pizza even if they get on their bended knees to him. Otherwise they won't eat their dinner when they get home. I will expect them back by six. Annabelle.

'Thanks,' I say to Brenda as I hurry past.

'They're such adorable girls,' Brenda replies. Her tone is accusatory. Men, hmmph.

Does she know that I have shifted out of the house? Perhaps she does. It doesn't take long for something like that to get around. No time to think about that now. My class is waiting. I open the door and there they are, eager to be taken over the rainbow and into the technicoloured land of filmdom.

'Let's get started,' I tell them. 'Today we are going to discuss the ways in which literature has been treated in film. We shall be dealing with Shakespeare's *King Lear* and how it has been approached by Richard Brook and Akira Kurosawa. Then we shall look at *Macbeth* and its various translations into film, in particular the Roman Polanski *Macbeth* and the Ken Hughes film noir *Joe MacBeth*.'

In this class the students are attentive, eager and accepting, unlike those in my usual afternoon lecture. Sometimes it happens that way. The interpersonal dynamics can make one lecture a pain and another a sheer joy. This class is one which likes to be involved in discussions, arguing concepts, interpretations and philosophies of film right up until the end of the hour.

Among them is Bright Eyes, so beautiful of spirit and physique that to look at him is to hurt. Only eleven or twelve years separate us. But was I ever so young and so much on the brink of the world?

The world is yours, Bright Eyes. Just reach out and take it, grab it all in both hands.

I begin with the argument. 'The play may be the thing but it is with film that we really catch the conscience of the King. True or false?'

Bright Eyes instantly responds to the thesis. 'True.' He gathers his argumentation, drawing particularly from Kurosawa. Catches my eye. Aquatic silk. Grins. Falters. Then continues, a brave determined voice expounding on the Japanese film director's vision.

4

THAT AFTERNOON, THERE is no answer when I ring the doorbell of my parents' home in Devonport. I go around the side and vault the fence to the back yard. Not even a yap from that excuse for a dog, the pampered poodle, given to my mother three years ago by my elder sister Pamela. But the ranchslider doors are wide open to the sun, the curtains billowing in the breeze from the sea.

'Is that you, David? Been waiting long?'

My father has come through the door, slipping out of his beach sandals. At seventy he is still a handsome devil, with the straight back and figure of a military man. His health and fitness are matters of pride with him. During the cold months he jogs morning and night. During summer he does a daily swim, ploughing vigorously to the wharf and back. He is the envy of men twenty years his junior.

'Dad,' I sigh, 'I've told you before about leaving the place with the doors open. You'll get done over one day.'

'Nonsense,' he snorts.

It's no use arguing with him. If he says something is nonsense, that is the end of the matter.

He has just come up from the beach. He wears a short robe over his swimsuit. A towel is draped over his arm. His hair is wet, slicked back. Fastidious as ever, he goes direct to the washbasket and throws the towel in.

'The children are down with your mother having a swim. Did you bring a swimsuit?'

'No.'

The beaches where I usually go are places where to wear a swimsuit is to be overdressed. Or coy. Or trespassing.

'Then take a pair of mine. In the bedroom drawer. Come to think of it, there may be a pair of yours there anyway.'

He is walking to the bathroom and doesn't see my reaction. The idea of wearing one of my father's swimsuits, pre-Speedo, does not appeal. But one of my own —

'Okay.'

From the master bedroom there is a panoramic view of this fashionable beach suburb here on the northern shore of the city. Prices for real estate have shot up since my parents first retired here seventeen years ago. Ever since, they have credited their good luck and sense.

The suburb itself is a few kilometres from the city, on the peninsula. It is an isthmus away, across the harbour bridge with its two-lane extension, dubbed the 'Nippon clip-on' because it was designed by Japanese engineers. My parents were among the first to build in what has, over the years, become progressively known by the property developers as the 'undeveloped' end of the peninsula. However, six years ago the *nouveaux riches* discovered the area and began to build palatial homes at midway or towards the boutique end, where the new tourist complex and yacht marina now stand.

The new rich have put increasing pressure on my parents and their neighbours to sell. But the older retired folk are all very happy with where they are, thank you very much. They like to think they represent a certain stability and tradition in the city. They consider themselves a bastion against the appalling consequences of the technological revolution and spread of McDonald's, Pizza Hut and other American fast-food chains. They represent good old-fashioned values in a crass world, a sense of British quality and style where the values of Commonwealth can be upheld.

The retired have structured their lives against change, against the New. Their strategies involve the time-honoured rituals of a cup of tea in bed at seven. Breakfast is at eight. One reads the morning paper until nine and does a spot of housework or tinkering with the boat. Morning tea is at ten and, after that, a visit to the library or the suburban shopping centre. One has lunch at half-past twelve, after which the men play golf or tennis and the women go to bowls. Afternoon tea is served at four. A nap might be in order, then a whisky before dinner at six. One watches the television news at seven and later the best British drama or comedy. To bed by ten with a book. Perhaps bridge on Friday. Or out on the yacht on the weekends.

Not a minute is left to chance. Every hour is accounted for. Otherwise something might get in between to disrupt, to subvert, to rock the boat.

I can't find a swimsuit in my father's drawer and his have button-up flies and flaps which are definitely not my style. Oh well, I'm wearing boxers today and they will be decent enough. Now a spare robe to wear in my stroll down to the beach. Open the wardrobe. The door is inset with a full-length mirror. As it swings open, the room revolves, bringing back memories of the parental bedroom. My sister and I were teenagers when we moved here. We always held this room to be sacrosanct. Its door was always closed and its privacy respected. Everything had its ordained place in the room. The bed, probably too femininely covered for my father's tastes, with floral eiderdown and scatter cushions. My mother's vanity unit, topped with skin cream, Dior *parfumerie*, powder puff and other assorted implements of beauty to 'gild the lily', as my father would proudly say. My father's clothes brush, manicure set, tie press, box of cufflinks and collar stiffeners on the side where he sleeps. His hair brush at hand, his thinning hair his only vanity. The traditional display of silver-framed photographs: sepia of my parents on their wedding day, my sister Pamela as a baby, swathed in lace, myself with Granny Jackson; colour of Annabelle and me on our wedding day, Pamela on her trip to Greece, and the two girls paddling in the sea the year Miranda just about drowned.

Whenever my mother was cross with my father she would retire to this bedroom and shut the door. If ever she had a headache the same convention would be followed. Mother always retired before Dad. Some sense of refinement, of delicacy was at work here, as if it was expected that women needed more time than men to prepare for bed. When we were in bed my father would check the house, cough, and himself go to bed. There is a poignancy, an old-fashionedness about their marriage, redolent of another time when passions were less heated and more innocent.

'You found a pair? No? Oh, you'll wear your boxers? Good.'

My father is there at the doorway, towelling his hair. His eyes show pleasure that he has such a well-formed son.

'See you later,' I say.

But his eyes flicker, bidding me stay a moment longer. When the words come they are as I would have expected. Thought out. Considered. Measured.

'We haven't seen Annabelle out here for a month or so. Whenever we telephone she seems happy to hear from us but she always says she's too busy to see us. Perhaps you might like to talk about it when you get back.' Oblique but firm. So. It had to happen. 'Your mother and I know something's wrong between you both but one never comes between a man and his wife. However, this afternoon when we were giving the girls a drink Miranda said something about your not living at home. Best if you were to tell us about it, son.'

'Dad, I —'

'No. When you return from the beach.'

The pathway to the beach is busy with schoolchildren rushing down for a swim. There is something about breeding and social standing which sets apart the children of the privileged. Finer boned and longer limbed, they replicate the grooming and sleek racehorse physicality of their class.

'Is that you, David?' Mrs Stockbroker and her husband, The Retired Stockbroker, are coming up the path. They live next door to my parents. 'Is Annabelle with you? No? The children are down with your mother by the Crocodile's Tail. They're simply gorgeous, my dear. Simply delightful.'

I wave in reply and hurry on down. The entire neighbourhood is besotted with the girls, who are the youngest children in the street. Already amid the shouts and yells of other older children I recognise the high, squealed commands of Rebecca and special piping sounds of Miranda. Then the beach comes into view and I see them.

The scene is pure picture postcard. Flame-petalled trees overhang the beach. Brightly coloured umbrellas spike the sand. Older children are launching their dinghies while grandparents watch. The sand is a golden dream curving around an impossibly azure sea. It is low tide and the rocks that have been dubbed the Crocodile's Tail ever since children of imagination began to swim here are exposed.

Rebecca is towing Miranda, in waterwings, toward the crocodile's jaw. Charmed, the retired on the beach watch with affection.

'I'm frightened, Becca, I'm frightened!' Miranda cries.

'Oh don't be such a wimp, Miranda,' Rebecca replies.

'But I'll drown.'

'No you won't.'

'It's such a long way to swim.'

'Don't you trust me to get us there? Just hold on tight, okay?'

When they make it, there is scattered applause from the beach. Rebecca makes a face and pulls her sister to safety.

My mother is sitting under a beach umbrella, the pampered poodle beside her, watching the girls as they clamber to the top of the Crocodile's Tail and claim it. She has sunglasses against the glare and is smoking a cigarette. She sees me approaching through the groups of sunbathers and children building sandcastles, and hastily stubs the cigarette in the sand.

'Hello, darling,' she says as I sit beside her.

She is a marvellously preserved woman who bears her years lightly. Her skin is slightly veiled with moisturiser but still has the sheen of vigour. She carries the signs of sixty-five years as does a vintage car — with grace.

Today, though, her nervousness makes her graceless.

'You don't have to hide your cigarette,' I answer.

'It's your father,' she says. 'He never likes me to smoke in the house. It's absolute agony waiting for him to go up from the beach so that I can light up.'

Her answer is evasive and she does not look at me. She takes another cigarette out of her beach bag. Her fingers shake as she lights the cigarette, inhales and breathes out the smoke.

'I know cigarettes are bad for me,' she says, 'but I just can't seem to give them up. The ones I buy have low tar, see? Are you going in? The water is lovely.'

She has not yet offered her cheek for my usual filial sign of affection. When I lean towards her she moves away.

'Go on now. Before the water gets too cold.'

My little princesses haven't noticed that I have arrived. I shall slip into the water, swim out to the open sea and sneak up on them from the other side of the Crocodile's Tail.

The water is liquid bliss. A quick duck of my head and I am totally immersed, body temperature taking on the sea's coolness. Then swift strokes seaward, careful not to be run down by the children's yachts whizzing out from the beach, around the lashing tail of the crocodile. There they are. In unguarded innocence. They have come down from the top and are entering the water again, ready for the perilous journey back to the beach.

'I can't do it, Becca!' Whimpering, Miranda slips into the sea and, straight away, begins a furious dogpaddle to the safety of the beach. 'Help me, Becca! Help me!'

Rebecca sighs and starts to push her sister, waterwings and all, through the water. 'See?' Rebecca says. 'As easy as pie.'

I go in for the attack. Underneath the water I can see pale legs just ready to be grabbed and eaten. I hold Miranda's left foot as she swims. She squeals and kicks out.

'Becca! A shark!'

'Nonsense,' Rebecca answers.

I hold one of her feet as well. Suddenly both girls are screaming for help.

'Grandma! Grandma! Save us!'

But my little princesses are too late. The Great White Pointer surfaces, has them by his teeth and is savaging them, gulp by bone-cracking gulp, tearing legs and arms from torsos, heads from bodies, oblivious of their cries of terror.

Then Rebecca says, firmly, 'That's enough, Daddy,' and the spell is broken. 'You mustn't do that to us, especially Miranda.'

Miranda is an asthmatic. Her attacks come randomly but she has an inhaler.

'Hello, Daddy,' Miranda sighs. She puts her arms around my neck, a wet bundle of curls and softness. 'It was you all along, wasn't it?'

Rebecca looks at her. 'Of course it was, silly. Anybody could see that.' Tenderly, she hugs me too.

Up on the beach my mother is shaking to pieces. She is breaking apart, her sunglasses flashing in the sun. Behind them her eyes are smoky, ablaze with fear and anger.

The girls run ahead with the pampered poodle and, by the time my mother and I arrive at the house they are already in the shower together. As usual, they argue over whether the water is too hot or too cold. When they get out my mother wraps them in towels and gives them a good rub-down. Then it's juice and biscuits, and they settle down to watch afternoon children's television.

My mother makes afternoon tea. We take it on the terrace. After idle small-talk, my father coughs and nods at me.

That is when I tell them that I have been living apart from Annabelle for some six weeks. Yes, I have taken a flat in the city. Yes, I will leave my new telephone number and am sorry that I haven't given it to them before now. No, I'm not sure if we'll get back together again. That is up to Annabelle.

My parents want to believe the best in me. They settle for the usual sympathies. These things happen. It may blow over. It will all come out in the wash. There are always occasional problems between a wife and a husband. It takes time before a marriage settles down.

Yes.

Clink of teacups.

Pity.

But it is not up to Annabelle, and because I crave my parents' respect and love, I just cannot tell them why I have left.

Oh yes, I could obscure the real facts by saying that the separation was something I had to do. I could say something to the effect that I had to work things out. Or that I had to find out who I was and what I wanted out of life. I could hide behind polite language.

But I would bring my parents' world crashing down around their ears, harbour bridge, suburbia, Uncle Tom Cobbleigh and all.

Behind the small-talk, fear.

5

BEFORE I GO any further I must describe Annabelle to you. I must make sure you have a fair and honest impression of her. I loved her once. I still love her. She has intelligence, beauty, strength and passion, and I could have chosen no better woman to be my wife and the mother of our children.

We bowed to each other most beautifully. I wanted to know what her name was and she told me. It was a sweet name. What's yours? she asked. Then, Where do you live?

I smiled. Second turn to the right and then straight on till morning, I said.

I was twenty, in my third year at university, and Annabelle was eighteen, when she came running into my life. That was eleven years ago. She looked like a young Emma Thompson. There was laughter spilling from her lips and long unruly blonde hair flying over her face.

We met during Capping Week. I belonged to a senior debating team. One day we received a formal letter from a first-year student group who charged us with being puffed-up and pompous and challenged us to defend our honour, not in a debate but in a Saturday cricket match. Being serious, we dressed for the occasion in our usual flannels and gear. When our opponents turned up, hanging out of two cars, we were stunned. All were women. What's more, they were dressed in feather boas and slit skirts, and sported an assortment of baseball bats, tennis racquets, hockey sticks and kitchen stirring equipment.

The effrontery of it astounded us all, for cricket was not to be made fun of. One of our number, Son Of The Lord High

Executioner, immediately demanded that the match be cancelled. There were hoots of laughter and glee from the sideline.

'Oh you *are* puffed-up and pompous, the lot of you,' someone shouted.

'One up to us!' It was Annabelle. She sought support from the sideline spectators.

'What say you all?'

'Hear hear! Hear hear!'

Then she turned to us with a twinkle in her eyes. 'Well, gentlemen, you are already down. Do you wish to play?'

Naturally, after that, we had to agree to proceed. We therefore took the toss and Annabelle's team elected to bat. They had lulled us into complacency and good humour and, by their dress, gave all the appearances of never having held a willow in their hands. They retired to the dressing rooms, and when they came out again they were padded and ready.

We were thoroughly trounced.

Little had we known that we were playing the top women's cricket team in the city. Annabelle was their captain and they hit fours galore. Not only that, but when it came to bowling, Annabelle had a mean spin. I wasn't going to let her bowl me out so easily though and we had a battle of wills on the pitch. Then she disarmed me totally.

'Listen, sport,' she winked. 'I've got a date in an hour and I haven't washed my hair. It takes an awfully long time to dry. Be a good boy and let me take your wicket?'

Then she went back, did her run up and:

'LBW!' she called.

She always thought I threw the game just for her. The truth is that she got me out fair and square.

You can still see this sense of fun, of the spirited trickster, in the photographs of Annabelle before we were married. Here she is mugging with friends out on the town. Here again, playing touch rugby with the boys next door — she herself was an only child. Here she is as a demure débutante, lifting her dress to reveal the red garter around her left thigh. This is the one the girls laugh over: their mother is the back end of the horse at a masquerade party. They also like the one of Annabelle crossing her eyes during the formal photograph taken at her graduation.

But the one they love best is the large photograph in the golden frame. Every family at some time or another enshrines itself in such a show of love and togetherness. This one was the result of a photographic session underneath the apple tree in our back yard. Annabelle and I are sitting in the dappled shadows opposite each other, laughing. Annabelle is a blue-eyed ash blonde in her late twenties, and her eyes sparkle with merriment. She is wearing an apricot silk blouse pinned at the neck with a ruby brooch and has a striking, womanly appeal. She is pointing at something.

The two girls are sitting in front of us, within the safe haven of lap and bended knee. They too are laughing, and are looking at the place where Annabelle is pointing. I think this is why Rebecca loves the photograph so much. We are playing Happy Family, Rebecca's favourite game.

The reason we are laughing is that Annabelle had hated the whole business of having the photograph taken at all. It was so middle-class to be sitting there, in our Sunday best, under an apple tree, of all icons. Then right in the middle of her grumpiness a bird, hidden in the branches of the tree, agreed with her and shat on my head.

Annabelle is not just a woman of beauty. Above all else she is animated by goodness. This is the quality that the photograph presents. Her animation brings light to her eyes and laughter to her lips. It is more precious and more lasting than the most flawless skin. Without it the face is a mere mask.

It was Rebecca's idea to bring the photograph over to the flat when I left them and moved out. Annabelle found her perched on a chair taking the photograph down from its usual place on the sitting room mantelpiece. Miranda was an accomplice, sitting gravely to one side.

'We're taking this over to Daddy,' Rebecca had said. 'Would you drive us there please?'

Annabelle had waited in the car, moody in dark glasses, while the girls came in. They walked past me, looked around the flat, and then Rebecca asked Miranda, 'Where do you think we should put it?'

Miranda pointed to the sideboard in the dining room. 'Just so you don't forget, Daddy,' she said.

I went with them to the front door, gave them a hug and watched as they clambered into the car. Just before they sped away Miranda waved her silly wand:

Abracadabra.

As if I could ever forget.

When Annabelle came into my life she didn't know that I had already had sex with men and that, in fact, most of my sexual experiences had been anonymous bouts with men. But my first sex had been with women and that, I felt, meant that I was heterosexual and that sex with men was just a phase. I was often astonished that I could give pleasure to both without being too conscience-stricken. My body had a mind of its own and was easily aroused by the touch of skin. Any skin. It reacted the same with a woman as with a man. My helpless, mounting erection wished only to find blind completion in another person.

But that was all before I met Charles, The Love Of My Life. He divined my secret. When having sex with a man I would put a wall up between the physical act and emotional involvement. Charles brought that wall down and made me love him. Until then I had refused any notion that sex with a man could lead to loving him. One could have sex with a man, yes, but one should love only a woman. Besides, I wanted to conform and to pass through heterosexual adolescence to the next plane — courtship, marriage and fatherhood. I felt that with the right woman I could give up men and become a responsible, contributing citizen. I wanted a brilliant career and to settle down.

Following that Capping Week cricket match, it was impossible not to notice Annabelle on campus. She was a laughing, carefree, spirited presence glimpsed with friends on her way to lectures. Or squirting tomato sauce into an unsuspecting boyfriend's cream bun and playing other practical jokes in the cafeteria. Or turning up in rugby jersey and gear, jug of foaming beer in hand, at one of the macho engineering students' hops.

There was a serious side to her too. In her second year she found her feminist voice. She spoke out during a rally on violence against women and called all engineering students rapists. When they pelted her with eggs she responded in kind, except that hers were very, very rotten, carrying a stench that lasted for days. I suspect she went through a brief lesbian phase but, after all, university was the place to find out and experiment.

At the time I was dating Corinne, Annabelle was dating a guy named Steve. Then Corinne and I split up after an argument about something or other. That left me hanging loose and, one night, Annabelle literally fell into my arms.

I was walking home from a student party. I happened to look across the street and caught sight of a woman in a red dress climbing out a third-floor window of one of the university men's hostels. She saw me and, putting her fingers in her mouth, whistled for my attention.

I was drunk and wasn't really too sure whether I was dreaming or not. But no, the woman was real. The woman was Annabelle. I crossed the street and peered up at her.

'What the hell are you doing up there!'

'What do you think it looks like, you bloody fool,' she answered. 'I'm trying to get down, of course. The hostel master's on the prowl.'

A half-naked young man appeared at the window and attempted to drag her back in.

'Oh no you don't, Stephen,' Annabelle hissed. 'I've just about had enough of you. Good*bye*.'

She kicked him like a football and he disappeared with a clunk. She pushed away a wing of her hair and glared down at me.

'Well, don't just stand there. Do something useful!'

You can never find a ladder when you want one, but I managed to direct her across the roof to a rickety fire escape. I was laughing so much because as she crawled and crept along she was muttering imprecations of the foulest kind.

'What's so funny!' she called. 'Here! Hold these!'

She threw her high heels at me and nodded, satisfied, when one of them hit the target and I yelped. Then down she clambered, her dress hiked up around her thighs. And fell into my arms.

Did I get any thanks?

'You copped a good look, didn't you!' she muttered as she slapped me and put on her shoes. 'Men. You're all the same.' She ran quickly to her car. Hopped in. Started the motor. And roared off.

After that, what else could I do except court, woo and win Annabelle from her other suitors? I seriously believed I loved her. My heart told me so, my mind told me so, my body told me so. The words 'I love you' came so easily to my lips, and when we finally made love we fitted so well.

We went back to her place. She wanted to be in control. She said she wanted to take a shower first.

I couldn't wait.

I saw her naked shape, like a gorgeous pale mermaid, rippling in the shower box. I shucked off my clothes and joined her. She started to laugh, her eyes filling with merriment, the water showering onto the floor.

'There isn't enough room!'

'Oh yes there is,' I said hoarsely. 'I'll show you how.'

'But I'm all wet!'

She tried to get out of my arms but I twisted my body into hers, kissing her protestations to silence. The water drummed over us. My cock was already straining up, arching, trying to find a way in.

'You know what they say about saving water,' I mumbled. I kissed her neck and breasts and licked her thighs apart.

When she was ready I lifted her legs onto my waist, locked them there and —

'Listen, sport,' Annabelle said against my shoulder, 'I'm pretty flexible but I'm not a contortionist. Before we go any further, I'm telling you that there isn't enough —'

'Wanna bet?'

I pushed myself into her. Lust took over, wanting me to ride her deep and strong.

'I can just see the headlines,' Annabelle said. 'Students found naked in shower, amid broken glass.' She started to giggle.

Ah well, improvise. Flex myself and make my cock jump inside her. Flex again. And again. Again.

Annabelle's giggles stopped. She started to gasp and then to whimper, trying to move away from the slow torture of a cock that was in control. Then she changed her mind and wanted to climb higher on me. She was ready to climax but I wouldn't let her do that. I kept flexing inside her and, finally, gave her a wink.

Then her eyes widened and she sucked in her breath.

'Oh you rotten bastard,' she said as she came.

She took her revenge later, in bed, when she sat on top of me, administered her own brand of ingenuity and brought me to the brink.

Then she hopped off me and asked pleasantly, 'Would you like a cup of tea?'

Annabelle the trickster sportswoman. I chased her around the bedroom, around the dining-room table and into the kitchen.

'While we're here, we may as well put on the jug,' she said.

I caught her on the stairs. By the time we finished, the jug had boiled dry.

Despite the great sex, Annabelle didn't want any emotional commitment. Instead of seeing more of each other, we saw less. I wonder whether my frustration at her reticence had anything to do with my being so ready for such commitment when Charles, whom I met soon after, insisted on it?

I now know that Annabelle had not wanted to fall in love with anybody. She had the feeling she was falling in love with me. She made dates with other guys on campus. She kept up her busy social whirl. She fitted me into her life but kept me left of the centre. She was trying to run away. She was trying to stay in control.

Then there was Tony, a friend of hers, who tried to talk her out of any relationship with me. He had good reason to do so. He and I had had sex.

A few months later, Annabelle told me that straight after her finals she was going overseas. I asked her to marry me instead. She said, 'No.'

Two weeks before she was due to leave, Tony committed suicide. Homosexual and out of the closet, he had been unable to stand the pressure of waiting for the examination results. Despondent and depressed, he took his sleeping bag to the side of the river, lay down in it, slit his wrists and drifted into oblivion.

Annabelle was asked by his parents to give one of the eulogies at his funeral service. Her delivery was simple and sweet, but there was a strength to it too. She encouraged us to think beyond Tony's death and to commit ourselves to become what he may have become. As I watched and listened to her I thought that here was a woman who, no matter which way the world was wagging, would never give in. She was a fighter. The world would never be able to get her down. Perhaps, from Annabelle's friendship with Tony, I may have also believed that she knew about me and would be understanding. I don't know.

Annabelle left for Europe. I did not hear from her for a while. I missed her intensely and I needed her. My relationship with Charles came to an end. I was so lonely. God, the things we do to each other.

Then one night Annabelle rang.

'Hello, sport,' she said. Her voice was soft and as sad as a dream. 'Do you still want to marry me?'

My heart leapt over the moon.

'Yes,' I said.

'Good,' she answered, 'because no matter how hard I've tried I love you, dammit.'

And so she came home. We were married soon after. On our wedding night she asked me to come to bed in silk pyjamas she had bought especially. She had sewn up the fly and there was no way out except down a trouser leg.

We managed to solve the problem.

Our marriage was supposed to save me. Both sets of parents and family were delighted at the joining of our two houses. In the business of building a nest and having children I relied on natural instinct and bonding to take me away from that Other Life. Ours was a match to delight the augurs and fill the air with zephyr breezes.

Rebecca was born by caesarean section during my first year as junior lecturer in the Humanities Department. Holding that bundle of squealing helplessness in my arms swept me away on a tide of gratitude and shame. I felt that I did not deserve such joy.

Two years later Miranda was born, the giggling funster of our household, carrying on her mother's tradition. By that time Film Studies had been established and I rocketed to the top of the academic totem when I beat out all other contenders for the directorship.

We bought The House On The Hill.

The only sadness to blight our lives was the death of Annabelle's parents in a car accident soon after Miranda's birth. At the graveside Annabelle looked at me with misted eyes.

'I have nobody else now except you.'

Now, even I am no longer hers.

I sometimes ask myself whether it was a mistake for me to marry Annabelle. Sometimes, in my darkest nights, I regret that I have turned our princesses into victims. I had seen Annabelle as a means of my salvation. She was supposed to be the prop for my conventional life.

But the question is academic now, and from our marriage have come two daughters. They are here, they are passionately loved, and they continue to be the most important people in our lives.

On the first night in the new house it seemed that all the stars were out. We were holding the girls and looking at that blazing night sky. I whispered a promise to them, saying, 'See, my darlings? That bright star second from the right? This is our Ship of Dreams, and that is where it is pointed. Always at that shining star.'

Once upon a time there was a Handsome Prince called David who had everything that anybody could wish for: looks, money, prospects. Well loved by family and friends, he sought, wooed, competed for and won the hand of the beautiful Princess Annabelle. All the bells in the kingdom pealed out on their wedding day. They loved each other and had two pretty daughters, Rebecca and Miranda.

They were supposed to live Happily Ever After.

6

THREE MINUTES PAST six, and the girls are giving me the silent treatment all the way home from my parents' house in Suburbia By The Sea. I stop the car outside the two-storeyed House on the Hill where the girls and Annabelle live. As we unbuckle and get out, the front door opens. Annabelle is lovely, wearing a high-neck cream turtle sweater and blue jeans. She leans on the door jamb and contemplates us as we cross the street to her. A lock of blonde hair falls over her eyes as she wags a finger at the girls. As yet she hasn't looked at me.

'You girls are late,' she says.

Miranda calls out, 'Daddy wouldn't let us have a pizza.'

Big bad Daddy.

Miranda runs through the gate towards her mother, who suddenly whips a water pistol from behind her back and squirts water at her and Rebecca. The girls halt, astonished. Then:

'Mum-*mee*!'

The girls yelp and scream with laughter. Annabelle keeps on squirting at them as they run past her and up the stairs to their bedroom. She chases behind them and I hear doors slam. Then, laughing to herself, Annabelle comes down the stairs and confronts me at the doorway. She looks at me thoughtfully. Tilts her head to one side. Her blue eyes are cloudy and deep. She brings her water pistol up. Squints. Aims. Pulls the trigger. Lets me have it between the eyes.

'Hello, sport,' she says. 'You can come in if you like.'

We are in the kitchen and Annabelle is about to dish out a

macaroni and salad meal for the girls.

All of a sudden, Miranda yells, 'Mummy! I can't find my wand.'

Annabelle grits her teeth and gives me an irritated look.

'Ever since you made that wand for Miranda it's been the bane of my life,' she says. 'She wants to take the silly thing everywhere with her.' She calls up the stairs. Sweetly. 'Have you found it where you put it?'

'You've moved it, Mummy. You've —' A cry of joy. 'Here it is! Here it is!'

Miranda comes to the banister and looks down at us. Rebecca joins her, grinning. Miranda looks at her and Rebecca nods. Miranda waves her wand, a wooden rod with a sparkly star at one end, its stem wrapped in rainbow cellophane, and spreads fairy dust over us.

'Daddy's staying for tea,' Rebecca says to Annabelle.

Annabelle stiffens.

'No, darlings,' I answer. 'I've got a heap of work waiting to do and —'

'Please, Mummy,' Rebecca asks.

Annabelle nods. Then, 'That child has got to stop blackmailing me like this,' she says. Not to me. To herself.

The girls come tumbling down the stairs and into our arms. Full of self-importance, Rebecca sets the table and takes me to my accustomed place at the head of it. Annabelle serves the meal, a spicy Italian dish, sits opposite me and watches the girls as they begin to eat.

'Mmm, this macaroni is delicious, Mummy,' Rebecca says, her face brimming with hope.

'You hate macaroni,' Annabelle replies.

'Not all the time!' Rebecca turns to me. 'Isn't it delicious, Daddy?'

We begin the desperate game of Happy Family.

The daylight is waning. Dinner is over and the girls are upstairs getting ready for bed. Annabelle is pouring tea in the lounge. The air crackles now that we are no longer diverted by the girls.

'How were your parents?' Annabelle asks.

'Fine. You know how they love their grandchildren.'

'One sugar or two? I can't seem to remember.'

'Two, thanks. It's always been two.'

'Milk?'

'You know I always have milk.'

'I never trust I know anything these days, sport.'

A clink of tea cups. The last of the sun flies out and away from the house. The lights come on in the street. Upstairs the girls are giggling.

'More tea?'

'Yes, thanks.'

'By the way, can you have the girls this Friday? A group of us are going out and I don't see why I should keep on waiting for you to come home.'

'Sorry, I can't.' Friday. The *Petrushka* premiere. 'Mum and Dad asked about us. It had to happen sooner or later. I told them I've got a separate place.'

'Oh yes. And did you tell them why?'

'No. Not yet.'

'So when will you tell them?'

'I don't know. They were pretty cut up as it was.'

'I don't want them to think it was my fault.'

'It wasn't.'

'Well will you do me a favour, David? Before you tell them could you let *me* know why?'

'You know why.'

'You left me, that's all I know. You said you were coming back. I thought we were working this all out.'

The night has fallen like a raven's wing. Hearing our raised voices the girls are silent.

'I'm really angry with you, David. It's been six weeks now. More, really. Years since we've really talked.'

'I think I'd better go.'

'That's always the way with you, isn't it? No sooner do I start raising the issue, than you try to duck out of it. Why haven't you been in touch? Is there somebody else?'

'I've been in touch.'

'You call a few telephone calls being in touch? Make more of an effort, damn you. We've got to talk about this.'

'Why?'

'Because I can't take this deceit, this wondering where I am and where I fit in your life. Wondering where the children are in your life. Don't you love them?'

'Yes, of course I do.'

It is happening all over again. Rebecca and Miranda are at the stairs. Looking down. Frightened.

'What do you want, David? What do you *want*? Do you love us?'

'Yes.'

'Do you want us in your life?'

'Yes.'

'And me?'

'Yes.'

'But not *that* way?'

'No. I don't know. Yes. No. There's another part of me that wants more.'

'Which part?'

'I'm leaving.'

'David, you can't place us on hold for ever. Life doesn't work that way. Even dogs get put out of their misery.'

'Anything you say, Annabelle, anything you say.'

Later, Annabelle and I sit silent. The stars are springing up to claim the night. Another attempt to reassemble the broken parts of our lives has failed.

Angry, Annabelle stands up. 'All I ever get from you these days is monosyllabic responses. You make me feel like an interrogator.' She calls the girls from their bedrooms. 'Darlings? Your father has to leave now.'

My nine-year-old Rebecca comes down. She asks, 'Isn't Daddy staying the night?' As if this is all Annabelle's fault.

'No, darling,' Annabelle says. Her voice is firm, passionate, raised, then recovering. Rebecca flinches.

Then Miranda is there, seven years of joy, jumping up into my arms. 'Will we see you again soon?'

My absence has become so much a pattern of her life that she regards this as normal.

'I'll arrange it with your mother,' I answer.

Already the girls have become the intermediaries in the conversations between their parents.

'Goodnight, Annabelle.'

A nod. Eyes locked on mine.

'Goodnight, my darlings.'

'Night, Daddy.'

I walk out into the darkness. Trembling. This is the part that always makes me want to cry out with pain. The girls and Annabelle stand in the light of the front doorway. The girls look so lost, and Annabelle is holding Miranda back. Rebecca has that frightened look, What have we done, Daddy? Then Miranda starts to sob.

I am halfway to the gate when Annabelle calls, 'No, *wait*.'

She comes running towards me and I open my arms to take her into them.

'What's happening to us, sport?' she cries. 'It wasn't supposed to happen like this. To other people, yes. But not to you. Not to me. Not like this. We were going to last for ever. Don't you remember?'

She kisses me and holds me tenderly. Then wrenches away, gathers the children in her arms and takes them inside.

Part Two

SECOND STAR FROM THE RIGHT

7

AT THE FLAT. Message light flashing. Rewind the tape and listen. The Slut again. Laughing down the line.

Beep. 'Hey, buddy, you avoiding me? Let's get together for good times. You know where to find me. Meet me in The Maze. Usual time. I'll be there.'

'Bang. *Bang.*'

Click.

There are three places in this city where I like to find sex after midnight. The first is The Steam Parlour. The second is The Fuck Palace. The third is The Maze.

Around this threesome there are the other establishments. The bars with their members-only Jack Off clubs. The X-rated gay cinema in the sleazy downtown area by the dock. Handcuffs (the S&M bar), Cowboys (the leather bar), the Powder Puff (the transvestite bar), Fa'a-afine (the Polynesian bar), The Tool Room, the two lesbian bars and the gay pubs. Two dance clubs close at three in the morning. So does the Muscle Gym with its small pool. Those who have not scored at The Teps go there when that piece of Victoriana closes at ten.

For those who still cruise them, there are The Bogs in the three public parks. Or you can always pick up the occasional nightwalker, backpacker or student walking the street.

Even the suburbs of this city have their delights. The most innocuous neighbourhood sauna can change overnight into one which swings both ways. In some of the high-class houses are the leather- and silver-studded Queens Of The Night. They are sleak and sinister *maîtresses*. Satanic goddesses of bondage and discipline. The whip women. The steel high-heeled dominatrix.

Tonight, The Fuck Palace. At the corner a couple of trade stand in poses of provocation. Their faces flare in the light of the eternal match.

'You got the time, bud?'

In front, streetkids play the video games, the machines stacked along the street. As I pass they look at each other and roll their eyes. Another fruit, another homo. Whizz bang kapow. The evil starvaders keep coming row on row down the video screen. Blast the fuckers out of space before they get ya. Spray them to stellar smithereens. Bam. Bam. *Bam*.

In The Fuck Palace are lots of men. The place is a shadowy version of Xanadu in the film *Citizen Kane*, with men slipping in and out of the sauna. But supermarket sex is not what I want tonight. Choose from the shelf. Each item has a Use By date.

Onward to The Steam Parlour.

We are all looking for Rosebud.

No sooner do I enter than The Spaniard's face appears above me. He grins. Waiting.

Up the stairs. Cross The Spaniard's palm with silver.

'A better night tonight,' he says as he hands me a towel.

In the painted vestibule are two pretty boy cowboys, one in red checked shirt and the other in suede leather jacket. Hunched over drinks and smoking. Eyes hooded in the dark. I go past them into the locker room. Begin stashing my gear.

The cowboys look at each other.

Nod.

Of all the rooms in The Steam Parlour, the locker room is the one that has changed the most since I first started coming here. All the locker rooms, everywhere in our world, are like this now.

The huge red words. WARNING. ACHTUNG. PRACTISE SAFE SEX. The big white posters. STOP. DON'T FUCK

WITHOUT A CONDOM. NICHT. NEIN. VERBOTEN.

Some of the posters are cutesy like the Cuzzie Bro Cock pulling a raincoat over himself: WRAP YOURSELF UP. Some are sassy like the two gorgeous bodybuilders smiling out at you and promising Paradise only if it comes packaged in plastic (but one of the bodybuilders is dead already, graphic proof that AIDS KILLS). A few are serious like the Grim Reaper scything away at sweet young things. DON'T END UP DEAD.

Sandwiched between the posters are the helpful hints. CONDOMS AT DESK. Or AIDS HOTLINE TEL: 3238 995. Or IT'S BEST TO TAKE THE TEST. The warnings have invaded the toilets too. You can't even go to the john without some reminder that IF IN DOUBT SAY NO.

But that's the way it is. Our kind is dying. Say a prayer for them. Say a prayer for me. Light a candle for our helplessness in the face of this compulsion.

SO MANY MEN, SO LITTLE TIME.

And if we are wilful and forgetful of the warnings? Ah hell, you can get killed just crossing from one side of the street to the other anyway.

SHINE ON, YOU CRAZY DIAMOND.

I am slipping out of my jeans when the cowboys from the foyer come in to join me. We look each other in the eyes. Size each other up. Hold the glances. The one in the red checked shirt wipes a hand across his lips. Sniffs.

The cowboys start undressing. Nobody speaks. The air is swollen with meaning. There is no need to talk, for the language here is almost exclusively physical. The accidental look as the one in the leather jacket bends to take off his boots. The bits and pieces of body shown as he stands and runs his fingers through his hair. Cheekbones. Vein pulsing on the neck. Eyes veiled by lashes. Undraping of pectorals from sweatshirt, releasing ripples of light. The red plum of a nipple, edible and ready to be tongued from the chest.

His partner, the one in the red checked shirt, is slower to undress. Fingers unbuckling a belt. The look again as jeans are slid from hips. That delicious arch of the buttocks to get the pants over the satin globes and down. In the ambient light a smooth alabaster

51

thigh, flexing. Something stirring and springing free as jockeys are slipped off, pulsing, drinking in the air. A dazzle of golden fleece. That moment of exposure, before the tucking in of the towel, which tells all. Whether the guy gives it or takes it.

Strength and vulnerability is more potent in the isolation of parts, the slow revelations of this or that. Together they are like pieces of an alphabet waiting to be locked into a sentence, a phrase, an exclamation, a gasp, by the fusing touch of another.

Another look my way and the cowboys exit into the lounge. I yank my clothes off. Nipples already stiffening in anticipation. Slip out of the underpants, give Johnny Boy a tweak and a couple of pulls to lengthen him. Let's get out of the Warning Zone.

THIS WAY TO PARADISE.

In the blue-lit television room, I pay my dues to the eternal boatmen, Always A Bridesmaid and Fat Forty And A Fairy. The two cowboys exchange glances and give me that look again. Always A Bridesmaid finds the situation irresistible and begins to whistle the theme from *The Lone Ranger*, alias the 'William Tell Overture'. As I pass by he whispers, 'Heigh ho, Silver —'

I grin and walk to the shower room. Take off my towel.

The Spaniard's towels are always white. If I press my nose into my towel and breathe deep, I can smell the other countless men who have used it before me. Big men, wiping themselves off, rasping the towel across their shoulders. Hunky men, flaying the towel across thighs and into the sweet crevices. Yuppie men, towelling armpits and chests, working the towel down, in and out, backwards and forwards. Laughing men. Chatting men. Erect men. Hungry men. Innocent men. Sated men.

As I am showering I hear the hiss of other showers being turned on. Through the spray I see the cowboys have joined me. I turn off my shower and idly look at them. One is tall and dark with hair running down to the cleft of his thighs. He is obviously the leader of the two. The other is smaller, blond and more compact. He sees me looking at him and turns his back, his buttocks clenched.

I hang up my towel. Stride into the world of steam.

Okay cowboys, follow the leader.

The red bulb is high up on the left wall of the steam room.

Around the glass the steam is a red stain like blood sprayed from an aerosol can. The spray is a suspension of tiny rubies. Further from the bulb the light becomes diffuse, less dangerous, less of a warning.

A wooden bench runs along three sides of the room. On the wall opposite the door is another, higher, bench. When the steam room is crowded there is room only to sit. But when there are few people, you can lie on your front or your back. Aficionados of the steam know that the higher bench is the one to go for. The steam is hotter, denser up there. It is a coagulate, a soup almost, nine parts water, one part body solution. All those liquids which give the body its distinct scent. You can drink in essence of man up there in that swirling broth. This must have been what it was like when God created us.

The benches also indicate what kind of sex you like, do or want. If you sit on the top bench you are a top or you want to be sucked. That is where the young hunks go, gay, bisexual, married or straight. Not into commitment, all they want is to get rid of their load and leave. In most cases it doesn't matter whose mouth does the job as long as it is moist and long in the throat.

The Bald One is known to give the best head. His main competitor is Snake Charmer, who can be top or bottom. His is a potent technique in the steam room. His Indian ancestry has given him glowing eyes which never look at the face or the body but right at the cock. I have seen a young hunk come in and sit on the high bench, unwind his eyes with interest at The Bald One but, on seeing Snake Charmer, become instantly mesmerised by his hypnotic low-cast eyes. Once the cock has been found, Snake Charmer's eyes brighten with concentration. Across the room he will send his gaze. After a minute, a twitch. Another minute, a stirring. A further minute, a sliding out from its phallic pouch. Broadening. Strengthening. Lengthening helplessly.

Then and only then will Snake Charmer stand, glide across the room to sit on the lower bench, watching the head beginning to sway and rear in that inevitable erotic dance to Snake Charmer's music. Waiting for his swift pounce and those mongoose teeth to shake, close over and swallow.

We asked Snake Charmer once, Hope Springs Eternal and I, for the secret of his success. He shrugged.

'A snake is a snake,' he said.

Poor Hope Springs Eternal. As I enter he looks up, squinting, and squeals out a broken, 'Old chap, hello.'

I nod to him, curtly, without answering. He understands and his eyes gleam in anticipation. Wet Dream Walking catches the nod and so do two others, watchers: Size Queen, with his raddled penis, and Once A Beauty, both older men who can no longer hack it in the competitive stakes.

Two steps and I am up beside Wet Dream Walking on the higher bench. He grins and slaps my palms in greeting. We settle back and wait.

The door to the room opens and, in a billow of steam, the cowboys enter. They take the lower bench and wait for their eyesight to adjust to the red darkness.

They find my eyes.

They find Wet Dream Walking beside me.

Yes, cowboys, one each. So who wants who?

Quickly, Wet Dream Walking and I get down to our sideshow. He pulls at my nipples. I pull at his. We begin to kiss, lapping each other's faces.

The cowboys cross the room. They have made their decision. When I look down, the blond has his head cradled on my left thigh, peering up and making his unspoken request. His friend is already at work on Wet Dream Walking, who breaks away from me with a gasp.

I smile with compassion.

Put both my hands around blond cowboy's head.

Give him what he wants.

In the morning, in the bathroom after a shower. I wipe the steam off the mirror so that I can see myself. I apply the shaving cream, rub it into the bristles and shave, following the contour of cheekbone and jaw. Stroke after stroke. Remembering bits and pieces of the cowboy last night. Smell of musk. Nice buns. Roll on the condom. Quick. Strong. Safe. The *coup de grâce*.

Damn, I have cut myself and blood blossoms on my chin. I staunch it, but it still bleeds. Still bleeds, ah. *Safe?*

My heart is pumping hard now and, fearful, I am peering eyes into eyes, searching the traceries of veins for any sign, any psychic hint. Extra furriness on the tongue or taste of death on the breath. Taste of his blood. Contamination. Looking down through the irises and into the red tide of my surging blood.

Lord, protect me from defects or rips in the rubber. From scratches of passion where contaminated blood might enter —

No. The bleeding begins to stop.

Mirror steaming up again. Open my mouth. Inspect. Something there on the tip of my tongue. A warning sign? Sprinkling of white like an early frost.

We are walking compendia of psychosomatic illnesses. Our fears are made up of rumours, hearsay, half rumours, folktales circulated among The Walking Well, triggered by the unusual, the slightest sign.

Frost. Tongue. Early. Blood.

When we have sex with a man, we are having sex with all the other men he has fucked with.

We dance with the man who danced with the girl who danced with the Prince of Wales.

8

WORRIED ABOUT MY sexual bout with the cowboy I diverted to see Left Dress at the Aids clinic. I expected tea and sympathy but got a lecture instead. Left Dress pushed me over the edge into self-loathing.

'Don't get me wrong,' he said, more gently. 'I'm not criticising what you are, only what you are doing. Being who you are isn't your fault.'

He pushed his wire-rimmed glasses up onto the bridge of his nose.

'There are four kinds of theories,' Left Dress said, 'explaining why we become homosexual. The first puts it down to genetic influences and, therefore, proposes that we are born this way and that there is nothing we can do about it. The second says that bio-chemical influences and the balances and levels of hormones are responsible. This presumes that if we rectify the balance we can become heterosexual. The third involves psychoanalytic theories, mainly that homosexuality arises from an arrested or distorted psychosexual development due to disturbed relationships with one or both parents —'

I looked at him askance. My mother would definitely not like *that* one.

'The fourth proposes that homosexuality is, like other behaviour, learned and not instinctive. Both its origins and continuance may be reinforced positively by pleasurable homosexual experiences or negatively by the avoidance of unpleasant heterosexual experiences. The main point is that all the theories agree that homosexuality arises from factors over which the individual has no control. The homosexual condition is morally neutral. It is not deliberately chosen.'

This would be a good place to set down the details of how and when the homoerotic imagery that defined my sexual preference for men began.

I think it started when my father's younger brother came to stay. My father had taken early retirement from the military and bought a cattle farm in the South Island, where the Alps crown the land. He had been a gentleman farmer before selling up and removing us northward to Auckland and to Suburbia By The Sea.

I was six, and my uncle was in his early twenties. One night he returned from a date with a local girl. He shared my bedroom and I saw him in the lighted doorway of the bathroom, after showering, slipping his towel from his midriff before getting into his bed. His hair was still wet. His muscles rippled with light. Nipples spiked the hair of his chest. His black hair caught the light in its curls. The light showered like a waterfall into his groin. He lifted his feet beneath the sheets and, as he pulled the blanket to his chest, grinned across at me and gave a lazy stretch.

'Night, boy.'

The smell of his skin and soap tingled my nostrils. The fantasies of what my uncle may have done with his date disturbed my dreams.

But nothing really connected until the year I turned eleven, when five seasonal stockmen came to help with the high-country mustering. Hairy and Beer Gut were the experienced hands, and Curly, Blacky and Redhead were first or second year in the business. I was at school but every afternoon would run down to the cattle yards to help out. I revelled in the smell of sweating cattle, tang of horses and swirling dust. Dogs yipped, calves bawled, stockmen whistled and whips cracked. All male country.

Every hot summer's night, when the work had been done, Hairy and Beer Gut would politely decline to use my mother's shower and, instead, go down to the river with Curly, Blacky and Redhead to wash away the day's dust.

One night Hairy, who was totally bald, yelled to my father, 'We're taking the young feller down to the river with us. Okay with you, boss?'

I assumed that my father, who did not think of the farmhands as equals, would say 'No'. But he was preoccupied and waved his hand in agreement.

Apart from my father and uncle I had never been in the company of adult males. From the very beginning the evening was pure magic. It was Walt Whitman territory, with the sun glowing orange in its downward flight, sending soft rays through the willows fringing the river. We walked together down the track, Curly strumming his guitar and whistling off-key. Somewhere on the track Beer Gut laid a hand on my shoulder, pulling me into the comradeship of the quintet.

We came to the swimming hole, where the sun seemed to be flaming in the water, burnishing the surface with gold. With a whoop and yodel and a flurry of dust, Curly slipped out of his work clothes and dived into the water. As he arrowed down, his body shed its dust like a second skin and was made suddenly molten, transfigured by light. Blacky and Redhead followed quickly after. When they undressed, slipping overalls from shoulders, I was startled by the pellucid whiteness of their skin. The sun had burned everywhere else to a red crisp: face and neck, lower arms, and chest where their shirts had been unbuttoned. Elsewhere was pallor of extraordinary sensuality, like sweetest milk.

Hairy started to laugh. Beer Gut pushed me, saying, 'Off you go, young feller.'

I was shy and did not want to undress completely. But Beer Gut gave me benediction.

'You're among friends, young feller. What you've got we've seen before, eh fellers?'

So, with gratefulness, and in the presence of men, I took my clothes off and, for the first time, felt the freedom of being myself.

There was nothing sexual about that time by the river. Hairy and Beer Gut went downstream to soap up and sluice themselves under a small overhang where the water foamed and thundered. Just before he hopped into the water Beer Gut stood to piss, his pizzle dwarfed by the gargantuan belly he carried on him. He was not a pretty sight, but the act itself was so unconsciously natural, like what a child would do.

I stayed upstream at the waterhole with Blacky, Curly and Redhead. Their masculinity was overpowering. They gave me my first lesson about all men not being born equal, for Blacky was large and Curly was medium. The well-built Redhead was circumcised, like I was. But they were equal in one respect. Their mateship. Their camaraderie. Their power was in knowing the strengths each could rely upon. Coming to help a mate in difficulty. Giving up your own safety for the other man.

I was profoundly moved. In the half light of the setting sun, I watched and envied as they horsed around, diving and splashing, having swimming contests from one side of the waterhole to the other. Slapping at each other's buttocks. Diving into the depths, twisting like mermen away from each other. Curly also taught me how to dive.

'That's the way, kid,' he instructed, 'arms outstretched. Head tucked under. Like this.'

Running ahead, Curly took four steps, launched himself in a flying wedge of shoulders, chest, taut stomach, balls and cock like ungainly undercarriage to bellyflop, intentionally, into the sun.

'Come on, kid. You can do it.'

Afterwards, with congratulations ringing in my ears, Beer Gut and Blacky teamed up to show me how to defend myself.

'It's a tough world out there,' Beer Gut said. 'Some guys are bigger than you. Stronger than you. Sometimes you have to have some tricks up your sleeve.'

'For instance,' Blacky continued, 'if somebody is charging at you don't try to stop him. Use his momentum *against* him. Like this —'

He motioned Redhead to rush him. As Redhead closed, Blacky sidestepped and pushed Redhead from behind and into the river. How we all laughed!

'Another trick, kid,' Curly added. 'You can fell Goliath simply by chopping at a guy's windpipe. If a guy is trying to breathe he's in no condition to protect himself. So once he's staggering around, knee him in the balls.'

Poor Redhead, who had just clambered out of the river, saw Curly feint at his throat. He yelped, put his hands up, and with another feint Curly had him wheeling into the river again.

'Hey you fellers!' Redhead spluttered.

'And sometimes,' Beer Gut said, 'attack is the best form of defence. Especially when you're outnumbered. Always go for the leader, kid, because sometimes the others are only as strong as he is. Okay?'

'Gee, thanks.'

We sat on the riverbank in the last of the sun. My heart was bursting with companionship. Then Hairy took out a deck of cards and began to play with the others.

Of all the bodies, Redhead's was the one with unconscious mystery. I could imagine myself looking like him when I was older. In one of those unexplained reactions, his was the one that caused me to stiffen.

'Ker-rist, you've got a big one for a young feller,' Hairy laughed.

I should have been embarrassed but I wasn't.

'Know how to use it, kid?' Redhead winked.

I will remember his smile, those green eyes like the sea, the way the sun set fire to his hair, the water jewelling his body, until the day I die. It was almost perfect. But then the sun winked out above the trees.

It was Wordsworth who wrote, 'Though nothing can bring back the hour of splendour in the grass, of glory in the flower we will grieve not, rather find strength in what remains behind.'

Perhaps I have been trying to replicate that late afternoon by the river all my life. For a shining moment all the world, the river, the hillside, the stars coming up, was apparelled in simplicity and in celestial light. All the tender earth was agleam with flowers, swaying in the lunar winds, their tubular petals drinking of the lifting moon.

'Time to get this young feller back to the boss,' Curly said.

We began to dress, putting on our mortality with our clothes. Just before leaving, Redhead picked up a stone and skipped it across the river.

Skip, skip skip, and it was over.

9

A NOTE SLIPPED underneath the door of my flat.

Remember me? I am on my way home after an awful rehearsal. You are never here when I call by. Don't forget Petrushka. Say hello to your fat friend. Chris.

Also a message from Annabelle on the answerphone:

Beep. Listen, sport, I've just had a telephone call from both your parents to say how sorry they are that we have separated. Your sister has also rung. They all hope that we can work things out. Frankly, I don't feel that I should be the one to tell your parents why you moved out. After all, you're their son. I'm just the girl you married. Not that I can tell them anyway because I don't know, do I. When your father asked me the reason I told him the only one who knows is you.'

Click.

Annabelle is right, of course she is right. It is time I told her and my parents the truth, the whole truth and nothing but the truth. But must it be so soon —

Then my sister had to interpose her formidable self into the situation. She has never been a believer in waiting to be told. I knew it was her as soon as I heard the Range Rover coming along the street and braking. A series of sounds indicated that she was parking in her usual authoritative manner: pushing the rear mudguard of the car in front and reversing to bash the front mudguard of the car behind until she had made enough room to fit.

Then, clip clop clip clop. And bang bang bang on the door.

She barged in, a twinset and pearls over a piece of prime steak.

Always pushing. Always demanding. Just because she's seven years older than me. I kept on remembering how much I had always disliked her and how I wouldn't give a stuff if we never saw each other again.

Although she was roaring and coming on like a lioness I knew my sister was just a pussycat. I had to kill a pussycat once, drown it. The owl and the pussycat went to sea. The pussycat scratched me as I pushed it under the water. In a beautiful peagreen boat. The pussycat looked at me with reproachful eyes. I wanted to grab my sister by the throat and push her under too.

So I took her by the scruff of her neck. Threw her growling into the tub. Pushed her under. Held her there.

'I have sex with men.'

Defied her to conjure up images of *fag, fruit, poofter, fairy, pansy, queer, homo*, of her much-beloved young brother mincing along the street, all at her peril. And, viciously, thought:

'Now cry all you want, bitch.'

Yet, after all that, there was something about being brother and sister that was different from being a son to a parent. Something that was more accepting of each other.

We were trying to reassemble our world. Piece by piece. One careful word building on another. Putting together a new vocabulary as if we had to learn how to talk again. Then she reached over and touched me.

'You can't leave them hanging like this. Mum and Dad. Annabelle, especially. You've got to tell her. It's not fair, David.'

The body has its own language. Her touch began a physical alphabet. Indicated that an acceptance, a beginning to speech had been reached. It was then that I cried and the whole ocean in me poured over the lip of my soul.

'Oh God, I'm so frightened. I keep thinking that if I delay another day then that's another day we can go on living as if nothing has happened. But once I tell them, there will be no going back. All our lives will change. Mine, theirs, yours, everybody's. And what will happen to the girls? Dear God —'

'You must do it,' she said. 'If you love Annabelle, your daughters, everybody, you must. What you're doing is hurting them. They're in pain, David. Do you want *me* to tell them?'

I sighed. Calmed down. Said, 'No.'

'So *when* will you tell them?'

'Tomorrow. I'll ring Annabelle and then Mum and Dad. Make a time to go to see them.'

A dry touch of lips on my left cheek.

And she was gone.

Somewhere I heard a tick tock tick tock as if, just around a corner, a crocodile which had swallowed a clock was coming.

Now tomorrow has come. Tomorrow and tomorrow and tomorrow this petty world creeps on apace, and this morning I have rung Annabelle but there is no answer. I have, however, told my parents that I am coming to see them this afternoon. That's all I can do for now.

So on with the jogging shorts and out.

I alternate my mornings between gym and jogging. This morning the first ten minutes of jogging are absolute agony. Everything refuses to move in unison. My lungs are saying, No. My legs are saying, Ouch. My chest is asking, Do we have to? My head keeps on asserting the physical benefits to them all, even if grimly.

From the flat my usual course is triangular. Along the main road to the suburban shopping centre. Then cut through the traffic, through the woods past the athletic park and The Teps. Finally, back via the motorway to the bridge, up the viaduct and the main road home again. Today I duck through the morning traffic and sprint to catch the lights at the intersections. The adrenalin of beating the lights makes my heart pump.

Then, coming in the opposite direction I see the familiar figure of Italian Stallion. It was at a party at his place that I met Chris.

'Go, David, go,' he yells.

He has shining brilliantine hair and laughs as I take up his challenge. Across and against the lights, the traffic already moving, weaving this way and that like an American gridiron player. Fend off a player here. Into the gap there.

Car horns burp, outraged, and brakes squeal.

Touchdown.

'Way to go!' Italian Stallion laughs.

His running partner, Now You See It Now You Don't, catches

up with him. He offers tantalising glimpses as he lopes along. He and Italian Stallion have been together for eight years now. After such a long time together they have become joined at the hip. Although true love has never run smooth, they have proven that by triumph of tenacity and will, male to male relationships can, and do, last.

By the time I reach the third side of my triangle my blood is singing and my breath steams in the air. On mornings like this the world is re-created in all its innocence.

Two elderly Asian women are performing Tai Chi movements in the park, slow-motion beauty in the dappling sun.

Then, zooming from The Teps and an early-morning swim, is The Noble Savage. Today not a flower in his ear but a piece of lustrous green jade. His car is filled with four young Maori boys and two women.

'Kia ora, David.'

As always, my heart leaps to see him. His is a new gay tribe working to uplift the causes of all Maori and Polynesian homosexuals, bisexuals, transvestites and lesbians. They are chanting as they come forward through their own homophobic world as well as ours. They are saying to us all, gay and straight:

Move over. We're coming through.

Onward to Film Studies where, despite impending endings, the world wags on. I now know how my secretary, the beautiful Brenda, found out about Annabelle and me. She is the sister of Mrs Stockbroker who lives next to my parents in Suburbia By The Sea. Her disapproval, however, has its positive side. She leaves me alone for most of the morning. Now I can get on with preparing my second lecture in the Shakespeare and Film series, catch up on the interminable correspondence, and do a fax to a Japanese film critic, Mister Nakamichi, confirming we would be happy to have him visit.

It's no good giving the fax to Brenda to take over to the mailroom. She is on the telephone, as usual, and from her frigid back it is obvious that it is still a case of nobody at home.

On the way across the campus:

'David? Oh David.' Spinster spies me and comes running. 'I was so sorry to hear the news about you and Annabelle. Would you like to have a drink after work?'

The news? Word is getting around *very* fast. No doubt from Brenda and her big mouth.

Then Predator comes clicking along the pavement in her red Fuck Me shoes. The high heels set up an undulation which goes from toe through hip and bosom to bouncing hair. She pushes Spinster to one side with a swivel of her curvaceous hips. If I was of a suspicious nature, I would conjecture that Predator has been waiting all day for my appearance. Wearing a tight green dress slit from top to bottom and fastened at the waist by a very precarious-looking button, she is Arnold Schwarzenegger in a dress.

'David,' she husks. 'Oh you poor darling.'

Predator has been wanting to show me her negative ion generator ever since she saw me *sans* underwear in the hot pool at the head of department's Christmas party. The slings on her shoes are sliding away from her heels. She is starting to undress before my very eyes.

'Sorry, ladies, I have a class.'

Get out of there.

Thanks to Brenda, the tea and sympathy have spread like a disease among my colleagues. *Everyone* seems to know that Annabelle and the girls are living in the family house. That I have moved to a flat. That all this happened about a month ago. What they are most curious about are the underlying and immediate circumstances and *why*.

Being academics and having a predilection for analysis, the sages among my colleagues have constructed two scenarios. The first is that Annabelle has either asked me to leave or kicked me out. In the second I have walked out. The former implies that Annabelle has found something out, or that I have been caught *in flagrante delicto* elsewhere. The latter scenario is similar except that Annabelle, not me, is at fault. Bets are no doubt already being taken in the staffroom about likely situations. But I have cultivated my heterosexual image to such perfection that I doubt anyone would guess correctly. Certainly not God's Gift To Woman. Or the Hellespont Ram who teaches Greek studies and wanted Annabelle's address so that he could ring and say how sorry he was. It takes one heterosexual to know another heterosexual.

They'll all know soon enough.

Meantime, my class awaits. Bright Eyes is there to boost my spirits and take my mind off facing my parents. Shuffle shuffle, cough, scratch of pen. All the students bend except Bright Eyes who looks up and listens. I wink at him.

Aquatic silk.

'I made reference, earlier in this lecture series, to Ken Hughes' film, *Joe MacBeth*, a much-underrated rendition of the Macbeth story in a mid-50s gangland setting. It is one of the two most interesting American attempts to film *Macbeth*, the other being the Orson Welles version. In it we have the King, Macbeth, played by Paul Douglas as a gangster, and the Lady, acted by the superlative Ruth Roman, as gangster's moll. *Joe MacBeth* is film noir. It revels in portraying a world of darkness, ambiguity, a netherworld of moral corruption, of gun-toting gangster and femme fatale wrapped in fur. At any moment you may be swept up in a vortex of sordid crime. I put it to you that *Joe MacBeth*, in its translation of the Shakespearean drama into this cynical, obsessive noir setting, is as potent a rendition of the conscience of Macbeth as the original —'

After the class, conscience, conscience. Yes, light thickens and the beacon that doth eternally course the heavens is spent. Take up the dagger, David. Do the deed.

'Twere well it were done quickly —

I pick up the telephone. Dial Annabelle.

Still no reply.

I call another number.

'Hello, Dad? It's David. Listen. I'm on my way.'

I go out to the car, wishing I had taken my sister up on her offer. Then I remember an anecdote of The Bald One's.

'When I came out,' he said, 'people just kept everything to themselves. There wasn't the need to make any great statement. But Barbara, my sister, was a righteous sort of person and insisted that our parents should be told. Foolishly I said all right.

'Both my parents were rather elderly. Our mother took the news well, but my aged father was rather more difficult. Being deaf, he couldn't hear what Barbara said at first. So she had to shout.

' "There's something I have to tell you, Father," she roared into his right ear. "You do know, don't you, that Geoffrey is bisexual."

'My parents would never have understood the word "gay".

'My father has always been rather irritated about Barbara, who can be very overbearing. He got very grumpy indeed.

' "You don't have to shout, Barbara," he said. "Of course I know that Geoffrey can speak French." '

10

SO HERE I go, driving away from the university to Suburbia By The Sea, listening to the beat of the city radio station.

Rock, roll, rap, bop and strut.

Across the isthmus and across the bridge. Below, the white shining yachts are like butterflies skimming the sea. On the radio, a news flash: our city of sails is to be visited by a nuclear-powered American aircraft carrier. A month and a half from now. A blockade of small boats is already planned to stop the carrier entering the harbour.

Now here I am at the parental home and my father is opening the door. He smiles, uncertain.

'Your mother has just gone into the village, David. I told her that whatever you have to say would be best said to me, man to man. Your mother is absolutely terrified about this whole business. But surely it can't be that bad, can it?'

He leads the way into the sitting room.

Coming out to one's parents must be the most difficult of all confrontations we have to face. Our mother is the only mother we have. We adore her and crave her maternal love. When we confess our predilection for men, we negate her sex and her maternity. Our father is the only father we have. We fear his anger, his disapproval and his brute force. He has brought us up in his own image. It is an image of patriarchal masculinity. When we confess our lust for men, he can only become punisher.

In my case, the relationships with both parents have generally been ones in which I have said 'Yes' to them and they have said 'No' to me. Thus I have never really been able to grow up.

Seated with my father I find myself faltering, hesitant, near to equivocation, to leaving it for another day. Yet I am an adult, intelligent, and have a career and confidence which should have thrown me clear of such a dependency. If I am so wavering, how much more difficult it must be for others, younger and braver than I.

Like Italian Stallion who told his folks when he was sixteen. His father locked him in the house and, when he would not recant his admission, threw him out into the street.

Or Always A Bridesmaid, whose mother has fabricated a life which he can never return to. She has told the rest of the family that he is dead.

Or bright, shining Chris. Being a ballet dancer was bad enough, but being a fairy was too much.

'Die of Aids, homo,' his brothers yelled as they beat the shit out of him.

When it comes to the crunch, coming out is the greatest of all confessions. Nothing is more difficult to acknowledge. When we become ourselves we reach right back to the time when we were conceived out of our parents' passion.

We murder their lives. There can never be any forgiveness.

Of course I have always loved my father, but my relationship with him has largely been regulated by my respect and fear of his authority and, therefore, by telling him what I think he prefers to hear rather than what should be said. Above all else I have desired his good opinion and have become everything he has wished me to become. Good sportsman. Fine student. Husband and father. I have replicated the model he provided. His discipline and example have made me masculine.

Yet intimacy has always eluded us and we have never really talked. In fact we have had very few skirmishes with directness or truth. Politically right wing, he accepts my left-wing tendencies as long as we don't talk about them. Adamant about the military, he cannot tolerate my revisionist views so we avoid discussion of them. We have been at stand off all our lives. Strategists in a command room, we jockey our forces into and out of sorties without engagement, yet without giving ground.

As now, for instance, when my father is waiting for me to talk about the subject so long avoided: the cause of my marital estrangement. He sits leaning forward, his face impassive. His whole stance is parade ground. At attention, not at ease.

Suddenly I am angry with him, for this is why I was unable to talk to him when sex began to lose its innocence. When beauty became bestial. When something natural became dirty, base, disturbing.

That was when I was twelve and staying over with the neighbours, their five sons and two daughters on the next farm. We were playing away from the house when, suddenly, I was pounced on by the boys and, at Tomboy's and Pigtail's orders, tied to a tree. Without undue ceremony my pants were pulled down and Tomboy inspected my circumcision.

'Does this hurt?' Pigtail laughed as her brothers pulled at me. 'Does it?'

Later that night, I was woken by whispered excitement. I opened my eyes to see one of the brothers, Pimple Face, standing by candlelight in the middle of the room. The other brothers were ringed around him, watching him. When they saw that I was awake they said, 'Ssssh'. Then they beckoned me to join them.

'Come and see. Shaun can do it now.'

Pyjama pants around his ankles, Pimple Face was pulling savagely at his cock.

'I've made spunk twice already,' he panted, proudly rubbing his tool with his right fist. 'And here it comes again —'

When I returned home I wanted to know what it was that had happened to Pimple Face. I was curious about this rite of passage from boyhood to manhood. Would the same thing happen to me? And if so, when? I asked my father, telling him about what I had seen. His reaction was to punish me. At the time I thought it was because puberty was shameful and dirty and asking about it was thus a sin. I now suspect that it was a reaction to the thought that his son might be involved in some kind of circle jerk with other boys. Whatever, I could never again speak to my father about sex. When, in turn, my own puberty erupted it was not something innocent and to be welcomed with joy. It was, rather, something already clothed with disapproval. Something not to be talked about.

So how to begin?

How to start talking to this man, this father, across all those years of not talking?

Then, a memory. Light. Amusing in its own way.

'Do you remember,' I begin, 'when we moved here from the farm? I was fourteen. The next year you sent me to Saint Crispin's boarding school. I made left winger in the First Fifteen.'

'Yes,' my father answers, surprised. 'You were a fine player.'

'Our squad was invited to travel upcountry to play against the Collegiate team. You remember that?'

My father is proud of his memory. 'Your school won, as I recall,' he says. 'Twenty-one to fifteen. A splendid effort. Your mother and I were delighted.'

'Just before our team left here on the bus I made an appointment with a doctor. In the city we were travelling to. I picked a name at random from the telephone book, telephoned, spoke to the doctor's nurse, and made the appointment. I called myself Mister Smith.' I smile at the memory. Mister Smith. 'That's why I asked for an extra allowance just before the trip.'

My father is puzzled but says nothing. He nods. 'Go on.'

'The reason why I made the appointment was because I was afraid. Oh, I could have gone to our own family doctor or to another doctor here. But I was frightened you might find out about it. Cities like this are smaller than you think. Anyway, when our team arrived at the other city we played our game and, as you know, we won. After the game, while the others went off to a celebration, I slipped out to keep my appointment. Of course, as soon as I walked into the consulting room the nurse knew my name wasn't Smith. Then when she asked for details it was quite clear that I was making them all up. But I was lucky, and she was a good sport. Obviously I hadn't made the appointment for nothing. So that when the doctor buzzed her, the nurse said to me, "The doctor will see you now Mister, ah, Smith." So I walked in.'

It was so long ago. Yet it seems like yesterday.

'The trouble was that when the doctor looked up and asked, "How can I help you?" I couldn't answer.'

My father looks at me, wondering.

'You see, I hadn't expected her to be a woman.' Ah, the foolish assumptions of youth. 'I had a question about sex. I needed to speak to a man about it. I needed to know why I was attracted to men.'

There. It's out. Slipped in and under his heart before he can feel the pain.

Even so, my father gives a deep groan and bows his head. Normally he never does this, self-conscious about his thinning hair. He is utterly vulnerable in a way that shames me. Yet he does not realise that I am being kind. Diplomatic. For if I was to tell him the truth it would be to admit that by the age of sixteen I had become a well-formed, sexually active young man. Family pressures, societal pressures, religious and peer pressures from Saint Crispin's had already moulded me into a heterosexual image and had led me to Sweet Kid, my first girlfriend and my first full sexual experience with either men or women. Then to sex with Anybody's in the back seat of her father's car. But something was missing from these encounters, something I couldn't put a finger on, until —

Choosing my words. Carefully. Tempering truth so as not to hurt his feelings.

'Long before I married Annabelle I had girlfriends. But I was attracted to men more than women. I never wanted to admit it then and I still don't like to admit it now. To all appearances I have taken the natural path. To find, marry and mate with a woman, Annabelle. To make a career. To have children, Rebecca and Miranda. I hope I have been a good husband, son and father. But my whole life has been a fabrication. A sham —'

My father begins to weep for himself.

'A counterfeit.'

He takes a handkerchief out of his trouser pocket and presses it to his eyes and mouth. I move on, quickly. While I have the advantage. While I have the strength.

'I have had another life, Dad. In the company of men.'

How much can I really tell him and how much does he really want to hear? With all my heart I can say that I wanted to be just like the rest of the guys. I looked regular, acted regular and was accepted by my peers as being regular. Above all else I wanted to be a lover of women.

It is so difficult to watch this man, my father, as he wrestles with the unbelievability of my confession. His broken sobs come from some dark place he has never known before. It takes him some time to recover. When he does, his back comes up. Control returning.

'Does Annabelle know any of this?' His voice is strong and peremptory.

'No.'

'Has she ever known?'

'No. I shall tell her tonight.'

He looks at me, angry. 'And what do you expect to do with your marriage? The children? Our grandchildren?'

'Whatever happens, they'll still visit you.'

'Is there no other way?'

'No, Dad.'

And now the words themselves. I've never actually said them before, even to myself. Just two words to acknowledge my self and my kind.

At first they are stones in my mouth. Heavy. Lodged in my throat. Delivering them is agony and, in the doing, the life that was becomes bloodied.

'I'm gay.'

Once more.

'I'm gay, Dad. Do you understand?'

And that is when he is upon me, backhanding me across the room, surprising me with his strength.

'What I under*stand*,' his voice rising, 'is that you will break your mother's heart.'

Not his. Hers.

'What I under*stand* is that you will cause pain to all of us.'

Shaking. Not giving ground. Filled with loathing.

'But what I still do *not* under*stand* is *why*.'

Fathers are such strange, uncharted territories. In the falling light my father is another country, a place of foreign coasts and archipelagos. Who knows *why*? I knew my lust for men was wrong but male beauty, and what men did to women, had already been imprinted on my sexual template and once there could not be removed.

'What I do *not* under*stand* is *why*.'

Behind my father is a photograph of the family: my mother, my father, my sister and myself in Saint Crispin's uniform. Slashed by falling light, there I am, a teenager. Tousled hair, green eyes. The earlier years of working on the farm had already filled me out. Swimming and lifting weights had started to work on the incipient man inside the boy, putting bulk to tissue, muscle fibre on bone. I followed a regime which sometimes alarmed my mother. Always pushing myself. Always lifting heavier weights. Always swimming extra lengths. Working out, pursuing fitness and athletic excellence with a single-mindedness others found admirable. What they did not know was that I undertook my training out of fear and hope. I had already started to punish myself for what I suspected I was.

Why? Why?

This is why.

Something was missing in my sex with women. Even at sixteen I knew it. I wanted to find that missing piece, that element my genetic makeup would say 'Yes' to, which my biochemical, hormonal or psychosexual personality would recognise. Or which would connect me with memories, skimming like a stone, of an uncle or of men swimming down at a river.

During another rugby weekend trip away from Saint Crispin's I went to a beach I knew men went to. I took off my clothes. Sat. Waited.

A man joined me. He stroked my thighs. Pinched my nipples. Took me into the sand dunes.

I stood. He kneeled in front of me. He cradled my balls in his left hand. Put his cool lips over my burning cock.

And everything in me said, *Yes*.

And I was gone.

Lost.

For ever.

That night, when I returned to Saint Crispin's, I waited for Lights Out. The moon was a galleon pointing toward the second star on the right.

Come on, said Peter. You will join us, won't you?

I hugged myself tightly, trying to stop the tears. I cried my eyes out, the ocean in me spilling out. Howling at the moon. Sobbing and shaking. Oh God. Oh God.

Someone in the dormitory heard me. There was a lifting of blankets on my bed. Someone shifted in beside me. Held me tight. Whispered, 'Sssshhh. There, there. Sssshhh.' Held me as I cried.

I didn't know who it was.

All I knew, and with terrible certainty, was that I had become one of The Lost Boys.

11

NOW I HAVE become a Changeling Prince, a thing of wolverine ugliness, waiting in the accustomed place beneath the trees on the other side of the street until the lights go off in the room where my little princesses sleep. The Ship of Dreams rolls in the swelling night tides, snapping the canvas, trying to pull away from its moorings.

I watch as Annabelle goes through the house checking the locks and turning out the lights. Until there is only one square of light from the main bedroom.

Get out of the car.

Time to tear limb from limb, to huff and puff and blow the house down.

Knock on the door.

Annabelle comes.

'Hello, sport. It's a bit late for a visit, isn't it?'

In her eyes, a glance of pure love.

And now I have told Annabelle and she has collapsed against the stairs.

'Oh sport, I think I'm going to be sick.'

Her eyes are glowing. She is trying to stop herself from shaking apart. She runs past me into the bathroom and throws up in the basin.

'I want you to tell me it isn't true. I want you to lie to me. Tell me anything you want. Tell me it's another woman. Tell me that you're having an affair with one of your female students. Tell me it's anybody else, but don't tell me it's a man.'

She is splashing water into her face. Splashing it all over herself. The water splashing everywhere. On to the mirror. On to the vanity. On to the floor.

'Lie to me you bastard, lie to *meeee* —'

Then she is flying at me, hitting out wherever she can. With anything that is at hand. Hitting. Hitting.

'Lie to me. Lie to me. *Lie to meee* —'

In the girls' bedroom Miranda, awakened by her mother, begins to cry. Grabs her inhaler. Begins to breathe *in*.

12

AMID ALL THIS pain and terror, with the world collapsing like a temple around me, I flee to opening night at the ballet. *Petrushka* itself. On the way I stop at a florist. Chris will be expecting flowers backstage. He is so popular that mine won't be the only bouquet. Two dozen red roses, tied with a huge red ribbon and sparkling in cellophane, should do the trick. Now a quick note:

'My fat friend wishes you good luck.'

'I warn you,' Chris grinned when we made our first date, 'that you'll have to book me well in advance. I'm very popular.'

We met at Italian Stallion's party, but I had seen Chris around the traps way before then. I hadn't known he was a ballet dancer. He was a striking six footer with eyes that sparkled like sun on the sea. In those days, he wore his dark curly hair in a fashionable ponytail. Tall, strong, masculine and not in the least effeminate as the ballet boys are supposed to be, his popularity was not to be wondered at. He looked more like a sleek rugby wing or ski instructor with that face of his, a size too small for his strong neck and deltoid build. But I should have realised, when I glimpsed him dancing a week earlier at The Club, that his movements owed as much to art as to spontaneity. I had been with Born To Boogie, no mean dancer himself. When he saw Chris, boogieing himself to a frenzy and scattering the light in dazzling coruscations, he had to admit to having met an equal.

You can never tell why it is that one person is attracted to another. Initially I had no designs on Chris, though I always admired the way he looked. He had a penchant for oversize shirts, carefully unbuttoned, pleated jeans and belts cinched tightly to show off his waist. On one occasion I saw him with one of his admirers running across the street in sweatpants and singlet of the kind that is designed to reveal everything. Just as the lights changed, his admirer dropped his shoulder bag and the contents scattered everywhere. The cars started to move but, grinning, Chris held up his hands to bid them, Stop. Then, he and his admirer turned the gathering of the things from the ground into a clown routine which had us in stitches. At the end, when everybody was applauding, Chris bowed low and then, with his admirer in tow, whirled like a Cossack around the crossing and into the crowd.

Then there he was at Italian Stallion's party and he was extremely irritated that I didn't know who he was or what he did. That, and the fact that I had brought Rebecca and Miranda with me, was what got us together.

Young girls at parties made up of predominantly gay men are enormously endearing. At the time I was still living with Annabelle and was babysitting while Annabelle was out with my sister. When the girls found out we were going to a party they jumped up and instantly demanded to be dressed in their best frocks. Miranda, in her white party outfit, had brought her fairy wand and went around asking everybody, 'Do you want me to change you from an ugly frog into a handsome prince?'

Most of the boys did not consider that any changing was necessary but, all of a sudden, Chris gave a loud *croak* and pretended he was an ugly toad. He shrank down to the ground, hopped up to Miranda, his body and face contorted and twisted. She screamed and tried to get away from him but he beseeched her with loud croaks and pitiful sighs:

'Please, princess —'

Miranda looked at me. It had all turned too real for her.

'Daddy, Daddy, I don't think I can —'

'Of course you can, darling,' I said.

She whimpered. Closed her eyes. 'I don't know the magic words.'

'Abracadabra,' Chris hinted.

She nodded, her eyebrows furrowed and she waved her wand quickly and ran across to hold my hand and watch.

The transformation took place. Chris began to grow and

79

unfold, reaching out from his toad-like form, miming the way the fairy dust was falling on him and changing him. At the end of the transformation he stepped through the boys to Miranda and knelt before her, his hand across his heart.

'Thank you, princess,' he said.

That is when Miranda bent down and gave Chris one of her devastating butterfly kisses, fluttering her eyelashes against his cheek. His face glowed as he received her benediction.

He looked up at her and asked, 'And is that how Daddies kiss?'

Miranda shook her head and showed him, which brought a roar of laughter.

'Hmmmn,' Chris said, 'I would think it must be really nice to be kissed goodnight by your Daddy.'

The *Petrushka* premiere is crowded with the glitterati. Rolls Royces, Mercedes, Bentleys and BMWs glide up to the entrance of the Aotea Centre and deposit their beautiful people. They are primarily thin and anorexic, unlike the portly opera crowd which tends to compete with the prima donnas. They are also superbly attired and coiffed in dramatic colours. The foyer entertainment at the ballet is an appropriate curtain-raiser to the main event.

I walk through the entrance and the flashlights of the press pop and explode — alas, not for me. The Mayor and Mrs Mayor have just arrived with the official party: the artificially tanned Mr Industry and Mrs Industry, the facelifted Mr Used To Be Big In Ballet and Mrs The Money That He Married, the crocodile-smiling Mr Arts Council with his wife Mrs Mediocre Potter, and Miss Television Personality and the smirking Mr Famous For Five Minutes. The wonderfully wicked Miss Felicity Ferret is in attendance, dipping her pen into delicious poison.

True to his word Chris has left a ticket for me at the box office. As I pick it up I pass the roses to the box-office clerk, an unprepossessing individual with bad teeth. He looks at the roses and the card, affects a bored yawn and calls for a messenger to take them backstage.

'More roses for delivery to Mr Christopher De Rosnay.'

This is the way all deliveries are announced to the dancers, each indicating that beauty or talent is being rewarded by floral tribute.

However, a Young Thing in the corner glances up at the mention of Chris's name. Another one of Chris's balletomaniacal conquests. If looks could kill, I would be dead on the spot.

I buy a programme. It is the usual glossy production, filled with advertisements and laudatory notes about the sponsors. There is an In Memoriam photograph of the recently deceased premier danseur. So young. So fine-looking. He has that perennial startled look that such youthful people rightfully have when they realise that Death has dared to mark them for debilitating illness and demise. The frontispiece announces that the first night proceeds will benefit the Aids clinic.

Further in are photographs of the cast. Mr Christopher De Rosnay has a small photograph with the other boys of the ballet. For a young man who started life as Bert Christopher Rossiter, a farmer's son, he hasn't done too badly for himself. His photograph is in the usual balletic genre: dramatically lit, his face is one of innocence made up with greasepaint sophistication. But the sense of joy and delight cannot be hidden. Chris is the most joyous individual I have ever known.

I go to the men's room to check out my appearance. Straighten my bowtie. Brush the shoulders of my dinner suit. The mirror is crowded with older men touching up eyeliner, confirming that toupees are straight or taking a breather from their corsets. Further in at the urinals there are the usual 'Oops' displays of mine's bigger than yours or someone keeling over as they try to take a gander at what's dangling next to them.

Then out again into the foyer and the rich and heady scented garden. The rich always smell sweet: of Dior, Lanvin, Passion, Yves St Laurent, Pierre Cardin, not a whiff of Old Spice or Armpit Au Naturel anywhere. You can tell the ex-ballerinas among the women: at fifty they have gaunt pale faces like Fonteyn, and tiny French rolls at long swan necks. When they walk up and down the staircase they seem to float three inches off the ground. The male ex-dancers are also fairly obvious. Returning from the men's room they are black and white penguins, sucking in their stomachs, hoping that nobody will realise that they have applied their mascara and the hair they are wearing is not their own.

The chimes begin. The performance is due to start in five minutes. Those who aren't in the know begin to enter, providing the audience for those who are in the know, who enter just before the lights dim. As I take my seat I see The Bald One who winks at me. Across the aisle Hope Springs Eternal solicitously guides an aged duenna to her seat.

There is a scattering of applause for the conductor. A rustling of silk and velvet as a thousand patrons settle into their seats. The last-minute entrance of the official party. The baton, a wand poised in mid-air, about to conjure magic. The overture, stealing into the dark. The quirky and spiky Stravinsky modulations, pungent, lean, surging and accelerating with full orchestral colour to a climax.

The curtain rises. The story begins of the puppet who comes to life. Another opening of the ballet.

By first intermission the production is assured of success. I have managed to uncross my legs and am now standing at the bar drinking champagne. The local Petrushka and the imported prima ballerina have achieved a *succès d'estime*, and Chris's contribution in the spirited *danse russe* has been warmly applauded. So too the second tableau with its stamping, swirling, angular choreography, so cleverly mimicking the brilliant concertante piano accompaniment. The compliments and congratulations are gushing and sparkling as freely as the champagne.

I smile to myself whenever I hear Chris's name being mentioned. He is dancing like a dream and looks stunning in his tights. From the stage he is unable to see me but he knows where I am seated. When he took his bow with the other boys he looked down, pretended to be a marionette and crossed his eyes.

'Who is that athletic young man third from the right? Ah yes, Christopher De Rosnay. Tough, sinewy, but his technique is good. Taught by Madame Czernay, I see. That explains everything. Raymond better look to his laurels. His *jetés* and last pirouette were less than impeccable. Though, mind you —'

Chris will be out of his tree when I retell the intermission gossip. 'Did they really say that? You're making it all up. Did they really? Of course, everybody knows that Raymond is on the way out.' Alas poor Raymond. Although distance lends enchantment there comes a time when age cannot be obscured by footlights and kind lighting.

Ballet is the realm of eternal youth. Of all the arts, it is the most ageist. Physical decay has no place here, nor truth; only beauty and illusion. Perhaps this is why gay men, themselves the most worried about getting older, have enshrined ballet above all other arts.

'Hi.'

A tap on my shoulder, and I turn to see Bright Eyes, so handsome in his dinner suit, white shirt and bowtie. He is slightly hesitant but flushed with pleasure.

'I didn't know you liked ballet,' I say.

He makes a grimace, a cross between a moue and a pout, crackling with unconscious sexuality.

'May I introduce my parents?' he says by way of explanation. To one side materialise Bright Eyes Senior and Mrs Bright Eyes. So this is how the son will look when he reaches his vintage years. Almost as bright of eye, and with that brimming healthiness that the well-to-do always seem to have. 'And my sister? Oh, and my friend Allan.'

The sister makes a small smile. As for Allan, he is a vain young man of the arrogant kind. We make small-talk.

'Are you enjoying the production?' Bright Eyes asks politely. 'Allan is a designer.'

He is also opinionated. 'The production is absolutely mediocre,' Allan pronounces to all and sundry. 'In Germany, where I saw this ballet last, the design had flair and originality. Not like *this*.'

Heads are turning.

'But Stravinsky's music,' Bright Eyes protests.

'He would turn in his grave if he heard how badly it was being played.'

Hmmmn. Faces are purpling all over the place. Tempers are rising. But Allan is saved from being lynched by the chimes. Ding ding ding.

'Well,' I say, 'time to return to our seats.' I turn to Allan to shake his hand. 'I do hope the second act will improve your opinion of the production.'

'I very much doubt it,' he answers unnecessarily.

'And I'll see you in class,' I smile at Bright Eyes.

His embarrassment is tangible but he returns my warmth with blushing cheeks.

'Come on Allan,' he whispers.

Looking at them both, I have a sense of who is master and who is servant.

So it is back to my seat. Despite knowing my preference for a seat as far back as possible, Chris has seated me right in the front row. There is an impish humour at work here, for Chris well knows my belief that ballet was the pornography of the eighteenth and nineteenth centuries.

All ballet is choreographed by desire. You cannot deny that one of the reasons why so many red-blooded men pretended that they were admirers of High Culture was because, at its most physical, ballet is public sex. It may be restrained but it is still public, taken to its highest pinnacle of taste and decorum. The women leaping around in their tutus, so fragile, so feminine, are figments of heterosexual fantasies. The men in their mindboggling tights are all that homosexual dreams are made of — strength coupled with grace.

When you're in the front row and staring up to the stage, the dancers may as well be naked, given the brevity of their dress. Alas, to have them so would be to make difficulties for composers of ballet music. As Sir Robert Helpmann has wittily pointed out, composers would have to add an extra beat after the male dancers had completed a jump.

I take my seat. I am sitting beside a young man who still has his programme over his lap.

'God, I could have done with a drink,' he says with a moan.

I begin to commiserate with him. Then a sixth sense makes me look up at the grand circle.

Annabelle is here and she has seen me. All the pillars and colonnades come crashing down. So this is why she wanted me to have the girls tonight.

We look across the expanse of the theatre. She is looking so beautiful. Her dress is sparkling silver. The lights are dimming, but her face glows like a pale star. She tries to smile. Then, wanly, leans over to one of her friends and whispers to him.

He nods. She takes his arm.

Leaves.

13

'SO YOU HAD a good seat?' Chris asks, tongue in cheek. 'A nice view?'

We are on our way to the car park. His arms are laden with bouquets of flowers. All red. All roses.

'Fabulous,' I answer. 'Who is that friend of yours, the one who almost split his tights?'

Chris laughs, knowing that I am kidding him. We have come in separate cars so he asks, 'Your place or mine? Better make it mine. It's in a mess, as usual, but I've got an early photo call.'

The whole evening has been an unqualified triumph. The *troisième tableau*, with its *danse de la ballerine*, was encored. The waltz, climaxing as the Moor lifts the ballerina high above his head *en attitude*, brought bravos to rattle the rooftops. With such accolades coming so early, the company was hard put to maintain the standard. But the *quatrième tableau* followed like a dream, with the *danse des nounous* winning warm acclaim. Then, of course, Chris had a superb solo, dancing during the jubilant finale. By the time the curtain came down on Petrushka's death the house was on its feet. Even Bright Eyes' vain young friend Allan was persuaded by his shining companion to stand.

In the middle of all the joy, the glimpse of two empty seats in the grand circle was one of the loneliest sights in the world.

Backstage, Chris was in seventh heaven. He was so intoxicated by the adrenalin rush of a fine performance that he scarcely saw me at first. His chest was heaving, his make-up smeared with tears and sweat. He hugged and kissed his way through his fellow dancers.

One moment of sadness and remembrance as the artistic director paid tribute to their deceased principal dancer. Then the streamers were flying, balloons were descending and champagne corks were popping for the onstage First Night Party. Our memories are not short, but we have to get on with life.

Through the streamers Chris saw me. His face glowed. He walked through his admirers and toward me in that familiar way that all ballet dancers have.

Eat your hearts out, guys.

He was already wiping off his make-up, emerging from behind the smeared mascara and face mask. Becoming a farmer's son again. His well-developed torso was streaked with sweat. Rivulets of sweat were running down his thighs.

'God it's good to see you,' he breathed in a low, hungry voice. 'We have to stay for the party but when this is all over, I want to burn lots of rubber.'

In Chris's third floor flat he is bucking beneath me, pushing himself, impaling himself further onto me. He is made golden by sweat, his body hair sprinkled with diamonds. He scissors his legs apart and across my shoulders. He is quivering in capitulation, wanting me to lift him off the bed.

'Oh yes. Oh yes.'

He moans as, half standing, I pull him up and lean my weight into him.

I am driving into him.Pound, then stop, pound, then stop, pound pound pound then stop. Pound pound pound, stop, withdraw to the tip then pound pound pound in again. In.

All of a sudden it happens. His eyes widen, startled.

'Oh —'

His chest starts to expand. His stomach muscles rippling in the moonlight. In that moment he is defenceless. Open.

Pull all the way out. Rest on the rim. He wants me back in.

'Please —'

His eyes close in acceptance.

This is when the last slow sliding in should come. Slow and sweet, feeling him mould over the curve of my length to where his navel is. Every inch *in*.

Then push again, feeling him clamp down and around.

The suction begins and he whimpers, howls and comes, aiding his climax with his hands, shooting to his shoulders.

I hold myself in him until he has reached completion. Then I lower him back onto the bed.

In a hurry now. Hissing with the momentum of it all. Take off the condom. Stand above him. Smell of rubber. Take my cock in my hand. Smell of sperm. Show him who is master. Quick pumps from tip to base and it starts.

My cock expands. Lengthens helplessly in its extremity of sensation. The head swells, opening up. From my balls comes the gathering, the slow gushing out. The pulsing river, the torrent, the flood in full flow, spasming onto him.

'Make it stop,' Chris cries in childish delight. 'Oh please,' as, with both hands, I direct my orgasm to cover him from neck to thighs, 'make it stop.'

But this is it. This tumultuous sensation of absolute pleasure, power and powerlessness. This spilling onto the man beneath me.

In orgasm neither Chris nor I are the Lords of the Dance. His is the rhythm, his is the choreography of lust, his is the decision when all is spent.

'When you die, you should leave your body to science.'

We are lying in bed, and Chris is looking down at me. Curious and with interest.

'You're not so bad yourself,' I say.

'I've never ever seen anybody climax like you do.'

'Look, I really think we should get some sleep.'

Chris is trying to get me interested again. 'How can I sleep? I've just danced my tiny tits off and I'm all excited. Do you think they really loved me?'

'Yes.'

'Was I really good?'

'Yes. At twenty-three you dance like a teenager.'

'And can we do it again?'

'No.'

'Are you trying to kill me?' I ask.

Chris giggles. 'Third time lucky. I warned you I wanted to burn rubber. So how was your week?'

'So so.'

'And the girls?'

'Saw them yesterday.'

'And Annabelle?'

'Okay. I've come clean to her and the folks about our separation. She was there tonight.'

'At the ballet?'

'Yes. She'd mentioned something about going out. I just didn't think we'd end up at the same place. I shouldn't have been surprised but I was.'

'Oh.'

'Are you okay?'

Chris is silent, the moon limning his shoulders. 'I should never have got involved with a married man. Should never have allowed it to happen.'

'You had nothing to do with our separation.'

'We'll never get any sleep if I stay.'

Chris is drowsy against my shoulders. 'Uh huh.'

'Goodnight.'

'Ring me in the morning,' Chris says.

'It *is* morning.'

'Oh God. Then don't ring me until tomorrow.'

'Goodnight.'

'Was I really that great tonight?'

'Yes. Really. Truly.'

14

WHEN YOU WISH upon a star, makes no difference who you are, anything your heart desires, will come true. If your heart is in your dreams —

Again, two o'clock in the morning, and I am returning home from Chris's flat. My memories are filled with Annabelle. They are made of nostalgia about past nights at the ballet and opera, sadness that those nights will never come again, and loneliness.

Thus I detour to the two-storeyed house where Annabelle and my little princesses sleep. It is a galleon tossed on stormy seas. All it needs is Tinkerbell to sprinkle fairy dust so that it can fly, someone to weigh the anchor and a strong hand on the wheel. A setting of course through the night sky and off it will go, a glistening Ship of Dreams, drifting upward. Toward that second star from the right.

Annabelle will be captain now. She will be crew and she will be navigator. She has two little children who must be given safe passage. They will stand beside her.

Isn't Daddy coming?

No, darlings.

But we'll get lost, Mummy.

We must be brave, darlings.

She was looking so beautiful. Her dress was sparkling silver. Her face a pale star. She leaned over to her friend and whispered to him, and together they —

Tick tock tick tock.

Annabelle, nothing at all can hide the truth that over two years ago the clock in the crocodile began to tick again. Perhaps it was boredom. Frustration at work. Lack of fun in the established routine of our lives. Perhaps it was remembering the potency of the sex act with a man. Needing to conquer and to be desired. Perhaps there is a passage in men's lives, whether heterosexual or homosexual, when the marriage bedroom and marriage itself become a confinement. All I know is that I felt I was growing old and I wasn't too sure whether I wanted that. Maybe I grew tired of the prospect of responsibility. I wanted to play truant. Not to grow up. To have adventures. Fight pirates. Rescue an Indian princess. Fly to Never Never Land.

I blow my nose. Turn the key. Take the steering wheel in my hands and —

The tears are convulsing my body and I cannot stop crying. For suddenly it seems as if the anchor chain snaps on that Ship Of Dreams and, in its surge away on the night tides, Annabelle and my two princesses are thrown, screaming, to the deck. The sails are flapping and the wheel is spinning and ahead are reefs as huge as galaxies.

Then Annabelle is there. Looking back at me.

'*Da-vid.*'

Calling from the top bedroom window.

This is all wrong but I cannot help opening the car door and running across the road to the house.

'I'm coming, Annabelle! I'm coming —'

Jumping aboard that Ship of Dreams. Banging on the door. Spinning the wheel away from danger. Annabelle opening to me. Her face, tear-streaked.

'Please, sport, don't let this happen to us.'

'Oh Annabelle, I'm so sorry.'

We are crying, kissing, holding each other, shivering. Moaning at the physical touch. Skin on skin.

'I don't care about anything,' she says. 'Don't go. Don't leave me. I want you home, David. Please come home.'

I am already kicking the door shut. Kissing her hungrily. Remembering the thrill of her skin. Pulling her nightgown from her shoulders.

'Oh God I've missed you,' she says. 'Missed *this*.'

I pick her up. Carry her up the stairs. My lips are sealed to hers. My arms hold her tight.

Pulling each other's clothes off.

'Oh yes —'

Kicking the bedroom door closed.

At the last moment, a condom. Her eyes flicker.

'Sport —'

A voice is crying out in my head that this is all *insanity*. But it is too late for that.

And in orgasm he is again triumphant:

The Lord of the Dance.

15

Wendy was wakened by the sound of sobs, and she sat up in bed to listen. She had seen Peter before, in dreams: so she was not a bit surprised to see him now. She asked him, quite politely, 'Boy, what are you crying for?'

He began to explain: it was because he could not get his shadow to stick back on. So Wendy fetched her needle and cotton and thimble, and sewed the shadow on to Peter's foot; she hurt him as little as she could help. When he found that it was now safely stuck on he danced about and crowed with joy. For, to tell the truth, Peter was very conceited. And instead of saying 'Thank you, Wendy, how kind you are!' he crowed, 'Oh, how clever I am!'

Annabelle has fallen with a long sigh into unconsciousness. All the tensions of the world have left her and she is gone, swooning into sleep.

Now, the moon is spilling through the window. She murmurs in my arms and, suddenly, wakes with a start, reaching for me to make sure I am there. Then, when she is reassured, she pushes me away. Stands and goes to the bathroom. When she returns she says, 'I hate it when you watch me while I'm asleep.'

Later, and it is my turn to wake. Annabelle's profile is etched in the light. Her eyes are wide and enigmatic. She is far away in a dark space beyond the moon.

'Can't sleep?' I ask.

'Just thinking.' She turns to me, accusatory. 'You *never* like the ballet.'

She is trying to be brave. Wondering what I was doing there. She is also remembering that tonight we made love with a condom. She is thinking, *why*.

Yet she already knows why.

Then, before we know it, we are into the morning after. Miranda, still trying to wake up, wanders into the bedroom and crawls between Annabelle and me as if I have not been away at all. But when Rebecca arrives her shouts of surprise and joy are so loud that the whole neighbourhood must hear her. She jumps in the middle with her sister.

'Rebecca,' Annabelle says, 'please get *out*.'

She is looking at me over the heads of the girls. My heart melts. I take her hands in mine. Kiss them.

But it is all madness.

The momentum of life takes us over the lip of insanity and shunts us into calm waters. I am showering and shucking on my clothes and moving out of the house and into the sun.

Annabelle is at the door. Looking at me.

'Well?' I ask.

She shrugs. A lock of her hair falls into her eyes. She brushes it back. 'I don't know,' she says. 'There's a part of me that hates you and will never ever trust you again, but there's a bigger part of me which loves you so much. I'm all mixed up between wanting you and not wanting you. And I'm angry, really angry. In all our years together I was never unfaithful to you. Never.'

I nod in acceptance and brush my lips against hers.

She turns away.

'Why did you do this to us, sport? *Why?*'

16

EVERYBODY ASKS WHY. But nobody asks how. To answer this question I need to tell you about my years at Saint Crispin's College. Saint Crispin's coincided with my adolescence, that time in our life which bridges the years of childhood with the world of adulthood.

Until puberty we are children of whom much is forgiven. After puberty there is no forgiveness. Our freedoms begin to have limits placed on them and our lives become channelled by education to approximate familial, societal, political and religious expectations.

For some unknown reason my father decided that the right bridge for me was Saint Crispin's. He had high hopes for me and must have been unhappy with the public school I was attending nearer our home. After discussing the matter with my mother, he arranged for me to attend Saint Crispin's, not as a day pupil but as a boarder.

I was fifteen when I entered the school's imposing gates with their heraldic shield, PLAY THE GAME. The headmaster, Batman, had shown no interest in me when my parents took me in for my interview. Everything about him was asymmetrical, from his lopsided appearance to his class-based decisions. It wasn't until he was aware of my father's pedigree, war history, income and where we lived that his interest perked up. Even so, some sixth sense must have alerted him to suspect that the slouching, glowering, long-haired adolescent, whose tie wasn't in a Windsor knot, would spell trouble. Only when he noted that I played left wing on the rugby field, did his eyes gleam with excitement. His voice boomed, 'Then let's give the boy a go, shall we?'

He thrust a hand out from beneath his voluminous black cape to shake my father's hand.

'What do you say, eh, young Munro?'

Parents are good at making unilateral decisions for their sons. I think my father expected that Saint Crispin's would teach me what was right and what was wrong for boys to do. In its hands my wild unruly spontaneity would be disciplined, and my body and mind would be moulded into the image of an upright, sports-oriented and educated young man of our class. He wanted me to succeed.

So I did, eventually, but I doubt that my father ever realised that Saint Crispin's would also be the place where unceasing collisions would occur between myself, authority and religion, and that much of the battle would be played on the dangerous ground dealing with masculinity and sex.

'So you're the new boy,' Wolf Man, the dorm master of Harrow, said when I arrived. He was bushy-eyebrowed, squat, top heavy, tightly muscled.

'Yes,' I answered.

I followed him up the winding stairs to the upper floor, watching the hem of his cape ascending.

'Sir,' he reprimanded. 'All masters answer only to sir, or to our surnames. You understand?'

'Yes.'

Pause. Angrily:

'Sir.'

Into a cold, unpartitioned room. Beds on both sides. Made. Tidy. An empty one near the door where it's draughtiest.

'This is yours,' Wolf Man said. Naturally. 'Put your suitcase in your locker. We are all at tea. Come, come.' Showing me his prominent teeth. 'I'm absolutely starving.'

Like most Anglican boarding schools, Saint Crispin's was modelled on English antecedents, Jolly Boating Weather, O God Our Help In Ages Past, Jerusalem, and all that. The school proper was a two-storeyed, ivy-clad, grey stone building like a 'U' enclosing a concrete quadrangle in the middle. Headmaster, staff and administration rooms were in front. The left wing housed arts, including

English, French, history, geography, music and religious studies. The right wing housed science and mathematics. The quadrangle opened into the playing fields at the back: four rugby fields, one soccer and one hockey. Tall chestnut and oak trees formed the outer perimeter of the college with the river and boatshed on the south side.

The three dormitories, or houses, were also two-storeyed grey stone at the far end of the football field, and huddled together were a separate ablutions block, dining hall and chapel. Appropriately enough, the dormitories were named Rugby, Eton and Harrow.

By the time I arrived that first term, all the beds in Rugby and Eton, the two top houses, were taken.

'School?' Wolf Man roared in the dining hall.

The hubbub of eating snapped into silence. One hundred and seventy-nine boys swivelling to look at me and Wolf Man standing at the door. Curious. Bored. Angry. Interested. Appraising.

'This is Munro. He will be in Harrow.'

I caught a movement at the corner of my eye. A big brutish boy, his mouth stuffed with meat, was making a contemptuous gesture, poking at his throat as if to vomit. My senses told me, Watch him. Then Wolf Man pushed me towards an empty chair. Nearest the door, naturally.

'School. Resume dinner.'

No teenager should ever begin late at a school like Saint Crispin's, where students normally start to board at eleven, where there are no family associations, and where friendships, relationships between students and teachers and sporting and social networks are already well established. All the inner circles are already full and the doors locked from the inside. By both masters and students. That includes the dining hall.

I wish I could say that my time at Saint Crispin's improved, but during the first term it didn't. I didn't mind that as a latecomer I was automatically shunted into the worst house, that disparate band of loners crippled in some way by lack of sporting abilities, intelligence, by wrong race or religion: the Hopeless At Sports, Sissies, Jews, Maori or Polynesians. But I *did* mind that my placement established my status.

'A new boy,' Dracula said, putting down his history text. 'And in Harrow, are you?' He was tall, wan, bloodless, avoiding the sunlight. 'We don't expect much of Harrow boys, do we, school?'

Titter, laughter, guffaw, haw haw.

'In Harrow, are we?' said Frankenstein, the English master. 'Perhaps this year Harrow will break its record for an all-time low in scholastic achievement.'

Ha ha, snort, what a comedian.

It did not help either that I began school in summer and not in winter, when my sporting prowess in rugby catapulted me to insider status. Nor that, at that age, I was not quite a senior but not a junior either. Not one of the favourites of the masters or one of the scorned, or one of the popular among the boys or one of the unpopular.

Thus it was that in my first term I was one of the boys of Harrow. One of the outsiders. But as an outsider I had four assets of value. One was physical strength. Another was that I began actually to enjoy my outsider status, revelling in being on the losing side. It made the measuring up, the proving of oneself all the more exciting. More fulfilling. Why start at the top and miss out on the fun of the climb? The third was that nobody else knew my strengths or weaknesses. And fourth, I despised bullies, and Saint Crispin's was divided into the bullies and the bullied. Rugby and Eton were the bullies, and Harrow boys were there to be bullied.

From my very first night I found myself ranged against the king of the bullies himself, the brutish boy I had seen at dinner whom everyone called Kong.

After dinner all the boys except those who were in summer training returned to their houses for study hour. That was how I met Nigger, a Maori who was in the bed next to mine; he took me in hand, introducing me to others in the top-floor dormitory. Stocky and stubborn, it was clear that Nigger was a protector, having inherited from his race an inclination to treat all those in Harrow as his tribe, his iwi.

'We may not be much to look at, eh,' he said to me. 'But all we got is each other.'

97

The 'we' whom Nigger referred to were the primarily lower-school boys, who had been picked over and consigned to Harrow. Those handful of upper-school seniors in the house had already abdicated their responsibility by virtue of their ineffectiveness as leaders. But that was at the beginning of it all; nothing inspires leadership more than having something to fight for — the honour of one's house.

It was already obvious that Nigger assessed me a protector too, having sized me up from the start.

'You can always smell a farm boy,' he said.

Indeed, I sometimes think that it was his and my patience and our ability to roll with the punches that helped us to survive those Saint Crispin's years. But Nigger had something extra: a stoicism and an attitude that enabled him to pick himself up and carry on. I owe him my survival really, because when the going was rough he was the one to come, pick me up and carry me away in a fireman's lift to safe ground.

'How come you're here?' I asked him.

'My father,' he answered, rolling his eyes. 'He thinks I should be a priest.'

It was after study hour that I faced off Kong. All the boys were marched off to the communal ablution block to shower, brush our teeth and change for bed. I was wondering why everybody seemed to be in such a hurry to finish. The lower school, particularly, simply washed behind their ears, gave a lick to their hair, put sponge to armpits and crotch, and then scuttled out.

I took a shower stall next to Nigger. I was soaping up and dreaming of being somewhere else when I heard the shower on the other side being turned on. Looking across I saw that the boy was thin and gangly to the point of anorexia.

'Meet Shylock,' Nigger grinned.

Shylock seemed very nervous. He'd been kept back by a master to tidy up the study room. 'We'd better get a move on,' he said to Nigger, 'before —'

But it was too late. Suddenly there was the sound of something banging on the tin walls of the ablution block. I knew then why the brutish boy was called Kong, for the sound instantly reminded me of the gong used to summon the giant ape on Skull Island. Then he was there, with fourteen or fifteen of his mates, returning from a training run. They came yahooing through the ablution block, bringing with them the musk smell of domination.

I had shampoo in my hair and my eyes were closed. But I knew that the new arrivals were throwing off their clothes and diving into the showers left and right of me. The water pressure kept changing, and I had to fiddle with the taps to keep the temperature constant.

There was a yelp to my right and, to raucous laughter, the sound of someone being thrown out of a shower.

Then it was my turn.

'You're in my shower!'

Someone grabbed my testicles, twisted, and before I knew it, pain and force propelled me out and into a fallen tangle with Shylock.

'Hey you fellers!' Nigger was beside me, helping me up.

I was blinded by the shampoo. I reached for a towel, wiping at my eyes. All around me, laughter. In the stalls, boys like horses steaming in a stable.

'Shut your mouth, Niggah,' a voice said. 'You'll be next.'

Kong. In my stall. Soaping himself up. Looking at me, gathering water in his mouth and fountaining it at me.

As I have said, one of my advantages as outsider was that nobody knew my strengths or weaknesses. Another was that I didn't know who Kong was either; if I had known, I may wisely have decided to bide my time and live to fight another day. All I saw was that he was big — but not *that* big. And the bigger they are, the harder they fall.

There's one way of getting a person out of a shower. Turn off the cold water.

'Thank you,' I said to Kong as he danced, yelping, out of the stall. I gave him a push to help him on his way, and stepped into the space he had so kindly vacated. Regulated the temperature. Began to hum. Arching my back. But listening. Alert.

Around me the laughter had died away. The sound of the showers thrummed on the tiles.

Then I heard Kong rage and bellow. Saw him speeding back towards me. Remembered Beer Gut saying, Use his strength *against* him. Saw Kong swing a punch.

Grabbed his fist. Yanked it forward and him with it.

Sidestepped.

And listened to his face *crack* into the tiles.

Finished my shower. Began to towel myself down.

'You've killed him,' one of Kong's boys said.

I sometimes wish I had. It would have saved me from the scragging I got from the rest of the sports team that night. Had it not been for Nigger and the anorexic Shylock, I might have joined Kong on the shower floor. What I had not appreciated was Kong's status. He was the front row prop in the First Fifteen; his hulking presence had assured Saint Crispin's domination of schoolboy rugby for two years now.

Worse was to come: a summons to appear before Batman in his office the next morning. The sports master and Kong had already been in and, as they came out, Kong had a smirk on his face which told me all.

'So, young Munro,' Batman said. 'I hear that you started a fight last night? Is that true?'

He was already reaching for the cane. Whatever I said would have no effect.

'Is that what Kong told you?'

'*Sir*,' he barked.

'Sir?'

'I could see with my own eyes the damage you inflicted on him,' Batman thundered.

Huh? And what about my black eye? And ribs? Did he tell you that his pals beat me up?

'But that's all we can expect from Harrow,' he added. He tapped the cane against the chair. 'Bend over, Munro.'

There is nothing more humiliating than being forcibly caned, bent over a chair and having six of the best whipped at your buttocks. The cane, slicing deep, is not the problem. It is the imposition of superiority and the application of physical force to maintain that superiority.

Afterward, I left Batman's office with as much dignity as I could muster.

Naturally, Kong and his mates were waiting outside to giggle and guffaw. Kong himself was rubbing at his buttocks in pretended agony.

Curly had said, Sometimes, kid, attack is the best method of defence. I walked over to Kong and his friends.

'Hey, Apeman,' I called to him. He looked at me, astonished. 'Yes, you,' I said, imitating an ape scratching at its armpits and crotch. 'You know your name, don't you?'

Claiming his and his friends' attention. Knowing that what I wanted to say was not for his benefit but for his friends'.

'So you told Batman that I started the fight last night?' Get him where his honour can be hit. 'You went crying to the headmaster.' Mimicking, dabbing at my eyes. 'Bad new boy. Poor Kong, boo hoo.'

His eyes began to shift with alarm. His friends looked at the ground.

'You're a coward, Kong.'

He came for me again. I chopped at his windpipe.

His hands went up. I grabbed his balls.

Twist.

I got another six of the best from Batman for that too.

Masculinity in adolescence is all about physical strength. About games of domination — who is dominant and who can be dominated — played at boarding schools by masters with pupils and by strong pupils over weak. Forget about academic achievement. The dux, the star of the end-of-year Gilbert and Sullivan production, the editor of the school magazine: none cut the same ice as the boy who is king by virtue of his physical or sporting prowess.

Kong. Kong. *Kong*.

17

A ROOM OF boys at night after prayers and Lights Out is a place of sighs and tears, snuffles and groans, giggles and suppressed laughter. The pillow fights have subsided, the tumblings over each other, the stories at bedtime of fellow boys and masters. Now, by moon's full light, each bed is a cradle upon which a boy can rock alone, contemplate, consider. He may think in triumph of his terrors and how he has been able to survive them another day. He may agonise over slights or faults in his classroom friendships. Alone with himself, this is the time when he considers his manhood. Takes his compass bearings. Decides whether he is measuring up.

Sometimes, the younger boys may feel sorry for themselves, indulging their sadnesses, trying to stop the sobs from being heard as they remember their mothers. There is no sadder sound than a voice weeping in the night. It is an admission that manhood comes at a sacrifice. It is the sound all of us try not to make when we become men. In those years we are not supposed to cry.

Looking back, it seems that not a day or night passed that first term when I was not pushed at, punched at, kicked at or beaten up by my nemesis Kong and his sycophants. He became my worst nightmare, and had it not been for the help of Nigger the Maori and Shylock the Jew Boy I might have been beaten into submission, choosing to leave the college rather than to stay on.

It was Nigger in the end who saved me, and all of us really. He called all the boys of Harrow together as a tribe, an iwi. 'United we stand, divided we fall' became the catchcry as the nerds, misfits

NIGHTS IN THE GARDENS OF SPAIN

and leftovers of Harrow rallied to protect me by pushing back, punching back, kicking back. In so doing they discovered the collective strength that a tribe has, and that the honour of our much put-upon house was worth fighting for. Honour is really only another word for masculinity. The Empire began to fight back.

Ironically, the rallying of Harrow around me served only to make me appear even more a troublemaker. A nuisance, a rebel, a boy with a disruptive influence on the rest of the school.

The masters might have been prepared to accept this when it was pupil to pupil. There were many matters among the boys, including Kong's bullying, to which they turned a blind eye. But when, in all innocence, I began to challenge their teachings during three special school assemblies, I set myself on a collision course with Batman himself.

'What's all this about?' I asked Shylock.

We had just concluded evening prayers and were being herded into the first special school assembly in the hall. Rugby in the front stalls, Eton next and Harrow, naturally, in its preordained place at the back.

'No talking, Munro,' Wolf Man called.

Before I could ask again, Four Eyes, the head prefect, saluted and squealed, 'School, attennn-*shun.*'

'Come on, Harrow,' Dracula screamed. 'Move along, boys. *Move!*' As if, being the last house in, it was our fault that we were not yet in our seats.

Between spiky heads I saw that Batman was ascending the platform. Behind came the other masters. All had grim expressions. Behind them the movie screen had been lowered.

'School, at *ease.* School, *sit.*'

'And *be silent,*' Wolf Man called. 'And keep your hands *in your laps* and *folded* at *all times.*'

We settled down. Batman nodded, as if God was there at the back of the hall. With the lights ablaze, a film began. As it was rolling, the masters patrolled the aisles.

The film was about stamens and pistils and how flowers were pollinated by bees. There were also shots of frogs croaking and hopping around and making a jelly substance from which, in fast

103

motion, tadpoles spilled out. Ten minutes later, and it was all over. The masters coughed discreetly. Batman heaved a sigh and nodded that assembly could be dismissed.

'So?' I hissed at Shylock.

It was his droll delivery and crossed eyes that undid me. 'Sex instruction,' he sighed.

I couldn't help it. I was a farm boy after all. Nothing, not even twelve of the best, could stop me from laughing.

The next week's special assembly was marked by a close monitoring of my behaviour. Wolf Man was on one side and Frankenstein on the other. Again, under the bright glaring lights of the hall, Batman ascended to address us. This time the topic was entitled Self Abuse.

Imagine a school of one hundred and eighty boys, patrolled by masters, stunned to silence by the fire and brimstone of a black-caped Batman. He thundered and exploded and pounded his words, and the male faculty nodded grimly at his every point.

'Cleanliness is next to godliness, boys,' he roared, 'and God can see into the heart of every unclean boy. He can see *all*, boys, everything that you do. Don't think that He can't. You must *save* yourselves,' he boomed while we all quailed. 'For the sake of your future wives, boys, do *not* deplete yourselves by *self abuse*. Every time you do it, your body needs two pints of blood to replace it.'

The masters began to nod, flapping their capes like the witches in *Macbeth*.

'If you feel Satan urging you,' Batman continued, 'think of God. If that doesn't work, think of your dear mothers or your sisters, boys. And if that doesn't work, have a *cold shower*.'

Again, ten minutes. And when he fell silent, huffing and puffing and harrumphing, he had scared the living daylights out of the lower school.

Of course, I knew what Batman was talking about, but I could see that the younger boys didn't. So when Batman foolishly roared, 'Are there any *questions*, boys?' I foolishly suggested one.

Standing, I said, 'Perhaps, Sir, you might explain what self abuse is.'

The school sighed audibly and Batman went scarlet.

'Why,' he thundered, 'it's — it's *masturbation*.'

'And what is masturbation, Sir?' Very few of the school would have known the practice by that name either.

It was worth the six I got just to see Batman flopping and gasping for a vocabulary that an eleven-year-old would understand.

The school motto was Play The Game. But Play The Game really meant by the rules of the masters or by the rules of Rugby and Eton. I had shown to both that I was not Playing The Game.

A single-sex boarding school run by sexually repressed males is not the best place for Changeling Boys. The controls that are placed on us mirror their repression. And most of the controls are the most frightening of any concocted: the Thou Shalt Nots of Christianity and the society that has sprung from Christianity.

Of course I understand, now, the *why* of the Saint Crispin's instruction. In that place of tears and sighs, of boys in the company of boys, it was important to enforce an acceptable heterosexual code of sexual conduct. Even worse, to educate senior boys to enforce that code on the rest of the school. To stop the crushes, the affections, the idealisations that boys often held of each other. To enforce gender roles and masculinity. To combat homoeroticism.

This was the patriarchy of Saint Crispin's. But for me it was already too late. I sublimated my crushes by being as masculine as I was supposed to be. In all the time I was there I lived in fear that I would be found out.

During the second term the First Fifteen's fullback left school and a vacancy came up in the team. Trials were held. Despite some team opposition led by Kong, I had undermined his sway to such an extent that I was successful in making it onto the bench. I was the only Harrow player in the team and my triumph paved the way for my and Harrow's revival at Saint Crispin's.

The physicality of the game, however, almost undid me. I developed a crush on Can That Boy Run, the perfect athletic machine who, one afternoon in a crowded dressing room after a game, asked me to apply oil to his back. He undressed to his jockstrap and lay face down on one of the benches. As soon as my hands touched him, I knew I was done for. I spilled too much oil and it ran golden over his shoulderblades and down his spine. He laughed, lifting himself on his elbows, and the oil spilled further over him like a river.

Then he looked at my eyes and we were both unmasked. All around, the other boys were laughing and joking and playing, reliving the match. But the ambience inhabited by Can That Boy Run and me was charged, tense, electric.

All of a sudden I snapped myself out of it.

'That's it,' I laughed, slapping his shoulders.

But from then on he and I avoided each other. I would not let my desires take hold of me. My masculinity had to be undoubted. I counted on it to save me from sexual scorn, abuse and thuggery.

However, nothing could have saved the bravest among us all, the beautiful Choirboy.

I should have known that first Sunday Evensong in the school chapel that Choirboy would be targeted by Kong. John Jones had arrived at the school later in the year than I had and thus had been placed in Harrow. But he had a physical and spiritual beauty more appropriate to Rugby or Eton.

'*O Seigneur, entends ma prière* —'

As soon as that boy soprano voice lifted above our heads, soaring in its crystalline perfection, some sixth sense made me look across the pews at Kong. He had been telling some joke to his mates and they were apoplectic with mirth, doubled over as if they were spewing in the pews.

'*Quand j'appelle, réponds-moi* —'

This was a voice of innocence. Of Eden before it was despoiled. Of a lark ascending to the top of the sky. Higher and higher. Kong became transfixed. Shushing his friends to silence. Looking for the source of the voice.

'*Viens, écoutes-moi.*'

What I was not prepared for was the *look* on Kong's face. I swear to you that it was love, although Kong would never have recognised it as such. But for those looking on, as he mooned after Choirboy, it was obvious that he had been smitten.

However, Kong's love did not last long, for at the headmaster's third special assembly Choirboy took his life into his hands — and made my own foolhardiness pale into insignificance.

On this occasion, Batman again ascended from his cave and,

cape swirling, took the lectern. He summoned the school Bible, placed it on the stand and solemnly began to read from the Old Testament: Genesis, Chapter Nineteen.

'*And there came two angels to Sodom at even,*' he declaimed, '*and Lot sat in the gate of Sodom. And Lot seeing them rose up to meet them and he bowed himself with his face toward the ground. And he said, Behold now, my lords —*'

The story of Sodom and Gomorrah is the touchstone of all emotional, religious and societal hysteria about homosexuality. In it, God sends two angels to investigate the outcry against the wickedness of the twin cities and the grievous sin therein. The divine messengers are received by Lot, nephew of Abraham, who presses them greatly to stay in his house and not to stay in the night streets.

However, the men of Sodom and Gomorrah, both old and young, from every quarter, ring the house and demand Lot to bring the two men out so that 'we may know them'. Lot pleads, 'I pray you, brethren, do not so wickedly,' and, instead, offers the men his two daughters, both virgins. The angels intercede. They blind the crowd of men. They then urge Lot to leave Sodom and Gomorrah, 'For we will destroy this place, because the cry of them is waxen great before the face of the Lord, and the Lord hath sent us to destroy it.' Attempts are made to stop them.

Lot manages to escape Sodom and Gomorrah with his wife and two daughters. God tells him not to look behind. Then God rains upon the twin cities of the plain brimstone and fire from heaven. But Lot's wife looks back and becomes a pillar of salt.

'*Ever since,*' Batman roared, '*God has set his face against the abomination of homosexuality. A homosexual is unfit for the Kingdom of God. Homosexual acts are against nature. They are a sexual perversion, boys. You must guard yourself against lustful thoughts for other boys. You must pray for the boy who has lustful thoughts for you. A homosexual is a sinner. He is a criminal in the eyes of God and of society. Do you all understand?*'

The masters, patrolling the aisles, fastened their beady eyes on us all.

'Yes, *Sir,*' came the unanimous reply.

It was ironic that such men should be so dogmatic about leanings they probably had themselves. Again, I understand now the reason for the third assembly: in Batman's fervid imagination we boys were bedhopping. But nothing will ever let me forgive the authoritarian, forbidding and clear assumption that They Were Right and that The Bible Was On Their Side, Thus Saith The Lord.

'Good,' Batman growled.

He was looking in my direction, expecting me to make some kind of intervention. Perhaps I might have, except that this lecture was not so much about sex as homosexuality and I was trying to hide that part of me. So it was that when Batman saw I wasn't going to laugh, ask a question or otherwise confront him he turned to the head prefect and nodded that the assembly should be dismissed.

That was when a clear voice floated from the back.

'There is nothing in Genesis which says that homosexuality was the sin which caused God to destroy Sodom and Gomorrah.'

'*Who said that!*' Batman roared.

The voice continued, trembling. 'The abomination referred to was not necessarily homosexuality. There is no word in Hebrew or Greek for homosexuality. The sin of Sodom and Gomorrah was larger than that. It includes many wickednesses, among them the threat of rape of angels.'

Choirboy. He was standing there, red-faced, but determined to have his say.

'I will see that boy in my office,' Batman signed to Dracula. Swirled. Exited. Tight-lipped.

'Schhhool dis*missed*,' the head prefect cried in a strangled tone, his eyes almost bursting from their sockets.

The assembly erupted. I looked back. Saw boys edging away from Choirboy. Saw the look of horror spreading across Kong's face. Saw Choirboy seeking support.

I wanted him to look my way. And not to look my way. I was afraid that he might see. Might know. But, at the same time, I wanted him to know.

His eyes locked mine. Frightened.

Then Dracula was there, speaking to him. He led him along the aisle like a falling star.

'*O Seigneur, entends ma prière.*'

Rape of angels, ah yes. It all came out, of course. Why Choirboy was at Saint Crispin's. He had already declared his position to his father. That he was homosexual. His father, fearful, had sent him here to make a man out of him.

'*Quand j'appelle, réponds-moi.*'

For a while Choirboy was protected because of his crystalline voice and the admiration of very important persons who attended chapel. Frankenstein, who also taught choir, was able to shield him with the cloak of the staff's approval. But out of staff range, he was constantly badgered.

'Hello, Girly,' boys would snigger.

'Sissy boy,' his own lower school would yell.

Give us a kiss. Pass the butter, Pansy. How about a piece, Fruit-cake? Oo, you *are* awful. Doing anything tonight, Sweety?

Nigger tried to organise Harrow around Choirboy, but found resistance. I did not know him well and God forgive me, even I was equivocal, reluctant. Afraid to be tarred with the same brush.

'What's wrong with you?' Nigger asked. 'I thought you liked losers? That you hated bullies. This is a brother we're talking about. You'd help me, wouldn't you? Or Shylock? What's the difference with John? Huh? Get wise, man.'

The difference? The difference is that for boys a Homosexual Boy is worse than a Black or a Jew because he has, so we mistakenly think, willingly given up the rights of the penis. He doesn't want to be a boy any longer. He wants to be a girl. And boys don't play with girls.

Even worse was Kong's reaction. His was the kind of anger that makes a boy kick a sandcastle to smithereens. To take the wings off a butterfly. To rape angels.

'*Viens, écoutes-moi.*'

Through all this Choirboy maintained an undaunted dignity. Then Easter approached and, with it, the special Easter service in the chapel. The choir was singing, Choirboy's voice soaring.

Then his voice broke and he was thrown to the wolves.

Late one night at the beginning of the second term, after Lights Out, a message came for Choirboy that his father had arrived unexpectedly and was waiting at the headmaster's office.

The path to the headmaster's leads past the dressing rooms at the far end of the rugby field. There, Kong and some of his mates were waiting. They had some jolly old fun. Took Choirboy into the showers and stripped him to see what he had: Hohoho, small, isn't it, boys? Got boot polish and blackened his private parts, Teeheehee.

It was Nigger who said, Something's wrong.

We could hear Choirboy's screams a quarter of a mile away. When Nigger, Shylock and I burst into the dressing rooms Kong had Choirboy's head down a toilet bowl and was yelling, 'Eat shit, Fag.'

One of Kong's cronies had a broom up Choirboy's anus.

Choirboy's face was covered in blood.

And excrement.

And piss.

At our arrival Kong and his pals took off, hooting with jackal laughter. I ran to Choirboy, who collapsed unconscious.

'Oh I'm so sorry, I'm so sorry.'

I cradled him in my arms. Wiped the urine away from his beautiful, wan face. Washed the shit out of his hair.

Choirboy stirred.

His eyes were filled with tears of humiliation. He tried to cover his nakedness.

'Thank you,' he said. 'For coming for me.'

There was an Inquiry. The school closed ranks. The boys who had been involved were exonerated. After all, they were fine upstanding young men. It was not their fault that they had been provoked into this assault by a sexual deviant.

Choirboy was in hospital for a week. After his release his father removed him from Saint Crispin's.

A friend once said, 'If you're not for me, you're against me.' Then she added, 'And if you stand silently and watch, you're as guilty as if you yourself were inflicting the punishment.'

In New York in the late 1960s, a group of transsexuals and transvestites threw bricks at Stonewall Inn and, with that act, Gay Liberation was born.

Choirboy was like that for me. When he was assaulted for being what he was, he became all that Stonewall represented. He did not hide what he was, as I did. He was the bravest of us all.

Part Three

THE FIRST DAY OF THE REST OF OUR LIVES

18

AN INTERNATIONAL FAX at work: *Hi. Long time since we saw each other. Stop.* It is from my Canadian friend, Oh My Goodness.

Two years ago when I was in Canada we saw each other. He was a tall blond bombshell with a disarming grin and it was yet another case of veni, vidi, vici.

The firm wants me to check out our operations in Australia and Thailand, so I am flying out there next month. I am hoping to take a few days in New Zealand first and hope you will have time to show me around. It would be great to see you.

I write a reply. Tongue in cheek. *Looking forward to extending the usual hospitality. Let me know time, date and airline arrival and I'll meet you.*

A surprising event. Hope Springs Eternal has fetched up in our academic waters. At first, when I opened the door to him at Film Studies, I didn't recognise him. He wore grey pinstripe trousers, black jacket and a bowtie, his sartorial elegance a complete contrast to the usual white towel around the waist.

'Old chap,' he said when I looked up.

'Hello,' I answered in mock heartiness. My reflex action was to wonder if Brenda had seen him come in. He caught my quick glance.

'Don't worry,' he said. 'I'm not here to blow your cover.'

I shrugged, ashamed. Motioned him to take a seat. 'So what can I do for you?'

'Nothing at all,' he smiled, 'nothing at all. Of all things I am now occasionally employed by the law faculty. The old professor — I was one of his students — put the hard word on me. He wanted somebody who could teach company law to the rabble and tempted me with an offer of my own office and a secretary. It makes a change from my usual day down in the city. And the scenery is just marvellous.' He leaned forward and, *sotto voce*, whispered, 'I've already been kicked out of the university sauna for ogling the boys.'

I grinned in spite of myself.

'Then I saw you yesterday,' he said, 'parking your car. The attendant told me who you were and which department you were in. So here I am. Just came to say hello.' He looked at me conspiratorially. 'I know this is odd, seeing as we often bump into each other in the Gardens of Spain, but we haven't ever been formally introduced, have we? May I have the honour? You can call me Jack. Everyone else does. Jack Alwyn-Jones actually.'

'Of course,' I answered, taking his limp hand.

Not only was Hope Springs Eternal one of the principals of the most respectable legal partnership in the city. He was also son and heir to the late Sir Always Boasting About Himself.

Then, 'Gardens of Spain?' I asked, puzzled.

'Oh, old chap,' he answered. 'Just an affectation of mine. You wouldn't know the orchestral and piano rhapsody by Manuel De Falla would you? An impressionistic piece describing nights in the Moorish gardens of Granada and Sierra de Cordoba?'

'No.'

'Ah well, never mind.' Jack flapped his hand and his grey eyes clouded with dreaminess. 'It just happens to be my pet name for all the glittering establishments where we heretics gather. The steam parlours, saunas, baths, beaches, bars. You know, in the old days an Inquisition would have condemned us to be burned

publicly at an auto-da-fé. Anyway, it saves me from explaining to
Mother when she inquires where I am going of an evening.'

Chuckling.

'She thinks The Gardens of Spain is a restaurant.'

Gardens of Spain. Yes.

19

THE NIGHT IS a river and I am driven to wander its banks. In spite of Annabelle and Chris I am like Orpheus, compulsive in my search for peace from the shades that haunt me. Within the whispering forest the maenads are gathering to rip my heart out and tear me limb from limb.

The Steam Parlour, The Fuck Palace or The Maze —

You would never recognise the entrance to The Maze by daylight. West of the city, it is a huge steel portcullis sealed between industrial warehouses where freight consignments await shipment: radiator specialists, lime merchants, meat slaughtering and storage companies, wool brokers and buyers, septic tank services, irrigation equipment, excavators, blacksmiths and farriers, hydroponics supplies, concrete pumping machines, coolstores and freezers, gaming machines, mining equipment. By day the area vibrates, pounds and thuds, articulated by the humming timetable of shipping arrivals and departures. By night it is a place slashed by sinister shadows.

In a previous incarnation The Maze was once the headquarters for The Grim Reapers, a bikie gang who used it as a shack-out, indoor race track and party place. It was the gang who bequeathed the portcullis and roller door as protection against the regular police raids.

Best to park the car beneath a street lamp. That won't stop the tyres from being slashed and windows broken, but it might prevent some prostitute having off her trick on your back seat. Then lock the door and cross over into the alley where The Maze is: opposite the laboratory promising Medical Equipment Servicing

& Calibration and next to the warehouse for Motor Accessory
Importers & Wholesalers. A logo is painted on the portcullis: 69,
the international symbol for oral sex. At night when the portcullis
is up and the steel roller door is opened, the logo disappears. But
when it vanishes The Maze's nihilistic creed takes its place. A sign
reading: ALL YOU NEED IN THIS LIFE IS A TREMEN-
DOUS SEX DRIVE AND A GREAT EGO. BRAINS DON'T
MEAN A SHIT.

Even before its present incarnation, The Maze had a reputation.
The cops repeatedly raided the bikie fortress. A body, decapitated,
was found floating in the oily water last week. Places like this
attract all that is murderous, diseased and suicidal in human
nature. It is not for the tourist, the faint hearted or the curious.
Yet we still come, to walk that inhospitable territory toward the
portcullis. There to take the first test: to seek entrance from
Robocock, the doorman.

Shall I go there tonight? No. Onward to The Steam Parlour.

I park the car in the side alley and return to the street, quickly,
because there has been a recurrence of gay bashings around The
Steam Parlour. Young men following you to your car. Pretending
to offer sex. Instead, placing switchblade to jugular vein, boots to
stomach, head and thighs. Knuckledusters smashing into skull,
eyes and crunching into nose. Eat shit, faggot.

The Spaniard has at long last got around to putting the 'u' into
the sign above the hatch. As I go to congratulate him he says, 'I
know, I know. I got Mark to do it before I fired him.'

Mark, The Young Thing. He had been decorative enough, flit-
ting between customer and customer with his tight butt. But
there was always something defensive about him which stopped
him from loosening up enough to relax and talk. As if he was
above this sort of shit. Only doing it for the money. Too good to
be performing for all these queers. His struts and poses were contemptuous of us. They reminded us of who we were by making a
mockery of what we did.

'I'm sorry about that,' I answer, automatically.

'Why be sorry?' The Spaniard responds. 'You know as well as I
do that a kid who is up himself is bad for business.' He passes me a

towel and key for a locker. 'Amateurs,' he spits.

The Spaniard starts to cough. Quickly he puts a white handkerchief to his dark lips. It is not imagination which colours the whiteness with petals of blood.

'Damn cigarettes,' he mutters. 'Bad for the health.'

I step away, quickly. Anything to escape his body fluids, the disease coughed up from and ejected out of his mottled throat. The gesture does not escape his attention and he smiles like a devil as I turn into the locker room.

DON'T SHARE NEEDLES OR MEN. A new poster advertises a Big Gay Dance Party: COME AS YOUR HERO AND DANCE YOUR TITS OFF.

Take off my sweatshirt. Nipples already stirring. Now my jeans. Cock swinging clear, starting to throb.

'Hi there.'

The New Young Thing. Perhaps nineteen. Nice. Tallish. Clear eyes and ready smile. Good shoulders. Good definition. A man's man. Refilling the condom dispenser. Trying to please.

'Have a freebie,' he offers. He palms me a condom in its foil wrapper. Just as natural as passing a piece of gum. Then a pause as he looks down at me:

'Come to think of it, this one's more your size.'

The Jumbo. Yes, kid, flattery will get you everywhere.

'Let me introduce myself,' he says. 'I've just started here. The name's Mar—'

Jesus, another one.

'But with a c,' he hastens. 'The American spelling.'

As if that makes a difference.

Past Always A Bridesmaid and Fat Forty And A Fairy, watching the latest Cadinot loop with nary the faintest stirrings of interest in their tightly towelled nether parts. They are like two swollen-bellied Egyptian mummies in the gloom.

'Nice kid, isn't he,' they ask.

I grin and nod in agreement, and they wave me through into the shower. Although staff are hands off, Marc has obviously passed the litmus test: to banter, to tease, to indulge in flirtation with Always A Bridesmaid and Fat Forty And A Fairy. Even the most unprepossessing of customers has a right to be respected, paid court to, made to feel special, desirable, wanted. And among the clientele of The Steam Parlour, Always A Bridesmaid and Fat Forty And A Fairy have a role important above all others: to offer tea and sympathy. Some of the guys who come here are not just after hot sex. Some want to talk, too. Have a friendly ear, pour out all their trouble and woes.

Open Sesame. The steam from the shower is like a billowing warm friend, embracing every pore and every part of my body. The Bald One and two other men are also showering, checking each other out. In one corner the ravenous Size Queen watches.

The shower room is for cocksmen to strut their stuff and to show off their equipment. Where sexual specifications are concerned, this place has seen them all. Some are short, some are long, some are thick and some are thin. Some are capped, some are uncapped. Some dress to the left, some dress to the right, some hang straight down, settling nicely into the groove between the balls. Some have big balls, some have small balls, some have no balls at all.

Some are brutish, some club-shaped. Some are conical, some crooked. Some are beautiful to look at, others could do with plastic surgery. Some take root from smooth alabaster thighs, others from hair so copious that the water does not penetrate. Some tuck there, others project out, but most conform to an unassuming configuration.

Nor, in sex, do they climax the same way. Some do so copiously, some dribble and some pour and keep pouring by the jugful. Some jet out to the shoulders and further. And some, by some enviable miracle of pressure, send fountains into the air, kaleidoscopic wheels spinning phhht, phhht, phhht, their bodies shuddering at each spout.

Blacks are generally bigger. Orientals are surprising sexual gymnasts. Scotsmen are to be savoured. Poles smell of hay. Dutchmen are collectors' items. Englishmen are apologetic until coaxed out. Americans are gorgeous and come with tans. Polynesians, by virtue of their sensual natures, are the best.

In early sex books, sexologists tried to convince that flaccid size was not relative to erect size. They opined that, erect, all of us approximate a median.

Ha. The experts were men who were ignorant of the likes of The Black, That Boy's Deformed or my friend Oh My Goodness.

I reach up to turn off the shower. The Bald One and the other two men are just about to go into the steam room, Size Queen in tow, when all of a sudden Snake Charmer, followed by a well-hung Out Of Towner, comes through the door. Everyone hesitates a moment and then casually returns to showering. Snake Charmer has already enticed Out Of Towner's cobra half out of its hairy undergrowth and it may be showtime, folks.

The steam drifts about us all. Out Of Towner looks a bit embarrassed about having an audience, twists the taps and clothes himself in a curtain of falling water. Snake Charmer, however, keeps up his mesmeric concentration and, slowly, the snake starts to uncoil and slither out again.

That's when my impish sense of humour gets the better of me. There's nothing like friendly competition to keep Snake Charmer's techniques up to the mark.

I leave my shower and stride between Out Of Towner and Snake Charmer, breaking Snake Charmer's concentration. I wink at him:

Toss you for him.

Then slowly I start to gyrate. To move my ass. To suddenly explode into a strut, pout, slide, jump, moonwalk swing and thrust that would leave Mick Jagger for dead.

'Oh wow,' Out Of Towner breathes.

For across the room Snake Charmer, no slouch himself in the dance stakes, is going into his own sinuous routine. Rippling his pecs and thrusting his buttocks, his cock whanging from side to side. Matching my every move. Getting into it, *yeah*.

The Bald One, Size Queen and the other two men watch avidly, calling their encouragement to us, Way to *go*. Out Of Towner is beside himself with excitement. Two hunks competing for him is the stuff of which legends are made. Then, the show's over and I am panting.

Okay, Out Of Towner. You've had your show. Time to choose, boy. His or mine. Waiting. Ruthless. Watching Out Of Towner making his choice.

Meantime, in the background comes the comedic patter of

Always A Bridesmaid and Fat Forty And A Fairy, doing a mock tap dance à la Gene Kelly:

'We're swinging in the rain, just swinging in the rain —' Then chortles of suppressed laughter, falling into silence and gleaming anticipation.

All Out Of Towner's birthdays have come at once. He comes padding over. But with a pelvic swivel to my audience I turn my back. Throw him to Snake Charmer's mongoose teeth. Yawn and flex my muscles. Making the conquest is all that matters.

Not tonight, fucker.

20

ON MY WAY to work, and I have just seen Chris off at the airport. *Petrushka* is going on tour for three weeks. I haven't told Chris that Annabelle and I have slept together and have talked about making a go of our marriage.

Chris is the last through the gate.

'Come *on*,' the others in the company yell.

He catches a glance from me and misinterprets it.

'It's only twenty-one days,' he grins, 'and I'll call.'

He gives me a hug and is off.

A week later and I have been shuttling backwards and forwards from the flat to The House On The Hill. Sometimes we make love, sometimes we don't. It is all insanity. When you want to do all the right things you do all the wrong things. We are two people who love each other, caught in a tragicomedy of passion, fear and anger, not too sure whether what we are saying is what we really mean or is what the other partner wants to hear.

'I want you back,' Annabelle says.

She has followed me out to the car, pleading with me to stay. Rebecca is holding Miranda on the doorstep of The House On The Hill, and Miranda is furiously waving her wand.

'I want to come back,' I answer. 'But I just don't know whether or not it's *right* for you, for me or for the girls.'

'Please stay —'

A rapping on the door of my flat. Annabelle is there, arms folded, looking across the sitting room to the bedroom.

'So this is where you live,' she says. 'May I come in?' I let her in. She stands with her back to me, shivering. 'I was just passing and I thought I'd drop in. Now I can see that it was a bad mistake. Is this where you bring them?'

'Who?'

'The men in your life, you *bastard*.'

'Don't do this, Annabelle. Don't do this.'

'Why did you let it happen? Whatever happened to good old self-restraint? Why did you give in?'

'You make my being gay sound like a weakness.'

'It *is*, sport.'

'No, it's a strength.'

'Well I don't give a damn any more because whatever it is, it's killing me. Killing *us*.'

Evening again, and I am at The House On The Hill. Annabelle and I have just finished making love, but this time something crawled into bed with us. The Thing turned the lovemaking into an act of utter joylessness.

Annabelle watches me unroll the condom.

'Have you had the test?' she asks.

I groan.

'I have a right to know.'

'No, I haven't.'

'Well, if we're getting back together, you'd better take it. I'm still in the dark about whether or not you're still having sex with men. Are you?'

'No. Yes. No. It all depends.'

'On what!'

'On what you call sex.'

'Let's give it a name then. Fucking.'

'With or without a condom?'

'Words, words, evasive words. *Tell* me.'

'Yes. I have *safe* sex. With men.'

She kneels in front of me. Stares me in the face.

'Nothing is safe, *sport*.' Then, 'And did you bring them here too?'

At the flat, and Annabelle has brought Rebecca and Miranda to visit. I have cooked dinner for them and, although the atmosphere has been strained, Rebecca and Miranda are trying very hard to make it all *work*. Meantime, Annabelle and I, punch drunk, trade blows in a ring while the girls, standing on the outside, seem always to be on their best behaviour.

'This is never going to work,' Annabelle says. 'There are so many questions I want to ask and am afraid to ask. So many promises I want to ask you to keep and am afraid to ask. All I want is for you to be happy.' She begins to weep. Signs to the girls:

'Get your coats, girls. We're going home.'

'Please don't go like this, Annabelle.'

She gives me a glance of love that pierces my heart.

'You're never going to change, sport. And I'm too proud to ask you to change. I don't want you to be what I want you to be. I want *you* to want that.'

'I don't want to lose you or the girls. I love you. I love them. Please forgive me.' Tears are streaming down my face.

'One of us has to be strong,' Annabelle pleads. 'One of us has to walk away from all this and set the other free. If it can't be you, it has to be me.'

She walks after the girls who wait huddling in the back seat of the car. Switches on the ignition..

'Girls, say goodnight to your father.'

I reach over and switch the ignition off. She switches it on again and we start a seesawing battle for the key.

'Damn you, David, damn you.'

In the back seat Miranda starts to whimper. She is too young to understand what is happening. Then with desperation Rebecca begins to yell at us both.

'Stop, Mummy. Stop, Daddy. Stop.'

She gathers Miranda in her arms. Already she has become the strong one of us all. Her father and mother are crying, thinking only of themselves.

'There, there, darling,' Rebecca whispers to her sister. 'There, there.' In a trice Rebecca has taken over the role of parent to Miranda.

Then she looks at me. 'Please, Daddy, it's time for us to go.'

At The House On The Hill, Annabelle and I have just finished making love again.

'This house is also yours,' Annabelle says. 'You can walk back through the door any time you want, but —'

There is always a but or an if.

'You can't have us — me and the girls — and men as well.'

The silence is palpable.

'Can't you understand, Annabelle?' I ask. 'That's why I got out in the first place. Being gay was ripping me apart.'

'Well isn't there shock treatment or something for conditions like yours?'

We stare at each other in the moonlight. Then we burst out laughing at the thought of my sitting in a chair with electrodes fizzing away in my skull, as if my gayness can be burnt out. But laughter can never keep the Thing at bay. Nor words made in the stomach of the night and spat out under duress and in fatigue. Nor pretending that everything will just go away.

The flat again, and Annabelle is there when Chris rings from Wellington, where *Petrushka* has had full houses. She waits while I talk. When I put down the telephone she says, 'Is Chris the ballet dancer?'

'Yes.'

'Is he the one you introduced me to? Is he the reason why you were at the ballet?' Her voice is rising with anger and fear. The force of her rage reduces me to monosyllables.

'Yes.'

'He's one of you, isn't he?'

'Yes.'

Then she shrugs her shoulders. 'Actually, I liked him.'

But one night the Thing crawls into Annabelle's dreams and she wakes up with a cry. Trembling, she turns to me.

'There are pictures in my head of what you do with other men. Make them go away. Please make them go away.'

Her weeping fills the house.

But when she falls asleep the weeping still keeps going. From the girls' room comes the sound of Rebecca getting out of her bed and into Miranda's bed.

Ssshh, darling. Ssshh.

Now it is morning again, fresh and sparkling, springing up out of the dark.

'Okay, sport. Let's try to forget the past. We can't go back. We've got to keep on going forward. Today is the first day of the rest of our lives.'

'I'll shake on that. But who is this decision *for*, Annabelle? You? Me? Or the girls?'

'I don't know yet, David. But I'm not going to let all those years of our marriage go down the drain without one helluva fight. I can't do it myself, though. You're going to have to meet me half way.'

'No promises.'

'But will you *try*, damn you?'

'I'll try.'

'I do love you, you sod.'

In the background Rebecca and Miranda are performing a frantic tarantella, holding hands and whirling whirling whirling like brightly spinning tops. Suddenly Miranda begins to cough and wheeze. Then, there she is, puffing on her inhaler, her eyes bright and feverish with hope.

21

TODAY I AM moving back to The House on The Hill from the flat. It is six o'clock in the morning and the telephone is ringing. My sister, at this godforsaken hour, haranguing and cuffing me like a female cub would a younger brother in the same pride of lions.

'It's the only time I can find you at home,' she defends herself, 'and I hate talking to answerphones. If I want to talk to a machine I can ring up the meteorological office and listen to the recorded weather report.' Then, 'So what I want to know is whether it's true?'

'What are you talking about!'

'I'm your sister, after all,' she continues. 'The least you could have done was tell *me*. You know you can talk to me.'

Not quite true. When you're sorting yourself out, family are not often the ones you can turn to. They represent the place of departure and not the place of arrival.

'Well?' she asks again 'Is it true?'

'About what!'

'What Mum and Dad are saying. That you and Annabelle are getting back together.'

Oh that.

'Yes.'

There is a long silence. Then my sister's voice comes down the line. 'Well, I don't know. You really take the cake.'

Click.

After all that, the day becomes just like any other. Ah well, now that I'm awake I may as well get the rest of my body up and moving. My half tumid penis thwangs from thigh to thigh as I pull on my shorts, my usual gear for the gym.

Time for a homemade cappuccino? Yes. A quick read through the morning daily too. So what's new on Spaceship Earth? Still en route for collision I see:

MASS BLOCKADE PLANNED TO STOP NUCLEAR CARRIER

The Navy has issued a plea to the organisers of the mass blockade of the harbour entrance to call off their protest. 'There is no way,' a Navy spokesman said, 'that this protest will have any effect whatsoever on the visit of the carrier.'

The carrier is scheduled to arrive in three weeks. At least four hundred small craft are expected to take part in the blockade. Wind surfers and small P-class yachts are also expected in the protest.

'Someone is going to get killed,' the Navy spokesman said. 'If so, it will be on the heads of the organisers.'

Around this headline and photograph is the usual depressing news of Political Crisis, Dire Economic Prediction, Pestilence, Death and Destruction, and Another Hole In The Ozone Layer. Welcome to our world. Then on page seven, a report from Canberra, Australia, that:

Research by a New Zealand scientist in Canberra may lead to a way of blocking the development of Aids and some cancers.

Dr Alistair Ramsay's work in the John Curtin School of Medical Research at the Australian National University has produced a genetically engineered method of repairing and boosting damaged immune systems.

Although not a cure, the research holds great potential of staving off the onset of Aids in HIV-infected people, and impeding the progress of some cancers.

Dr Ramsay's research, reported in the influential American journal *Science*, has produced promising results in laboratory animals, and will be tested in clinical trials of HIV-infected humans in Sydney and Melbourne this year or early next year.

Working with Dr Alan Husband of the University of Sydney and German scientists in Freiburg, Dr Ramsay is using a system of inserting new genetic material into a harmless virus, which may then be able to counter the damage caused by the HIV virus and cancer.

'It shows the potential for immunotherapy to help either throw off the disease, or prevent the onset of serious problems,' Dr Ramsay said.

'Our aim would be to keep parts of the immune system intact, to prevent or put off the onset of the syndrome of Aids in HIV-infected individuals, which is when the immune system collapses finally.'

Rip it out for the file. You never know. Another piece of information to add to the fearful conversations we have with each other. The life that you save may be your own.

Now pack my suitcase. I may as well take it over to The House On The Hill after I've been to the gym.

On the way, The Noble Savage again, cheekily driving across my path. His eyes are glowing and his grin is as bright as the sun. In his emerald-coloured pareu he looks as if he has been born with the dawn.

'Kia ora, David. Do you want to come bowling this week?' he asks. 'We've got a fundraiser for the Prostitutes' Collective.'

The transvestites and transsexuals of The Noble Savage's tribe are stunning. Lithe and supple, they are without the square shoulders, Adam's apple and knobbly knees that are a dead giveaway in their white counterparts. But they are careless, giving sex without condoms.

'Can't this week,' I answer.

'Ah well, send in your donation anyhow,' he winks.

He zooms off. He is son of the morning.

Into the gym and up the stairs. Poor Miss Cellulite still pedals away and Mister Gargantua looks as if he's been at the rowing machine forever. What's amazing is that Left Dress showed me a photograph of Mister Gargantua when he was younger and he was *some* hunk. Something happens to men in their thirties, some acceptance by the body that it must succumb to the imperatives of genetic inheritance. A giving up takes place. The teenage stunner who once had masses of jet black hair has lost it by the time he is thirty-five. The boy who was captain of the swim team has developed a barrel gut, his unused muscles turned to jello. The dreamboat voted Most Likely To Succeed exhibits the tics and mannerisms which indicate a long battle with nervous breakdown. Noses that were aquiline become meaty. Cheeks that were planed become fleshy, and what were once firm jawlines are now jowls. The skin starts to fold, crack, blister, crater and lose its youthful sheen. Hair goes grey, recedes or disappears altogether. Waists thicken and the muscles of arms and legs lose definition. Perhaps this is how it happened with Hope Springs Eternal.

But no time to sit and be sad. Get myself going and thank my lucky stars for skinny parents. Through the main floor I dash.

I am late again and The Black has already begun his punishing routine.

'You want it fast dontcha fuckers! Then start *mooovinnn* before I *kick ass*.'

The floor judders and heaves as the aerobics class jump, skip, stretch, flop, jiggle and plop.

As for me, working on the circuit has to be achieved gingerly. However, even slower is heterosexual Big Balls, who has forsaken the aerobics class for a workout on the weights. Every stretch and pike tightens his skin and sends signals of pain. His face and arms are fiercely red.

'Looks like you got some sun yesterday,' I say to him.

'Went out yachting,' he puffs. 'I forgot to watch myself.'

He certainly did. When he is getting changed in the dressing room he glows all over like the apple the Wicked Witch gave Snow White to eat. At the sight of him, All American, who is going for a shower in the nearby stalls, makes a gesture of mock horror, putting his fingers across the O of his mouth.

'Burny *burny*,' he says, pretending to flick his towel at Big Balls before he steps into the communal waterfall.

'But not where it really matters,' Big Balls answers, revealing a tiny tanline that shows a jockstrap has protected his crotch. We all laugh. Then:

'Lucky *lucky*,' The Hulk interrupts. Already showering, he turns and flexes his muscles, sending bullets of water to ricochet over Big Balls' body. Every squirt sizzles like rain on a hot tin roof, and Big Balls yelps and crashes naked into others in the dressing room, hiding behind a startled Bright Eyes. The Hulk grins. He would never be in danger of sunburnt vitals. Uncircumcised, his dick has a protective umbrella.

Meantime, Bright Eyes looks across at me, exposed. For the brush of Big Balls' body against his, skin against skin, has made his cock storm out in helpless surging. Quickly he steps into the shower next to me, turns the cold tap full on and disappears under the waterfall. I catch Left Dress looking at him and me with an inquiring glance. Bright Eyes catches the look as he emerges from the chrysalis of water. He colours. Dresses. Looks neither left or right. And is gone.

So now I park the car in its accustomed place. I take my suitcase out and walk through the hot sunlight to The House On The Hill.

The door opens. Annabelle is waiting there, holding back the girls. But my little Miranda wriggles away from her grasp and is running through the sunlight, a bundle of delightful curls and joy. Then Rebecca too.

'I'm glad you're back, Daddy,' Rebecca sighs.

Although the suitcase is too heavy, she and Miranda pull it out of the back seat of the car and through the gate to the doorstep where Annabelle waits.

'Hello, sport,' she says, her voice quivering. 'I burnt the toast, the shower has developed a leak, Miranda has been impossible this morning but otherwise —'

We hold each other. Afraid and awed by our arrogance in attempting to thwart the compulsion that is breaking us apart on this the first day of the rest of our lives.

22

And after the reconciliation, no great change seems to have occurred. The sun hasn't stopped in the sky. There has been no portent, no sign of malediction or of blessing to mark my reunion with Annabelle. Nothing at all. Instead, the return to the routine of taking Miranda and Rebecca to school.

'Bye, Daddy! See you after school?'

'Yes, darlings,' I assure them.

Even so, they wave and wave and wave as if they are not too sure themselves.

It is almost as if the weeks we've been apart have never happened. For here I am up at Film Studies and this could be a day just like any other day. Indeed, the world wags on.

Then, a glance at the calendar. Almost forgot. The Japanese critic to whom I sent a fax earlier is coming to my film class this morning and Ronald, my assistant, wants a meeting: URGENT.

The telephone rings.

Chris again, this time from Christchurch. He is bubbling over with excitement.

'Guess what happened!' he yells. 'Raymond injured his left leg and I had to go on last night in the *lead*. And they loved me, David. They simply loved me —'

His boyish exuberance makes me yearn for him. I should tell him now, while I've still got the strength and will, about Annabelle and me. But the words refuse to come, and before I know it he has hung up.

Tell him when he returns. Yes.

I walk out to Brenda who has started to put on her face. Now I'm irritated about Chris. I watch Brenda, cross with her too for the cold shoulder I keep getting over Annabelle, and meanly think that plastic surgery or reincarnation are better bets for her.

'If it is not too much to ask,' I begin, 'can you tell me if there have been any messages?'

'Your life insurance broker has rung,' Brenda replies. She applies a top lip with Jungle Desire. 'You've some mail, which I've put on your desk.' Bottom lip in a different gloss of Irresistible. Then the following is enunciated with a wide mouth, pursed and waiting for her lips to dry:

'An don' 'orget the 'orning 'ea.'

Among the usual clutch of bills and memoranda is a letter in its familiar grey envelope from the longtime partner of The Love Of My Life. They live on the outskirts of Napier where Longtime Partner was an orchardist:

'David, do you think you could pop down and see us soon? I know that Charles is keen to see you.'

Pleasant. Light. But beneath the lightness is an invitation that cannot be declined.

The staff morning tea is in full swing. That is, the usual people have turned up to the usual boring farewell. This farewell, however, is marked by all the celebrants trying to keep as far away from the guest of honour as possible. A teacher of linguistics, he is not named Bad Breath for nothing.

What with trying to escape his pestilential gums, and at the same time avoiding the repeated offers from God's Gift To Woman to take cake, we are faced with a difficult choice of whom to avoid. Bad Breath seems to be winning, which means that today his breath can turn one to stone. So, like the others, I join the crowd around God's Gift, who is revelling in his new-found popularity by telling one of his appalling bargain basement jokes.

'What do you call a mushroom with a twelve-inch penis?'

We shake our heads, fearing the worst.

'A fun guy to be with.'

Fun guy. Fungi. And he has the audacity to laugh at his own joke. Jesus.

Oops, and now Predator flashes me a dazzling smile. With her right leg crossed over her left thigh she looks like Rhonda Fleming, a Hollywood siren of the 1950s. The shoe on her left foot is, as usual, dangling from her heel as she swings in a suggestive movement.

Everything is normal, so normal. Like the calm place in the eye of the hurricane.

Back at Film Studies I can see that Brenda is entertaining the Japanese critic, bowing and saying 'Hai' to everything he says. I signal that I am back. I gather my notes, readying myself for class. Already I can see them going into the lecture room. Among them, Bright Eyes, who sees me and waves. His semaphoring hand showers the corridor with light.

'Hi,' I call. I am tempted to refer to the incident in the shower room at the gym this morning but instead, 'Been to any good ballet lately?'

He grins ruefully. 'We keep on being kicked out,' he yells. Then, referring to his friend, Allan, he adds, 'He goes back to London tomorrow.'

And good riddance.

The Japanese film critic has heard our exchange and, seeing me, begins to shake Brenda's hand and bow.

'Mister Nakamichi?' I ask. 'So delighted to have you at our humble establishment. Would you care to follow me?'

Into the lion's den. The class is settling down, curious about their guest. Bright Eyes is poised, alert, shining.

'Okay everyone, we shall now turn from Shakespeare and Film to a new subject. In the next few lectures we shall be tracing the ways in which the indigenous American film form has been adapted by the non-American film industries around the world. Notably India, which has the largest film-making industry internationally, Japan and, of course, Australia and New Zealand. Today we shall discuss the film industry in Japan and,' turning to the Japanese critic, 'we have the pleasure of one of that industry's foremost critics, Mister Nakamichi.'

A hum of appreciation. Mister Nakamichi grins from ear to ear and nods vigorously, making sure that everybody knows it is he we are talking about. As if it could be anyone else.

'Mister Nakamichi is a well-known scholar of the work of Akira

Kurosawa, whose Shakespearean-inspired films of *Macbeth* and *King Lear* have earlier been discussed. He was a personal friend of the actress playing Lady Macbeth, she who rustled from room to room like a black mamba —'

The lions are tamed. Time to feed them.

After the lecture the applause for the Japanese critic is overwhelming and well deserved. He has been erudite, witty and provocative. Bright Eyes has led a vigorous discussion on some of the points he has raised. A group led by our young tutor, Stephen, is engaging Mister Nakamichi in further questions. Stephen is angling for an invitation to visit Japan. Bright Eyes is attractive and animated, running his fingers through his hair, nodding or wiping his brow in body language which indicates perhaps, yes and of course, it's so obvious.

Then it's time to rescue Mister Nakamichi, say sayonara to him and slip Stephen some cash from the department's visitor entertainment budget to take him to dinner.

'So there you are, David.' It is Ronald, my assistant. 'I left you a note,' he adds, disapprovingly. 'Marked *urgent*. Didn't you get it?'

I take Bright Eyes' example and wipe my brow — *of course*.

Then I listen to Ronald as he describes, with as much enthusiasm as his Scottish caution will allow, a new find.

In the old days, pre-1920 and before the era of motion films, Victorian entertainment came in the form of fifty-foot loops that ran through the Edison Company's peep-show kinetoscopes. These were the early pioneering days of film, before the birth of film narrative, when short film subjects were little actualities, slices of real life, taken from popular entertainments. A music-hall conjurer pulling a rabbit out of a hat, a burlesque queen bumping and grinding out of her corset, a travelling show's knife-throwing act or a vaudeville singer crooning in flickering silence. Sometimes well-known personalities would be featured in tiny animated fragments of action: Annie Oakley taking potshots at clay targets, Indians from Buffalo Bill's Wild West Show re-enacting a war council, or Gentleman Jim Corbett in a championship boxing match.

'Laddie,' Ronald says, with a light in his eyes, 'a cache of these kinetoscope films has turned up in a farm basement in Eketahuna.'

A day's drive away. Don't blink as you pass through, or you will miss it.

'That's great,' I breathe with awe.

'Apparently an old codger there, when he was young, lived in New York. He inherited his father's collection of kinetoscopes. When he married and settled in New Zealand after the First World War, he brought the collection with him. He died a month ago aged ninety-eight and, when his son was cleaning out the basement — on his father's farm just outside the town — he found the films.'

'Wonderful news,' I respond. 'So do you want time off to go up there to pick them up?'

'To start with,' Ronald says.

'To start with?'

Ronald leans forward, unable to keep his excitement in.

'Laddie, we are talking here about a major find. *Major*. I need three trucks.'

'Three?' My own excitement is rising.

'And lots of money. All the films are remarkably preserved, apparently, but they are all on nitrocellulose stock. Some have deteriorated but most have maintained their chemical stability mainly because the basement had ideal temperature and humidity conditions. We've struck it lucky.'

'How much money do you need?' He takes my breath away.

'Thousands of dollars. I want to start on preservation as soon as the films get here. I am relying on you to get it. Once we start moving the films out they will become unstable. We will have to rig the trucks to duplicate the current basement conditions. We're going to have to refit and extend the laboratory and, again, duplicate the conditions where the films are in situ. I'll need two trained assistants —'

I try to sound as calm as possible. 'You'd better explain,' I begin. 'How many films are there?'

A pause.

'The biggest ever found anywhere in the world. This will be the making of Film Studies, laddie. The Americans are going to spit tacks when they find out.'

'So how many?'

He has died and gone to heaven.

'Two hundred, maybe two hundred and fifty of the little beauties,' he whispers.

There's a saying about this country that we are where baby Austins go to die. Not only baby Austins but also steam trains, biplanes, model T Fords, paddlewheel steamers. On a smaller scale 78 records, forgotten artworks, antique silver sets, antiquarian books. All the garbage, the trash, the detritus that the world throws out, heigh ho, seems to find its way down here. We are the well at the bottom of the world.

Oh you beautiful clean and tidy world.

I am in a state of euphoria as I walk to my office. Obviously we'll have to keep the lid on Ronald's discovery until the legal documents have been drawn up assigning ownership to the university. Then we'll work quietly away at restoration and have a premiere at the end of it. The international interest will be gigantic. Film archivists from all over the world will want to be here.

The money, the *money*. How shall I raise the *money*? The university must get it for us. Or I must. By hook or by crook. Beg, borrow, steal.

Brenda sees me coming. Buoyed up by Ronald, feeling magnanimous, I tell her that Annabelle and I are back together. We are working things out. This is the happy ending Brenda's movie soul has been craving, and her lips start to quiver. With a look which spells 'Good Boy,' she dabs at her eyes and picks up the telephone. Great. The sooner this new bulletin goes out the better.

Then, 'You have a visitor,' she says, motioning to my office.

I open the door, smiling. It must be Hope Springs Eternal. He has become a regular visitor now for coffee or possibly lunch:

Just stopped by for a chat, old chap.

But as the door swings open I see the glow of a cigarette and hear the sound of laughter, rattling like a black mamba.

He waits until I have closed the door behind me. Raises a hand like a gun, levelling it with his eye. Until I am in the cross sights. Sights down the length. Cocks a finger, slowly: click.

'Bang. *Bang.*'

His voice is like a whistling on the wind, bringing malediction to the day.

'Hi there.'

Every boy has a Hook in his life. Mine is The Slut. Sitting there. And today is no longer like any other. It has whiplashed upon itself, drawing blood.

His eyes are snakelike. He wants to spit poison in my eyes.

'Listen, *fucker*,' I answer.

The Slut starts to laugh, his laughter coiling in my ear.

'This *is* my lucky day,' he says.

'I told you before not to come to my office or call me here or anywhere. You hear me, sleazeball?'

His laughter echoes louder, rearing through the afternoon.

'But baby, bay-*bee*, you've been avoiding me. So I thought I'd come to see you. Don't you wanna have good times any more? Don't you wanna go to the moon no more? Wouldn't you like some nice fairy dust to make you fly?'

My heart is beating fast. 'Don't fuck with me,' I say. 'Don't try me again.'

'Oh baby, baby,' The Slut croons. 'You know I like it when you talk bad to me. Bay-beee —'

He strikes. His lips curl back, his eyes are a maelstrom of rage and he spits. I put my hands up to protect my eyes. His yellow poison splatters my face, burning.

'Meet me in The Maze, baby —' Rustling out of the office. 'For goo-*ood* times.'

I made a mistake and he is making me pay. He has always been charismatic. Our sex was stunning. Then one night he introduced drugs into our lovemaking. It was a potent cocktail that shot me over the moon.

He knew what he was doing. I became his. Or so he thought.

I still could be.

On this the first day of the rest of our lives —

Ah yes, we must indeed be arrogant to believe that we can thwart the compulsive presence of our past.

Shaking.

Dear God.

23

LIFE HAS BECOME a roller coaster and sometimes it's simply a matter of holding on tight and trying to keep your eyes open at the bends. Today I have a city appointment with Mister Arts Council at his grand city office. I park my battered car next to a Bentley in the visitors' carpark. Then up the external elevator, a glass tube fixed to the outside of the building, all the way to the top floor. Money or status buys position in this city and, as the lift ascends, all the world opens out beneath my feet.

There are real flowers and shrubbery in the foyer. The young female receptionist tells me, 'Mister Robertson will see you shortly.' She waits a mandatory minute and then:

'You may go in now.'

I straighten my tie and take one quick smile in the mirror to make sure I don't have something stuck in my teeth. Ronald, Stephen, Brenda and the Film Studies team are relying on me. I walk through the door and wade through the plush carpet.

Mister Robertson gets up from behind his desk and its twelve telephones to greet me.

'Ah, Mister Munro,' he says. 'I understand you are seeking a grant from our council for some important film project of yours. Why don't you start from the beginning?'

During the last three weeks Ronald and I have worked carefully and painstakingly to secure the legal rights to the films he has discovered. Ronald went down to the town to do an inventory and telephoned back to tell me, 'Laddie, there's more than we expected. Would you believe two hundred and seventy of the little nitrate beauties?' He sounded as if he would burst into tears.

Like every eager hick-town lawyer, the solicitor handling the deceased estate of the owner has been extremely pedantic. A money transaction is not expected but certain other assurances are. In particular there must be appropriate acknowledgement of the bequest and a certain amount of bowing and scraping to the heirs. I have handled the business side of the transaction with as much diplomacy and tact as can be mustered. Ronald has been champing at the bit on the sideline. I have even managed to find monies within existing Film Studies budget lines to hire and fit out three trucks to collect the films. All that is needed is for the heirs to sign on the dotted line and the wagons will roll.

'You will, of course, come down personally,' the lawyer has asked, 'to thank the descendants for such a beneficent gesture?'

'Yes, of course.'

Bow, scrape, grease grease.

Just get the signatures, man. All I want is the signatures.

'Meantime,' I tell Mister Arts Council, 'my Film Studies department have been keeping all this closely under wraps. We don't want our American colleagues to find out and come in over our heads with promises of big bucks to the heirs.'

Mister Robertson nods and purses his lips.

'And that's been the main problem,' I add.

The university is strapped for research funds and has been unable to come through with finance to turn Film Studies into a processing centre for the films on arrival. Nor can we go to our usual American sources because we don't want them to know yet.

'How much do you need?' asks Mister Arts Council, rocking his chair back and forth.

Say it quick before it sticks in my throat:

'One hundred thousand dollars for phase one.'

Gulp.

If the window had been made of cellophane Mister Arts Council would be crashing through it and falling.

'Oh dear,' he answers. 'Oh dear dear *dear*.'

We have to move fast, I tell Mister Arts Council. Ronald has ascertained that most of the films are in a volatile state and, once they leave their current atmospheric conditions, will deteriorate fast. Careful storage in temperature- and humidity-controlled vaults will slow the process. The vaults, however, will need to be built. Then we need to transfer the films from their nitrate materials to acetate, safety stock. In some cases it will simply be a matter of transferring a good nitrate print to a more permanent acetate negative. For the majority, the original materials will require repair or painstaking restoration work before preservation masters and reference prints can be struck. Ronald needs the facilities. He also needs at least two assistants in phase one to do the transfers. He cannot do it all himself. We will be working against time and could be in danger of losing films to the destabilisation process. They cannot wait.

Mister Robertson starts to hedge and smile like a cornered rat. Have we tried the banks? Yes, but they will only offer loan finance. What about the corporate sector? Not everybody, but there has been an overall shrinkage in disposable money owing to the recession.

Finally, 'Thank you for coming,' Mister Arts Council says. 'I'll put your request before council at its next meeting.'

'Next meeting? That will be too late.'

'It's the best I can do.'

Brenda and Stephen are waiting for me in the office of Film Studies. All of a sudden, Ronald is there at the doorway. His eyes are wide with hope and expectation. He sees my face.

'We didn't get the money, did we,' he says.

'There are other avenues,' I answer.

'You can only do your best.'

Then he is gone.

24

IT COULD NEVER have lasted, the uneasy joining together again that Annabelle and I tried to do with our lives. Too much had happened between us and Annabelle's trust had been destroyed. And too much of me, my gay eidolon, was trying to get out from behind the facade we had erected. My shadow, sewn on with such slender thread, was wriggling free, the thread popping out of each hole.

But we tried, and my parents and my sister were happy but puzzled. The girls, of course, were over the moon. They were solicitous, as if we were invalids recovering from a long illness.

It was all a journey to Never Never Land, a journey of confusion, anger, silent rages and frigidity as we tried to prop up the day-to-day structure of our lives. We'd decided that we were being selfish and that the girls came first. Children needed a stable environment to grow up in, we said. They need us, we agreed. We should have won Academy Awards for best actor and actress in the game of Happy Family. We carried on with the familiar timetables. Dropping the girls off at school. My going to the university while Annabelle got on with the job of being housewife and mother. We went out together to dinner with friends and resumed seeing my parents together. We tried to work something out. We went round and round in circles. There is no doubt in my mind that of the two of us it was Annabelle who put the most effort into keeping us together.

But Annabelle could never really cope with the strain of the unanswered questions. The real problem of my having sex with men was still the Thing that existed between us.

I knew it was happening the night before Chris returned. Annabelle woke up screaming. She was sweating, her body clammy with the wetness. She turned to me with horror palpable in her eyes.

'I don't think I'm going to make it, sport. The pictures in my head won't go away. They just won't.'

I held her tight until she fell to sleep.

I guess I had been waiting for it to happen. All I felt was a deep and tender sadness.

'There there, Annabelle. There there.'

Two days later, Chris called me at the office.

'Where have you been? I've been ringing your flat and your answering machine isn't on either. When are we getting together? How about Saturday?'

'I've promised to take Rebecca and Miranda somewhere on Saturday.'

'Including Saturday night?' His tone warns me not to say yes.

'I'm afraid so.'

A frigid silence.

'So how are you doing?' I ask.

'Fabulous,' he says. 'I've made lots of new friends.'

So there, David. If you're not around, there are other fish.

'Great.'

'So. The girls huh?' Waiting for an invitation.

'Yes.'

'Not six foot two and eyes of blue?' Somebody's told him about Bright Eyes but not about Annabelle.

'No. Small and pretty and want to get out of the city. I was thinking of taking them up to the hot springs for the day.'

'Have you missed me?'

Out of the blue.

Of course. I've truly missed his company.

'Chris —'

Too late. 'Listen, I'll come with you and the girls.' He is hesitant.

'No.'

Although Chris has sometimes joined us, I've never liked to mix my lives up. I've always tried to leave the girls in one box and my other life in another. And now that I'm giving that up —

'Oh come on.' Hopeful. Then, 'Come and pick me up. We'll be back in town in time for my Saturday evening performance, won't we? Good. See you then.'

I put down the telephone. Yes, tell him this Saturday.

Yes.

That Saturday morning, just before leaving to pick up Chris, was when I knew it wasn't going to work with Annabelle. We were having breakfast. We were laughing and joking and in the middle of it all Miranda took up my unfinished glass of milk. Something flashed through my mind, something Alien-like, slipping from my throat and into the milk. And I reached over in a panic and swept the glass from Miranda's hands.

'Daddy!' Miranda chortled.

The milk splashed over everybody and everything. The plates, jug, sugar bowl, spoons, cereal packets, jam, everything crashed on the floor.

The girls thought it was all a riot and went into peals of laughter, but Annabelle knew. She took the girls up to the bathroom to clean them up. When she came back she looked at me calmly.

'I know you can't get Aids from toilet seats or from touching other people who have Aids,' she said. ' I guess the same must go for milk. But if my daughters ever catch anything off you that might threaten their lives, so help me God I'll kill you with my bare hands.'

'Are you girls ready?' I yell up the stairs. Above I can hear Miranda racing to bang on the bathroom to hurry Rebecca up.

'Becca! Becca! Time to go.'

'Enjoy yourselves, darlings,' Annabelle calls as the girls race out of the house and jump into the car. Slam. To me:

'I'll see you soon.'

Out of habit I lean to kiss her.

'No don't,' she says with a fierce determination.

'Come on, Daddy,' Rebecca wails, flicking at her hair. 'We're late enough as it is.'

Rebecca, who has always cited car sickness as her reason, is sitting up front with me. She has become a compendium of psychosomatic illnesses, of moans and plaints of one kind or another. Mirroring the turmoil of her outer world with pretences of her own. I start the motor and we move away from the curb. A wave of a hand, a bend in the road, and Annabelle is lost from sight. Miranda starts to sing in the back seat:

'There were ten green bottles, sitting on the wall, ten green bottles sitting on the wall.'

Together, Rebecca and I join in:

'And if one green bottle should accidentally fall, there'll be nine green bottles sitting on the wall.'

Later, Rebecca is nestling up close to me, purring like a cat. The sun is streaming in the sky. Her face is beatific.

'We always have a nice time when we're together, don't we Daddy?' she says. It is like a mantra, a prayer of reassurance.

Time to tell her. 'Do you mind, darling?' I ask. 'A friend of Daddy's wants to join us today.'

'Who?'

Rebecca is instantly on the offensive, and so is Miranda, who puts her arms around my neck.

'Chris.'

'Yay!' Miranda murmurs. 'He buys us ice creams.'

But Rebecca is silent. Then, 'We never ever have you to ourselves, Daddy. Never.' Her bottom lip quivers, reproving.

Chris is waiting in singlet and trackpants, with backpack and baseball cap, on the kerb outside the high-rise block where his apartment is. As soon as the car stops he starts to bark like a dog and run around the grass and through the shrubs. People walking along the footpath watch, amused. Then Chris comes bounding toward the car, whining to be let in the door. He is making it right, trying to make Rebecca accept.

'Woof,' he says, giving a yearning look.

'No dogs allowed,' I answer.

'Oh let him in!' a bystander calls.

'Mean Daddy,' he mutters out the side of his mouth. 'Then Miranda or Rebecca will have to change me back into a human, woof.'

'But Mummy wouldn't let me bring my wand today,' Miranda cries alarmed.

'A scratch under my left ear will do,' he hints. He looks soulfully at Rebecca who hesitates and then scratches, wrinkling her nose as she does so. In an instant Chris is transformed. He jumps into the back of the car, arms around the girls and says in his best British accent to me:

'Right! We're off! Let's get going, my good fellow, and don't spare the horses!'

To scattered applause we head on out into the blazing day.

Chris leans forward. Reflected in the rear vision mirror, his eyes are smouldering. He breathes on my neck, soft and warm.

'God, it's good to see you.'

25

'*Eight green bottles sitting on the wall, eight green bottles sitting on the wall, and if one green bottle should accidentally fall there'll be seven green bottles, sitting on the wall —*'

Ever since they were babies the girls have loved The Hot Pools. Some thirty kilometres from the city, the trek out there means a day out, occasioning anticipation of ice creams, swimming, chasing each other down the water slide and having a game of minigolf before returning home. Once upon a time it also meant being a Family. A mother. A father. Two daughters. Together.

Today, still not a Family.

The Hot Pools themselves are fed by thermal water springing from the base of the mountains. In the old days people would come out to 'take the waters' for medicinal purposes. Since then a settlement has sprung up around the pools, and local entrepreneurs have turned the natural beauty into a mini Walt Disney complex. Ideal For The Family. Children Free. Cut Lunches Available At Our Kiosk.

The Hot Pools are a blue and white tiled aquatic hippodrome. There are seven pools, all at various temperatures and painted blue at the bottom to give the water its colour. The five original pools have names like Diamond, Oasis, Shalimar, Opal (the Movie Pool) and Fountain Of Youth, and are decorated accordingly — in all-purpose plastic tack. To enter Diamond, for instance, one passes through a huge ring topped by a fluorescent imitation of a real diamond. Shalimar has cutout camels and palm trees which get blown down in the slightest wind. These are the pools where the elderly and the parents lounge in swimsuits bought ten years ago,

146

for you don't actually go to The Hot Pools to swim. Rather to sit, float, scratch, burp, flop, bloat, fart and tip, and to be stirred occasionally like pieces of meat floating in a casserole.

The two remaining pools have been added to attract the young. The Bambi pool is for the young children and on a hot day smells of urine. The Choobs is Olympic size, sporting two diving platforms at one end and 'One Of The Biggest Water Slides In The Southern Hemisphere'. This is where the young bucks and would-be hunks head for.

But even complexes like this aquacade have their illicit side. Beyond the Fountain Of Youth is a huddle of concrete-blocked spa pools, rented by the half hour to couples who wish to use them. Not only that, but you can cruise or be cruised here as expertly as anywhere else in Christendom. At the end of the day, the sun, frustration and desire have all had their effect on the couples and the spas have long waiting lists. Every now and then the woman on the loudspeaker system dryly announces availability, as if advising trains leaving a railway station:

'Mr and Mrs Brown, Spa Number 1.'

Or for those not in the know:

'Mr Wilson and Miss Allen, Spa Number 2.'

Or even more revealing:

'Mr Jackson and Mr Williams, Spa Number 7.'

Part of the fun of the complex is to lie watching the red-faced couples as they hasten sheep-eyed to their assignation.

Today The Hot Pools are filled to the brim. The girls are screaming as Chris pursues them up the zigzag tower to the top of the water slide. Below, the whole complex is listening and smiling, amused. There is no sound happier than young children enjoying themselves.

At the top Miranda grabs a foam mat and, kneeling on it, begins the circuitous slide down through the Choob to the plunge pool far below. I am waiting there to help her out before she swallows too much water. After her comes her heavier sister, Rebecca, lying on her stomach for more speed. Then, zooming after them, is Chris. In the tube of the water slide his voice booms out like the giant who chases Jack down the beanstalk:

'I'm coming to *get youuuuuu.*' The screams escalate, echoing from the open trumpet of the tube as if it was an ancient gramophone player. Already Rebecca has caught up to Miranda and is yelling:

'Out of the way, Assassin!' This is one of her favourite lines from *Dumbo*.

Then Chris is upon them as they round the final bend, he gathers the girls in a huge gruff:

'Yohoho and I'm going to eat you all up!'

Until with a tangle of screams and legs and flailing arms they splash into the plunge pool.

'Daddeee!'

I leap into the froth, grabbing at Miranda. But Chris has scooped her up and saved her from swallowing too much water.

Laughing, splendid, boyish Chris, flinging Miranda into my arms.

'Come on, Daddy, puh-lease.' Rebecca tries to pull me up and after her and Miranda. The girls want to go up the water slide again. But with me, the Daddy this time, not with Chris.

'No,' I answer. 'I've drunk about half the pool as it is.' The taste isn't all chlorine either.

Chris and I are lying on the side of the Champagne Pool. We have been taking turns chasing the girls down the water slide and now, despite their pleadings, have piked out. Chris is looking stunning, the water glistening over his body. He looks as if he has been poured into his new kingfisher blue and slightly see-through Speedos. He is being cruised outrageously by a woman of indeterminate age and, more interestingly, a young man who has taken off his wedding ring.

'Daddy's a party pooper,' says Rebecca. She gives a disdainful sniff and, raising her chin, an imperious lowering of eyelids. 'Come on, Miranda, we don't need him anyway.'

'No we don't,' says Miranda.

Ah yes, off with Daddy's head.

Together they scamper back to the water slide. Chris cranes to watch and shakes his head in wonder. The cords in his neck toughen and his chest muscles ribbon with washboard tautness.

'God they're exhausting,' he muses. 'Don't they ever stop?'

'Nope,' I answer. 'They bop till they drop.'

Chris leans back with a sigh. Then, 'I really needed this,' he says, shaking the drops of water from his hair like a puppy dog. 'To be away from the usual crowd. The people at the ballet. The boys. Among real people for a change. With a family.' His voice is pursuing an impossible dream. Then his eyes flicker open and the depths within are limitless. 'Thank you for having me along. I know how much you love your daughters and how jealous you are of the time you have with them.'

He stares at me a while before tilting his head and closing his eyes.

'Five green bottles —'

I sometimes think that Chris fell in love as much with the girls as he did with me. The Bald One once said, with insight, 'You come with a ready-made family, David. For those of us without, you become doubly desirable.'

Chris is right. Of course he is right. I do love my two daughters. Nobody who has ever witnessed the birth of his own flesh and blood can possibly be unmoved by their vulnerability. The ugly squealing mass of wet redness, being unwrapped from its cawl and trailing its umbilical from its mother's womb, is part of your own creation myth. When that young child is placed in your hands, so tiny, still outraged and gasping for air, its fontanelle pulsing, its heart pumping in its tiny cage, the imprint is eternal. No counterfeit child can replicate the smell, the touch and the special psychic identity instantly recognisable as your own.

That moment of birth was when I loved Annabelle most. It was she who had taken the major burden of carrying and then bringing forth our children into this perilous life. When Rebecca was born I was so overcome that I did not really understand when Annabelle whispered at her birth, 'I'm so sorry that I have not given you a son.' Then, when Miranda came along, she whispered, 'Third time lucky.'

There never was a third time, nor did I ever regret that. The girls as they came were just perfect, fulfilling our biological expectations and presumptions about having a family. They confirmed our marriage by completing us.

Every moment with my daughters is precious. Rebecca is right. We never get enough time alone together. Never enough time to reassure each other of our love one for the other. Chris is right too.

Yes. I am jealous.

Chris rolls over onto his front and disappoints the woman of indeterminate age as his penis gives a plaintive yell and disappears from sight, crushed against the concrete. Far away I can hear Rebecca's voice:

'Gangway!'

When she and Miranda emerge from the foaming plunge pool I wave. But they do not see me.

Then Chris's voice comes out of some place often hidden, some yearning place.

'I envy you having children.'

Nothing more. Only that. Bringing with it the typical gay dream. Find a lesbian who wants a child, impregnate her and bingo. That's where the dream begins and ends but as men with children will know, that is just the beginning. There is the bringing up to get through, the fearful running to the child crying in the night, the attending to all the unknown ills and pains of the young. There is much more than mere fathering which bonds parents and children.

Then, 'I'd love to be a father.'

Chris's voice drifts, reminding me of the pain and the shame of our kind. For to some, male to male coupling is a biological and societal affront. It denies the prospect of reproduction. It is the end of the line for families. I remember The Noble Savage telling me how his mother keened and wailed in her Maori fashion. When he asked her why she was taking it so hard, she said that she was mourning not for him but for the line, the whakapapa, that would end with him.

We who couple with our own sex carry the grief of the children we could have had. If we are the last of the line, ours is a choice of courage.

And now, even though I have the feeling that Annabelle and I are not going to work, Chris's innocence compels me to tell him:

'Chris, I've moved back with Annabelle.' His body tenses. 'We've been trying to work something out.'

He looks up at me. Sits up. Then stares far beyond The Hot Pools into the distance.

'So that's what this has all been about. I knew something was wrong —'

The girls are laughing in the background, the laughter like tinkling charms.

He sniffs. 'And where does all this leave me?'

'I don't know.'

'You don't know?' He stands. Trembling. His shadow falls upon me. 'I'll tell you where it leaves me.' His whole body is shaking apart. 'Where I've always been with you. Nowhere. In limbo. Never Never Land.'

And quickly he turns, takes two steps, dives, enters the water like a knife and churns away in a powerful overarm to the other side of the pool.

Now we are speeding back into the city. Oh the trials of trying to please everybody at once: we are all cross with each other. I have to get Chris back on time for his performance tonight and the girls complained, 'Why do we have to leave so early?' We thus had to curtail our usual game of minigolf, which was a disaster anyway because I had forgotten to tell Chris it was Miranda's turn to win. To top things off, Miranda's ice cream fell into the Champagne Pool. And Rebecca refused to talk to me because a boy made fun of her and she thought it was because her swimsuit was old-fashioned.

'Please buy me a new swimsuit, Daddy, before I die of embarrassment.' I refused.

Even so, Chris tries to brighten us all up. He starts to sing, an unfailing optimist:

'And if four green bottles should accidentally fall, there'll be —'

But today is cancelled owing to lack of interest. The song waits for a chorus to join in and, lacking the requisite voices, ends with a whimper.

With relief Chris looks at his watch and sees that we have made it back with an hour to spare before curtain up. In an attempt to cheer the girls he tries a last valiant lob to their fantasies.

'I know you're taking the girls to dinner now, but would they like to meet the Princess in the ballet afterward?'

His eyes tell me to say yes. Since I told him about me and Annabelle we haven't talked the implications through.

Rebecca is unsure, but a faint gleam of interest appears in Miranda's eyes. I had taken them to a matinee of *Petrushka* and they had adored the girl dancing as the Princess who across the footlights had looked so young and beautiful.

'We're not dressed to meet a princess —' says Miranda anxiously.

'Nor have we had a proper invitation,' adds Rebecca who is a stickler for protocol.

'Oh, but I told the Princess,' Chris replies, 'that you might look in on her and she said you'd be most welcome.'

'In that case,' Rebecca says, 'perhaps you might tell the Princess that we shall come after our pizza.'

Three-quarters of an hour later Chris met us at the stage door, ushering us past the doorman. He was in full make-up and costume, and the girls were alarmed at the transformation.

I should have known then too, that our meeting with the ballet princess would be a disaster. Although Chris attempted to set the scene with magic, bowing low at the princess's feet, nothing could have saved the moment.

'Your Majesty,' Chris said, 'may I have the pleasure of introducing the Princesses Rebecca and Miranda.'

At which the forty-five-year-old prima ballerina, paper white and wrinkled, extended a crooked hand with wicked fingers and the girls recoiled with alarm.

Ah, my poor Chris. Your dreams should stay on the stage side of the footlights where they belong. There, in that world, illusion is master. Here on this side I am the master of illusion. You should leave me if you can.

'*Three green bottles —*'

The girls have recovered from their alarm and are now playing with the costume props and being dressed up. Chris and I are in the front seat of the car, looking out at the night.

'I should never have got mixed up with you,' he says. His voice is filled with self-loathing. 'I always told myself that I should stay clear of married men. I came between you and your wife. Between you and your children.'

'You had nothing to do with the breakup of my marriage,' I answer. 'The way I feel about myself, about Annabelle and about the girls was happening for a long time. Long before I met you.'

'I love your daughters,' he replies. 'I admire Annabelle too. The best thing for you is to go back to them. I see that now.'

He is looking straight ahead and, at that moment, a car turns into the alley and I see Chris's face in the glare of the headlights. The light etches his profile, seeks him out from behind the stage make-up and the spangles in the corners of his eyes. He clenches his right fist and begins to pound at the dashboard.

'Damn, damn, damn it to hell, *dammit.*'

I try to take him into my arms, for bodies have a language of their own. But bodies also have needs which, having once found fulfilment in one lover's arms, yearn for that fulfilment again and again. And the signals become confused.

Chris pushes me away. 'Your children come first in your life.'

Then, to himself:

'I was really caught this time. Really, truly caught. Oh God.'

And he is gone, wrenching the door open and away.

Did I ever tell Chris in the early days that I loved him? No, and when I moved out of The House On The Hill I rented the flat and set up in it by myself.

'I need time,' I told him.

All communication is mutual disclosure. I now know that I have never entirely disclosed my hand to Chris. Or to Annabelle. Or to anyone in my life. Ever.

But there has always been one never-changing truth. The girls will always come first.

Always.

26

'*Two green bottles* —'

On our return home the girls went straight to bed, Rebecca complaining about her swimsuit and Miranda that Chris had won at minigolf. Now Annabelle and I are in the sitting room. She is pensive. Leans forward, hair catching fire in the light. Angry.

'Why didn't you tell me that Chris was going out to The Hot Pools with you?'

'I meant to, but I wasn't too sure how you would take it. I wanted to tell him about us.'

'And did you?'

'Yes.'

'Good.'

The night is drenched with sadness. When I place my hand on Annabelle's hip she moves it away.

'Your coming back to me has not changed the fact,' she says, 'that you still prefer men, don't you? Or that your life is filled with secrets. Who are you, David? Tell me.'

I guess I could have evaded the question but there was something about the way Annabelle had asked it that got through my defences. I knew that if I didn't tell Annabelle now I never would. So I told her about my uncle and the time at the river. About Saint Crispin's and the knowing which eventually led me to a beach where I knew men who had sex with men went. About going to university and meeting her and how I fell in love with her and thought those other times were over. When I told her about Charles, oh God, I hated myself for my duplicity. But I kept going until it was done. The dam was broken inside me and I went on to tell her about my nights in the Gardens of Spain. About Chris. Then I told her of a rash that had appeared in my groin. As it turned out, the rash was a minor non-sexually transmitted matter.

'I went to see a friend at the Aids Clinic about it. He took the opportunity to ask me if I had multiple partners. I said, Yes, but that I was planning to change my behaviour. He asked me if I practised safe sex with you, Annabelle. I said, No. He asked if I practised safe sex with men. I said, Yes. He asked if I realised I was placing you at risk. I said, No. He told me to think about my answer. When I did I realised that I was. That is why I had to leave, the first time. I realised I was placing you at risk. That I had already put myself on a path that I couldn't get off, but that I could push you and the girls off it before it was too late. It was not too late for you but it might already have been too late for me. If anything ever happened to you or them, I would kill myself first.'

Looking at Annabelle. The salt from her tears leaving crystals on her face.

'I love you and our daughters more than you know.'

She howled and slashed her hand across my face.

'Don't you ever say that word to me again. Ever.'

Now, hours later, Annabelle has found a kind of acceptance and stands at the door of the girls' bedroom, looking in at them. The light from the hallway glows on her. I join her. She stiffens, then sighs and puts her arms around me.

'Do you remember,' Annabelle says, 'when Rebecca had her seventh birthday and we promised to take her to see the elephant at the zoo?'

'Yes. Pamela had given her a pink and green stuffed elephant. And when we got to the zoo she was so cross. She said, "Daddy, this elephant is too big and it's not" —'

'Pink and green,' Annabelle giggles. She is giggling and weeping at the same time. And she is pulling my arms tighter around her and finding it difficult to talk.

'And do you remember when that other horrible little child,' she says, referring to Miranda, 'cut off all her hair?'

'Yes. We put her in a pram and took her to the hairdresser's. The streets were so busy and everybody kept looking at Miranda and edging away from us as if we had mutilated her ourselves. And all the way we argued about who was going to push the chair. You or me. You kept saying to me, "She's *your* child," and I kept saying to you —'

'She's *yours*.'

We are both laughing and crying.

Then Annabelle leans back against me and sighs. For a moment, she doesn't speak. Then:

'Oh, sport. I think I need to ask you for a divorce.'

I kiss her neck and breathe her in.

This time it is my turn to say, 'Yes, Annabelle. I know.'

'And if one green bottle should accidentally fall, there'd be —
No green bottles standing on the wall.'

Part Four

DUELLING IN THE RIGGING
OF CAPTAIN HOOK'S GALLEON

27

SO NOW I have lost both Chris and Annabelle, but not Rebecca and Miranda. I am moving back to the flat and Rebecca asks Annabelle, 'Why are you letting Daddy do this, Mummy?' She is so angry. Arms akimbo, she looks like Rumpelstiltskin. If she stamped her foot hard enough she'd go right through the floor. She doesn't look at me at all as I take my clothes out to the car. Only at Annabelle, as if this is all her fault.

Later, after a lot of grovelling and pleading, Mister Arts Council has agreed to call a special meeting of the Arts Council to discuss the Film Studies application. I have sought a special grant to cover transportation and restoration of the cache of films that Ronald has found.

Then Mister Arts Council's secretary is on the telephone.

'Mister Munro? Mister Robertson asked me to let you know that unfortunately your application for assistance to the Arts Council for your film restoration project has been declined blah blah blah.'

Damn. So where to now?

Five minutes later, and I put down the telephone after talking to the finance manager of my bank. I have asked for a short-term personal loan of, gulp, one hundred thousand dollars. He pauses, checks my account, asks questions about collateral and says that on the basis of my 'loanability' the bank could go so far as fifty thousand dollars.

'Will that do for now, Mister Munro?'

Done. Half the money for phase one is better than none.

Then the Hick Town Lawyer rings.

'Mister Munro? I am very happy to inform you that the transfer documents on the films have been signed by the heirs to the deceased estate of their father. Your university and your Film Studies department should count themselves very lucky indeed. The documents are being couriered up to you today. Please let us know when you expect to be here to take receipt of the films.'

My heart is beating fast. I walk casually to the door and wait until Brenda looks up. She knows instantly that I have news. Already she is calling down to Ronald and Stephen through the department intercom.

Simply, 'They're ours.'

And Ronald's dour visage crumples into relief and happiness, his Adam's apple like a plumb bob in his throat. He takes my hand and pats it.

'Oh you beautiful lad,' he says, 'you big, beautiful jock.' Over and over again.

Then, when he has calmed down, I really make his day.

'Obviously,' I say to him, 'we shall all be taking our cues from you. So, if you don't mind, I would like you to be the project director. Okay? Does everybody else agree?'

Stephen and Brenda nod with vigour. I turn to them.

'It seems to me that Ronald knows what is required in terms of transportation of the films and construction of the vaults to receive them.' I turn back to Ronald. 'We will wait on your plan of action, Ronald. Meantime, congratulations. Will your network of film buffs help us?'

I extend my hand and Ronald pumps it up and down. His voice is stuck in his throat. He has a whole support group of intense film votaries, who meet in rapt silence to watch The Classics Of The Golden Age Of Hollywood.

'How about using some of our senior students? I suggest that you begin building your laboratory and storage vaults *now*.'

'What about the money?' Stephen asks.

'I can assure you of half now. The rest will come later.'

Where from, God knows.

'And the transportation of the films here?' Ronald asks.

'Our lectures and tutorials can't simply stop while all this is happening,' I agree. 'I think we should plan to drive down to get the films during the long weekend break.' Two weeks away. Some of our senior students might want to help —' I am thinking particularly of Bright Eyes. 'But not just anybody, mind. These films are volatile.'

Then I turn to Brenda and smile.

'Of course,' I say to her, 'I am expecting you to co-ordinate the operation. Will you?'

Brenda loves it when I am being so masterful. She preens, she purrs, she pouts with pride. She becomes the efficient secretary of every 1950s film you've ever seen. Once a star, always a star.

'Okay?' I ask. 'Then what are we waiting for?'

I get out the plastic cups and the bottle of Moët that has been waiting for an occasion like this. I'll figure out a way of getting the extra fifty thousand dollars for phase one later. Meantime:

'Let's break out the champagne!'

Afterwards, I call longtime partner of The Love Of My Life.

'Hello? It's David here. Look, thank you for your letter. How's Charles? As it happens, business calls me down your way. I was thinking of dropping in —'

Then I try Chris. Nothing venture, nothing win.

He is not in.

28

A FAX FROM Oh My Goodness in Canada: *I am delighted that New Zealand can extend the usual hospitalities to its fellow Commonwealth nation, Canada. Please be assured that Canada will be fully prepared for every eventuality and hopes to reciprocate all hospitalities in kind. Will be arriving for two days exactly beginning morning of* —

The dates follow. Two days together. Soon.

A week later. Back at the flat. Only one person rings at this time of the morning. I turn onto my stomach, pulling the pillows and blankets over my head. My voice invites callers to leave a message. Then the beep and there she is: my sister.

'I know you're there, David, so pick up the phone. *Pick up the phone, David.*'

Nice try, Sis.

'Okay, little brother. Nobody said working all this out was going to be easy, did they? However, at least you tried reconciliation. Mum and Dad know that now. They'll get over it. Time heals all wounds. Meantime, I'll keep softening them up. Okay?'

Silence.

'Okay. And if you *are* there, David, may you grow a huge wart on your nose.'

Click.

Up and at 'em. Rise and shine. Get the milk and newspaper, delivered to the front door. Think of Chris. I haven't seen him now for over two weeks. I've called. He hasn't called. It's over between us. Ah well, no use crying over spilt —

The morning newspaper has devoted its entire front page to

photographs of the blockade being planned against the American aircraft carrier. My God, the carrier is due in today. It is storming across the horizon, having punched past the moon and through the swarm of stars into our Never Never Land. If an accident happened with its nuclear reactor, it could blow a hole in our harbour.

Even so, the small events of our lives go on. This morning, the jog. No visual delights from Italian Stallion and Now You See It Now You Don't. Nor The Noble Savage. Rather, the strange vision of That Boy's Deformed running a three-legged race down the hill to The Teps to make me smile. In the midst of life, a sense of the ridiculous. Then just before leaving the flat for Film Studies, a call comes from Annabelle. She wants to remind me that we have an appointment with our lawyer later today to talk about divorce proceedings. Although the decision has been made, life goes on. No barriers yet. No incivility. Rather, we are remaining in touch. We are not cutting off all communication. We are working through the process without undue histrionics and in an adult fashion. Is this the way that divorce should be managed? The truth is that you muddle through, making judgements as best you can, each judgement driven by fear, kindness, anger, hope, jealousy, love, hate.

Behind Annabelle's voice I can hear the usual sounds of Rebecca and Miranda being pushed through the morning and out the door to school.

'Oh yes, don't forget,' Annabelle says, 'you're also picking up the girls later this afternoon? It's your mother's birthday soon and they want to get her their presents.' There is a scream, a yell and a wail. 'Come to think of it, why don't you have them for keeps.' Annabelle gives a rueful laugh. Then, 'Here, Rebecca wants to talk to you.'

'Is that you, Daddy?' Rebecca says. 'Miranda got into my wardrobe and left it in an awful mess. She's *always* doing it. When can I have my own room?'

'I'll talk to your mother about that,' I say. 'But I've got to go, darling. I'll see you later today. Goodbye.'

A tussle once more. This time, Miranda.

'Yes, darling?'

'You said goodbye to Rebecca,' she says, 'but you haven't said goodbye to *me*.'

'Here's a kiss then,' I answer.

I blow a kiss along the telephone line, strong enough for it to speed its way to the little princess, waiting at the other end to catch it and hold it against her heart. 'See you soon, darling.'

I go to put down the receiver. But —

'Daddy?' Miranda asks. 'When are you coming home? Daddy?'

She cannot understand that this time the separation is final. The world turns to ashes.

'I'll see you this afternoon,' I answer. Say anything. Cover up the question. Divert her away from it.

'Yes, Daddy. All right. Goodbye.'

I put the telephone down and try to rebuild my world, piece by piece. Restore its balance. Open the door and out.

Driving to work along the beach highway the sight of yachts skimming the harbour takes my breath away. All the wings are white butterflies come to alight upon the green crystal water. They are a thousand butterfly kisses sent by Miranda to soothe my sadness.

The yachts are not the only craft on the sea. Among them power boats buzz and manoeuvre like wasps. Even the courageous wind surfers are there, fluorescent dragonflies slipping between the bigger craft with astonishing élan and bravura. All are moving toward the entrance to the harbour known as The Heads. I switch on the radio. The DJ reports:

'US naval authorities still refuse to confirm or deny whether its naval force is nuclear armed or nuclear powered. Anti-nuclear protests are already underway, with thousands of small boats and yachts and, yes folks, even wind surfers, moving out to block the entrance.'

The previous blockade produced spectacular derring-do. Piratical power boats slipping in and under the warship's hull. Wind surfers like buccaneers riding the bow waves beneath the awesome guns of the nuclear galleon. Yachts trying to engage grappling hooks against the grey sliding giant. Say a prayer for our sailors today. We who live in Erewhon are jealous of our freedom and fiercely protective of our environment.

This is our patch, Yanks. Take your ships and anchor them in the Hudson.

I am not winning today, and the coming of the carrier has filled my whole world with unease. At university no car park is available in the staff parking area. Finally, after a quarter of an hour I am able to squeeze into a space vacated by a student who has somehow scored a staff pass. I know, now, why Jack The Ripper went on his murderous spree. And Freddie.

'Old chap,' a familiar voice calls. 'Surely you're coming the wrong way? The fleet's in.'

Hope Springs Eternal is pulling out of the carpark in his grey Jaguar. The latest model, naturally.

'Oh my, American marines,' Jack continues. 'I have cancelled all my appointments to go down to see the ships come in. All those wholesome American-as-apple-pie sailors to play with.'

'You are incorrigible,' I pronounce.

He smiles, leaning out of the car window. By a trick of light the sun lends him handsomeness and stirs my memory.

'How about lunch next week?' he asks.

'Okay.'

He nods. Starts to drive away. Then, 'Actually, your secretary will tell you that I was at your office just a moment ago. I looked in to see if you wanted to come with me. You're sure you won't? The sailor boys are only here for two days. While there I took a phone call for you in your office. Some fellow wanting to talk to you about some transaction or other.'

Bang. *Bang*.

My blood runs cold.

'We had a lovely chat,' Hope Springs Eternal says. 'He sounded rather nice. He left a telephone number. I made a note of it in your diary.'

All of a sudden I want to cry out a warning:

'*Jackkk* —'

But it is too late. His foot is on the accelerator.

'Next week then? Good.'

Into Film Studies. There, Brian, head of Theatre Studies, is killing himself with laughter. I have missed the coffee break where, apparently, God's Gift To Woman was trounced by Predator. He was telling one of his usual penile jokes and let slip that as a student he'd slept with Predator. She overheard and was enraged. 'You think your penis was a great deal?' she asked him. 'Personally speaking I've gotten more thrills from a banana. And I'll tell you what. At least with a banana I can eat it and it tastes better.'

I give a low whistle. Wow. Attagirl, Predator.

Truth games and they hit home, bringing a perspective to my day. I am no better and no worse than any other man. I have been playing power games of my own with Annabelle, with Chris and with my life.

All of us play power games. That is our masculine estate. If not propelled by our penis then we are propelled by our war toys.

It is almost as if the aircraft carrier has come crashing through my life like some avenging angel.

'Naughty naughty,' Brenda tsks as I slam the door and walk through into my office. 'Your friend waited for ages.'

'I know. I saw him on my way in.'

'And we forgot to call our life insurance broker again, didn't we.'

She is playing Judy Holliday in *Bells Are Ringing*.

'I'll call him back soon. Can you give me a rundown on where we're at with the films?'

Brenda becomes secretary incarnate. The cheque from my bank has arrived and been deposited into a special account. The three trucks have all been booked and paid for. A *very* good price for the hire. A notice has been posted asking students to volunteer to go down with us. Oh yes. A warehouse down by the railway station has been found as storage space for the films on their arrival. A lease has been taken at a *very* good price, and paid for. Ronald himself has organised the fit-out and already his team of dedicated film buffs is on the job.

'Splendid,' I tell Brenda.

She is pleased at my compliment and blushes. Then, 'How-*ever*,' she says, 'we will have cashflow problems unless the rest of the money comes through. Ronald wants to set up a restoration laboratory here in Film Studies as soon as possible. He is drawing up plans to convert one of the classrooms and —'

'No worries,' I tell her. 'I'm working on it.'

Too many other things have been occupying my mind and I haven't done a thing. *Help.*

In the office I finally ring the insurance broker.

'Have you had a chance to look over the forms I sent you?' he asks. 'Do you want to update your policy?'

The timing could not be more ironic. The impending meeting with the lawyer and the initiation of divorce proceedings, not to mention the arrival of a nuclear threat, have turned my thoughts to my changing world. Death is a constant and I should make provision for the children.

'Everything looks straightforward enough,' I say, 'but I haven't given the matter sufficient thought.'

An evasion. In fact the forms have a Yes or No format and slotted in among the questions are: Have you suffered or are you suffering from night sweats or unintentional weight loss or persistent fever, diarrhoea, or swollen glands? Have you worked as a prostitute at any time since 1980? Have you engaged in male-to-male anal sexual activity on any occasion since 1980?

'Okay,' the broker answers. 'Just fill in the form when you have the time and send it back to me, signed. Okay?'

To answer the questions or not answer the questions: that is *the* question. I pick up the telephone, ring the Aids clinic and ask for Left Dress. 'I've got a favour to ask of you.' I tell him about the clauses in my insurance policy. 'What's it all about?'

'If you tick Yes to the questions you run the risk of being denied life cover or being charged considerably higher than average premiums. You will definitely be asked to take the test. Even if it is negative you might still be charged higher premiums.'

'But why just questions about homosexual activity? Why not about heterosexual activity? '

'The life insurance companies have been panicked by Aids. It's the huge payouts. Millions of bucks. Millions.'

'That must be the same with other life-threatening diseases, surely? Cancer? Heart disease?'

'Dear friend, the difference is that Aids taps into the basic taboos. It's transmitted in socially stigmatised ways, either by homosexual activity or intravenous drug use.'

'Jesus. I didn't think it had come to this.'

'The irony is that the companies are targeting those clients who are already practising safe sex. They're still not picking up heterosexual risk, or encouraging high-risk bisexual or closeted men to be honest. We are definitely fighting any policy which has an Aids-exclusion and won't pay out in cases of Aids.'

'So what do I do about this policy?'

'Forget it. Telephone your broker and tell him that you've looked it over and you don't want to update your current policy. Well, is that it? I have to dash. Welcome to life, and life insurance in the age of Aids,' he says good-humouredly. 'And be a good boy, put an overcoat on him when he needs it and —'

'I know —'

'Stay alive with safe sex.'

The clinic's motto.

I put the receiver down. In the midst of life we are in death. Anger, frustration, rage take hold of my emotions.

Why have I been so afraid to take the test? Why? Because I am not just afraid I might test positive. I am also angry that taking the test is a enforced admission of my sexual practices and a public declaration of my homosexuality.

The insurance policy is in front of me. To hell with it. I take up my pencil and slash fiercely at the boxes of the questionnaire.

Duelling in the rigging.

No.

No.

But, oh, *yes.*

Out the window I can see the American aircraft carrier and its destroyer escort arriving at dock. In its wake a thousand butterflies flutter. They are drowning in the sea.

29

IN THE AFTERNOON I drive back from the university into the city for my appointment with Annabelle at the lawyer's office. The traffic is hellish. The American aircraft carrier has anchored. Down on the harbour anti-nuclear protesters are fighting the police and pro-nuclear supporters.

'Yankee go home!' they chant. 'No nukes, no nukes!'

Above, the aircraft carrier towers, cutting a wedge in the sky. It is an awesome, palpable presence, a sea-going military city bringing with it resonances of all those gung-ho John Wayne movies. *Flying Leathernecks. The Green Berets. Sands of Iwo Jima. Battle Cry.*

I park the car in the multi-storey carpark, take the lift and exit into the sunlit street, past the cluster of passers-by looking at the television news coverage of the blockade. A brief glimpse of a huge grey juggernaut slicing through butterflies' wings.

'Have you heard? One of the yachts was run down in the harbour and two wind surfers are missing.'

Over to the coffee house where Annabelle and I have arranged to meet before going on to Farquhar, Martin & Chuzzlewit. She hasn't yet arrived, so I take a table and order a cappuccino for myself and Earl Grey for her. Ah, there she is. Standing in the doorway. Checked grey and white suit, white blouse, white shoes, hair in a French roll. Pearl earrings. Restrained. Nice.

'Hello, sport,' Annabelle says.

This is a different Annabelle today. No nonsense. No emotion. Businesslike. Measured.

I stand and pull out a chair for her. Her face is a mask made up of blush and lipstick.

'I ordered tea for you.'

'I might have wanted coffee,' she says quickly.

'You don't like coffee.'

Sparring.

'From now on, don't assume,' she says, pulling her chair in.

Silence is the only response to that one. I look at my watch. We are due at the lawyer's office in ten minutes.

'So. Here we are,' I venture. 'You look very attractive.'

'Do I? I would have been here earlier but I just couldn't decide what to wear. Black would have been too gloomy and something bright didn't seem appropriate.' Her voice is still brittle but then she sighs, 'Look, I'm sorry if I'm short with you, but I don't exactly feel on top of the world.'

'I suppose we really have to do this —' Trying to find a way out. 'But it's not as if there's anybody in your life —'

'You leave my life out of this.'

'And there's no real hurry, surely.'

She is firm. 'Yes there is. It's for the best.'

Mouthing platitudes.

Annabelle takes up her cup. It is a symbolic gesture. Thus saith the White Goddess. Puts the cup down. Signals for the waiter. All bow to the White Goddess.

'I'd like coffee please. Black.'

Mister Charles Farquhar Senior has been the family lawyer for years. He should have retired years ago but some reluctance to hand over to his son, Charles Farquhar Junior, has forced him to stay on. A friend of my father's, he set up practice straight after the Second World War. He ushers us in with a peremptory nod to me and a solicitous one to Annabelle.

'So,' he says, looking down his spectacles. 'I presume, seeing that you are both here, that you wish to proceed with this business? You are quite sure?'

'Yes,' says Annabelle.

'And you, David? Is that your wish also?'

When you wish upon a star. I'm wishing for the one I love. A dream is a wish your heart makes.

'Yes.'

He coughs, shuffles some papers. Sighs. Then, 'Let's proceed then shall we? Presumably neither of you will contest the divorce. The grounds —' He already knows I'm gay but glosses over this. 'Will be incompatibility I take it?'

You can take it where you want, Mister Farquhar. Up your nose. Up anywhere your heart desires.

'And settlement will be based on equal share of matrimonial property? Good.'

And I suddenly remember that this is one of the reasons why I delayed so long in telling. That it would set in motion forces over which I would have no control. That it would be the beginning of the end. That —

Is there no escape?

Ever since I came out I have been forcibly put in a maze. It's for the best. Trapped there. The girls and I have to get on with our lives. All the exits have been blocked up, and there is no way out except the way I am meant to go.

'You do understand, don't you, David?'

A big bulbous face is peering down at me where I stand small in the maze, looking up at him.

'I beg your pardon?' I haven't really been listening.

'You will have to get your own lawyer. I shall represent Annabelle of course.'

She, too, is looking down at me where I am scrabbling in the maze. Stroking me with a sad finger.

'Oh.'

Really?

'Yes.'

Three bags full, Sir. Let me out, Sir.

'Then I shall draw up the necessary papers, Annabelle,' the lawyer says, excluding me already. 'I shall present them to David's lawyer when he has one.'

Who cares anyway, because God's great grey galleon is coming down the maze and slicing through my screaming skull. No little sword of mine, no daring derring-do, is ever going to stop it.

30

LATE AFTERNOON, AND I am picking up the girls from The House On The Hill so that they can buy their birthday presents for my mother. Rebecca has seen a lovely bracelet. Miranda, of course, has her eye on a plastic tiara which will make Grandma a queen.

I am having a cup of tea with Annabelle. We are both still simmering from the visit to the lawyer. Waiting as Miranda looks upstairs for her fairy wand. The whole business with the lawyer was a question not of what Simon says but what society says. Society was coming down on me like a ton of bricks. Don't give me any of this crap about everything being for the best. What was at work now was the machinery to support convention. Annabelle had to be protected and I had to be punished. All my worldly possessions must be sliced in half. My little princesses too, no doubt. Which part would you like, David? Left or right? Why not have one of each: Rebecca's right side and Miranda's left? Glue them together and, hey presto.

'Darling,' Annabelle calls up the stairwell to Miranda, 'do you really want to take the wand? Your inhaler's more important. Have you got that? Why don't you leave the wand at home for me to look after? Where it's safe?'

Miranda looks over the balustrade. She whimpers, 'But you might go out.' She pulls at Rebecca's skirt.

'She wants to take it,' Rebecca says, looking at me. 'You don't mind, do you, Daddy.'

The way she phrases it is not a question. On the way out a peck on Annabelle's cheek but, 'No, sport. Don't.'

'Is Chris coming with us?' Rebecca asks as we approach the car.

'No,' I answer.

'Good,' she says. She opens the front passenger door and sits down. Reaches for the seat belt and clips it on.

'Didn't you like Chris?' I ask.

Miranda is clambering in the back, clutching her wand tight.

'He was all right, Daddy,' Rebecca says. 'But he wasn't part of the family. Not part of Mummy, Miranda, me and you.'

I shrug my shoulders. 'Okay,' I say, starting the car. 'I am your humble driver. Where to first?'

'To Grandma's,' Miranda orders.

'Your wish is my command, o my princesses,' I answer.

Then Rebecca screams, 'We forgot to bring the tape measure.'

We are going to measure the circumference of Grandma's head. After all, it's no good getting a tiara for a queen if it won't fit, is it. And that, too, is not a question.

'I'm sure Grandma will have one,' I answer.

'Why?' my mother says, wide-eyed and innocent. 'What do you want my tape measure for? Are you girls planning to do some sewing? Is that it?'

'No,' Rebecca answers. 'We just want it to measure, um, Miranda's wand.'

'Yes, yes,' Miranda screams conspiratorially. She claps with glee at her sister's cleverness.

'Well I'll just get my sewing basket,' my mother says. Then, 'Oh, I'm so tired, I think I might take a little nap over there —'

She yawns ostentatiously and points to the couch where her head can conveniently loll over the back.

'Oh please,' Rebecca says excitedly. 'Do go to sleep if you wish to.' Already a plot is hatching in her mind. She is whispering in her sister's ear, While Grandma's asleep you can take one end of the tape and I'll take the other and —

My father and I retire to the back patio.

'Would you like a beer, David?'

Ever since this business began he has ceased calling me son.

'Thanks, Dad,' I answer.

We sit in the deck chairs, positioning them so that we can see through the French doors where my mother is going through her charade.

'So how's the university?' my father asks.

'I've a problem on my hands right now,' I answer. 'I don't know the outcome.'

'I understand you've taken out a huge loan,' he continues.

I nod. How does he know? Ah, the family lawyer.

Inside, my mother has just given another huge yawn, as if she was a soprano trying to hit a top E flat. Then she pats at her hair, looks with some surprise at the couch as if she hadn't realised it was there and lies down on it. Two little heads peep around the door. Rebecca sees me and puts a finger to her lips: Sssssh. Then Miranda waves her wand. It has sleeping dust on it and that should send Grandma off to dream land.

'They're such pretty girls,' my father says. 'Crackers, both of them.'

He watches affectionately as my mother suddenly becomes overpowered by the sleeping dust. Although she is too much of a lady to snore, she attempts a few sighs and snuffles before settling into a deep slumber. Rebecca is tiptoeing over and looking down at her. She motions Miranda to come, Yes, she's sleeping now. And Miranda trips: *bang*. Frantically waves her wand again. Puts old Grandma to sleep again. Phew.

Then it comes out of nowhere.

'I despise what you're doing, David. I can barely cope with your being a homosexual. But what you are doing to those little girls and to Annabelle defies decency.'

Oh Miranda, bring your wand and save Daddy.

'Your mother is on medication prescribed by the family doctor,' my father continues. 'Even so, she still sometimes gets out of bed in the middle of the night. She can't stop crying. I cannot believe that you have done this to us.'

Inside, Rebecca has spread the tape across Grandma's head. Grandma conveniently turns so that the tape can be slipped under. Miranda looks out the window at me, Aren't we clever?

It is time for me to face down my father.

'And how do you think it's been for *me*?' I answer. 'Do you think this is easy? *You* think you've got a prior claim on grief? You know nothing about grief. This has been the hardest thing I've ever had to do. I want to start living an honest life. Not a lie.'

Success. The girls have managed to take the measurements. Cautiously they slip the tape from underneath Grandma's head. Retreat to the hallway. Wave the wand to wake her up.

I turn to my father. 'This is my life, Dad. I'm trying to live it the best way I can. Make the best decisions that I can. They may not be the same decisions that you might make, but I am not you. I suggest that you and mother accept what has happened. Make the best of it too. Because if you or she ever upset my daughters with your own selfish complaining and grief, I warn you, Dad, you will answer to me personally. Nothing must upset them. Do you hear me? Nothing.'

My father is as stiff as a rod, but his lips are trembling. My mother senses something. One look at him and she knows. She wakens from the couch and comes rushing out.

'How dare you raise your voice to your father. You watch your words, David. I will not have you arguing with him. He is right and you are wrong. You hear me? You are *wrong*.'

She is shaking apart. Tears spilling out from between the cracks. Go on, mother, say it. *Say* it.

And she does: the words that have been held inside. They come from the womb in which I was conceived. From all those years when she nursed me. All those years, betrayed years, of a son given the silver spoon. Betrayed by a son who should have known better. Who took advantage of her love, her guardianship, her many acts of protection. Who, once upon a time, she would have died for.

'I wish —' My mother is cracking apart, shard by shard. 'I wish you had never been born.'

And into the middle of a world that is breaking apart, the girls come running.

'Never.'

Now I tell the girls it is time to go. Miranda runs to sit on my father's lap. Rebecca comes to whisper in my ear.

'Grandma's got an awfully big head,' she says. 'I hope we can find a tiara that will fit.'

'So where are you girls going now?' my father asks Miranda. She looks up at him solemnly.

'I want to shop till I drop,' she says.

The things she comes out with.

My mother turns to me. 'Will we see the girls soon?' For a moment her eyes are fearful. Both she and my father look forward so much to having their grandchildren around.

I should tell them both, No. No more. Not ever. But breeding always will out.

'Yes, of course.' Then, 'Girls, give your grandparents a kiss.'

My mother offers a cheek. When I embrace her she brushes the air with her lips. Just enough to ensure a semblance of decorum. To fool anybody who may be looking on.

The games we play.

And again I feel my life is being sliced and diced, and right in the middle of it my daughters are disappearing down a huge mincing machine. Conventional society is claiming ownership of them, taking them away from me piece by piece.

Before they belong to anybody else they belong to me. Dammit, nobody gets them without a fight.

Duelling in the rigging.

Then it is evening and I have stopped by The Club on my way home for a drink at the bar, not knowing whether I've won or not. The Club is really rocking. The strobe lights are silver scalpels dissecting the patrons. Youth is the premium on the dance floor. Among the patrons I see Born To Boogie, dancing up a storm. He is indulging his usual taste for guys who look exactly like him. As he said to me once, I'm the only guy I really like.

I wave to him as I am leaving. And just as I go out the door, Chris.

'Oh.'

His face flares like the sunset.

Now I am back at the flat. I returned via the port. The American aircraft carrier loomed overhead. Avenging angel.

All of a sudden I think of Annabelle and —

Go for it Annabelle, dear. Straight on till morning.

Then just as I am putting out the light, there is a knock at the door.

Chris. Standing there.

'I'm so sorry,' he shivers.

'So am I,' I whisper. I am so glad to see him.

'When I saw you tonight I —'

'Yes. So did I —'

We are in each other's arms. Reaching hungrily for each other. Kissing deeply.

Trying to salve the wounds of the heart and of the day. Trying to find a centre, a harbour, that is our own. That nothing and nobody can touch or take away. Kicking shut the door.

31

AFTER TWO DAYS in our city the Yanks have gone home, slicing away in the morning light. I was staying over at Chris's apartment. I left his arms, padding across to watch from the third floor window. The carrier assumed Darth Vader perspectives, an intergalactic craft thrumming powerfully away from us. Winking out and over the sea.

Having a relationship with a man is like walking in a minefield. The games of power, dominance and control are much more complex when it is not man and woman but man and man. Someone submissive one day may be dominant the next. Someone strong one day may be weak the next. There are no established roles, no protocols. Only two men, each fiercely independent yet wanting to love and be loved without dependency. A minefield.

A man who loves other men is a world colliding with other worlds. Driven by fears of his own mortality, and not able to replicate himself and thereby achieve some sense of immortality, he is a wayward star.

So Chris is back in my life.

On the day after the American carrier left, he was pall bearer at the funeral of a close friend, All The World Was In Front Of Him, who died after a debilitating Aids-related illness. A violinist in the city orchestra, All The World was a vivacious presence among us, someone who discovered his gayness late and kept gasping at the joy of it, as if he had always been holding his breath. He revelled in flirtation and in sexual affairs and, five years earlier, had visited San Francisco where he had met a 'marvellous' man.

Every new man was 'marvellous', but this one had the virus. It crawled out of his blood and nested in All The World's blood, hatching out its own razoring young.

All The World had been very close to Chris. One afternoon they had been running across a pedestrian crossing together and he'd dropped his shoulder bag.

I went with Chris to the funeral service. A small string group played one of All The World's favourite compositions, Ravel's evocative Introduction and Allegro for strings and harp. Many of his old friends, lovers and colleagues were there. Left Dress represented the Aids clinic. Mister Arts Council made a short, rushed visit to express his condolences before going on to another service. He was like veteran actress Linda Christian, the well-known 'star of stage, screen, television and funerals'.

All The World's cousin gave the eulogy, expressing anger that all our artists, our bright shining dancers, painters, novelists, sculptors and theatre designers were succumbing to this affliction.

Then Chris and All The World's other friends placed the casket on their shoulders. Took All The World to his final rest. Scattered white rose petals and watched the falling earth.

Back to bed. Slip in beside Chris. He is whimpering in his sleep, asking me to hold him closer and tighter. Do you love me? he asks. Do you want me in your life? I need to be loved. I need someone to love. Don't ever leave, will you?

Picking up on all the trumpets and alarums of the world.

Last night we went to dance at The Club. We arrived right in the middle of scandalous excitement. The patrons were all abuzz at the appearance of Ruck, a well known All Black. There were nods of oho and aha. He wasn't the only newcomer, I noticed. Bright Eyes was there too.

Chris was oblivious to them all. The music had stopped. Chris walked onto the floor. As soon as Born To Boogie saw him coming he shrugged and vacated the space, leaving it all to Chris.

Strobes flashing around him, he stood there alone. Deltoid build. Tightly cinched belt. He took everybody's breath away, including Ruck's, with his rugged handsomeness. Clicked his fingers. Then called to All The World:

'This is for you, Simon.'

As if by magic, the music began, and with it Chris started to whirl around the room like a Cossack. People began to shout and scream. He showered the night with sparks of delight and thankfulness for his dead friend.

Dancing a tarantella on All The World's grave. Cocking a snook. Thumbing his nose.

But tonight, a minefield.

32

AT THE RECOMMENDATION of Spinster I have engaged her lawyer, The Most Boring Man In The World, to represent me in the divorce proceedings. He and the family lawyer are already locked in battle over how the matrimonial property should be shared between Annabelle and me.

For instance, two sets of valuations have been taken on The House On The Hill, one by the family lawyer and the other by The Most Boring Man. The valuations vary, and so does the advice on what we should do with the property. My lawyer wants me to sell it and split the proceeds. Annabelle's lawyer wants us to come to some agreement whereby Annabelle and the girls remain there and she pays me rent. Both Annabelle and I are agreed that it would be less traumatic for the girls if they stayed in the house. My suggestion has been that I transfer my share to her and that she take on sole ownership. Can this be done?

Alas, my lawyer advises against this because I am virtually giving away my share in the house. And, anyway, the law doesn't work that way. Some financial arrangement must be entered into. I must be bought out. But with what? Annabelle has suffered the fate of many married women. She has no savings, stocks and bonds, property or anything of her own. All she had has been invested in husband and children.

So it has gone on. The legal sawing through our lives, house, car, bank accounts, household effects, my income, how much maintenance I should pay and for how long, what should happen if or when Annabelle remarries, blah blah blah. Everything is being valued and stickers placed on items signifying either Hers or

Mine. And, for the moment The House On The Hill is Annabelle's, available to me by invitation only.

In spite of this, Annabelle and I try to maintain some sense of context for Rebecca and Miranda. We have decided not to tell them. Even so, there is no doubt that the world has changed. Not only the children, but the world is being divided up. On one side, my rights. On the other side, Annabelle's. On one side, my share. On the other side, Annabelle's. On one side, my space. On the other side, Annabelle's. Our lawyers are our arbitrators of who gets what and when.

Meantime, the children occupy Annabelle's space. After all, Annabelle is their mother.

'At some point, however,' The Most Boring Man In The World warns me, 'we will have to consider visitation rights. Who has the children and when. Times. Dates. Arrangements. Until that happens, try to be sensitive to the situation.' Everything is being separated out. The trouble is that sometimes life doesn't quite work out this way. Try explaining it to children. They know nothing about being split down the middle.

The next week, a second fax waiting for me at the office from Oh My Goodness:

Two days in New Zealand may not be long enough, he writes. *Why don't we continue our discussions* (hah!) *in Australia? I would love to have you join me there at the conference so that we might come to some agreements of mutual benefit.*

The offer is tempting but the timing is not opportune. What with the divorce proceedings and now the discovery of the films I'll be hard pressed for time.

There has also been a message from my life insurance broker. I ring him back.

'We notice,' he says in an embarrassed tone, 'that you have engaged in male to male anal sex.'

'Yes.'

'I am afraid that company policy requires us to ask that you take the Aids test.'

'And if I decide not to update my policy but leave it as it is? Will you still require me to take the test?'

'Uh, but now that we know —'

'You haven't got a leg to stand on. I've taken legal advice and neither you nor anybody else can change the conditions of my current policy. I'll consider your request.'

I hang up. Then ring Left Dress.

'Why didn't you take my advice?' he sighs.

'Because I refuse to pass as heterosexual in this society any longer. It's about time I took the test anyway.'

He's heard such brave, foolish and unrealistic rhetoric before. Talk is cheap.

'I'll make an appointment for you. Later today? Good.'

Eat, drink and be merry. Tomorrow we may die.

Meantime, planning and progress on getting the cache of films up from the back of beyond to Film Studies has gone by leaps and bounds, and I have had to mortgage myself by another twenty-five thousand dollars. The bank manager, regretfully, can do no more. It will have to do unless I can obtain some gelignite and actually rob the bank.

We are one week away from collecting the films and the warehouse down by the old railway station has been turned into a vault specially constructed, and temperature and humidity controlled, to maintain the films against deterioration. Ronald has left nothing to chance and I was told by Stephen that he actually stayed locked in the vault all night with a thermometer to check there was no temperature variation.

Now, carpenters bearing Ronald's detailed instructions are banging and crashing around Film Studies, converting one of our classrooms into a restoration laboratory for the painstaking and difficult transfer of the films from their volatile nitrate condition onto safety stock. Brenda is in her element. She has decided to be Sigourney Weaver, issuing orders to the workmen as if she is chief executive of some corporate giant.

From my office I watch progress with growing elation. I think of Chris; if he walked in right now I'd have him clothes off and flat across the desk.

Then the roof falls in.

Staff meeting, and the room is surprisingly animated. In one corner I see God's Gift To Woman offering cake, so naturally veer toward the opposite side of the room. Spinster comes bearing a cup of coffee. She cocks a beady, sparrow eye at me and gestures with her head at God's Gift.

'Beware the Ides of March,' she says. 'Foul deeds are to hand. Dastardly plots being hatched.'

God's Gift is talking to the head of department and Brian, the head of Theatre Studies.

'I'd watch my back if I were you,' Spinster continues.

The head of department calls us all to order and we take our seats. The usual preliminaries are quickly dispensed with. Introductions of new tutors; a report by the head of his last meeting with the Vice Chancellor; matters concerning the staffing, student and accommodation problems of our own department. So far so good.

Then out of the blue God's Gift asks the head, 'Might I ask through you —' He swivels a crocodile smile in my direction. 'What is happening at Film Studies?'

Uh oh. I am found out. Stonewall, David, stonewall.

I smile at the Head and lie through my teeth. 'I sent you a memorandum last week.'

'A memo? I've not received it.'

'It must have been lost in the system.'

If all else fails blame the luckless registry staff.

'So what is happening?' God's Gift presses. 'I've had reports that you've had tradesmen and carpenters modifying one of your classrooms and outfitting it with rather specialised equipment.'

'Only reports?' I ask him. 'You haven't come to see for yourself? I wouldn't believe all I heard if I was you.'

God's Gift shrugs at the titters from the staff. 'Can you verify the reports? After all,' he plays to the gallery, 'it wasn't too long ago that we were discussing the space constraints we were facing.' So that's it. 'The increase in my own roll of students who want to take American Literature has brought me to crisis point. And I know there are others in the same predicament.'

I see. If he can't have extra space, neither can I. Time to be authoritative.

'You've got it absolutely wrong,' I say to him. 'I am not increasing my space or encroaching on your space. What I am doing is modifying the current layout of Film Studies to enable practical, hands-on experience for the senior students in our curriculum.'

All said with wide-eyed innocence.

'Hands-on?' the head asks. 'What area of the syllabus are you talking about?'

'Research and development.'

Brian, head of Theatre Studies, takes sides with God's Gift.

'And what budget has this, ah, modification come out of?'

'My own. But —'

Brian has always wanted to take over Film Studies. Is this the bid? Get me thrown out for mismanagement?

'Hmmmn,' the head says. Then, suspicious, 'I really wish that memorandum of yours had turned up, David.'

God's Gift and Brian keep pushing. The killer question.

'And how much has all this so far cost?'

They have a mole somewhere. When I find him, the carnage of my revenge will outdo the final scene of *Bonnie and Clyde*.

'Seventy five —'

'Oh, that's all right then,' says the head.

'Thousand dollars.'

The head's words die on his breath. He blanches. Looks like he will keel over and have a heart attack. Recovers.

'I think I'd better discuss this with you in my office,' he says, closing the meeting.

In the background God's Gift and Brian nod, congratulating each other.

The head's discussion with me is short and sharp. I outline the significance of the find, the contribution that will be made to international film history, and say that I have needed to move fast because of the highly vulnerable nature of the material. I tell him that the magnitude of the find, two hundred and seventy films, has required a major laboratory contruction programme.

But even as I talk I know that the head is correct. Of course I had no right to spend such an amount or to embark on such a major modification of the Film Studies space without his prior authority. I have far exceeded my own level of financial authority, which is five thousand maximum. The fact that I have raised most of the money in a personal loan does not obscure the issue. Nor that I have employed private contractors to do the work. There are channels that I should have negotiated, and such a major project as this should definitely have been discussed in the University Committee. Not only that, but to divert my students into assisting with the modifications jeopardises their own studies.

'I shall have to take this matter up with the Vice Chancellor,' the head says. 'In the meantime, all further activity on this project should cease.'

'But —'

'No buts, David. I am ordering you.'

I take my leave.

God's Gift and Brian, who have been lying in wait, pounce on me and play penitent.

'Sorry, David,' they say. 'We didn't realise —' I turn on them. Who cares that the corridor is crowded.

'Gentlemen, why don't you both go and fuck each other?'

I have been completely thrown by the staff meeting and the telephone conversation with my insurance broker. I lose it totally in my morning lecture on film-making in Australia and New Zealand. For some reason Bright Eyes questions the validity of my judgement of Geoff Murphy's *Utu* which, for the purposes of the course, I have compared with Merata Mita's *Mauri*. My thesis has been that the Murphy film is a Pakeha perspective on a Maori world and that Mita's film is a Maori film within a Maori perspective.

'But surely, Sir,' Bright Eyes asks vigorously, 'you cannot possibly compare the one film with the other. *Utu* is a historical film and *Mauri* is contemporary.'

'I'm glad you noticed,' I answer, and he colours. '*Utu* is set firmly in the American tradition of the Western. Except that Maori replace Indians. Murphy himself accepts that film narrative tradition. Mita does not and attempts to subvert film narrative to Maori purposes.'

'Can you really say that? The characters in Mita's film are not unlike Murphy's. For instance, the gang members. Surely they are only carbon copies in the same film narrative tradition as, say,

Peter Fonda's *Easy Rider*?'

Bright Eyes defends. He pushes a lock of hair out of his eyes. And in that moment I am angry at his innocence.

'Aren't you listening?' I ask. 'I said that Mita *attempts*. I did not say that she has been entirely successful.' The rest of the class has grown extremely silent. 'Of course Mita, just like any other film-maker, is constrained by the entire film tradition. Of course she has inherited the same narrative straitjackets. But what distinguishes her film-making are the nuances, the small illuminations which makes *Mauri* a truly indigenous film. You cannot say the same about Murphy.'

'That depends on your definition of what an indigenous film is,' Bright Eyes murmurs. His quietitude is resolute. He refuses to give in.

'And are you saying that your definition is better than mine?' I ask.

'Murphy's *Goodbye Pork Pie* is just as indigenous as *Mauri*.'

'Oh for crying out loud,' I answer. 'Haven't you learnt anything at all? Class dismissed.'

I am absolutely fuming as I storm out of the class and back to my office. Up the stairs and —

'David, wait.'

Nor am I in the mood for Predator, trying to run after me in her ridiculous shoes. I stop, leaning against the stair rail.

'I'm sorry about this morning,' she says. Her green eyes dilate, underlining her emotion. 'You know I'm on your side.'

'Thanks,' I answer. 'I appreciate it.'

I start to move away. But she puts a restraining hand on my arm. Tender. Soft.

'Listen,' she continues, 'I've also heard why you and Annabelle are divorcing.'

I push her hand off me. So she wants to smirk and scoff, does she? Play the woman scorned? What a bitch.

'That's nobody's business except ours,' I say. 'Now if you'll excuse me —'

'Look.' She is determined, standing her ground. 'I know what you men say about me. The last thing I want to do is get into your or any other academic's underpants. Got that? Can't a man

185

and a woman be friends without sex coming into it?'

I am taken aback. Slightly miffed but also embarrassed.

'That's all I have ever wanted from you, David. Friendship. Interesting company. Intellectual discussion. I can't say that I'm not disappointed you like men. But —' She smiles, uncertain about my reaction. 'If you need me —'

She lifts herself as high in her shoes as she possibly can, teetering dangerously, and kisses me.

'God,' she grins. '*Men.*'

The head's order has finally reached Film Studies. I should have told everybody but just didn't have the heart.

'Is it true, David?' Ronald asks. He is panicky, close to tears. He has been cow-eyed with trust and confidence in me. Damn him for trusting. 'Laddie, do we have to close down shop?'

Brenda and Stephen hover close by, awaiting my answer.

'Laddie, don't let them do this to us. The trucks are all set, everything is set. Laddie? *Laddeee —*'

His voice howls after me as I turn and walk away.

The clinic is right by the park. When Left Dress made the appointment, he gave me a *nom de plume*, saying, 'It's standard practice. To protect individuals who take the test from those who might discriminate against you.'

There are two small waiting rooms, no doubt to ensure further privacy. I wait in one room and pick up a magazine. But my thoughts are racing ahead of me. I haven't exactly been a saint. What if I have the virus? What then? As you sow, you reap.

The doctor invites me into his surgery. He is young, professional, anonymous. When I leave the clinic I can't even remember what he looks like. He does some counselling and asks questions about my partners and whether I practise safe sex. Assures himself that I really do need to take the test.

'How long before the results are known?' I ask.

'We've made it easier on the nerves,' he says. 'Once it used to take three weeks. Now it's a matter of days.' Then, 'Please roll up your sleeve.'

He loops a plastic tube around my upper arm to distend the

veins. Takes a hypodermic needle. Presses it into the skin. The blood fountains red, shockingly crimson, so full of life. A Red Sea opening up to let Moses through.

'Come back on Friday,' he says.

Try to keep out the fears. No use worrying until then.

Then back to Film Studies.

'Call Ronald and Stephen up, will you?' I ask Brenda.

She nods, gives a choking cry and dabs at her eyes.

When Ronald arrives he doesn't want to look at me. He stares out the window, his Adam's apple working up and down.

'I'm sorry I walked away like that,' I apologise.

'That's all right, laddie. You're under a lot of strain. We appreciate what you're doing.'

Then I explain the situation.

'Yes, laddie,' Ronald says. 'Speaking on behalf of us all, we know you'll do your best. You'll think of something —'

Yes. I always think of something.

God, I could do with some tea and sympathy. I try to ring Chris but there's no answer. On the spur of the moment, I try Jack. We were supposed to be meeting sometime this week anyway.

'I'm sorry, Sir,' Jack's secretary says. 'Mister Alwyn-Jones is unavailable. He has just come out of hospital —'

'What!'

'And is recuperating at his mother's.'

33

THE NEXT AFTERNOON I have taken a few hours off and plan to take the girls to The Teps and then to see Jack.

'Hello, Daddy.' Miranda has her mouth crammed with muesli.

'They won't be long,' Annabelle interrupts, adding, 'I hope,' under her breath.

Miranda is trying to eat an apple at the same time.

'We're *not* going swimming again, are we?' Rebecca asks with a toss of her head. 'I am *never* going swimming again. In the sea or the baths. In my life. Ever.' Unless, of course, nice Daddy buys her a new pair of togs.

Annabelle is in a rush.

'So,' I ask. 'Where are you off to?'

'I've joined a women's group,' she answers. 'It's a support group, actually. We have to keep together. We have a counsellor coming today to give us assertiveness training.' Assertiveness training? Then, grabbing a beach bag, 'And then I'm off to the gym.'

'The gym?'

'Don't worry. Not yours. A women's gym. I started last week. It's just what I need.'

This is the Annabelle I have always admired. She is picking up the pieces. Taking control of her life. Getting back in top condition to battle the world to protect her cubs. Out with the old. In with the new. She is getting on with it.

Drawing the line.

Later, I park my car in the street and climb the steps to Mrs Alwyn-Jones's house, bouquet of flowers in hand. I whistle appreciatively as the house appears from behind its curtain of lush ferns. For a fleeting moment there is the illusion of France, the Côte d'Azur. The two-storeyed stucco villa is painted apricot, with green shutters, blue awnings and green door. A portico of bright blue canvas leads to a glass conservatory on the side that gets the sun. Miles of wisteria climb the house. A pebbled drive and pathway appear amid neatly clipped lawn. In the centre, a small cherubim fountain.

I press the intercom button at the entrance.

'David,' Jack answers. 'Come through, turn left down the hall and on into the conservatory.'

The door clicks open and the illusion is gone, for without doubt the interior design is *le style anglais*. There are black and white tiles in the entranceway and smoothly rounded balustrading like a swan's neck curving to the second floor. Wood panelling in the hall. Chintz curtains against alcoved windows. Delicate watercolours of sporting scenes, framed in heavy gilt. Brussels weave carpet, painted porphyry.

'Down this way,' Jack calls.

He is sitting in the sunlit conservatory at the end of the hallway. Past a little red library and bedroom with French windows for maximum light.

'Lovely to see you, old chap,' Jack greets me, shaking my hand. He puts aside his newspaper. 'Did you read today that an estimated ten per cent of our population is of our persuasion? It's absolutely disgusting, don't you think? What is civilisation coming to!' He laughs, winces from his stitches and continues, 'Mother has gone out. She's like an old hen. I shall be glad to get back to my own townhouse in the city. Would you like a gin and tonic?'

He waves me to a seat at the dining table. He has prepared chicken marbella and a salade niçoise.

Jack is not a pretty sight. His face is purpled and swollen, with gashes from top lip across left cheek. He had been leaving The Steam Parlour when the gay bashers jumped him. He had suspected rib fractures from being kicked while down. Had it not been for a bunch of American sailors from the nuclear vessel, he may have sustained graver injuries. One of them, Chip, a Virginia farm boy who had joined the Navy to get away from his Bible-belting folks, had been a regular visitor while he was in hospital. Friendly and courteous with his 'Yes Sir', 'No Sir' bedside manner, Chip had completely swept Jack off his feet.

'You all get well now, you hear?' Chip had told Jack on the day before the fleet had shipped out. And was gone.

Half an hour later and I am beginning to relax. The week has been strenuous and, in its own way, stressful. I find I am unburdening myself to Jack. I can get rid of my load by placing it on him.

'So that's the story,' I say. 'The most magnificent discovery in film history, at least in this country, and no likelihood of support from the Arts Council. Or the Film Commission. Or Film Archives. Though everybody, naturally, is as excited as we are. But —' I hold out my hands helplessly. 'No funding agency can really cope with the project that simply falls out of the air. Which hasn't been planned for. Or put in the budget. But we're going ahead anyway.'

'How?' Jack asks.

He leans forward and his neck slides out from his shirt, showing the wattling of his skin. There are spider veins around his chinline where the bruising still shows. Yet here in his own milieu, his own setting, I am aware of how right it is and how wrong he appears when he comes to The Steam Parlour. He has the credentials to belong here, with his breeding, his understanding of finer things, his upper-class manners. But *there*? The clothes do not maketh the man.

'I've taken a bank loan,' I shudder. 'God knows how I'll pay it back. Whether the head stops the project or not, the piper will still have to be paid, I guess.' I smile, bravely. 'But, Dorothy, at the end of it there surely must be a rainbow. Things might not be as bad as we think they'll be. If the Vice Chancellor agrees, we'll carry on and, when rainbow time comes, have a major premiere. Invite a big Hollywood star. Clint Eastwood or Robert Redford or somebody like that. We'll get there. Cross fingers.'

Jack fingers his gin.

'That's what I've always admired about you,' he says. 'Your confidence.' He is silent a moment and then raises the glass to his lips. 'May we drink to the success of your project?'

We raise our glasses and toast the venture. The gin is strong with a piquant dash of lemon.

'Now let's eat, shall we?' he asks. 'And while we eat, perhaps you can give me some advice.' His eyes are aglow. 'A wonderful man has come into my life. I think I'm in love.'

Jack is sitting there, chatting about his new man. No, it is not Chip: Jack is sensible enough to know that an affair with a sailor, who no doubt has a guy in every port, is not the basis for a long-term relationship.

'So where did you meet this man?' I ask.

I am trying to feel positive about Jack's news. But his is not the physical presence or emotional personality which attracts anything like love. Not only that but his neediness, his headlong rushing into 'love', makes him vulnerable. He *wants* to be in love.

'I know what you're thinking,' he answers.

I must be cruel to be kind. 'Well, a guy you pick up at The Steam Parlour or The Fuck Palace is hardly someone to fall for.'

I try to say it with lightness, with a knowing smile, but it comes across too strongly. I know full well Jack's usual sex partners, not to mention the assortment of fly-by-nighters who also make up his fare.

'I didn't meet him in the Gardens,' he responds. 'Old chap, I've been around long enough to realise that the men who go there are not after love.'

'So how did it happen?' I try the light touch again but my sarcasm is scarcely veiled. 'He isn't one of your hired boys, is he?'

When all else has failed, Jack has been known to consort with trade or one of the escort agency stables of young men.

Jack stares at me. 'I thought you'd be pleased for me,' he says. 'I thought you'd be happy for me.'

I reach over and pat his shoulder. The anxiety I feel at his news surprises me into realising that since he has been tutoring at the university we have become closer friends than I had thought.

'I guess I just don't want you to get hurt,' I answer. 'I've got to know you well enough to know how vulnerable you are. Sex is one thing but love is another. It's a rainbow, Jack. And you have a habit of believing in something that was never there in the first place.'

'This is different.'

'That's what they all say.'

'No, it is.'

'Jack, you're always chasing rainbows. A guy shows interest in you and you're in love already? Give me a break.'

Jack looks away from me.

'Okay,' I sigh. 'I'll suspend judgement. Why don't you tell me about him?'

Jack is quiet for a moment. Then his eyes glow with hope and expectation.

'He came to see me in hospital. I've known him by sight for quite some time but have never spoken to him. When he heard I had been assaulted he came right over. We started to talk and —'

'So your romance started in hospital?' I interrupt. 'Jack, that's too fast, much too fast to fall in love.'

'But it did happen,' Jack answers. 'Not straight away, of course, but over the following days he kept coming back. Always kind. Always gentle.' A relaxing of his lips. 'And his basket is somewhat oversized.'

'What does he do?' I ask, still doubtful.

'He's in the export business. He's in Thailand and Malaysia right now, which is the reason why I can't introduce him to you.'

'Convenient.'

'But he's returning in a week,' Jack continues. 'I'm planning to throw a dinner party to introduce him to my friends. I would very much like you to come, old chap. Will you?' He is looking up at me, earnestly. He is ripe for love. Ripe for being picked off. Ripe. 'Only once in my life have I ever been in love,' he says. 'I had a crush on one of the boys at my very first school. They say you always remember your first love.' His voice is like driftwood on a sea of dreams. 'Since then I have only had sex, never love. It's all right for you, David. You have looks, a personality and confidence.'

'But you've got money,' I say, trying to inflate his self-worth. Trying a joke. 'If you're rich, I'm single.'

He shakes his head. 'Money has never bought me love. It buys sex, I know that, but I'm getting tired of that. I want somebody to come home to. Somebody who looks forward to my coming home.'

'And how does this guy feel about you?'

'What do you think?' asks Jack with terrible honesty. 'Friendship right now, but who knows? I want to say "Yes" to this one, not "Yes but". What he's giving me is more than I've ever had. Ever. In my life.'

We are sitting opposite each other, Jack and I, in the afternoon light, and all of a sudden I have a terrible feeling about all this. Nevertheless:

'Well, Jack, you have to find love wherever it is, and once you have it, *grab* it.' He nods at me and smiles. A tremulous smile, quivering. 'Only, please keep your head. Okay?'

'I've got to take the chance,' Jack whispers. 'I've got to jump, old chap.'

It is time for me to go. At that moment the light pierces through the conservatory. A thin pencil of light like a memory.

'Jack,' I ask, 'have we ever met before? Before The Steam Parlour, I mean?'

'Old chap,' he answers fondly, 'wouldn't you have remembered if we had?'

Yes, we all take the chance when we fall in love. But some of us have certainties of success. Sitting there, talking to Jack, all I can sense is a man who is always grabbing at what is never there. Hopping up and down on a chair, grabbing at the insubstantial air.

Hop hop hop.

And then

Jump.

34

THE NEXT DAY at university I see Brian, head of Theatre Studies, across the campus. He waves but I can't be bothered responding, stuff it.

No sooner am I in my room than Brenda has the head of department on the line.

'The Vice Chancellor has called a meeting to discuss the Film Studies matter next week. I would advise you to be prepared.'

Clipped. Abrupt. Here comes the axe to chop off David's head. I call the staff together.

'I need your help,' I begin. 'Our best strategy, I think, is to try to achieve a balance between convincing the university of the international importance of our project while, at the same time, acknowledging that we didn't go through the proper channels to get it underway.'

'It sticks in my craw,' Ronald says, 'to eat humble pie. But if that's the way it has to be —' Then, 'As it happens, the old man who collected all this stuff also left a stack of film posters. Some are priceless. That could mean extra income.'

'So what do we do?' Stephen asks.

'I don't want more questions,' I respond. 'I want some answers. I want all of you to develop some briefing notes for me. Give me some arguments to take to the Vice Chancellor. Some justifications. Make it so watertight that we can get away with it with just a slap on the wrists. Otherwise —'

Brenda takes over. This is just where she excels. 'Okay, fellers,' she says in her best Marilyn Monroe imitation, 'you heard the boss. Let's have our first session this afternoon.'

I have a few moments in my room before this morning's lecture. I have been trying to understand why I had such a hostile reaction to Bright Eyes' arguments yesterday.

I realise that my anger was driven by frustration that he is coming out and has become one of us. He is easily dazzled by excitement. He is so filled with optimism, idealism, expectations and trust. Yet ours is a world where a man who says he loves you one day might leave you the next. Where youth is a commodity and sex simply a throwaway carton.

Here is another young man on the brink of becoming, like I had become a few years ago, one of The Lost Boys.

We already know, intuitively, that we are kindred spirits. Even so, it had hurt to see him in all his innocence and beauty, at The Club last night, in that place of darting glances and flashing lights. He had come over to the bar to say hello. After he left Wet Dream Walking and Italian Stallion had both sidled up, wolf whistled, and asked me about him.

'Who's that?'

'One of my students. Just a baby.'

'Some baby.' Eyebrows lifted, looking at me.

'No,' I respond. 'Students are a no-no.'

'There's always a first time, man.'

No time to think about it now. Go on to my class. Everyone seated. Bright Eyes, unusually, at the back. Head down as I come in. Ashamed that I showed him up in front of the class.

'Today,' I begin, 'we will continue our discussion on indigenous film-making in Australia and New Zealand.' Take a deep breath. 'But before I do so, I need to apologise for my behaviour yesterday. A very fine student expressed cogent arguments which I unfairly trashed. He was right and I was wrong. There are of course many definitions of what constitutes indigenous. Now —'

Bright Eyes is like a pale star gleaming.

Turn to the subject at hand.

Go well, Bright Eyes.

'All further activity on this project should cease —'

I have made up my mind. I call Brenda, Ronald and Stephen together again.

'When the head issued his directive,' I begin, 'his exact words were that all further activity on this project should cease. My understanding of the word "further" suggests to me that any work already underway *before* his directive can still continue. We are therefore going ahead as planned.'

My three co-conspirators can hardly believe their ears.

'Thank you, laddie,' Ronald answers.

'And,' I continue, 'just to make sure we won't be stopped, I want to bring forward the date the trucks go down to get the films.'

My words are straight out of any 1940s war movie you would care to name. *Operation Burma. Bataan.* Brenda is looking at me as if I was Errol Flynn.

'The trucks leave tomorrow.'

35

SO NOW I have parked my car outside The House On The Hill and have come inside to tell Annabelle and the girls I will be away for the weekend. And I am in absolute terror because Annabelle has asked me to stay with her and tell the girls, finally, that we are divorcing each other.

'Can't it wait until I get back?' I ask.

Annabelle's hair is spun of gold by Rumpelstiltskin. We are sitting in the lounge. Above our heads the girls are racing like little elephants, screaming and yelling. Such are the joys that I abandoned when I left them.

'Please, sport, let's do it now. Get it over with.'

'But they won't understand.'

'Perhaps you need to make them understand.'

'Why?'

Annabelle's eyes are glittering with determination.

'Why? You ask, Why? Not a day goes past, David, when either one of them talks about you. Rebecca will say over breakfast, "When Daddy's home again I want him to put a new shelf on my bookcase high enough so that Miranda can't reach." Or Miranda will say, "Daddy will let us have a kitten even if you won't Mummy, won't he, Rebecca?" But now that it will be divorce, they need to understand. They *must* be told.'

Annabelle is up from her chair, fearful yet clear about the proper thing to be done.

'Then you tell them.'

'Oh yes, take the easy way out. Leave me as usual to do the dirty work.' Her jibe drives deep. Makes me feel ashamed. 'You don't realise, do you, how difficult this has been for me. I am still here in this house. I have to answer to people who still don't know about us. Have you ever thought of that? Oh no, you were over the hills and far away, and never mind about *me*. Did you bother to tell people that you'd gone? The telephone still rang for you. Letters still came for you in the post. Some of our friends still send invitations to both of us. Old Mrs Potter thought you were away overseas on business. Whenever she asked me where you were, it became more convenient for me to say that you'd gone to America. Better that than to have her say, "I'm so sorry, dear, I didn't know." Better to tell anybody who asked that you were still away on business. One of the things you did, David, was to turn *me* into a liar. But I'm tired of lying. Tired that your deceit has turned *me* to deception. Tired of always taking it on myself. Tired of always lying to the girls. From now on you can do your own lying.'

'I didn't tell you to lie for me.'

Above in their bedrooms the girls are piping laughter down to Annabelle and me where we sit facing each other.

'Of *course* I know it was my own fault telling everybody that you were away on business. I suppose I did it because I kept on hoping that you would come back to me. To us. To our life together. But we're past that point. We've tried. Been there done that.' She is being tidy, heigh ho, out with the rubbish. 'And as for the girls, we can't keep them believing, can't keep them hoping that we will get back together. Every time we argue, something dies in them.' She is disarming me. 'They are starting to blame themselves, David. We have the chance to stop them from doing that. We can only do it, however, if we make everything clear to them.' Leaving me defenceless. 'They say to me, "It's because we did something wrong, isn't it, Mummy?" '

Reducing me to silence.

You want me to tell them that Daddy's gay?

Oh no you *don't*, Annabelle. I know what you're up to. You want the girls to start hating me, don't you? You want to show me up for being homosexual, don't you? See, girls? Your Daddy doesn't really love you at all. If he did, why would he leave you? You think I don't know what you're up to, Annabelle? You want *my* daughters to turn against me. To despise me, for having left them.

I won't do it. I want them to love me for ever. For ever.

Annabelle's eyes are weeping tears of gold. 'If you truly love us, set us free. Please.'

36

MY EYES ARE streaming with tears. Once upon a time there was a Handsome Prince —

I promised Annabelle I would tell my princesses. Now I have.

'Mummy and Daddy are getting divorced.'

'NoMummyNoNoNoNoNO.'

Rebecca is standing in the centre of the living room, shaking her head, snap snap snap, and stamping her foot. Her eyes are grim with determination as she stands with her hands on her hips.

'Darlings,' Annabelle is saying, 'everything will be okay. It will all work out, you'll see. All it means is that Daddy will have his house. And Mummy will have her house. And you two girls will have two houses, not one, to live in.' Annabelle's voice is bright and shiny. 'Tell them, David.'

'ThisisDaddy'shouseherewith*us*Mummy.'

Miranda is whimpering. She doesn't understand what is happening. All she knows is that something is wrong. She watches her bigger sister where Rebecca grimly holds her ground.

'Of course it is, darling,' Annabelle is pleading, 'and we will always make him welcome when he comes to see us. We still love him and he still loves us.' She turns to me, 'Don't you, Daddy?'

My mouth is full of blood and I cannot answer.

'Idon't*care*whatyousayMummyIdon't*care*.'

With a scream Miranda has run to Rebecca and clutches at the hem of Rebecca's dress.

'What'swrongBecca?What's*wrong*.'

Miranda looks from me to Annabelle to me to Annabelle, her head cracking this way and that.

'Darlings,' Annabelle cries, 'whatever Mummy and Daddy do to each other doesn't mean that we have stopped loving you. You are the two most wonderful daughters in the whole wide world. Tell them, David. *Tell them.*

Blood. Mouth full of.

'ThenwhyMummywhyMummyWHYMummmeeee.'

'IfyouloveusandDaddylovesusthenWhy.'

'We'vebeenbadgirlshaven'tweMummybadbad*bad.*'

The girls are screaming and crying and shaking apart.

This must be what innocence looks and sounds like when it has been murdered.

Two little girls holding each other like lost babes in the wood. A mother, holding out her arms to them, trying to remain strong, trying to hold back her own grief. And in the absence of a father's reassurance, taking it all upon herself.

Fluttering to the ground with an arrow in her breast. Resigned.

'No my darlings. It's not you. Hush now.'

Annabelle has been holding her arms across her chest and, when she raises them to her children, she hopes they will not see the ruby blood that spills there.

'It's not you at all, my darlings — it's Mummy who's been bad.'

Part Five

LIFE, NEVER NEVER LAND, AND A MAN THAT DREAMS ARE MADE OF

37

THERE IS NO refuge in the cold flat. I drive to the local take-away bar and grab a pizza and beer. Then back into the car and over to The Fuck Palace, crumbling on the edge of the world. Through the empty streets, past the Town Hall to the place where children sometimes watch with pink rats' eyes the shadowed alleys and the men who come to gasp out their pleasures.

Into the foyer with its huge defaced 1950s movie posters of pulchritudinous men and women. Steve Reeves in *Hercules Unchained*. Maria Montez in *The Cobra Woman*. Edmund Purdom in *The Egyptian*. Rhonda Fleming, reputed to have been one of the most beautiful women in all history, as Semiramis in *Queen of Babylon*. Virginia Mayo in *The Silver Chalice*. Kirk Douglas as *Spartacus*. Lana Turner, pearl-beaded within an inch of indecency in *The Prodigal*, and poor old Victor Mature with Hedy Lamarr in *Samson and Delilah*, about which movie mogul Harry Cohn remarked: 'I never go to see a movie where the guy has bigger tits.' Those were the days when actresses were not allowed to reveal their navel. Men were men and women were women, and something was wrong if you couldn't tell the difference. All slashed now, hieroglyphed with graffiti, splattered with urine, penned with names and telephone numbers. Defiled.

Now into the locker room. But it is a place of ghosts. The men sitting there are lost in its dimensions. The lockers are like metallic caskets which have burst open. All the ornate trappings that once were here have been stripped away. Gone, the black and gold fittings along the walls. Gone, the small cameos of scenes from epic films. Gone, the coloured glass that was inset decoratively in the ceramic flooring. Yet, once upon a time, men thronged here. Eager. Bright. Hopeful.

The Fuck Palace is indeed Charles Foster Kane's *Xanadu*. The survivors of the seventies still live on in this place of Time Remembered.

Tonight I am not seeking the past. Only the present. The parade has well and truly passed by. Atlantis will never rise again from the sea.

Onward to The Steam Parlour.

The hatch opens. The florid face of The Spaniard smiles like the devil. Pursued by conscience and the sound of a world shaking apart, I seek forgetfulness in this netherworld.

'Haven't seen you for a while,' he says. His gold teeth gleam in a blood-red mouth. His tongue is swollen, engorged, and stippled with yellow mucus.

'I've been busy.'

He hands me a towel. 'A word of advice,' he says. 'Don't get it on with the Indian. I don't know whether I should have let him in. He's beginning to smell.' He makes a gesture with his fingers, clamping his nose tight shut. The movement is contemptible. Odious.

I sway slightly at the news. Alas, Snake Charmer. The garden is blighted by disease, rusting the white rose petals. Angrily I eyeball The Spaniard. I want to say something like, You've been taking his money so far and haven't complained, you bastard. Or, He probably picked it up from here, fucker. But The Spaniard outstares me, his lips slashing a slit in his face. His smile seems to say, You'll be next.

Away from the vestibule, past Always A Bridesmaid and Fat Forty And A Fairy lying in the shadowed Stygian gloom.

'Have you heard?' Always A Bridesmaid asks.

I nod. Fat Forty And A Fairy sighs and brushes at his eyes. He and Always A Bridesmaid are already preparing Snake Charmer's shroud, the cloth to wrap him in, the gold coins to put on his eyelids and to push into the purse of his mouth when he is dead. I feel like hugging them both. They are not only a friendly ear or the voice of humour. They are also chorus. Just as I am leaving them they begin to tell affectionate stories about Snake Charmer. His first night here and, 'Ever since,' Fat Forty And A Fairy rolls his eyes, 'there has scarce been a week when somebody has not flown Air India.'

When I need to have payment made to the eternal ferryman so that he might take me across the river of death, let the paymasters be Fat Forty And A Fairy and Always A Bridesmaid. They are the finest among us all.

Then, past Marc, the new boy, giving me a hi-five as I pass through to the dressing room. Out of my jeans. Into the shower and quickly through the door to the steam room and its welcoming warmth and wetness.

Stained red, the steam eddies and swirls away from the door. Through the steam I recognise The Bald One and Wet Dream Walking. A dude is kneeling in front of Wet Dream Walking, his hands on both Wet Dream Walking's knees, his head lifting and falling in the slow silent choreography of sex. Size Queen and Once A Beauty match their hand strokes to the dude's motions.

Two other people are in the room. One a Succulent Stranger. The other must be Snake Charmer. But I cannot see his eyes, glowing in the steam. Then I hear him:

'Oh Christ. Oh God —'

I take the high bench and listen to the sighs as they are sucked out of Wet Dream Walking. The Succulent Stranger looks at me. His gaze is enough to tell me he is interested. Suddenly he gets up and walks out the door. For a brief moment his profile is wreathed in steam, showing a jutting cock. Time to go after him.

Out in the shower room, The Succulent Stranger looks as if he has been standing there since the beginning of time. Waiting.

Turn on the shower. Look The Succulent Stranger over.

It would be great to have the wattage lowered. But that would defeat the purposes of the shower room. The brightness is not only to expose the strength or beauty or ugliness or the commonplace among the jocks who might be showering with you. It is not just to allow you to check out whether the guy who has come on to you is all that he looked like he was in the steam room. No. Not only that. The light also enables you to check for the tell tale marks. Blotches. Purple stains. Paper skin. It gives time for your second sense to consider whether a sex partner's purple traceries of veins are to do with the steam or with something infinitely more insidious. Something hatching inside. Even the healthy may have it.

The shower room is second chance land. Here you can surrender to your decision to take or give sex. Or you can smile and step back with a slow sad lingering caress of the potential partner's thigh. 'Listen, uh —'

Not tonight. Succumb to the succulence and to the slow teasing. Yes, for this is what homoeroticism is all about. This silent, slow seduction of a stranger, trying to coax his own hunger open like the petals of a flower.

The techniques depend on the stranger because all men are different, with their own set of likes and dislikes. Unlike women, men do not go for whole body sensitivity or appreciation. This is the age of photography, of the close-up, the freeze frame, the slow-motion shot, the segmenting of parts into tits and ass, cock or snatch. Gay men are no different from straight men in localising what they like. Some like nipples, some like buns. Some like smooth, some like thatch. Above all, there has been a genitalisation of the male. As if the sum of a man is his balls and cock. Thus some prefer cut, some uncut, some like it large, some like it small. Some equate large with better. Prefer young not old. Dark, not blond. Compact, not tall.

So show him what's there. Turn, tuck, pose, pout, strut. Give him a range of choices and, even though I might not quite be the sum of all the parts he likes, seduce him into thinking that they are all there. Show it all by making love to myself. Lick my armpits. Twist my nipples. Take the soap down and show the muscle definition. Further down now to the butt, the head on the hammer, eager to nail his arse with my dark swollen stake. Let him see. Let him take a good look.

Now look at him.

Oh yes, he's easy in his skin, easy-assed and riding high. Every male has a sense of homosexuality about him, and The Succulent Stranger is no different. He is confident inside his body. His assets put him on my plus side. Nice butt, sweet curvature of spine, a smouldering sensuality. Flared nostrils. Hooded eyes. Easy smile.

This is what happens when we are at The Steam Parlour. This assembling of the parts to make up a Fuck for the night. Like Frankenstein. So return Succulent Stranger's smile. Walk over to him. Take up the soap and start soaping him. Move behind him. Let your skin touch his skin. This is the final seduction.

If you've seduced him, this is your prize —

Meld.

Later. Freewheeling into the accustomed place beneath the trees on the other side of the road. Above, the Ship of Dreams, tugging in the night winds. The bedroom windows are dark.

I blow two kisses to Rebecca and Miranda, blowing them up and into the room where they sleep.

Has Annabelle remembered to —

My darlings, in this world you are the sweetest, most innocent and most perfect of your father's accomplishments.

Sleep well.

38

A SHORT DESCRIPTION of Eketahuna, The Town Back of Beyond: 'This picturesque river township of 600 was one of the pioneer settlements developed by Scandinavian migrants who came in the mid 1800s by oxcart and bullock team to establish New Daneland. Its Scandinavian name, Mellemskov, was discarded in favour of the indigenous original, meaning 'to run aground on a shoal'. The fine community hall, built in Scandanavian style, and the old church, are witness to the town's antecedents, as well as the fair-kinned and blond population. Main industries: orcharding and horticulture. Main entertainment: river rafting and bungy jumping. *See*: Siegfried Tours.'

A bright morning. On the road and all is well. Ronald is ahead, driving the first truck, with Brenda as navigator and one of Ronald's covey of film fanatics as co-driver. Following him is Stephen, who has an eager Bright Eyes and another student with him. I am Tail End Charlie, barrelling this antiquated machine along the main highway. Behind, the city is receding like a multi-winged yacht tacking to starboard.

I would dearly have loved Bright Eyes to drive with me, but I shall be detouring around midday and Ronald will need all hands on deck when he arrives at the farm where the films are waiting for us. Early this morning, before we left the city, I telephoned The Love Of My Life. I knew that either he or his longtime part-ner would be awake. Country folks get up with the sun and go down with the sun, especially when there's shearing, harvesting or orcharding to be done.

'Hello, David,' Longtime Partner answered. 'You're on your way then?'

'Yes. I should arrive by four this afternoon.'

'Travel safely. Can you can stay over?'

'I really wish I could, but I'd better not chance it. I need to be there to thank the people who have bequeathed the films to us and supervise their loading. Then afterwards, I have invited the lawyer there, the family who owned the films and our workers to dinner. The least I can do under the circumstances.'

'Well, any time you can spare. We know how busy you are. Charles is looking forward to the visit.'

In convoy Ronald, Stephen and I negotiate the early Saturday motorway traffic. Away from the hi-tech canyons of tall black glass towers, past the container port and railway station, along the motorway and hideous conglomerations of corridor towns and suburbs which fuel our city with their manpower. The traffic is filled with quick-tempered danger.

This morning was a tangle of farewells. Fractious. Filled with the criss and cross of mixed signals.

I was sleeping over at Chris's place. I reached for my watch in the tangle of clothes on the floor. The time was six-fifteen. Time to hit the road.

'When do you expect to be back?' Chris in his waking minutes was absolutely desirable. In the curtained light of his apartment his face was an enigma.

'The day after tomorrow.'

'I'll miss you. Can't you get back earlier? You're never here when I need you. Wish I could come.'

'You can't. Your rehearsals.'

The *Petrushka* season was over. The ballet company, however, planned to send small touring groups out to the provinces with a programme of ballet highlights. Nothing fancy. Something from *Swan Lake*, *Giselle* and *Petrushka*, something modern as well. Ten dancers per group with a director/publicist and pianist. Something old, something new, something borrowed, something blue.

I bent to kiss Chris. Each kiss drank of his lips, the honey of his mouth, as if endeavouring to coax out his mysteries. This is what seduction is all about. Holding a man close, chest to chest, nipple grazing gently across nipple, wanting him to let you in. Waiting for that unconscious tremor which is the sign that the way is open.

Then, 'I love you,' he said.

Shifting sands. Quicksand. Shifting tides.

The Maori say that the country was a giant fish hooked up from the sea by the half-god, half-man trickster Maui. The fish was later hacked about by Maui's brothers, explaining why there are so many ravines and switchback mountain ranges. The backbone of a half-eaten fish, the skeletal frame was snapped and broken by the hunger-ravaged brothers.

From the city the plan is to follow the Main Highway all the way down to Eketahuna. We shall go through the Waikato, past the mysterious Mountain Of Kings, where Maori royalty are buried, and along the River Of A Thousand Serpents, as winding and as imposing as the Mississippi. We plan to stop for a brief morning tea at Hamilton and then get going towards the heart of this dark country. Another brief stop for lunch at Taupo and then on again to the crossroads. A physical landmark which I have always called Sphinx Mountain rears just outside Taupo.

Ah yes, the riddle of the sphinx. Man as crawling child, upright man and then in old age with walking stick. Or —

After dressing this morning, Chris took me to Film Studies, where the trucks were waiting. On the way, however, two stops. The first at The House On The Hill.

'I'll wait in the car,' Chris said. He looked up at me. Reflective. Watched as I knocked on the door and Miranda opened it and jumped up into my arms.

'Will you bring me a present?' she asked. She was as shiny as a polished button. She was also coughing a lot, but trying not to show it.

'For goodness sake,' Annabelle said to Miranda. 'It isn't Christmas or your birthday. It's Grandma's.'

Oh God, I forgot. Today.

'Your mother expects to see you at the very least,' Annabelle said. 'But it's your life. Look, I'm taking the girls over there later. You know Miranda, the party animal. I'll buy your mother a book and tell her it's from you.'

'Thanks.'

'Don't thank me. I'll just add it to the settlement.' Ouch.

'Look, David, last night was awful, just *awful*. How dare you do that to me. To the girls. It took me ages to calm them down.' In the background, Rebecca had her back to us. She was firm. Unmoving. Unforgiving. 'There's a lot we've got to work through and I'm going to have to put some distance between us. Okay? You're way ahead of me in adjusting to all this and I'm far behind. But my anger is beginning to catch up.'

Annabelle was beginning to draw the line. She on her side, me on mine. We were divorcing, after all. Remember?

I put up both my hands. 'You're the sheriff,' I said.

A hug from Miranda. Then, just as I was getting into the car, Rebecca came barrelling past Annabelle and flung herself into my arms. 'I love you, Daddy,' she said. She wrapped herself around me and held on with a fierceness that made me grieve.

Chris and I drove on to Suburbia By The Sea. Chris was still brooding, pensive. He had watched the girls and Annabelle waving in the sunlight.

'I forgot to tell you,' he said. 'The last time we were all together Rebecca said to me, "When Daddy is home for ever, who will love you, Chris?" '

My darling Rebecca. Behind that laughing smile is a whole universe that I do not know filled with expectations and assumptions undreamed of.

'You know what young children are like.'

He nodded. But, 'You know, David,' he said, 'it's really hard for me sometimes. Really hard. I matter too.'

I matter too.

At Suburbia By The Sea, Chris again stayed in the car while I got out and walked to the door. A rapid banging and then my father was there.

'Hello, David.' He was relieved that although I had become a Changeling Son I had not forgotten those rituals around which the game of Happy Families is conducted.

Behind him came the voice of my mother. 'Is that David?'

An intake of breath, pleased, and she was there, in pink dressing gown and slippers, standing behind my father. Opening the door wider. To reveal my sister as well.

'Happy birthday, Mum.'

A warm embrace. A woman of soap and lily water.

'You *never* remember Mum's birthday,' Pamela said suspiciously. I ignored her.

'Just a quick visit,' I said. 'Annabelle and the girls are bringing my present later —'

Suddenly my mother stiffened. Gave a small bird-like cry. She must have seen, over my shoulder, Chris sitting in the car. She pushed me away. Clutched at my sister. Went down the hallway. Away.

My father imprisoned me with his eyes.

'You're always welcome, David,' he said. 'This is your home and we are your parents. But your mother and I do not want any of your fairy friends around.'

Pamela sighed. 'God, brother, when will you ever learn?'

It can all happen so quickly. Like lightning striking on a summer's day. A person turning to salt.

I walked back to Chris. We drove to Film Studies. I tried to explain to him.

'Sometimes it's hard for me too, Chris. I feel as if I'm caught in the middle and things happen so quickly and it's so hard to know what to do. I think it must be different for single gay men. Not so many people to answer to. To answer for. With me, it's a matter of working through with one person at a time and —'

'But will I ever come first?' Chris interrupted. 'When will you ever get around to *me*? Do I come after your kids, Annabelle, your folks and —' touché '— students or the other guys you're seeing in the places you go to? I'm not stupid, David.' His voice caught. He took a deep breath. 'I think I'd like to take a break from seeing you. There's a few things I have to sort out.' He put on his sunglasses. Started the car. Silence. Then, 'Okay? Yes, well. Look after your fat friend.'

To run aground on a shoal.

Past Taupiri Maunga, the Mountain Of Kings, and along the River Of A Thousand Serpents, and our convoy is ahead of schedule, penetrating ever deeper into the heart of darkness. The landscape is filled with millions of trees, green arrowheads thrusting at the sky. Logging trucks rumble along the highway. But there are also signs of forest fires, blackened, scorched, like skid marks through the swathe of green. Life is like that too, with its angers, passions and pain. Tangled. Criss-crossed. Marked by scorch trails.

Three hours run and we are in the centre of the country, cupped by the vast, tideless Lake Taupo created by a volcanic eruption greater than Santorini or Krakatoa. Across the lake are snowcapped mountains, a gleaming pillar between earth and sky. Every kilometre brings with it a sense of freedom, a throwing off of responsibility, and we are indeed making better time than we had expected. After lunch, Ronald and I consult the map. From here we had planned to skirt the lake, drive right down the middle of the country, past the military camp and thence to the crossroads. But Bright Eyes finds a quicker route for me. Highway Five will take me to the other side of Sphinx Mountain and I will get to The Love Of My Life's earlier.

'I've never been that way,' I tell him.

'The road looks okay,' Stephen says. 'It'll take you through some desolate country. You'll be travelling through the Tuhoe area, the place of The People Of The Mist. Why don't you try it?'

'I'd love to come with you,' Bright Eyes says. 'We could talk and —' He blushes. But, no. When we reach the crossroads I wave him and the convoy onward. I turn into Highway Five, marked by a dead tree, white as a witching bone.

I have always loved long journeys. The mere act of leaving accustomed surroundings with their own known context is a release from real time, real life. You can place that accustomed life on hold, freeze it, secure in the awareness that it will be there waiting for you when you come back. Every journey thus becomes an opportunity to explore your parallel lives, those other, optional lives which have always been there too. The rooms inhabited by the other people in your life. Where the beds are made, waiting for your return, for you to come back.

Beneath the shadow of Sphinx Mountain I have left Chris, Annabelle, the girls and That Life behind. And ahead lies Charles.

All highways are peopled by ghosts. By memories, hitching, waiting by the side of the road to be picked up. Or emerging out of the cumulus castles in the air. Or slashing down as a hawk does on its roadside prey. Or kicked up into the windscreen by a passing car. Or, as now, like a haze of summer mist which lifts, revealing a hitch hiker in front of me. Stepping out to thumb me down. He is a farm boy, smelling of sweat and honesty, and isn't going very far. But he has, by simply being there, fulfilled his role as seer at the crossroads, because long after he has stepped down from the truck I remember that this was how The Love Of My Life and I had met. On a road like this in a summer twelve years ago.

Then I arrive in Charles's town and the memories have slipped away, momentarily, with the farm boy laughing, 'Thanks for the lift.' But the momentum is still there, churning up memories of Charles as I drive towards a small orchard just outside the town limits. And because I still love Charles, every kilometre closer to him brings a sense of fear at having to face the reality of him and his longtime partner, Dennis.

When some people travel they aim at the destination. That is not as important to me as the getting there. I am a yachtsman at heart rather than a powerboat enthusiast. But my judgements about wind direction, strength of tide and weather conditions have often left me, as now, stranded on quicksand and shifting sandbars. Not there yesterday, the shifting sands threaten the old maps, the compasses and sextants of navigation. This has always been the terror and *fatalità* of my life. And as the kilometres have gone past, the memories have unwound like the shroud from a necropolis.

The truth is that I have not seen Charles for two years. Now that I am approaching the farm, I am afraid. Angry. Ashamed.

We said we would always love each other, no matter what. Even after we had stormed our separate ways, he to Dennis and me to Annabelle, we said —

Drive up the tree-lined road to the house. A sturdy California-style wooden bungalow, recently painted, with garage and other sheds around. Down a slope, willows fringing a river. Further along, the orchard.

Apply the brakes, and watch the dust swirl slowly past and settle.

Get out. Stretch. Dogs come to bark and jump.

'Gidday, David.'

Dennis, in overalls and battered hat, sloping out of the packing shed. His handshake is firm. His eyes crinkle in the sun.

'We weren't expecting you until four,' Dennis says. 'But never mind, it's great to have you.' He pushes me in front of him towards the house. 'Come in, come in. Have you seen Charles yet?'

Before I can stop him, he begins to call. As if we are playing a game of Hide and Seek.

'Charles? Charles? David's arrived.'

All around dogs are barking. I haven't had a chance to find a place to hide. I want to cry out, Don't come yet. Don't.

But it is too late. A shadow looms out of the darkness.

Coming ready or not.

39

'CHARLES! CHARLES? DAVID'S arrived —'

A shadow looms out of the darkened hallway. But not Charles at all. Rather, a young woman in jeans and check shirt. Butch haircut, freckles scattered across an easy smile. Nose peeling from the sun.

'Eva?' Dennis asks. 'Is Charles —'

She puts a finger to her lips. 'He's sleeping on the couch down by the river.' She looks up at me from wire-rimmed glasses. 'You must be David. Charles has talked a lot about you. He thought he'd take a rest before you arrived.'

'Eva lives in town,' Dennis explains. 'But she or her lover Sue comes out every day. Without them I —'

Eva shushes him with a hug. She puts an arm around his waist. Says to him, 'Why don't we let David spend some time alone with Charles? I need you to help me with the bed upstairs. It's time we brought it down and put it in the front room.'

'Let me help with that,' I say to Eva.

'No,' she answers. 'We'll manage.' She gives me a firm push. 'Off you go.'

'Piangea cantando nell'erma landa piangea la mesta, O salce, salce, salce.'

Down by the river, and I am remembering a song of willows weeping beside the slow swirling current.

I was hitching back to Auckland from Mount Maunganui. I'd just finished a vacation job. The long summer break was over. A white sports car came buzzing down the road like a light aircraft. Then Charles was braking at the corner where I stood, rucksack on back and thumb out.

'If I leave you here,' he said in his droll, twinkling fashion, 'somebody else will pick you up. And we can't have that, can we?'

The path to the river is like a track to a place where mermaids sing. At the end of it, dappled in the emerald light of river and willows, is Charles, his back to me, asleep on a couch draped with a light sheet. When I am halfway towards him he sighs and turns. I hesitate, looking back to Eva and Dennis for support. But they have gone inside. There is nobody in the world except myself and Charles and the rivuleting chuckling river.

There is a chair next to the couch. I sit on it, listening to Charles's uneven breathing. Gaze upon him.

That was how we met, but I recognised him as soon as he stopped his car. He was at university too and I had seen him around campus. Charles must have known that Annabelle and I were dating each other. He had been a friend of Tony, who had committed suicide and whose funeral oration had been delivered by Annabelle.

'We've never been formally introduced, have we?' he asked as I stepped into the car. 'My name is Charles.'

I extended my hand and he chuckled. Reached for it and grasped it firmly. Pulled me towards him and, eyes looking into my own shocked eyes, kissed me, taking my breath away.

'I never shake hands on a first date,' he said solemnly. Then, echoing Bette Davis in *All About Eve*, 'Fasten your seat belt, this is going to be a bumpy ride!'

Now here we are, some twelve years later. Sharing the shaded cool of a summer's day down by the river. And I am again intoxicated with remembering the aphrodisiac of Charles's body.

No two men are alike. Every one is distinct: that is the wonder of God's creation. Each brings his own garden of earthly delights, his own hair, own perfume, own textured skin. None ever brings the same light, temperature, shadows or gesture. Each is an infinite variation on a common theme. With Charles, however, God created one of a kind and then broke the mould. His skin so seamless and pellucid, and its natural scent like salt water licked off the air.

His frame so tall, so finely constructed of chiselled bones and light-catching planes. His eyes so startling in their smokiness, clearing occasionally in unaffected delight. His hair, mouth, lips, throat, all crafted with joy and then animated with splendid and bold animal appetite. Not the most handsome of men. But a man among men.

By the time his sports car had turned into the drive, I was hooked, lined and totally sunk.

'Goodbye,' he said gravely. This time, extending his hand. 'I do hope we meet again.'

No sooner had I stepped out of the car than he was off. Tyres scorching the road.

Gone.

Charles sighs again in his sleep and shivers. Without thinking I am reaching for the blanket to tuck it around his shoulders. It is an old patchwork blanket made of brightly coloured squares. In so doing I graze his right hand. Automatically his fingers open. They could be waiting for anybody's clasp, resting there, flexing. I place my hand in his and the fingers close gently into mine. Content now, he remains in sleep.

Oh God, and the memories begin to rush out like a raging river. For it wasn't too long after that that I rang him at the hostel where he lived.

'Hi,' I said. 'This is David.'

'David? David who?'

Teasing, playing with me.

'You know. The hitch hiker.'

'Oh, *that* David.' Pretending, feigning ignorance. 'So what can I do for you, uh, David?'

'I thought you might like to go out. To a movie, dinner or something.'

There was a pause. Then, gently, 'Oh David, you'll have to do much better than that.' After a moment, sighing. 'Look, do you like swimming? Come with me to the beach this weekend. Okay? I'll pick you up. I remember where you live.'

I telephoned him back an half an hour later. By that time my voice was strong and certain. 'The weekend is too far away,' I said.

'How about tomorrow?'

He laughed. 'That's *much* better.'

The beach was a shrine to our sun-seeking personalities. Although we spent most of the day seducing each other with talk, laughter and flirtation, we knew that we sought more from each other. But something held me back. Sensed that this would be different for me. That by capitulating to Charles I would not escape so easily. So that, as the afternoon waned and the beach became a place of intimacy, it was Charles who made the move.

We were lying on our sides, facing each other. Our eyes connected. He traced a finger down from my neck to my groin. And kept it there. He was direct.

'If I asked you for a fuck, what would you say?' he said.

There are three answers to that question. I took the third. 'I don't know.'

He smiled. 'Oh, *not* a good answer. You can do better.'

He slipped his hand into my swimsuit. I gasped for breath.

'Yes.'

'*Scorreano i rivi fra le zolle in fior, gemea quel core affranto . . . l'amara onda del pianto.*'

The fresh stream runs between the flowery banks like bitter tears. Holding Charles's hand reminds me of that first burning touch of skin on skin.

'Yes.'

And that is when he moved, pulling me into the sand dunes, ripping off my togs so that I bounded free. By that stage I didn't care who was looking on. I allowed him to take me in his arms, push my legs back and, with a slow thrust, seal me to him.

We gasped out our climax, our semen ribboning over our shoulders and into the sand. The impact shocked both of us. Something psychic as well as physical had happened. Some deep communion had been sounded, like a whale deep-diving, extending our known depths, making us feel the pain of loss when the embrace was over.

'I must use that line more often,' Charles said afterward. He was lying on his back looking up at the sun.

'What line?' I asked.

'If I asked you for a fuck,' he laughed. 'My first time out I was asked that question. By a young guy who tried to pick me up at the beach. Like you, I didn't know what to reply either. But I didn't have a second chance like you did. However, the next day I went back to find him. He wasn't there, but an older man was. He said, "Do you want to come out for a swim?" I said, "Okay." As we were swimming out there among the breakers he said, "You won't need these, will you?" And yanked off my swimsuit. He was my first partner. I was so ashamed of what I had done. It was worse when I saw him the next weekend at church. He was assisting with the sacrament. You know what? When he passed me the wine and the wafer I looked up into his eyes. He didn't even recognise me.' Charles paused. Looked at me ruefully. 'I think that that's what made me angrier. Not being remembered.'

Not remembering Charles is something of which I will never be guilty. In those days, before the virus, many gay encounters were hit-and-miss affairs, of having sex first and then getting to know whether you liked the guy. But ours was ordained by Lady Luck, and there was no turning back. We just couldn't get enough of each other. Annabelle had by that time left for Europe and, although I missed her like mad, Charles reactivated that other part of me. I would sneak into his university hostel after the doors were closed and get into his room. He was such a prankster; one night he persuaded a friend to wait in the bed to find out whether I would be able to tell the difference.

'Your friend is bigger,' I said, attempting an air of bored sophistication which I hoped would teach him a lesson.

On Sunday afternoons he would come around to the house when my parents were out playing golf. On one occasion we found in my father's den his collection of erotica and the medical manuals which passed for sex books in my parents' day. One should never underestimate the sexual proclivities of one's parents. The greatest discovery was a copy of the *Kama Sutra* and a well-thumbed Japanese pillow book, filled with faded but graphic drawings, hidden among my father's military books. The mere presence of the books attested to my father's lusty manhood, further alluded to in poignant and yearning letters to my mother when he was in active service. The understatement of phrases like 'At nights I think of my Bunny and want to frolic' belied a groaning, scarcely-able-to-be-suppressed sexuality. Charles and I spent over an hour indulging our curiosity and overheated imagination in consulting my father's library. The pillow book, with its anatomical drawings of men having their engorged organs joined into supine women, was something to fire our helpless senses to holocaust proportions. Although composed of delicately drawn and brush-coloured men and women, the ruthless animality of the men made me stiffen and plead Charles to investigate my rampant condition. He suggested that we adjourn to the caravan. But when it started rocking and rolling, popping the fuses in the electrical connections between the caravan and house, we moved back inside to my bedroom, scattering clothes everywhere. My bed became the playground for our ravenous appetites. There we plundered the riches of each other's bodies.

'Mmmmn, that feels nice. Oh yes, *yyesss*.'

What made it so exciting was that our erogenous zones kept moving. Chasing them and locating them was part of the fun. We never used the same techniques to find them and developed intricate strategies to coax out our ecstasies. With one eye on the clock and the other on what we were doing we would postpone our climax until the last moment. Only then would we lever and tip each other like wheelbarrows into orgasm.

Once, I came home with Charles to this very farm, for it has always been in his family. His parents were away for the week. We pitched a tent by this river and made love by candlelight, entranced by the shadow patterns flickering against the canvas. The nights were warm, and often we would slip into the river to delight and swim. When he came out of the water naked, he looked like a white gleaming fish with dark weed at head, armpits and groin.

Of all the memories that is the one that I shall hold the longest. Of making love that night by the river. It did not matter that the next morning we found ourselves in agony from mosquito bites. Or that in our boisterous lovemaking we rolled into a patch of thistles. That was all part of the charisma, the boldness, the spontaneity of Charles.

'Oh.' He whimpered.

His face shone silver in the moonlight. It was grim, fierce, suffused. He was sitting astride my thighs, looking down at me. His cock arched a huge shadow like an eclipse across the moon. I have never seen its like again. Then his chest muscles clenched. His buttocks squeezed tight sucking at me. And all of a sudden it was upon him. His cock swelled. The spasms began. Comets flaming in the sky, across the face of the moon.

There's no doubt that I loved Charles. Yet I also maintained my relationship with Annabelle by letter. It was so easy to believe that Charles and I lived on an island outside reality. And so we did. Until even the island itself was destroyed. By Charles.

I had made the mistake of thinking his love for me equalled mine for him. One night, when I was least expecting it, he said, 'David, it's time for me to move on. You have to get on with your life. I have to get on with mine.'

'No. No,' I cried.

He smiled gently. 'Definitely *not* a good answer, David.'

Skip, skip, skip and it was over.

'Solea la storia con questo semplice suono finir: Egli era nato per la sua gloria io per amar . . .'

Charles was born for his glory, I to love. He let me go gently back into the world. He himself followed his sexual imperative, submitting to his promiscuous nature, to whoever and wherever it led him.

I hated him for a time and cried like Orpheus. I found solace in marriage to Annabelle and in fatherhood. But I have always been searching the underworld for another soul of his magnitude. I have never found it. He was and always will be The Love Of My Life, the chiaroscuro which gives light to my personal history.

And as I look at him, the tears flow from my eyes. It is not only the chromosomatic imperative that is to blame for his rapid hair loss. For the slackening of face muscles, once so taut. For the diminishing of nose to cartilage and bone. For the deep and dark necrosis of skin around the orbs of eyes. For weight decrease and body realignment. No, in the natural order of things I can accept that one's physical heritage will finally burst through the chrysalis skin of youth, the illusory beauty of one's first incarnation. The actress Jacqueline Bisset once told how her doctor father gently guided her from vanity by pointing out that her beauty had nothing to do with any self-achievement; that beauty alters, matures, fades. Our inherited genes print out the physiognomy and physiology that is no more and no less than the cumulative programme of our past.

If the way that Charles looks now was natural, I would rest easy in this legacy of biological man. Had Charles and I remained together I suspect that I would have loved him more the longer we lived, for with aging would have come vulnerability. Longevity of love should never be equated with unmarked skin or unblemished innocence. Confused with the necromancy of the beauty industry or the nip, tuck, lift and suction of plastic surgery.

This is the place where mermaids sing, '*Salce, salce, salce.*'

The wind disturbs the willows. Makes them rustle and flick like warning whips across the surface of the water.

Charles awakens.

'Who is this?' he asks.

He is blind, reaching for my face, to trace its contours.

'Hello Charles.'

And all of a sudden there is the sound of the mermaids diving, diving, diving, like silver dreams into the river.

40

IT WAS LATE by the time we returned to the city. Ronald, Stephen, Brenda and Bright Eyes could see that I was depressed but did not know why. I tried not to let my sadness about Charles spill over their own happiness as they finished unloading canisters of films, packed in temperature-controlled cylinders, into the temporary warehouse down by the railway station. Ronald had telephoned ahead to his film-buff friends and they were waiting for us. When he stepped down from the truck and they began to applaud him, it must have been the greatest moment of his life. They shook his hand, patted him on the back and then, with reverence, four men per cylinder, unhooked the cylinders from the slings in which they had been placed for transport and carried the films into the warehouse as if they had just come out of Tutankhamun's tomb.

'Be careful,' they hissed to each other. In everyone's mind was the terrifying thought of those precious images flaking from the reels like gold leaf from an Oriental buddha.

Brenda organised coffee. We sat around talking. In one corner some of the film buffs were going into ecstasies over the cache of old movie posters, all in absolute mint condition. Bright Eyes was with them, eager faced and gesticulating as they outlined the significance of the find.

Of course. I didn't realise. You're absolutely right. Wow.

He was having such a good time that I didn't want to disturb him. Nor Ronald, who wanted the sweetness of this moment to last. But I had to get to Jack's dinner party at which he was bringing out his new friend. Showing him off. Just before leaving,

Ronald pumped my hand.
'Laddie —'

The siren song of mermaids singing pursued me, even to Jack's.
'I thought you'd never get here,' he said.

Behind Jack I could see his dinner guests standing and chatting in small groups, and they were all laughing. At me. At Jack. At nothing. At everything. At the tragedy and comedy of life.

'Please tell me,' I whispered to Jack, 'that all this is just a joke. Please —'

I was already shivering. Sweat beaded my brow. I knew some of these guests. Glowing eyes. Febrile, nervous gestures. Among them Pin Cushion, Once A Beauty, Mouth, Robocock. Even more sinister, the addicts, the hookers and the hooked. They woke only at night. Slept in coffins by day.

'Come in, come in,' he said. 'Don't stand there. Somebody open up another bottle of champers!'

Jack's manner was grotesquely buoyant. Although his face was still somewhat scabbed from the assault, he had applied some kind of pancake make-up which gave him a ghastly ochre colouring. He was wearing pinstripe and bowtie, as if he was getting married. In his lapel was a green carnation, the *fleur du mal*.

The way opened before me. A man was standing in the middle of this vampirical crowd. Jack was beaming with pride and adoration as he began the introductions. Wanting me to approve his choice. Wanting my validation.

Warrick has always been extraordinarily mesmeric. His handsome profile was strong and clean cut. On his trip overseas to Thailand and Singapore, he had blonded his hair so that it shone with golden filigree. His eyes were black. Impeccably dressed in an Italian suit, he looked made to measure for Jack's lifestyle. His manner when he was introduced was deferential.

'Of course you know each other,' Jack said. He moved Warrick toward me, his eyes were pleading.

'We've met before,' I answered.

Jack smiled at everyone and said in a loud voice, 'If it wasn't for David I would never have met Warrick.'

All the time, I watched Warrick's unblinking eyes. Mocking.

Saying, If I can't get at you one way I'll find another.

Then Warrick was being edged past.

My eyes narrowed with anger and fear. I played the perfect guest, but when I saw Jack going to his bedroom, I followed, closed the door behind me, took him by his throat and shoved him against the wall. Hard.

'You stupid, pathetic sod,' I hissed. 'How did this happen?'

He tried to pull my hands away. 'In your office,' he coughed. 'While I was waiting for you one day. He called. Seemed upset. We met. Then I was in hospital. And he brought me —' I took my hands off his throat. 'Flowers.'

'Don't you know what he is? What he does?'

'I want you to be happy for me.'

'Happy? God, Jack, don't you understand? He's bad news. Really bad.'

I couldn't help shivering.

'Jack —'

Later that night I went to The Maze. I searched for Warrick in the dark tunnels where men whispered and touched and clung. Looked for Warrick in the arena where The Sling was. Waited for Warrick to exit.

When he slid out of his trapdoor I went for him with a wire, flipped it around his neck and *pulled* so that it cut into his throat.

'I wouldn't move if I was you.'

He gasped. He put his hands up and tried to squeeze his fingers through between the wire and his skin. I gave another *tug*.

'I thought you might turn up,' he said. He tried to look back at me. Chuckled. Leaned back into me like a lover. 'Hey, I've got some top grade stuff, man, all the way from Thailand. You and me, huh? Shoot you past the moon?'

He was looking fabulous. His blond streaked hair. Iago must have looked like this. He had not yet sloughed off his skin. My resolve wavered. Then flared strong again.

'Listen, fucker, you harm one hair of Jack's head and I'm coming after you. You got that?'

A twist of the wire. A gurgle.

A nod, 'Yes.'

Fear and desire were fuelling my adrenalin. I let go the wire and he fell to the ground, clutching at his throat. I should have garotted him then.

Bang. *Bang.*

Just as he was putting his hand on the cup, Tink shrieked, 'No! Don't!'
  'Why not?'
  'Hook has poisoned it.'
  'Nonsense! How could Hook get down here?'
  Tink could not explain that; but she said she had heard Hook muttering to himself in the forest, and boasting that he had poisoned Peter. Peter said, 'That's perfect rubbish. Hook could not have been here without my seeing him: and I haven't been to sleep.' Tink could not stop to argue. She got between his lips and the cup, and drank the medicine at one gulp. Then she turned pale and staggered, while Peter was shouting, 'How dare you drink my medicine!' 'It was poisoned,' Tink whispered faintly.

41

THE NEXT AFTERNOON after my return from Eketahuna, the girls and I go to see a re-run of the cartoon feature *An American Tail*. At the end of it, Miranda turns to me, her tears glistening, as Fievel the mouse is reunited with his family.

'He's found his Daddy,' she says.

And now the girls and I are back at The House On The Hill and Annabelle has not yet returned.

'I've got a key, Daddy,' Rebecca says. She wiggles it in my face with proud self-importance. She is pleased with herself. Not only has she got a new bathing suit out of Daddy but she has her own key from Mummy.

My heart shrivels with sadness. The world is filled with solo mothers with children who have to let themselves out in the morning and in at night. I have turned my daughters into latchkey children. Rebecca, however, handles it all with aplomb. Opens the door.

'Well, darlings —'

'You're not leaving us, are you Daddy?' Rebecca asks. 'What if Mummy is late?'

'Or has had an accident?' Miranda continues.

My daughters' lips are trembling and their imaginations are conjuring up horrible images of Mummy lying dead underneath a truck or on a pedestrian crossing.

'I'm not allowed in, darlings,' I tell them. 'Not unless Mummy invites me in.'

'But she's not *here*, Daddy.'

And so I melt. Nod my head; 'Okay.' Step across the threshold.
Where Rebecca takes my hand.

'Would you like a cup of tea, Daddy?' she asks.

'Yes. Thank you.'

Meanwhile Miranda has run upstairs to take her swimming togs
to the washbasket and put her waterwings back on top of the
wardrobe in the bedroom she sleeps in with her sister. Fearing that
she might fall, I follow after her, up the stairs and past the bedroom which I once shared with Annabelle.

And my heart lurches because the 'new' Annabelle has spring
cleaned my presence away. There is a new cover on the double bed.
A book of new curtain fabric for Madame To Choose From is on
the bed. The desk where the accounts and correspondence were
handled and which used to be in the corner alcove, has been moved
to the other side of the room. There is a new sofa beneath the back
window overlooking the park. All the photographs of me are gone.

There is no longer the sense of a bedroom still lived in by husband and wife. That place of sighs and caresses has been put into a
storage area where all failed or lost dreams go. All those dreams
have snapped off their stalks and are freeze dried like flowers.

In the girls' bedroom I find Miranda getting a chair to stand on.
Balancing on it. Reaching up on her tiptoes to put the waterwings
up there along with Rebecca's pink and green stuffed elephant.

'Let me, darling,' I offer.

She shakes her head. 'No, I can do it, Daddy. Mummy says we
have to do everything for ourselves, now that you don't live at our
house.' She grits her teeth, stretches up and reaches high, almost
overbalances but — 'There. See, Daddy?'

And starts to fall. But I am there, as I once used to be, catching
her and cradling her in my arms.

Miranda laughs. 'Put me down, Daddy. Put me down.'

And is off, humming and running down the stairs to her sister.

Leaving me shaken and alone.

Looking at this jumbled mass of girls' clothing and a bedroom
bursting at the seams. Two beds, brightly covered with duvets,
nightdresses tucked under pillows. Posters on the walls, crystal
ornaments on the two bedside tables and a photographic gallery
made up of photos that Rebecca has taken with her Instamatic.

Rebecca is right. She needs a separate bedroom.

Miranda's inhaler for her asthma is half screwed up in the middle of a dirty handkerchief. How can she find it in all this mess? What happens if she has an attack. If —

I go to call Miranda. To reprimand her. Then remember. I have no rights in this house. When I left it, I relinquished all. Committed my little princesses to the mercy of the world. To whatever might come knocking: Wicked Witch or Big Bad Wolf. Something with slavering jaws. Axes and knives. Off with their heads.

'Daddy?' Rebecca is at the doorway, balancing a cup of tea proudly in her hands. I take it from her. She puts her head against my side. 'When are you coming home, Daddy?'

Still the same question. Always the same question.

A slam of the front door.

'Girls?'

Annabelle comes running up the stairs. She sees me there in the doorway. Her hair is tied back with a ribbon. Her face is flushed and bright from a shower.

'What are you doing up here?' she asks me. Her eyes are smouldering. 'You've crossed the line, David. Crossed the line.'

Is this how it must always be?

Annabelle and I are in the kitchen. Annabelle has made a much stronger cup of tea and strained it so that it is blessedly free of the tea leaves of Miranda's offering. But the anger still flows between us.

'I only came in because you weren't here and —'

'The girls are perfectly capable of looking after themselves when I'm not here. Goodness knows, they've had enough experience over the last few months.'

'And what if something had happened to you? What if —'

The girls are up on the balcony, listening.

Annabelle bangs her fists on the table. 'Oh, *what if*! The girls and I can't live our lives on bloody What Ifs! If anything happens to me, they know how to use the telephone. They have your number, their grandparents' number, your sister's number. And there are always the neighbours. And anyway, I'm here, aren't I?' Annabelle pauses. Her assertiveness training is doing wonders.

Then, 'I'm not apologising for being late. Why should I! I just don't want you in the house when I'm not around, that's all. You have no right, sport. No right.'

'Fine,' I answer. 'Next time I'll wait outside while Rebecca opens the door and she and Miranda are inside. And if the place bursts into flames I'll just wait until the Fire Service gets here. No doubt you'll have given them permission to come inside.'

Miranda is waving her silly wand.

I have put my coat on. I stalk towards the door.

'You're being stupid, ridiculous and difficult,' Annabelle says. 'And why do you always walk away like this? Stand still when I'm talking to you! You know what I mean.'

'No I don't.'

'You don't? Then let me spell it out for you.' She pulls at my arms. Spins me around. She takes me by surprise. 'I've been disempowered by you, David. Not only personally but also politically and sexually.'

'Keep your counselling jargon for your sessions, Annabelle.'

But she is not taking *that* lying down. 'When we were married I relinquished myself into your hands. Now I have to take my life back. That means drawing the line. And I am drawing the line at this house. This is our territory, the girls' and mine, and you are crossing it, *sport.*'

'Mummy? Daddy?'

Miranda is looking down at us. Rebecca is close to tears.

'I'd better go,' I say. 'We're upsetting the girls.'

Annabelle bars my way. Her eyes are wide with anger. 'My counsellor tells me that you must have been planning to leave me months before you actually did. Is that true?'

I should lie. I should cheat. But I am so angry.

'Yes.'

Oh God. Forgive me, Annabelle. She steps aside, as if hit. And Rebecca is flying down the stairs.

'Daddy, Daddy. This is all my fault.'

Annabelle is remote. Takes Rebecca aside. Breathes deep.

'Your father has to go now.'

Slams the door.

42

SO NOW I wake up in my flat to yet another morning of another day in this my life. Switch off the alarm. Stretch. Yawn. Amble into the bathroom. Look in the mirror. Inspect my teeth and tongue. Angle my forehead to see how much more light is filtering through the curls. These are the years of falling hair. Get the milk and newspaper in.

Well, whadd'ya know, the Anglican Bishop has made a brave plea at the Forty-sixth Synod for understanding on the question of the Church and homosexuality.

'I don't believe,' he says, 'this is the time for more rules. Confrontations are unhelpful. Fear paralyses. I suggest dialogue, openness to new truth, a sense of trust in one another as persons and Christians; a desire to love, to listen carefully to what we at present disagree with. It is important, as we discuss and find ways forward, that we include gay men and lesbian women in that discussion, face to face. They have stories to tell, perceptions to offer, questions to ask. We need to become more life-giving.'

Then back into the bedroom. Catch a glimpse of the photograph of Annabelle, Rebecca and Miranda and me sitting underneath the tree.

Blow my little princesses a kiss.

I.

One kiss.

Love.

Another kiss.

You.

Yesterday morning, the jog. Today, the gym. Nothing seems to have changed. As always, the first ten minutes of the workout are tough, but after that I find the balance between breath and body to vault into a good rhythm. Keep my heart and pulse rate up.

Down on the main floor, The Black has begun another aerobics class. Time to kick ass. By this time I am breathing deep, enjoying the sweat and the thrill of a body that is performing well. Then into the shower room where Bionic Cock is doing his usual tricks with his silicone implant and All American swivels this way and that, scattering the water like cartwheels among the laughing men and boys. All the sons of Adam.

Taking coffee in the gym coffee lounge, I see Bright Eyes talking with Left Dress. I know that Bright Eyes is disappointed that, as much as I would like to, I have not pursued our friendship. A student is a student. Neither Left Dress or Bright Eyes sees me and, anyway, I want to do a Greta Garbo. Slide my shades over my eyes and take a seat close to the window. There idly to consult the latest edition of our own gay magazine, *Top And Bottom*. I see that the Mister Gay New Zealand contest is being held soon and will be judged on 'confidence and personality blah blah blah' — a likely story. And look here, another fuck palace has opened, but in The Shining City, further to the south:

The latest place to go in Christchurch met with a huge response on its opening night last Wednesday. Over one hundred and fifty increasingly enthusiastic guys turned up and jammed the two floors of Fellas in a relaxed and uninhibited atmosphere. There seemed no doubt that the hottest spot to be by far was the second floor, where a collection of theme cubicles for all tastes in a maze-like layout provides a very cruisy atmosphere!

The shop on the first floor stocks mostly imported items with labels like Oz, On and Audace, as well as cards, videos and the usual accessory items. Fellas is stockist of Ultimate Fresh and Blast aromas, and Smooth lubricant for the budget-conscious.

Fine tuning in response to various comments is still taking place. Members will be pleased to know the lights are now well down and the holes in the corrugated iron have been filled!

Basically we are an indoor beat where gay and bisexual men can express their sexuality in a situation that is both safe and reinforcing. We are very affordable price-wise.

Must check Fellas out next time I am in The Shining City.

Time for me to find out about my test. I drive over to the clinic, where the doctor asks me to step inside his office. His look is worried, as if he doesn't want to tell me what I already know.

'You've tested negative.'

My blood leaps with relief. Reprieved. A stay of execution. Firing squad at ease. Insurance company, up yours.

Liberated.

On my way out and:

'Yo, David.'

A car that used to be green once turns into the curb. The Noble Savage, and my heart catches at his strength. He gets out of his car and comes over. 'I'm glad I caught you, man. You got time to talk?'

'Sure.'

Although I must get to university, an invitation to sit and talk with The Noble Savage is not one to be dismissed lightly. We move over to a bench and look over the park where children are flying a superb aerobatic kite.

'I'm leaving town,' The Noble Savage says. 'But I wanted to tell you before I left how nice it has been to know you.'

'When are you coming back?' I ask.

'I don't know. My people are hurting out there. I need to go home to my iwi.'

'What about your work with the Prostitutes' Collective?' I ask, astonished. 'And with the clinic?'

'There's more. I'm getting married, David.'

Married? The idea is not preposterous because I can see that The Noble Savage would make a wonderful father. His body is carved from earth and sky. Its angularity is made for holding children. Its strength for sheltering a family.

'It's been arranged for me,' he says. 'By my mother. She wants grandchildren.'

'An arranged marriage? In these days?'

'Actually,' he laughs, 'the idea isn't so bad when you come to think of it. Why shouldn't gay single men be able to marry and have children? We're trying it out, anyway. Her name's Leah.'

What had happened was that The Noble Savage had accompanied his mother to a funeral of a distant uncle in another tribal area. That was a year ago and, at the funeral, his mother noticed Leah, an unmarried woman of twenty-eight, who had nursed the old man in his last years. She made some judicious inquiries, spoke to Leah's family, and the marriage was agreed upon with the family.

'Four weeks back,' The Noble Savage says, 'my mother asked me to go home. I didn't know what she had done until, one afternoon, Leah's people brought her to me. I was angry at first. My people know all about my being gay but think it's just a momentary aberration. You and I know that it isn't. But then Leah asked if she could talk to me alone.'

She was, to The Noble Savage's surprise, a strong, articulate and passionate woman.

'I know you are a homosexual,' she said, 'and so I do not come to this blind. But my womb is crying for children, as greatly as your mother weeps for grandchildren. You must realise that your line will die if you do not have a son. You are a fine man and your sexuality has a strength of its own which you can bring to a relationship not only with me but with any children we may have. We are both too old not to accept this arrangement. I want a son. I can give you a son. You are my last chance. I am yours.'

'When she put it like that,' The Noble Savage says, 'I realised she was right. I've made my choice.'

'What choice is that?'

He smiles and embraces me. Turns to get back into his car. 'I've already kept you long enough,' he says, as he starts the engine.

'I asked you a question.'

'The choice not to be selfish, as your society is, David. If I was to choose between being Maori or being gay I would have to choose to be Maori. That is how I was born and that is how my people will bury me. Not as a gay person. But as one of the iwi. I guess, when it comes to the crunch, my cultural registration is more important than my sexual registration after all.' His face gleams like a bronzed sculpture. 'It's been nice knowing you, David. God go with you. Goodbye.'

Up at university there is a message to ring Annabelle. The anger between us still simmers like a summer storm. Forked lightning and thunder clouds and air filled with crackling electricity. But we are also struggling to find some accommodation.

In the end, 'I'm sorry,' I say.

'No, you were right,' she says. 'If you had left the children and something happened to them I would have blamed you.'

'I can't win either way. But I still shouldn't have come in without your permission.'

'Well, it's in the past now, David.' Then, in an attempt at conciliation, 'Are you doing anything on Saturday afternoon?' Three days time. Oh My Goodness arrives tomorrow but he'll be gone by then. 'You're not doing anything? Why don't we take the girls out on a picnic. To the Crocodile's Tail. Get out from under all this terrible business between our lawyers.'

I laugh out loud. Our lawyers are eidolons of ourselves, sent out to do battle, clashing like titans.

'Good,' Annabelle says. 'The girls will be so happy. And I want to talk to you anyway.'

'What about?'

'Ask me no questions and I'll tell you no lies.' She giggles. 'You'll just have to wait.'

Then, just as I put the telephone down, the wrath finally comes down from the head of department.

'David? I told you last week that any further work on this film project of yours should be stopped. You well know that the matter has gone to the Vice Chancellor and the University Committee. Now I have reports that you went down to get the films during the weekend. You have deliberately gone against me. Until that meeting I am closing you down. You hear me? Down.'

43

AT MIDDAY THE ringing of the telephone. Jack.

'Feel like lunch, old chap? Good. I've booked a table at The Fisherman's Café. Come straight over.'

He is sitting by the window looking out across the sea. The café is crowded and, as I make my way towards the table, the patrons watch with disdainful arrogance. Obviously not one of us. 'David,' Jack calls, 'my infamous enfant.'

'Not so much an enfant,' I respond, sitting down. 'Same age as you, Jack.'

But you look much younger, you hateful man. Gin? Or shall we go straight to the wine list?'

'Wine, I think.'

He is recovering very well from the assault. The stitches have been taken out where his cheek was cut open, but the scar will remain for a long time. He motions me to sit opposite him.

I glance out the window. 'I see you've picked the table for the view.'

Outside sailors, shirts off, work on the rigging of an old sailing ship.

'Everyone loves a sailor,' Jack answers. 'Speaking of which, I received a postcard from Chip the other day. Isn't he a dear boy? His ship is in Manila right now. Ah, lucky Manila —'

The waiter attends us. Jack puts his tongue in his cheek. Eyeballs me.

'May I recommend the fisherman's basket?' he says, without blinking an eye. 'It has so many goodies in it.'

We are half way through our meal when Jack says, 'I hear you're in a spot of bother.'

'Oh?' An oyster teeters on my fork.

'Your films,' he continues. 'You know what university politics is like. Everybody knows each other's business. If you want to keep a secret, don't tell an academic. I hadn't realised, though, that you would go so far as to defy your head of department. Nor take out a second mortgage.'

'So you know that too?' I remember the family lawyer. 'Obviously lawyers have big mouths too.'

'Mother has her sources.'

Jack has tucked the napkin around his neck and every time he waggles his fork food flies off in all directions. One of the privileges of the rich.

'So the gardening circle knows also?'

'Old chap,' Jack whispers sternly, 'I wouldn't let mother hear you describe her committee like that. So how serious is it?'

'I walk the plank on Friday.'

'Is it that bad?'

I lean back in my chair. For no reason at all, tears of frustration rush into my eyes. It's so ridiculous, really.

'Oh shit.' I try to laugh. 'Sorry about this, Jack. But I had to overstep everybody. This is such a magnificent find. All these films. They're bits and pieces of our history that nobody has seen since they were made. Ever. They're the film equivalent of, oh I don't know, opening up Tutankhamun's tomb. The trouble is that they're not made of gold or lapis lazuli. If they were, the university would be taking the credit and damn the red tape. We were running out of time. I had to do it. If the university doesn't allow us to continue, they will miss out on accolades undreamed of.'

'Are they that special?' Jack takes a glass of wine. Spills it, but doesn't care.

'Yes, Jack. Although they're just old silent films they do talk. They talk to our hearts. They speak to our intellect. They're like runes. We found them in the dust of an old house in a place back of beyond. That they've survived at all is an absolute miracle. We've got to piece them together. And when that is done, their secrets, their divinations will be unlocked. They whisper to our bones, Jack.'

He tries a joke. 'None of them would by any chance, even by the remotest chance, be somewhat, er, risqué?'

'I don't think so.'

'Art never is,' he sighs. 'Ah well —'

He lifts his glass again. As he does so, I notice his left wrist.

Burn marks.

Somebody has stubbed out their cigarettes there in the ash tray of that soft white flesh.

It is happening already.

'Did Warrick do this?' I ask. I have reached out and taken Jack's wrist in my hand.

'Old chap —'

'I told him not to harm you in any way,' I whisper. 'Did he do this? Did he?'

'We were just playing around. Using little toys. You know what it's like. He got carried away.'

Yes, I know what it's like. The lethal combination of drugs and sex and sado-masochism. I've been there before. Seen Warrick and his sicko ways. His enjoyment of other men's pain.

The waiter approaches. We are creating a disturbance.

'Is anything wrong, Sir?' he asks Jack.

'No,' Jack answers. 'I was just showing my friend here how bruised I got when I went sailing last weekend.'

The waiter hesitates, unsure. Walks away. The restaurant begins to piece itself together again. Smoothing its feathers. Really, the clientele who are coming to this place.

Jack is trembling. 'Would you like some dessert?' he asks.

'Just coffee,' I answer.

I reach for his arm again and he flinches.

'I love him, David,' he says with determination. 'I know you were his lover once. Warrick's told me all about that —' I go to interrupt but he hurries on. 'And I know what he is now and what he has been in the past. But you see only the bad in him and I see both the bad and the good. Certainly he has been violent with me, but that's my business not yours. What people do in the privacy of their own bedroom is their choice. I expect you to respect that privacy. I will not have you talk against him.'

I stroke Jack's wrist. Lace my fingers through his and who cares if anybody notices. Two men holding hands. Nothing sexual. Rather in friendship and with affection.

Oh Jack, when I began to have sex with men during my marriage I hated myself so much. When I reached for help Warrick was there, smiling. But the hand that helped me to stand the pain had a needle in it. The hand said, Try this for all your pain. I did, and was shot over the moon.

Then when I went to see Left Dress about Annabelle and my personal lifestyle he said:

'Let me see your arm.'

He hadn't believed me when I had told him I was not taking drugs.

'Jack, you've got to get away now while you can.'

The following day, however, Jack rings me up. He has made another step. Warrick has told him he has nowhere to stay, so Jack has invited him to move in with him. I fear that Jack is under the spell of make-believe. Of enticement. Of dreams.

'What's your poison?' Jack asks.

He has come around to Film Studies to celebrate with expensive champagne. The bottle pops. Champagne rushes out like a river. His optimism is so ridiculous that I could hit him. That stupid red face like Smee's, the foolishness, the inanity, the horror, oh Jack —

Tink managed to flutter to her little room in the wall, and sank upon her couch. Her light grew weaker every moment. Peter knelt by her tiny doorway, and sobbed: 'Oh, Tink, you did that to save me!' He could see that she was nearly dead. If her light went right out, nothing could save her.

Then he thought he heard whispering in a wee thin voice, that she thought she might get well again if children said they believed in fairies.

And he called out to all the children in the world: 'If you believe in fairies, clap your hands! Hurry or Tink will die! Do you believe?'

There was a sound of clapping — it was far away, but certainly it was clapping, quite a lot of clapping. It stopped as suddenly as it began; and behold, Tink was well again! Her light grew bright again, her tinkle came back, and she popped out of bed and went flashing round the room —

Oh Jack. I don't think I can help you. Nor all the clapping in the world.

44

THE GARDENS OF Spain by night, The Beach by day.

Oh My Goodness has finally arrived on his two-day stopover. I am waiting for him to come out of Customs, planning to take him to our beach for the day. Restorative and redolent of innocence, The Beach is the playground where we are able to take our conspiracies into the sunlight.

I am looking forward to the break. From thinking about anything. Annabelle. The films. Chris. Jack, who has become such a part of my life. From all that's going on. What I want. Who I am. Even from thinking about the girls.

Like all our beaches, The Beach is on the very edge of civilisation, out beyond the wildest dreams. Beyond constraints. Beyond respectability. Beyond the country of decorous behaviour. To get there you must drive for hours, out beyond the tall black-glassed towers and away. Past the suburban beaches with their swimsuited heterosexual carnivals, family tummy bulge and babyfat picnics. Past even the nude heterosexual beaches, bacon and eggs being burnt to a frazzle in one huge sandy frying pan. To the Forbidden Zone.

The history of our beaches has always involved a pitched battle between ourselves and the rest of the world. Some lone pioneer, either in an act of frustration, foolhardiness or bravery, staked a claim for all of us many years ago by taking off his clothes. Another joined him and another, making a beachhead, establishing a camaraderie, a spirit of conspiracy of us against them. The word got around and before you knew it The Beach had a reputation. It was a place to go on a hot summer day. To meet other men. To mark the place with our own scent.

None of our beaches has ever been taken without a battle. Our forebears have been arrested and charged with lewd or illicit behaviour or consorting in unnatural acts with other men. Even now The Beach is still subject to the occasional sweep of authority. Wet Dream Walking was chased recently, as bare-arsed as a bunny, by a warden on a beach further to the north. When the warden failed to catch up with him, he waited at Wet Dream Walking's pile of clothes. But his intention to arrest was defeated by numbers. Other men, seeing what had happened, silently surrounded the warden, eyeballing him into leaving.

Most of us have our first anonymous sex on one of our beaches. Unsure adolescents, we park our bikes or borrowed cars on the road and, cheeks blazing, climb down the rocks to where we have been told to go. It has taken us weeks to pluck up the courage. Trying to act casual, we saunter around the first two bays to the third. There, we see the beat.

Our resolve falters and, instead, we sit on the sand in a spot where we can spy from and be spied upon. Heart thumping, we take off shirt and, gulp, jeans, exposing pigeon chest and skinny legs. Then, if we're lucky, there is a voice and a stirring of someone coming up on us from behind. We look up, hoping he's the kind of guy we have dreamed about. If he isn't, we stand and move away like scared jackrabbits. But if he is, then, oh boy, this might be the time to lose It.

'Hi.'

His voice is smiling but uncertain. Rejection is so exposed out here in the sand in the middle of the sun.

'Uh, hi.'

He is not what you have dreamed of but the approximation is sufficient.

A spreading of a towel next to yours. Then the immortal words:

'Listen, could you put some oil on my back?'

Whether you say yes or whether you say no does not matter. Capitulation may not come the first time or the second or the third. But once this far, there is no turning back. No turning back from the ecstacy of the experience and agony of the conscience-stricken aftermath. No turning back from the terrible beauty that compels you to return. Eventually to initiate, in your own turn, remembering with appreciation the completeness of your own.

Our beaches are hard won. Once gained they can never be given up. They are the playgrounds of our innocence. Innocence lost, innocence found, innocence regained. We all have a vested interest in maintaining the beaches, for they are the shrines to our sexuality, our past, present and our future.

The Beach, wherever it is, is our Eden.

Then there he is, Oh My Goodness, coming out of Customs and looking as excited and as anxious as a cocker spaniel. He is a six-feet-four stunning grey-eyed blond and turns heads with his boyish healthiness. He sees me and comes loping over.

'I was worried you didn't get my fax.'

'Which one?' I answer drily.

'Is your car handy?' he laughs. 'I've got a helluva lot of luggage. Four suitcases.'

'Planning to stay, are you?' I ask.

'Samples for the conference in Australia but —' He winks. 'You never know your luck.'

At the apartment Oh My Goodness is eager and nervous. I show him his room and he asks, 'Is this where you sleep?'

I shake my head. The light vacates his eyes a moment. Then, 'You know,' he says, 'I sometimes have bad nightmares. I might have to climb in with you.'

'It's a single bed.' I look down at the V of his jeans. 'And there's not room for the three of us.'

He laughs and grabs me in a playful hug. 'It's so great to see you and to have you take the mickey out of me. So what's the pro-gramme today?'

'I've packed a picnic. I thought we'd go to the beach.'

'How about staying home?'

I know he is disappointed. But the day is hot and I need to be in the heat.

'You've got a one-track mind. Dirt track.'

'Don't you want to take advantage of my fabulous body?' He

starts a slow bump and grind, parodying a male stripper.

'Beach first. Then if you're a good dog,' I pat him on the head, 'I'll give you a bone.'

'Woof woof,' he answers.

The motorway north is packed. A lime-green beach buggy, filled with six young bare-chested beach bunnies, zips in and out of the traffic with gay abandon. The guys are painted up with fluorescent zinc sun block. Like Indians on the warpath.

'Is this it?' Oh My Goodness asks.

I turn the car into the verge at the top of the rise. The Beach is crowded today. Cars are jampacked along the road including Size Queen's Veedub and a Peugeot owned by the self-destructive Pin Cushion. Pricked by a poisoned pin, he now walks with the undead on his own hyperbolic arc to oblivion.

'Not yet,' I answer.

I reach in the back and toss Oh My Goodness a pair of sneakers. Reach for my backpack. In it are towels, cans of juice, fruit, magazines, Walkman and tapes, lubricant, condoms. Supplies for the entire day.

'We've got a bit of walking to do.'

Stash my wallet in the boot. The cars here are regularly done over by kids or louts, and you're asking for trouble if you leave wallet and credit cards under the seat. This is what happened to Chris during a visit to San Francisco soon after we started seeing each other. Listen, he said on the telephone, could you cancel my Amex and Diner's for me? Bemused, I listened to him putting the best gloss on the incident. No need to explain. Life is life. A beach is a beach. We cannot change the compulsions that we have, even if we are in some kind of commitment.

'Down there?' Oh My Goodness asks, unbelieving. He stares down the cliff face. I join him, shoving a backpack in his hands. We walk past the cars. Some have pencil and paper under the windscreens. Hello, hello, the lime-green beach buggy is here too.

'Yup.'

The hedonistic impulse has always ensured that The Beach, wherever it is, is a variation on the same theme. A long climb down from a cliff and a leisurely walk around the rocks to the best sand that God ever made. In this case three sandy bays where the sand backs up against the trees and, at the third bay, dunes and tussock. Sea shelving shallowly from azure to inky blue.

'Are you okay?' I ask Oh My Goodness.

'Sure.'

On the way down I look for Grasshopper. Denizen of the beach, he has been lookout and unofficial deity for years. Lizardlike, his skin is a tanned carapace, softening at the pelvic join. There is no part of him that has not been burnt brown by the sun. He is as much a guardian as Fat Forty And A Fairy and Always A Bridesmaid. He looks up and waves us on. Far below I see the six beach bunnies have reached the bottom of the track and are running across the sand. Their high spirits echo in the natural acoustics. We carry on down the track.

'So, how was your flight?' I ask.

Oh My Goodness replies, regaling me with stories of delayed connections and bad service, made tolerable only by hunky air stewards. We are moving past decorum into the country of shared intimacies, trying to cement our separation by time and space as if it had never existed.

Looking at him and listening to him, I am amazed that I didn't take him straight to bed when he arrived. He is a blond bombshell of the kind associated with erotic fantasies. Aquiline features, strong open face, gleaming hair that isn't out of a bottle. His body is well defined, a golden arrow stippled with reddish fuzz across his chest and down to his navel. The sun is opening his pores and drenching him in the honey smell that I remember so well from our first encounter.

Perhaps having had Chris in my life has changed the usual pattern of lust or desire. Or the preoccupation with the divorce proceedings may be having a dampening effect. Then, of course, there is the certainty of sex between me and Oh My Goodness. When it is predictable, the excitement level is reduced, the actual timing of the event irrelevant. Is this what happens with marriages too?

Then we reach the sand. Rest. Panting. Perspiring in the sun.

'You've got a choice,' I tease Oh My Goodness. 'The first beach is Paradise. The next is Heaven. Further around is Hell.'

He laughs. He knows I'm having him on.

'Like Mykonos, huh? You're such a magician,' he says. But his imagination is into overload as he thinks about the various delights that might be available at each. With a grin, 'Let's go straight to Hell.'

At Paradise, the beach is a yellow sickle scything at the sea. The Golden Oldies are out in force. They wear tennis hats and look over the mound of bellies moulded by middle age. They lie packed together like a double-decker geriatric gourmet sandwich. Each one is leathered by the sun, his skin already a country claimed by melanoma. Handkerchief Head is among them, and so is Glory Hole. No doubt, as the day deepens, Glory Hole will wander from this old man's territory to take a look in Heaven and Hell.

Onward to Heaven, where space is at a premium. The beach is carpeted. When bodies are piled up so much, they lose their individuality. Become sexless. Nevertheless, there are some wonderful shapes and sizes. The Doctor is with his Patient; they have finished short-term consultations and are now settling into a long-term practice.

'The water's great,' The Doctor calls.

Indeed it feels silken and cool as I walk its edge with Oh My Goodness. We watch as couples chase each other out to sea. Then they are diving in, porpoising around and eventually clasping each other between scissoring legs in the deep contentment of love.

Opera-addicted Madama Butterfly is also taking the sun with his ever-forgiving Chinese Takeaway. Exiled from Hong Kong, Madama Butterfly is an Etonian rice queen with a continuing avid taste for younger chop suey.

Then, with surprise, I see Jack. He is beached among all this brown flesh like a white dolphin. Lying next to him but pretending not to be with him, Warrick. When I get closer I notice the bruises on Jack's body. From the assault outside The Steam Parlour? Or from Warrick?

'I want you to meet a friend of mine,' I say to Oh My Goodness. He shrugs his shoulders, Okay.

We step around the bodies in Heaven and, as we approach, Jack's face lifts up in a glad, welcoming smile.

'Hello,' he greets us in a voice of enforced brightness. 'Isn't the day simply splendid?'

'Christ,' Warrick mutters. Jack's voice has a carrying power which belies the small pouch of body from which it comes. Nevertheless Warrick looks up as we approach. He scowls at me but his eyes fix on Oh My Goodness with relish.

'This is my friend from Canada,' I begin.

Once the introductions are effected, we chat. But I am so angry with Warrick, *and* with Jack for being so foolish. I realise that I really do care about Jack. Apart from his bruises, he is one of those people who should never sit unprotected in the sun. The light either poisons them or alters their body chemistry, producing pustules or other skin malignancies. It drains hair of elasticity so that it droops like dying weeds. Jack is one of the pale tribe. Put him in the sun and he burns rather than browns, slowly cooking as if in a vast solar microwave oven. Already his face is popping with red sores, and crimson weals are developing across the hairless expanse of his chest and upper legs.

'Don't take too much sun, Jack.'

'I brought a hat.'

'I told him,' Warrick says with a laugh, 'to bring a paperbag and put it over his head.'

I ignore him. I turn to Jack. 'I'll ring you tomorrow.'

Onward to Hell.

'That's an interesting situation,' Oh My Goodness says of Jack's relationship.

'It's just begun.'

'Does he pay the younger guy?'

'No. Not that I know of. Though, come to think of it, a strict commercial transaction wouldn't be a bad idea.'

'Well he must be getting something out of the relationship.'

'That's what he tells me. That's why he is still clinging to it. He loves him.'

'I know the feeling,' Oh My Goodness murmurs.

We cross the channel and reach the rocks framing Hell. The tide is high and Oh My Goodness and I have to swim with the packs around the rocks to a platform made slippery by seaweed. One step. Then another, and The Beach opens in all its wonder.

Oh My Goodness gives an appreciative whistle.

There are mermen in the sparkling water. This is man made godlike. Man before the Fall when he became ashamed to look upon his nakedness. Man at his most natural and beautiful and, paradoxically, his most brutal. Striding the beat, the rim of dune between sand and sky. A whole world of games and power flows here in this place where one man meets another. But here we are free to be what we want to be.

Today, The Beach is filled with fun. The six beach bunnies are horsing around in the surf. As we walk up the beach, some of the guys start to wolf whistle at Oh My Goodness. Among them are Italian Stallion and Now You See It Now You Don't. The former is going to be put out when Oh My Goodness strips off. With his shorts still on, Oh My Goodness's physique and sassiness present only the curtain raiser. Purposely I walk to a spot where Size Queen reigns. Just behind him are the eternal watchers, sun flashing from their binoculars. Although there are some well-equipped men around, no one's seen anything yet.

'This will do,' I tell Oh My Goodness.

We unshoulder our packs and spread our towels. Sitting down, Oh My Goodness flips open a can of beer. The froth overspills from his mouth.

'This is really nice. Really. Nice.' He looks at me and asks, 'You coming in?'

'No. Not yet. You go ahead.'

This is the part I love.

'Okay.'

Oh My Goodness slips his shorts off, showing a tan line. Letting out a Calgary yodel, 'Yee*haa*!' he is off and speeding toward the surf.

'Holy shit,' one of the beach bunnies calls.

'I think I've just fallen in love,' someone else murmurs in a daze.

As for Size Queen, he is having a heart attack.

All eyes are on Oh My Goodness and the mongaloosa which slaps down past his knees, left and right, as he runs.

Oh My Goodness is lying on his back. Water and sweat bead his body like pearls. Since his return to the beach there has been a veritable barrage of binoculars behind us. On the sand the population has slowly started to drift closer and closer to us. Every now and then the beach bunnies kick sand as they sprint past. But Oh My Goodness is not interested.

'Would you look at these jocks,' I say, flipping the pages of *Mandate*. 'They're real fantasy material. Why do they all have to be blonds?'

'What's wrong with blonds?' Oh My Goodness asks.

'Haven't you heard?' I reply. 'Look, what's the first thing a blond does in the morning?'

'Don't know.'

'Goes home. And how does a blond turn the light on after having had sex?'

'You tell me.'

'Opens the car door. And what does a blond say after sex?'

'I'm dying to hear.'

'So, all you guys in the same team?'

Oh My Goodness pretends mock horror. Then he says, 'But there's a great difference between those blonds and moi.'

'What is that?'

'Five inches longer, twice as thick and no pimples on the bum. Anyway, a cock in the hand is worth two in the bush. Why look at pictures when you can have the real thing?'

'Oh, puh-*lease*. Put it away before it strangles itself.'

Oh My Goodness has an infectious laugh. His teeth gleam white in the sun and his tongue is pink with health.

'You know I love it when you treat me mean. And you're the only one who hasn't fallen in love with me for *this*.'

'I hate to tell you, but as big as you are there's always one bigger. And give me a break. Do you really think you have a brain for me to be interested in?'

Oh My Goodness starts to have hysterics, kicking up sand with his feet.

'Watch it or you'll tie yourself up in knots,' I say sarcastically.

He wriggles closer to me.

Size Queen has been cruising backwards and forwards outrageously, hoping to catch my attention. But I have been ignoring his obvious expectation to be invited over.

'Actually, I've had offers,' Oh My Goodness says. 'To be in porno mags. Even movies.'

'I can guess.'

'But it never amounted to anything. The horrible dark places where they wanted me to put my pecker. Just as well I didn't. I'd probably be dead by now. All those guys dying. You know.'

When you watch the X-rated movies, say a prayer for the professionals. For most are dead now. All those wonderful bodies, freely given, freely taken, all gone into the night.

We lie close together for a while. Oh My Goodness begins to stroke my thighs. Dipping between them into the sweet places. My sex drive starts to carry me toward that place postponed this morning. Then I notice seagulls are beating the air above us, hovering, ready to fall. Eyeing the gulls, I whisper to Oh My Goodness:

'Can I make a suggestion? I'd put my hands over that mongaloosa of yours if I were you.'

He looks up and his laughter spills over and into the air.

'Time for a cold shower,' I continue, biting his left ear.

With a yelp he is up and after me. Together we race toward the surf. As we plunge in, The Reverend looks ruefully at his own partner and good-naturedly yells out to me, 'Oh you lucky, lucky son of a bitch.'

Later, and I can't wait. We are resting half in and half out of the water among the rocks. Kissing. Fondling.

'Listen,' I ask, tonguing Oh My Goodness's nipples. 'What's your attitude to public sex?'

'Try me,' he answers.

We join together like Siamese mermen.

Around us binoculars falter and *flash*.

45

I DON'T WANT to think about anything, really. I just want to escape the world a while. Not grow up. Not be responsible. Enjoy myself. Oh My Goodness is just the intermezzo that is needed. Here today, gone tomorrow.

After The Beach, I take him on the town. Among the tourist sights, the baths at The Fuck Palace.

'Whadd'ya reckon?' I ask him.

He is standing by the pool where the erotic ambience lives on. Every now and then the sauna opens and a man comes to dive in the pool. Splashes of pearls. Falls of diamonds. Glittering arpeggios.

'Places like this were closed down years ago in Canada and the States,' Oh My Goodness says. 'Do you people think you're invulnerable? That you have some exemption from God?'

We move on to The Club. I am never quite sure about Oh My Goodness's reaction to the scene. Sometimes he is eager, but occasionally his sense of propriety gets in the way of enjoyment. That's what first attracted me to him when we met three years ago in Canada. The Saskatoon 'aw shucks' farm boy with a shiny nose and innocent curiosity was irresistible. Although he is somebody who could be seduced by life, he still retains his natural modesty. In later years this has become transmuted into an academic decency and sensibility which puts reputation first. And what still remains a pleasant diversion for me has become something more serious for him. Something to be approached with caution. Something he is unsure about.

The Club is really rocking. Youth is, as ever, the premium on the dance floor. Born To Boogie comes across with yet another twin in tow. I wonder why he bothers. May as well bring a mirror.

'You disgusting animal,' Born To Boogie says. 'The whole place has been buzzing with what you and your friend got up today at the beach.'

I laugh because Born To Boogie is much better known than I for public displays. I introduce him to Oh My Goodness and invite him and his friend to join us at the bar. It is not too long before Born To Boogie comes up with his own Blond jokes:

'What does a blond wear behind his ears to attract a man?'

We shake our heads.

'His ankles.'

Then comes the killer. 'What is the useless piece of skin at the end of a penis?'

Again we shake our heads.

'A man.'

I can't take any more. 'I need to go water Horace,' I say to Born to Boogie. 'Do you mind keeping my Canadian friend company?' As if that will be a problem. Size Queen has already spotted Oh My Goodness and is rushing across to meet him.

I am not long at the urinal before I am joined by an aging gay of Size Queen's vintage. At the mirror he looks at himself, pokes at his hair and sighs:

'I've just been dancing with a younger guy. Doesn't he know it's taken me the whole day to look like this?'

By the time I return, Oh My Goodness is positively surrounded. Being poked at, prodded at, invited, sampled. I go to the rescue.

'I don't think I want to stay,' he says. His face has clamped down. He has put up a sign in front of it: Nobody is home.

'Okay,' I answer. 'Let's get out of here.'

We push out of the crowd and I bump into someone. Spill his beer.

Ruck, laughing with his retinue of admirers. His arms are around the shoulders of a familiar figure.

Chris.

The visit is too soon over. A second day at The Beach. Another night on the town. Then the next morning, back at the airport to say goodbye.

'Come with me to Australia,' Oh My Goodness says. 'No, come back with me when I return to Canada. We get on so well together. We're so right for each other. Emotionally. In every way.'

'No.' The chemistry is right for him but not for me.

'I could organise a teaching position at the best university. I've got a friend who can get you through immigration. No problem.'

'There is. I can't leave. I have commitments. A career. Kids. All that baggage that we bring to relationships.'

'Do I have to spell it out to you?' he asks, pleading.

'You're the ideal combination, really,' I answer. 'You're every gay man's dream come true. Everything that anybody ever wanted. Beauty, brains, money, a career *and* a mongaloosa.' I'm trying to make him lighten up, but he slips to his knees in mock proposal.

'Dammit, everything that's happening to you and Annabelle is for the best. You'll be free to be whoever you want. I'm the best offer you'll ever get. With me you could have the best of all possible worlds.'

'Get outta here.'

Even having everything may not be enough. It is time to get on with life.

46

SO NOW IT'S Friday, Black Friday. Film Studies is silent. Everybody goes around on tiptoes as if the floor is made of eggshell. This morning the Vice Chancellor, the University Committee and the head of department consider what is to be done about 'the Film Studies business'.

Tsk, tsk, David. Bad boy, *very* bad boy. Here comes the chopper to chop off your head.

Come midday, high noon, the sun at its apex, Ronald, Stephen and Brenda crowd into my office. They are joined by Bright Eyes and other cohorts of Ronald's.

The telephone rings. Everything comes to a standstill, like a film that has stopped. Brenda has her mouth half open. Ronald's eyes are wide with despair. Bright Eyes looks like Jesus in an attitude of prayer. Freeze frame.

'David? You have friends in high places.' The head of department. He sounds cross. 'Why didn't you tell me you knew Lady Alwyn-Jones?'

'Who? I don't know —'

'Of course you know Her Ladyship! Her late husband left a bequest to this university.'

I nod. The Sir Always Boasting About Himself bequest which enabled the commerce wing to be built.

'Lady Alwyn-Jones happens to be on the University Committee. She is also the sole trustee of her husband's bequest. She has instructed that two hundred thousand dollars be diverted to Film Studies. Of course the Vice Chancellor has agreed. I wish you'd told me all this before. It would have saved a lot of trouble.'

The penny drops.
Amid the shouts of jubilation I telephone Jack.
'That's some gardening circle your mother has.'

Part Six

STRAIGHT ON TILL MORNING

47

THE WEEKEND. SATURDAY is stormy. Not swimming weather. Seagulls wheel and skirl across the beach at Suburbia By The Sea. Rebecca has managed to pull Miranda through the low tide and up onto the Crocodile's Tail. Now Rebecca has gone on, climbing the whole length from the jaws, snapped open on the beach to the tail, lashing out in the deep water. Meantime the tide has begun to come in again and part of the Crocodile, where the body and tail are joined, is submerged. Poor little Miranda is trying to gauge when to wade across. Every time she starts to venture, another wave comes crashing through the gap.

'Becca,' Miranda wails. 'Becca!' Even her wand is ineffectual against the might of Neptune.

Annabelle and I are on the beach, watching from afar. I go to help, but Annabelle restrains me.

'No,' she says. 'They'll work it out.'

Indeed Rebecca, sighing that 'Why do I have such a hopeless little sister' sigh, climbs down. Her instructions to Miranda drift over the waves to us:

'When I count to three, darling, jump onto *that* rock and then *that* rock. Okay?'

'Come and carry me over,' Miranda sobs.

'You can do it,' Rebecca answers.

'I truly can't, Becca.'

Rebecca surprises me with her sharpness. Perhaps her mother's assertiveness training is rubbing off on her.

'Miranda, you are such a wimp. Now, one, two, *three.*'

Before she can even think about it, Miranda is splashing across the gap. Whoosh comes a wave, but too late, ha ha ha! Miranda is across, and rushing up to the top of the tail.

'I'm the king of the castle and you're the dirty rascal!' Her piping voice ends in a little wheeze and cough. Quickly she reaches for her inhaler and takes a puff. Looks at us, hoping we haven't seen.

I settle back on the sand. The picnic food looks as if it has been machinegunned by Miranda's mouth. The blanket is littered with half-eaten buns, pizza and half-consumed bottles of soft drink.

'That younger child of yours,' Annabelle says good-humouredly, excluding herself from the parental process. 'She's become a terror with food. Picking one thing up and putting it down. And she won't go anywhere without that silly wand.'

'We shouldn't stay out too long,' I say. 'I think she's coming down with something.'

'Oh it's just psychosomatic,' Annabelle answers. 'She was coughing a little just before we left the house. Anyway, we have to fend for ourselves now.'

Annabelle starts to clear up. As she bends and reaches I notice how much slimmer she has become.

'So how much have you lost?' I ask.

'Can you tell?' she answers, pleased.

'It looks good,' I continue. 'Obviously going to the gym and whatever else you're doing is paying dividends.'

'I'm getting on with my life,' she answers, nodding to herself. 'Yes.' Finishes packing up. 'Let's go for a walk.'

'What about the girls?'

'They'll be okay. Come on. I'll race you to the point.'

With that she is off, sprinting down the beach, her toes digging into the sand. I sprint after her, and people on the beach yell encouragement:

'Go, go, *go.*'

She is like Diana, the Roman Goddess of the Hunt. And, like

Diana, she has golden apples, one of which she tosses, just as I am coming abreast of her.

'The girls!' Her eyes register alarm. She points to the Crocodile's Tail.

I falter. Look behind. The girls are waving and shouting in the sun. Then I feel Annabelle shoving me in the small of my back. I trip and fall, and the trickster Annabelle sails gaily on, silvering the air with her laughter.

Now we are returning from the point. Annabelle has threaded an arm through mine. It is just like old times. If anyone was looking on, they would not know the turmoil that lies beneath this happy picture. Rather they would see, simply, a man, a woman and two lovely children.

'So what did you want to talk to me about?' Annabelle has been chatting happily, but now stops. Colours. 'Come on,' I nudge her. 'Don't be coy.'

She looks at me sideways. Watching me carefully. The Crocodile's Tail has always been the place where we have been able to confess the small intimacies of our lives.

'I've been asked out on a date.'

I laugh out loud and she is offended.

'Don't you think I'm attractive enough for men?' she asks.

'No, it's not that,' I answer.

'Then what!' She takes her arm from me. Stops on the beach, arms akimbo.

'God,' I sigh, 'you take the cake. I'm happy for you, that's all. You take my breath away.'

She stays apart, still uncertain. Then takes my arm again. 'It's just a date after all,' she shrugs. 'Nothing serious. But it's a validation. I've been really bruised, you know. When a man leaves a woman for another woman, that's bad enough. But when it's for another man —'

We walk on a while in silence. This is the first time that we have been able to talk unemotionally about my homosexuality.

'Is he anyone I know?' I ask.

'Actually, yes,' she confesses. 'Do you remember George?'

The Hellespont Ram, from the Classics Department. Oh no.

'He's been divorced for a while. Anyway, we bumped into one another a few weeks ago. He's been pestering me ever since.'

'I'll bet,' I say, and Annabelle catches my cynicism. 'He asked *me* for your telephone number. Had I known —'

Annabelle's temper flares. 'Look, sport' she answers, 'the world is full of solo mothers. It's really hard out there. I have to take my chances. I'm not looking for anything more than a nice man to take me out to dinner at some warm restaurant, and nothing more. Okay?'

I nod and pull her close to stop her from being hurt. She pokes me with a finger.

'Oh, *you*,' she says. Then, 'My counsellor has told me I must start looking forward. Sometimes the only way I've been able to manage that is to pretend to myself that you have died. Not left me, but died.'

Her words sound so flippant. Careless.

'Well, thanks.'

'I know that might sound harsh, but thinking of you as dead makes it much easier to stop hoping that you'll come back.'

I stop and stare at her. She looks back at me. I can see Rebecca staring at me from out of those eyes. Tears spilling. 'Damn you, sport. You were supposed to look after me. But you didn't. You forgot to hold me tight. You let a gap happen, a space for the wind to come between us. And by the way, Miranda says you come around to the house sometimes. Do you know that she often waits for you to turn up? I found her one night, watching out for you. I said, "Go to sleep." But she said, "No I can't, Daddy hasn't come yet." It's got to stop, sport. You've got to set us free.'

'You always say that. I only do it to make sure —'

'We can look after ourselves, David.'

The afternoon is turning cold. The clouds are hurtling across the sky. The waves are white tipped and the Crocodile is trying to dislodge my two princesses into the sea. There to snap them both in half with its jaws.

'Girls?' Annabelle calls. 'Time to go home.'

'Okay, Mummeee —'

Rebecca clambers down and, when they get to the gap in the tail, piggybacks Miranda across. Miranda is coughing as she runs up to us.

Rebecca's eyes are shining with joy and happiness. Although the light flickers when I drop her, Miranda and Annabelle at their house, it returns again with all the energy she can muster.

'It was good to be a family again, wasn't it, Daddy?'

'Yes, darling. Yes.'

As I drive away, I catch a look between Rebecca and Miranda. Something is going on, as if they are still hopeful that Annabelle and I can get back together. One can never know with children. They inhabit a different world, of wishes made by closing your eyes and crossing your fingers. Where dreams can come true if you believe hard enough.

48

BACK AT THE apartment and I am parking the car. The world is not only filled with solo mums. There are solo dads as well. This is the price one has to pay. I have my key in the lock and am turning it to open the door when I hear someone coming up behind me.

For a moment I think it is The Slut. I turn swiftly, ready to defend myself.

Chris. In workout tights and sweatshirt, tote bag over his shoulder. He is perspiring and sweat stains his armpits. He puts his arms up. His eyes are afraid.

'Hi,' he says. 'I was just passing and I —'

My heartbeat subsides. It finds another stream. Warm. Relieved. Glad.

'It's so good to see you,' I answer.

We stand on the step, awkward with each other. Then the telephone saves us.

'Come on in,' I invite him.

'Well, only for a moment.'

The telephone ringing and ringing. Annabelle. Behind her, Miranda is screaming. Coughing. Hysterical. Coughing again.

'David, Miranda didn't by any chance leave her wand in the car did she?'

Then Rebecca has taken the telephone. 'Daddy, please find Miranda's wand for her. It's her security blanket, Daddy. She really needs it. Please find it. If anybody can, you can. Oh Daddy please. Find. The wand.'

'Do you mind if I come with you?' Chris asks.

The Crocodile's Tail is lit by the moon. The jaws are wide open, ready to snap, snap, *snap*. The waves curl and hiss around the rocks. Snap, curl, slap, hiss.

Chris and I are out with the torch, in the dark and cold, with the rain drizzling, looking all over and around the Crocodile's Tail for that damn wand.

'Someone must have found it and taken it,' Chris says.

'Who'd want to do that! All it is, is a wooden rod wrapped around with cellophane and a big pasted star sprinkled with glitter.'

After half an hour we still cannot find the stupid thing. Chris has slipped a couple of times and his trackpants are splotched and wet from the waves.

'The sea must have swept it away,' I tell Chris.

'Let's give it one more try,' he answers. 'Miranda really loves that wand. You know what children are like.'

The sea surges against us both and I reach up and —

'Here,' he says.

Grabs my arm. Rescues me. Grins.

'Did you find it, Daddy?' Rebecca asks when I knock on the door. 'Did you? Did you?' She sees Chris waiting in the car.

'No, darling.'

Behind her I can see Miranda staring at me, frightened. It is the end of the world. Daddy always finds things. He's never failed before. Daddy can do anything. Anything.

Her sister intercepts the glance. There, there, Miranda.

'But —' I have had one hand behind my back. 'Ta-ra!'

Luckily I remembered that Film Buff has a collection of memorabilia, including a wand which could have been used by the Good Fairy in *The Wizard of Oz*.

Miranda's eyes brighten a moment. Then they fade. And I remember a certain Christmas when Miranda had asked for a new dressing gown. We had thought we could give her one that Rebecca had grown out of, and Annabelle sewed on new buttons and bows. But those little eyes faded on that morning too. Thank you Mummy, thank you Daddy, Miranda said, it's a pretty dressing gown with its new buttons and bows but it's still Becca's dressing gown not mine.

Nevertheless, Miranda accepts the new wand. Lifts her face to be kissed. Goes off hand in hand to bed with her sister.

'She'll get over it,' Annabelle says. 'She was getting too attached to the old wand anyway.'

'Thank you,' I say to Chris.

I have taken him out to dinner and now it is after midnight. We have adjourned to The Munchbox coffee bar, a pink crate of bleary neon, and are having a positively terrible cup of cappuccino. No wonder the place is deserted. Just us, and a couple of drunk businessmen eyeing up two prostitutes. Lettuce and tomato quick sex on a sandwich to go, and easy on the mayonnaise.

'That's okay,' Chris answers. 'Only too glad to help.'

He has put on a jersey over his sweatshirt. His eyes glisten in the light of the bar.

'So. How are things with you?' I ask.

'Fine. We're in rehearsals. Almost ready for the tour now. Just extracts of course. Dancing with piano. Not the same thing as having an orchestra, but we'll do our best. It's so difficult, when you go to schools, to create the fantasy of ballet. We're too close. And the piano doesn't exactly hide all our grunts. But you know all this. And you? You got the films, I take it? How's the restoration coming along?'

All small-talk, hiding what we really need to say to each other. Pride getting in the way. Anger.

'I'm much the same. The project has had a few hiccups.'

'I'm sure you'll work it out. That's what I've always admired about you. You're a man who makes things happen.' He looks at me quickly. Then away.

'So how's Ruck?' I ask. It is hard not to keep the jealousy out of my voice. Nobody likes to be thrown over.

Chris throws one back at me, gotcha. 'And how's your Canadian friend?'

He makes a small moue and shrugs. Leans back in his chair. Slides forward. The movement is irresistible.

'I've stopped seeing Ruck. I've been too busy. And anyway I don't like threesomes.'

'Why didn't you ask me along?' I ask jokingly.

The joke misfires. Chris stares at me, uncomprehending. 'Is that what I've meant to you all along?' he asks. 'Just another sex partner in your life?'

I can't answer. I don't want to answer.

'I knew this wouldn't work,' he sighs. 'You just don't want it to work.' Shoulders his tote bag. 'Can you take me home?'

'Sure.'

We sit in the car. Just outside Chris's place. A siren wails in the night. It seems as if we've been sitting here for ages. A city going to sleep is a lonely place.

Chris tries again. 'I suppose it would be a dumb move to ask you in for a cup of coffee?'

'I think so.'

He is silent. Then he jerks the door open. Brutally.

'Okay. That's it then.'

He gets out of the car. Walks away. Does not look back.

Just like that.

49

NOW IT IS two-thirty in the morning and I am back in the apartment. I have spent most of the midnight hours at a grotty X-rated cinema in Sleaze Alley. Security grilles, fluorescent painted entrance. Deserted foyer except for the ticket vendor. Amplimesh decor and an interior made up of sparkling Glamatex. A few patrons watch the climaxes on the screen like spritzer foaming up and out.

I am angry with myself in this Sleaze-O-Rama. For not finding the wand. For not fulfilling expectations. For not —

The message light is winking on my answering machine. If one of them is my sister I'll —

OhmyGod.

Beep.

David, this is Annabelle here and the time is nine o'clock. Could you call me at home, please. Thank you.

Beep.

It is now nine-thirty, David. You must be out. Look, Miranda's temperature is up and she has suddenly started to breathe very badly. Perhaps she caught a chill out at the Crocodile's Tail today. Her inhaler has run out. I think I'd better take her to the doctor.

Beep.

David, are you there? If you are, *pick up the phone.* The doctor has given Miranda an injection to get her over her breathing problems. He's slightly anxious about her temperature but thinks she should be all right now. I am taking her home. Oh, it's now nine minutes past ten.

Beep.

Daddy? This is Rebecca here. Mummy can't raise the doctor. She is getting Miranda ready to take to hospital. We have called a taxi. The hospital is . . . Which one, Mummy? Mummy says the one we were born in. I have to go now. Please come, Daddy, please.

Beep.

Son, this is your father here. Miranda has had a very bad turn. It's not her usual asthmatic condition. She has some sort of infection now and it is stopping her from breathing. Don't worry. Your mother and I are here at the hospital with Annabelle and Rebecca. It is now ten forty-five. No doubt you'll be home soon.

Beep.

David. Where *are* you? It's Annabelle here and it's after midnight. The doctors are extremely anxious about Miranda's condition. She does not seem to be responding to the drugs they are giving her. She's on oxygen right now. Oh David . . .

Beep.

You need to get down here as soon as you can, son. It's two-thirty. The doctors are proposing to operate. Miranda's nasal passages have clogged up and she can't breathe. The doctors want to do a [obscured] . . . I think it's called. Open up her throat and put a tube down into her lungs.

Beep.

DaddyDaddyDaddyWhereareyouDaddy MirandaisdyingDaddy *Daddddeeeee*.

Beep.

Out and into the car.

The key won't go into the lock. My hands are trembling so much. Start, damn you, *start*. The engine catches. I back out into the road. Burn rubber, David.

Across the city in the dead of night. Not much traffic around. Taking chances. Through all the red lights. Then onto the motorway ramp. Roaring along the steel ribbon of road. To the hospital turnoff. Through more red lights. *Get out of my way*. The hospital is ahead. It is lit up like a birthday cake. Careen through the car park. Out of the car. Into the foyer. Duty nurse.

'Miranda —? Oh yes. That's the little girl who —'

OhmyGod. Please let her not be dead. Not dead.

Third floor. Forget about the lift. Up the stairs three at a time. A wolf has got my little girl. Is shaking the life out of her. Through the doors and into the third-floor corridor. Everything is quiet. Still. But far at the end of the passageway is a family group. Grieving.

'Whereissheeee?'

Rebecca looks up.

'Oh, Daddy. It's my fault. Miranda wasn't feeling well even before we went to the Crocodile's Tail but we had been planning it for ages because we knew how much you and Mummy liked it there and —'

My father is trying to calm me down. He is shaking me hard. Takes me to one side.

'Get a hold of yourself, David.'

He tries to tell me what has happened. He, my mother and my sister all begin to talk at once. Beyond them I can see a small hospital room. Annabelle is there and —

'Are you Miranda's father?'

A young red-headed doctor. Professional. Dressed in white.

'Yes I am.'

'Good. We're preparing the operating room for your daughter. We need you to sign the papers approving the operation. Your wife has already signed.'

'You're operating?'

'Yes.'

'Let me *see herrrrr.*'

The hospital room is dimly lit. In an aureole of light is a high bed. Looking so small in it is Miranda. She has an oxygen mask over her face. A monitor is measuring her heartbeat. Tubes feeding blood have been attached to her arms.

Sitting beside the bed is Annabelle. She smiles a welcome at me. I go to her, standing behind her, looking down at this little girl who is fighting for her life. Miranda's attempts at breathing seem to fill the room.

'Ah ah ah —'

The heart machine sends out small pips of alarm.

I put my left hand on Annabelle's shoulder. She pats it. Laces her fingers through mine.

'Do you remember, David, when I was pregnant with Miranda? We weren't too sure that we wanted another child, were we! And when she came, she was absolutely *awful*. So ugly too, with those monkey features and loud crying and —' Annabelle cannot continue. Tears stream down her face.

If there is a God, take me instead of this young girl. Let me be the one to die. Not this perfect child.

Suddenly, the doctor and two orderlies come into the room.

'We're ready now,' the doctor says.

Annabelle looks up at me. I nod. There are stones in my mouth. Hard. Aching.

The orderlies prepare Miranda.

'We're going on a great adventure now,' one of them says. 'Across the city, past the moon and way out to a star second from the right.'

At that, Miranda murmurs something. The orderly bends to hear. Strains. 'She keeps on asking for something,' he says.

Annabelle sighs. 'Her wand.'

'Do you have it?'

'No. She lost it.'

'Ah.'

The nurses wheel Miranda out of the room. There is a small moment when my mother and father bend to kiss her.

'There's a good little girl,' my mother says gaily. 'The doctors will make you as right as rain.'

Miranda winces in the bright corridor light. She looks around. Sees Annabelle. Sees me.

'Dad-*dee*.'

The doctor bends to her. 'Well, little one, let's go then, shall we?'

Miranda starts to thresh her head.

'Becca! *Becca* —'

Rebecca takes her sister's hand. When Rebecca tries to release herself, Miranda won't let go.

'There, there, darling,' Rebecca says. 'You just do what the doctor says now. There, there.'

That's when it happens.

At the far end of the corridor, where the stairway is, the lift doors open. The lift looks empty at first. Then silver glitter is falling like gentle rain and a figure dressed in dazzling gold steps out. He wears a fabulous merman's mask and his tall body shimmers. He looks like a god, and when he sees us he bows low, his star-spangled cape flowing like a dream.

He is the Lord Of The Dance. And as he steps proudly towards us, his feet seem to float above the shining floor. Every now and then, he pirouettes. His cape swirls out like a huge sea flower, scattering more silver rain and dazzling light. Along the corridor he comes. Dancing towards us.

But his hands are always firm, always in front of him, clasping a wondrous gift.

As he come nearer, Annabelle begins to weep again. She weeps at the generosity of this dancing lord. His bounty. His magnanimity. His majesty. She whispers to Miranda.

'Look, darling.'

Twirling, advancing, bowing, the dancer comes, a vision of magic. Giving the performance of his life.

The doctor wants to take Miranda quickly. Then he sees the wondrous gift and understands. He helps lift Miranda a little so that she can see.

Then the dancer is there. He kneels as lords are supposed to kneel, head bowed. His mask is decorated with seahorse wings. His neck is draped with luminescent paua, shimmering with many colours. His merman scales glitter in the light. As he kneels, he holds his wondrous gift toward Miranda.

'Princess Miranda,' he says, 'I cannot stay because I am of the sea and even now I have difficulty breathing.' His breath rasps in and out.

Miranda nods, 'So do I,' behind her own face mask.

'However, my master Neptune, King Of The Sea, has sent me because the mermaids of the southern ocean found something which he believes belong to you.'

His chest rises and falls as if he has swum many leagues under the sea to get here. Then he stands, looks at us all and, gravely, winks. Silver glitter rains about him.

'It is my honour, Princess Miranda, to bring you the best wishes of my master. His Royal Majesty also extends his homage to all who love you. But most of all, to you princess, my master sends this small token of his esteem, affection and respect.'

He places the wondrous gift in Miranda's hands. Her fingers curl around it. Close tight.

'My wand.'

It is dawn when I get to Chris's place. I take the lift up, knock on the door and he opens it. He smiles at me, wan in the first sunlight. He doesn't look as if he's been to sleep at all. Then he yawns. Scratches his hair. Silver sparkles fall out and he shakes his head vigorously.

'Is Miranda all right?'

'Yes.'

'Did they operate?'

'Yes. It was successful. They'll keep her in hospital under observation for a week. She'll have a scar on her neck. But she's breathing now and out of danger.'

'I went back, you see. To the beach. After a party, around midnight. Yes I know, a stupid time to go looking but Miranda loves that wand. Anyway I found it. Nowhere near the Crocodile's Tail! Under a tree. I took it around to Annabelle's house, planning to leave it at the door so that Miranda would find it in the morning. She'd left a note on the door for you to say she was taking Miranda to hospital. I rang you, but you had obviously gone on. Anyway, I had this little old thing, this Neptune costume from last year's Christmas party, so I just put it on and came over.'

'Thank you.'

'My pleasure.'

'I thought you ought to know. She's okay now.'

I turn to leave. Take a few steps. Chris is watching me as I wait for the lift to come. When it does, I wait too long and the door shuts.

I go back to Chris. There are star spangles at the corners of his eyes. I bow to him. Wobbling a little. Bending low.

'The emissary of the Princess Miranda,' I begin, 'pays homage to the emissary of the King Of The Sea and begs his forgiveness and —'

Chris puts a hand on my shoulder. He helps me to stand. For a long time we look at each other.

'Oh Chris —'

He puts a finger to my lips: Ssshh.

'You can't even *bow* properly,' he says.

Tenderly, he takes me into his embrace.

50

A WEEK LATER, and Miranda is out of hospital. She has enjoyed all the flowers, sweets and attention so much that she is trying to remain an invalid at home. Her sister is *very* cross.

Today, however, my mind is on Charles, The Love Of My Life. It is his birthday, the date is ringed with red ink on my desk calendar, along with the birthdays of Rebecca, Miranda, Annabelle, my father, my mother, my sister and Chris. I pick up the telephone. I have waited until late afternoon, with the sun touching the spires of the university like light to candles.

'Why, David.' Longtime Partner's voice is light with forced happiness. 'Your roses and card arrived this morning. You never forget do you? Charles will be so delighted that you called. Yes, I'll give him your love.'

I put the telephone down. My hands are shaking. Nothing can stop the grief that flames and gutters into night.

'Cantiamo, cantiamo, il dolce funebre —'

I have delayed too long in telling you of how I left Charles when I went to see him at his farm, in that place where mermaids were singing. I should draw a curtain on my final moments with him, but that would be dishonest. Even a person dying of Aids should be allowed the dignity of being described and not hidden away behind decorous silence.

He woke up, of course, as I was sitting there with him. There was no smile of greeting. Rather a sudden sneezing, spasmodic convulsion which brought Eva and Dennis running. He drew raucous breath, before vomiting blood and reaching for oxygen. Nor was there any look of welcome when his eyelids flicked open. The eyes beneath were opaque, twitching windows of the blind.

'Who is this?' he asked.

'Hello, Charles,' I answered.

I was spared watching him eat.

I remembered that I had seen a sheep like this. Its brain half eaten away by maggots, the sheep had staggered, snuffled, spasmed and careered a staggering course, bleating loudly for death. It had been Curly who, with indrawn breath against the stench of rotting brains and eyes averted from the maggots that spilled from its cranium, had taken the knife and slit its throat and put it out of its misery.

I hated this heinous taking away of Charles's strength and vitality. This Thing rampaging through his blood stream, devouring all his goodness. This Creature stalking his bones, sucking out their marrow, snapping him in two. Growing purple flowers in the garden of his skin.

Later, Dennis told me that he had already said goodbye to the Charles he had loved.

'This is not Charles,' he said.

We were sitting on the verandah, having a beer, in the dying sun. Eva was preparing Charles for sleep in the new bedroom. His voice was querulous, mean, waspish.

'We were talking about his order of service,' Dennis continued. 'I wanted to know what hymns and readings he wanted. At first he didn't want to talk about it. Do what you like, he said. Or about the friends who should be there. I don't want anybody to know, he said. Then I asked him if he'd like somebody to sing an aria. You know how much he loved opera.' Dennis paused, remembering. 'I thought he might choose that final aria from *Orpheus and Eurydice*, but he didn't. He said crossly, I want a Beatles song. So we're having *Lucy In The Sky With Diamonds*.'

It seemed embarrassing under the circumstances, but both Dennis and I burst out laughing.

'And *then* —' Dennis was wiping at his eyes. 'He said he wanted to sing it himself.'

That set us off again.

'Ah me,' Dennis said. 'There have been times when I've hated him. Wanted him to die. Not hang on like this. And then when I think of him gone, I wonder how I will —'

He looked away. Tears welled up in his eyes. The last sun twinkled out over the lawn. A flash on the river and it was gone.

I didn't stay much longer after that. When Eva had ministered to Charles, I went in to say goodbye.

'Charles?' Dennis said. 'David has to go now.'

Charles's eyes swivelled in my direction. Flickered. Dulled. I kissed him on the cheeks and forehead.

This man had truly been The Love Of My Life. My capitulation to him had set us both on a storming, passionate, no-holds-barred ride that Bette Davis never dreamed of. Its possession of me had been total, and everything before or since was rendered a pale shadow. He had never denied his sexual orientation and, by revelling in it, had for ever changed mine. We had once been each other's safety belts, until he had released the catch. Now it was my turn.

'Thank you, Charles.'

He had said something to me once, and it came back to me. He had been angry that a sexual partner at the beach, whom he saw later at church, hadn't remembered him. I thought about that as I said goodbye to Eva and Dennis. I told them I hadn't minded at all that during the entire visit Charles hadn't remembered me.

'Yes, we know,' they said. 'We understand.'

For a moment I lost control and started to weep.

And all of a sudden Charles jerked his head, listening to my sobs, and addressed me like a querulous schoolmaster.

'You'll have to do better than that.'

Yes, Charles. Tears. I'll have to do *much* better.

'*Cantiamo, cantiamo. Il salce funebre sara la mia ghirlanda.*'
The green willow shall be my garland.

51

OH MY GOODNESS has sent a postcard from the Land Of Smiles, Thailand. The postcard has two colour views, one of Grandpa Stone and the other of Grandma Stone at Koh Smui, Surat-Thani.

'Hi! Am now recovering from my business in Australia in the relatively cool clime of Thailand (which is of course pretty hot in other ways!). I go back to Canada tomorrow. Whenever I look at the sky at night I shall think of you to the south. Whether you like it or not, I'll be back. Love.'

Work has resumed at Film Studies on converting one of our classrooms into a laboratory where we can restore 'The Films', as everybody calls them. The word about the find has leaked out, and we have been inundated with calls from film institutions in America, Great Britain, France and Germany offering financial support, technical equipment and qualified personnel. Some want to attach senior technicians to us and offer exchange fellowships to our students. We've also had offers to purchase the films, sight unseen, as is, from a foundation in California. Megabucks.

Brenda has never had it so good. She has unilaterally decided she must have a new title to deal with all this, so now calls herself my Personal Assistant. She has taken to wearing leopardskin and is the envy of the other departmental secretaries. She is always on the telephone, sparkling, scintillating, purring and sighing as she talks to big-name companies and men she has only read about in film magazines. Like Robert Redford for the Sundance Foundation or Karl Malden for the Academy of Motion Picture

Sciences or Ted Mann, owner of the huge Californian Mann theatre chain. My suggestion that she should have an assistant brought daggers to her eyes. Share all this fun with somebody else? Get off the grass, boss.

As for Ronald, he has taken all this with his usual Scottish imperturbability. Every now and then, though, Stephen, Bright Eyes, who has become fully employed on the project for his thesis, and the rest of the team come sidling into the office to support Ronald when he says to me, 'We're big enough to handle this ourselves, eh laddie.' The stern manner in which he delivers this statement indicates that it is not a question.

The university has been taken by surprise. On a 'just in case' basis, a lawyer has been appointed to handle all the legal niceties. The head of department is over the moon, and Brian and God's Gift have been shunted off to one side at our staff meetings. The head has been suggesting that more room should be taken from *them* and given to Film Studies.

I guess this must be what winning is like.

Then, all of a sudden the banging and crashing stops. With a gulp, Ronald realises that the time has come to begin the restoration process.

And Annabelle and I move beyond anger into quieter waters. We have been lucky. Not all divorcing couples manage it quite like we have. Annabelle has taken control of her life and struck out from me into independence. There are still times of anger but, generally, there has been little rancour. The girls now come to stay over with me in the flat.

At first it is a novelty. Then, when Rebecca begins to redecorate, amusing. After a while, it becomes exasperating when, at the weekends, Annabelle drops the girls off as if they are two bags of groceries:

'All yours, sport!'

Where she goes I never know. The gym. Counselling. To dinner, the cinema or bowling with friends. She is also being dated. The only time I am curious about her dates is when she goes out with George. Ice floes come crashing down the telephone.

'Now I know how he got his nickname.'

'The Hellespont Ram?'

'No. The other one.'

I know never to ask again.

Chris is not perturbed by all this. He fits himself around the girls' visits with frightening ease. Even so, there are times when I prefer to keep that life apart.

He rings my flat at ten. He is leaving tomorrow on the ballet tour.

'Hi. Are you still up? Good. I'm coming over.'

Half an hour later I hear Chris arriving in the street. I creep carefully around the divan in the sitting room where the girls are sleeping and open the front door. Chris is locking his car. He is looking gorgeous. He has had his hair cut short. Tweed jacket. Faded blue jeans. Open-necked shirt. When he sees me waiting, he grins and waves. Then he is striding up the path and through the front door, closing it as he comes in. He backs me against the door, kissing hungrily. Breath sweet with mint.

'You're supposed to be at rehearsal,' I say.

'Got cancelled.'

His tongue seeks mine, circling around it and darting deep into my throat. Already he is shouldering out of his jacket and kicking off his shoes. Manoeuvring me around and —

'This is not a good idea,' I tell him.

'Why not?' he answers. Then, 'What the hell.'

We have almost tripped over the divan.

'The girls are here,' I tell him.

He pauses. 'Why didn't you say so over the phone!'

'You didn't give me time.'

He shrugs. Keeps on going. Pulls at his shirt. Moves me back-wards into the dimly lit bedroom. Moaning.

'Look. This really isn't a good —'

Unheeding, he propels me toward the bed. His lips are en-gorged, sucking on mine. He is in a hurry now. Unbuckling his belt.

'Oh, tough,' he answers. 'I need you too. I won't make the bed-springs creak. And if I'm too noisy, just stuff something in my mouth.'

Whimpering. Yanking his jeans down. No underpants. Skin as

smooth as alabaster. Cock colliding with mine. Hissing between clenched teeth. Guiding me between his thighs. Falling onto the bed, pulling me onto him. 'Oh fuck me.' Hoarse with desire. 'Please. Fuck me.'

I don't know how long we are asleep, but when Miranda starts to cry, Chris is instantly out of bed, naked, and stepping swiftly into the sitting room.

'God, she's so gorgeous,' he whispers when I join him. Daddy has taken some time to find a dressing gown underneath Chris's pile of clothes.

All Chris's protective instincts have come out and he holds Miranda tightly, soothing her, as if she is his. Then, just before she drifts back into sleep, he gives her a butterfly kiss.

The next morning Chris is supposed to leave by seven. Instead he rolls into me and before I know it I am reaching for him, pulling him into me, searching for his lips. My tongue is lapping at his eyelids, wanting him to wake up. He moans, we roll over each other, fighting for each other and —

'What are you doing, Daddy?' Miranda is at the doorway.

Uh. 'Hello, darling.' I pull the blankets over us, Chris shakes with mirth, trying to suppress his laughter.

'Daddy?'

'We're, uh, wrestling, darling.'

Miranda goes back to the sitting room and I hear her tell Rebecca, 'Daddy and Chris are wrestling.'

Giggle, giggle.

Chris's eyes stare into mine. 'Wrestling, huh?'

'Yes.'

'Cute, David. Cute.'

Later, when Chris is dressed, we walk out of the bedroom. The girls are watching morning television.

'Hi, girls!' Chris says.

'Hi, Chris,' they reply, as if there is nothing unusual about him being there. He gets some cereal and joins them in the sitting room.

'Can I watch too?' he asks.

'Sure.'

'Oh, great. Snagglepuss. My *favourite* cartoon.'

Afterwards I walk him to his car. He starts to grin.

'Sometimes I wonder about you,' he says. 'Keeping me in one box and the girls in another.' He waggles a finger: naughty, naughty. 'Well, it isn't going to work. Wrestling. Huh. And stay away from students with bright eyes.'

He thinks I am still struck on Bright Eyes. But a student is a student and I have put Bright Eyes in a box labelled friendship only. With sex out of the question, our friendship has deepened, and Bright Eyes has been free to accept the overtures of others.

With a snort Chris is off. Bright shining Chris.

He is getting the measure of me. Forcing me to grow up.

52

MEANTIME, THINGS ARE not going well for Jack. I am help-less, watching as he accepts everything that The Slut dishes out. Warrick is a main chancer, spitting out his venom but every now and then sweetening it with a little bit of love and fairy dust. Just enough to keep Jack on line and besotted enough to accept the public abuse, masochistic cruelty, drug dealing and the turning of his life into a place where Warrick is master and Jack is servant.

Lately, I have heard rumours that Jack and Warrick no longer have sex. Instead, Warrick is bringing his tricks home. Living off Jack. Beating him up whenever he objects. Shunting him into a corner. Making of Jack's own home a steam parlour.

Then Jack telephones me, his voice wan.

'Old chap, could you possibly spare a moment to dine with me at lunch? Good. I shall meet you at The Teps.'

The Teps is an old Victorian building just beneath the motorway. It has been here since the early days of colonisation, when people preferred to swim in the comfort of warm saline broth than in the sea. Thousands upon thousands of city swimmers have since swum in one of the two pools. Ten years ago the complex was extended to steam room, sauna, spa and solarium. Now, a mezzanine floor has been built, encircling the whole building with gym, track, masseuse and healthetaria — one of those hideous word combina-tions to define a café that serves non-alcoholic beverages and veg-etarian mush.

The café at The Teps is overflowing with animation. From the doorway I can see past the entrance counter, beyond the glass partition, to the pool beneath. This is the Yuppie Hour, when the young hunks from the high-rise offices come to put in an hour at the pool. Tall and trim, capped and goggled, they plunge in and swim back and forward in the lanes. The under-surface lighting transforms them into green phosphorescent mermen.

'Over here,' Jack calls.

He has a table near the window. Dressed in suit and tie, with a white carnation in his lapel, he is oddly formal and disconcertingly radiant. Again I am struck by a feeling that we have met before. As I approach he stands and extends his hand. His grip is strong, then wavers. He motions me to sit.

'What will you have?' he asks.

The café doesn't serve alcohol so I name my usual aerated poison.

'You'll note, I hope,' he winks, 'that as usual I have chosen the position that affords the best possible views.'

I laugh, taking in the young men in the mezzanine gym, popping their muscles on the rowing machine. One of them is wearing very brief shorts, and every time he flexes his legs there is a tantalising glimpse of inner jockstrap and sweat-beaded thigh. Lunch hours are made of such fleeting joys.

'So,' Jack begins. 'I understand that restoration of the films has already begun. Splendid. Splendid. You know, Mother is taking this as a personal feather in her cap.'

'And so she should.'

'She has the University Committee eating out of her hands. It is not often that an investment of theirs pays back such a rich dividend.'

I look at him tenderly. 'Thank you, Jack. It would never have happened without your help and your mother's —'

'Gardening circle?'

We laugh together.

Our drinks arrive. I raise the glass to my eye, keeping it level with the pool, so that when a Young Thing dives the trick of perspective makes it appear that he splashes into my drink.

Then, 'So how about you?' I ask Jack.

A quiver quickly masked. 'I've been fine. But you know, of course, that Warrick and I aren't sleeping together any more.

Haven't been, in fact, for quite some time. It's hard with him now downstairs.'

'Why don't you just kick the fucker out.'

Jack flinches from my raised voice. 'Oh I couldn't. He's got nowhere else to go. And anyway, don't you realise that I adore him? I'd much rather have him in my life than not in my life.'

He looks toward the pool. Three guys are sitting on the side, chests heaving with exertion. Their wet Speedos accentuate the obvious, moulding the tuck, size, curve and dress.

'He's started to bring guys home.'

'So I've heard.'

'Dealing from the townhouse. When they haven't got enough cash, having sex with them. Sometimes he lets me have one or two, and he laughs and laughs and laughs —'

Raucous laughter splits the air. The three guys start pushing one another before sliding back into the pool.

'You've got to put a stop to it, Jack. Now, while you've still got the chance. Before you get —'

'Hooked? Addicted? Too late, old chap. Once on the fairy dust or a toke or a hit and it's so jolly hard to give it all up. So very jolly hard.'

Jack doesn't want to look at me. He is a soft, passive, ridiculous apology of humanity. I feel like I could backhand him right now and knock him out of his foolishness. But he starts to quiver and quake, and before I know it he is sobbing and the ocean in him is spilling out.

'Oh God, David —'

'Jack, listen. It's not too late. I know people who can help you. But, first of all, you've got to help yourself. You've got to get rid of him. I'll come over and help you throw him out. There are other fish —'

'For you, perhaps,' Jack interrupts. His voice is filled with terrible self-knowledge. 'But me?'

His eyes circle the room. At this moment all the young, the beautiful and the innocent of the world seem to be here, wearing their sexuality with insouciant carelessness. The Teps is the birthplace of innocence and idealised beauty beyond recall.

I try to lighten the mood. 'You're in a bad place, Jack. You've got to get out of it. It doesn't matter what you look like, there's—'

'Always someone who's into your type, yes, yes,' he says. Then, 'He treats me bad because he loves me.'

The bravado with which he says this makes me reach over and touch Jack's wrists. 'But —'

Jack straightens. 'You're right, David, and I still have my self-respect. And there's Mother's reputation and the family reputation to think of. So I have come to a decision to end it all before it gets any worse. Have done with it.'

Beyond the glass partition, a splash and crystal cascade of another diver fountaining into the pool.

Of course I should have realised that Jack did not mean what I thought he meant: that he had decided to end his relationship with Warrick. But he kept up such entertaining chatter over our lettuce leaf and tomato that his real meaning became hidden.

'Did you know,' he whispered, 'that The Teps is actually listed in *Spartacus*?'

I pretend innocence, saying, 'Our old Victorian swimming pool? In an international gay travellers' guide? Surely not.'

'Old chap, it's because of the showers here. The exhibitions. My God.'

Then, when he asked me to come by his townhouse at seven-thirty that evening, before Warrick got home, that too was a signal I didn't decipher. I thought he was taking up my offer to help him when he gave Warrick his marching orders.

'You're my best friend,' he said as we parted and shook hands. 'I can rely on you.'

I was embarrassed at that, because I had never really been as close to him as he to me. I had never realised that he felt so strongly about me.

When I stood up to leave, Jack told me he was going to stay at The Teps awhile.

'Don't ogle the boys too closely. You know that only leads to trouble,' I called.

He winked and waved a limp hand.

As I left, I thought I saw him making for the counter. He was framed for a moment, as if looking into some vast luminous aquarium. Mermen frolicked and played there, light dappling their thrusting, racing bodies with unattainable magic. His face was filled with delight and regret, for he was not a swimmer. He cupped his hands to his left ear as if he was holding a seashell, the better to hear the siren songs from that sunken world. The light from the pool dappled his face and, for a moment, he was transformed, made beautiful.

It was then that I thought I knew who he was, though it wasn't until I got to his townhouse that night, and saw his school tie and school photograph, that the penny dropped.

I left Jack around two in the afternoon. I know, now, that as soon as I left, he left also. In the next four hours he visited all his Gardens of Spain. Then went back home.

The police say Jack died just after seven o'clock. He made the final preparations, tidied the townhouse, wrote a note to me and another to Warrick and then had a bath. He had obviously been planning it for weeks. Everything was so immaculate and thought through. The suit he wanted to be buried in was on his bed. His will was on the desk in the hallway. He had taken an enema before having his bath so that, in his death throes, he would not soil his clothes or leave any mess. He had always been a fastidious person. Some last-minute nerves must have hit him, though. He had drained a bottle of whisky sometime between six forty-five and seven.

I like to think that Jack went out of this world as high as a kite. I can imagine him absolutely blotto, tripping over things and falling down the stairs to the spare room. There he has already slung the rope over a beam and placed a chair beneath it.

One hop.

Then another.

And he is standing on the chair like a rotund little rooster, reaching for the rope.

Settles it around like a neck tie.

Tallyho.

And

jump.

And

but itsnotsupposedto*hurt*.
And
snap.
Oh
Warrick.

I arrived right on the dot, half an hour later. The door was open
when I went to knock. The letter was propped up on the hallway
table beside an envelope enclosing his will.

'Don't come any further, old chap. Call the police. When
Warrick arrives at 8.30, please comfort him. Sorry about any
inconvenience.

'P.S. I have left the bulk of my estate to trustees. You are one of
them. Other bequests have been made to Film Studies, the rest of
the family and some personal gifts to friends. I am leaving a legacy,
including this townhouse, to Warrick. I know you never liked him
but he gave me all and more than any other person.'

He had left me a Picasso I had much admired.

Of course I didn't heed his instructions. I went from room to
room until I found him. He was not a pretty sight.

'You poor, stupid, pathetic sod,' I thought.

I didn't call the police straight away either. I waited until
Warrick came home with his latest supply and his trick for the
night. When Warrick asked for Jack I replied, 'He's downstairs.'

Why should Warrick have it easy, have it tidy for him? I prayed
that the sight of Jack swinging there would haunt him for the rest
of his life.

It was worth it just to hear him puke his guts out.

I pocketed the will too, but I should have realised that Jack's
lawyer would have the original. I hadn't wanted Warrick to benefit from a man he had driven to death. After all, isn't that what
best friends are for?

There was an inquiry of course. GAY SUICIDE, the tabloid
headlines screamed. The police visited The Teps and were told
that someone had seen him throwing a white carnation into the
pool. Others were questioned in steam parlours, saunas, jack-off
clubs, bondage rooms and bars, all Jack's beloved Gardens of
Spain. He had been a pale ghost, radiantly smiling from out of the

dark. Having been consumed by love, sex with strangers was no substitute. That's the trouble with love. Once you've experienced its highs and lows, and if your self-image is such that you don't believe you'll ever experience it again, there is no other course, really, except to self-destruct.

I went to the funeral service. It was High Church and filled with people, some I vaguely thought I knew, bankers, accountants, city men and women. We all have other lives. Fond tributes were paid to him, lying there in his coffin in the aisle, more accolades in death than he had probably ever had in life. I wanted to ask, 'Where were all you fine people when he needed your help?' But the question would only have hurtled back at me. 'Where were *you*, then?'

Warrick was there, playing the widow for all he was worth. He let out a stifled sob when the choir began to sing 'O For the Wings of a Dove'. He had already become famous in some of our circles as 'the one whom his partner committed suicide over'. As if he possessed some desirability, some fatal sexual technique that drove other men to their deaths. I had hoped that the police might find his drugs; he must have been tearing his hair out trying to hide them before the police arrived that night.

I vowed I would have the last laugh. If Warrick thought he was going to get more than the townhouse, he would have to think again. Over my dead body. As it was I already had it in mind to forestall settlement on the townhouse as long as possible and then only to drip-feed Warrick with promises of 'possibly more' for the rest of his life. Get him hooked on expectations and hopes in the same way as Jack had been. That was if the police didn't find out about him first.

I couldn't stand it all. I got up from my seat, paused in the aisle with bowed head, said a prayer for a man who had regarded me as his best friend, and left.

Oh yes. The letter he'd left me went on:

'Old chap, you never ever really knew did you! But you almost found me out today, I suspect. I'm glad you didn't. So let me confess that, yes, we knew each other many years ago. We shared the same dormitory for a little while. Once late at night I heard you crying. I held you in my arms. You also tried to defend me against bullies. I have never forgotten that. I shall never forget you, old chap. Sincerely. Jack. P.S. My real name is John, the same as my father's, but people here in Auckland have always called me Jack to distinguish between us. You knew me as John, John Jones, at St Crispin's.'

'*O Seigneur, entends ma prière.*'

I rushed to his bedroom. In his closet, the school tie.

'There, there. Shhh. Shhh.'

On the wall, a photograph of Saint Crispin's school choir.

'*Quand j'appelle, réponds-moi.*'

Choirboy.

53

AFTER JACK'S FUNERAL, at Film Studies. Brenda has a telephone call which makes her drop the receiver and give a cinematic scream. She comes barging into my office, takes my hand and pulls me down the stairs to the Film Studies theatrette.

'What's going on?' I ask.

Ronald and Stephen are waiting. What passes for excitement is written all across Ronald's dour Scottish face. Bright Eyes is in on the secret too. He keeps running his hands through his hair.

'Take a seat, laddie. Take a seat.'

Stephen gets the lights. Brenda sits next to me. On the other side, Bright Eyes grins as Ronald starts the projector.

'We've been working all day and all night on the first film and, just this morning, we have a print. It's not perfect, we still have to iron out some problems with the computer program, but sit down, laddie, and watch.'

The lights go down. The screen starts to flicker. All of a sudden images start to jerk to life. Old black and white film has a magic which, when released on screen, is overpowering in its simplicity and truth.

Hopi Indians have been filmed at a secret ceremony. They are dancing in the hot sun. Beating drums. Feet stamping the desert sand. There is a closeup of a Medicine Man cupping his voice and calling soundlessly into the desert. Something begins to move out there. Like a flood across the sand. Glistening. Dissolving into thousands of snakes. Being called into the dance. Hastening now into the circle. Black. Striped. Mottled. Being taken up by the dancing Indians. Draped around necks. Held. Kissed. The communion of serpent and man. Joining in the dance of life and death. As it must have been once in Eden. Before we placed our heel on the serpent's head.

The film flickers and dies. Ronald is there looking hopefully into my eyes.

'So what do you think, laddie?'

I wish we could turn back time. God, I wish we could regain that awesome innocence of Eden. Why did the sons of Adam have to go and stuff it all up? Why?

My heart is bursting with ecstasy and tears. Ecstasy because of the terrible beauty of the film and tears because —

'Laddie?'

I nod my head. Give him the thumbs-up.

He punches the air.

Oh, Jack, do you know *why*?

54

THREE WEEKS LATER. Something is happening in Annabelle's life. Whenever I go to The House On The Hill to pick up the girls she is bright-eyed, sparkling and full of giggles. She's had painters through and redesigned the living room. She also seems to have reconstructed herself. Going to the gym, working out and involving herself with friends and in the world is transforming her. She is emerging from the long chrysalis of grief.

This metamorphosis does not go unnoticed. Whenever the girls and I are shunted out to 'Have a nice day', Rebecca rolls her eyes and compresses her lips. Who would want to have parents.

'It's Barry,' Miranda says one afternoon.

We are having ice cream. Lick, curl, sniff. Rebecca shoots a warning glance. But Miranda, who is angling for another ice cream, decides to bargain.

'May I have another, Daddy?'

No more information unless more ice cream. Deal?

'Okay,' I say.

Miranda wants possession of the cone first. Then:

'So who's Barry!'

'Mummy's aerobics instructor.'

Jesus.

'You weren't in mourning for long,' I say to Annabelle in tones slightly edged with sarcasm.

'Which of the girls was it!' Annabelle gives a mock scream. 'It was Rebecca, wasn't it! She dobbed me in, didn't she? There's something going on in that girl's head. I shall have to talk to her about it.'

'No, it was Miranda.'

'Miranda? Oh well, I suppose you would have found out soon enough. Better now I suppose.'

'Yes. But. An aerobics instructor?'

'Is that what Miranda told you?' Annabelle laughs.

'Isn't that what he does?'

'Oh no. He works at the gym. He's my hairdresser.'

Even worse. Then Annabelle starts to giggle. I throw a cushion at her.

'You always did have a wicked sense of humour,' I say. 'So. What does he really do?'

'Well, he *is* an aerobics instructor,' Annabelle confirms. 'But that's only part time. During the day he works.'

'Will this get worse or better?'

'At the City Council.'

'Worse. Sanitation? Or is he a lawn manicurist?'

'No,' she laughs. 'He's an engineer.'

'Better. When will I meet him?'

Shadows dance across Annabelle's eyes. She asks, 'What's it to you? Do I have to get your permission? Your approval? You're out of my life now. Out.'

At the door I go to peck her cheek.

'Oh no you don't,' she says.

And closes the door.

The next weekend the girls and I are on our usual visit to my parents. Annabelle telephones and says that she feels like another walk along the Crocodile's Tail. Would we like to meet her there?

When we arrive, Annabelle is already on the highest part of the Crocodile's Tail, looking out to an opalescent sea. Rebecca and Miranda dash off by themselves to collect coloured glass worn to softness by the waves.

'Hi,' I call.

Annabelle waves back and when I am near I can see that her eyes are flecked with a sad radiance.

'Isn't it a lovely day for a walk in the sun?' she asks.

The girls are screaming with delight, fossicking and discovering the jewels that the sea has made. Annabelle chatters on for a moment, recovering. Then she threads an arm into mine and leans into me.

'I think the next great love of my life is about to begin.'

From afar, Rebecca is watching us. She has always loved the Crocodile's Tail with its memories of being a family.

'Barry?'

'Yes.'

So, after George, Michael and William, other dates of Annabelle's, this is the one that won't go away.

'I'm glad.'

But the truth is, I'm not. I feel desolate. I want Annabelle to be happy, but there is a part of me which wants her to love me all the time. Which dislikes the idea of her going on to another man. Even so, I know that this must be the way.

'You're much too wonderful to live all alone. You deserve to be happy.'

'He loves the kids.'

'And does he love you?'

'I think so.'

For some reason my desolation makes me bitter. Perhaps it has something to do with the grey sky and skirling seagulls. Or with the foaming sea.

'And is he good in bed?'

Annabelle stares at me. Uncomprehending.

'God, you're a shit sometimes.'

Instantly I feel ashamed. 'I'm sorry.'

'That's not good enough,' Annabelle answers, spirited. 'You walked out on me, you bastard. You damaged me. I'm not looking for sex. That might be what men do when they are looking for a substitute for the little wifey they've just discarded. But that's not what women want. Do you know how difficult it is for me to even think of having another man in my life? Do you? I won't have you thinking of any relationship I might get into in *your* terms.'

She is facing me now, strong and determined. Her voice rises to disturb seagulls. They clatter and shrill above us. The girls are running to join us.

'Daddy! Daddy!' Miranda cries. 'We've found lots and lots of blue glass!' The precious ones. The ones that are difficult to find.

'I want you to be happy for me. Are you?'

'I —'

'Please, David.'

She wants my blessing. Why is it so hard to give?

'Oh Annabelle.' Let her go. 'Yes. Of course. Be happy.'

With a sigh, Annabelle moves into my arms and, for the first time for a long time, we are able to hold each other without confusion. And in my mind, all in an instant, I see pictures of our life together like a film unfolding.

People say that this is what happens just before you die, too. This unfolding of memories.

Another weekend and I am dropping the kids back to Annabelle again. Through the glass door I see she has a visitor. When I ring the bell Annabelle starts. She floats before the door, fingers combing back her hair. She is flushed and preoccupied.

'Aren't you guys back early?' she asks.

She bends down to hug Miranda. But Miranda has seen the visitor. Trackpants. Sweatshirt. Sweat stains at the armpits. Strong build. Black wavy hair. Casual authority. Getting up from the table. Taking a few steps.

'Barry!' Miranda calls. She runs towards him to be thrown into the air and caught.

'Hi there, Button.'

Button. My Miranda, defecting already. Button.

''Scuse me,' Rebecca says. She kisses me. 'Bye, Daddy.' She glares at Annabelle and runs up the stairs to her room. Slam.

Helpless, Annabelle stands there. However, unlike the old days it is not to me that she looks for support but to this other man who puts Miranda down and says to her, 'Why don't you go upstairs?'

Then he comes towards us both, Annabelle and myself. He slips an arm around Annabelle and she closes her eyes and leans against him. He will not be compartmentalised. He in one box, and me and the girls in another. He looks at me and nods.

'You've got fine daughters,' he says. Then he extends his hand, 'The name's Barry.'

'Yes. I know.'

And so it is done.

By me, this formal relinquishing of possession. By Annabelle, this acceptance of a new emotional contract. By the new man, this taking on of a woman and her children.

'Do you have time for coffee?' Annabelle asks.

'Another time.'

I turn to go and, this time, it is Annabelle who pecks my cheek.

After that, the city becomes so small. Wherever I turn I see them. Annabelle and Barry laughing in a restaurant. Or munching popcorn during the interval of a movie. Or at the market with the girls, Miranda hoisted high on Barry's shoulders. Or driving past on the way to the beach. Laughing. Sunny. Smiling. Playing Happy Family. The way it is supposed to be.

I guess this is how Annabelle must have felt whenever she saw me with Chris.

Sometimes, there are sadnesses. The girls, particularly, want to feel secure. Rebecca rings every day now.

'Daddy? Daddy? When are you coming to pick us up again? Can Mummy come with us when we go out?'

As if she already knows that Barry will change our lives.

One night, when we are all at the house together, Miranda asks me, 'You'll always be my Daddy, won't you?' Her eyes dart from me to Annabelle to Barry.

'Yes, of course he will,' Barry says.

'You'll have two Daddies,' Annabelle says. Then instantly wishes she could cut off her tongue. But Barry just laughs.

Rebecca is beyond persuasion. 'All I've *ever* wanted is one Daddy,' she says. Her lip trembles. Her eyes imprison mine with her accusation.

Barry is becoming a permanent fixture. Friends and family are realigning themselves to accommodate the succession. Annabelle has arisen victorious. It is all the better that the new Prince Charming is not an ugly frog but some virile, vigorous, undoubtedly heterosexual male.

Our divorce comes through. In court the agreement is signed, sealed and delivered. Clean, antiseptic, painless. Annabelle is looking beautiful but wan. She has asked Barry not to come to court. My parents are at home minding the girls.

'Now take me home, sport.'

It starts as soon as we are in the car. We sob like two adolescent kids for all the dreams we once had, all the future that we had planned. At the house, we tell the girls that it is done.

Rebecca takes Miranda's hand and walks up the stairs. Then, at the landing, she turns. Her eyes dilate with anger and, before I know it, she comes screaming upon me, beating at me and flailing me with her fists.

'When we went on the Crocodile's Tail I saw you and Mummy hugging. I don't understand, Daddy. I don't understand.'

'Let it out, darling. Let it all out.'

There are no longer stones in my mouth. It is time for me to be strong. To take the responsibility. Not Annabelle. Me.

'Why are you *doing* this to us, Daddy? Daddy? *Daddy?*'

Miranda is sobbing. 'Becca,' she calls. 'Becca —'

'Why are you *doing* this to us, Mummy?'

Screaming, hitting, kicking, head going snap snap snap. Then, suddenly, Rebecca is still. She walks back up the stairs. Takes Miranda by the hand. 'There, there, Miranda, darling.' Dries her sister's tears.

Shuts their bedroom door.

'So. Barry's asked you to marry him?'

'Yes. But right now I could do without men.'

'You can't cope by yourself.'

'Oh no? You just try me, sport. Now get *out*.'

Part Seven

SHIP OF DREAMS

55

THE WORLD WILL never be the same again. Although divorce has set me free to be what I want, the price has been paid in pain. For the phoenix to hatch, does it always have to be like this?

I have decided to stop going to The Steam Parlour. It was always part of the freedom I sought, but I have discovered there is a world beyond. I have to find it and my place in it. Acknowledging that I am gay is just a start. *Being* gay is something else. It is not just about sex or having sex. It's about being a whole person.

Time to start looking.

And so I come for the last time to The Steam Parlour to say my farewells to Fat Forty And A Fairy and Always A Bridesmaid.

Night and rain. The street is busy with buses and traffic. Headlights pop like flashlights: Gotcha. The anonymous black door. Through and up the stairway.

LET US STEAM CLEAN YOUR BODY.

The hatch slides open. The Spaniard's face appears. He watches as I ascend. Grinning. Gold tooth flashing. Earring glittering in dyed black hair.

The Spaniard signs me in, hands me a towel. I walk with it

through the familiar vestibule, wall-to-wall tackiness, and into the locker room. Marc smiles a greeting but is puzzled when I do not get undressed.

'Not staying?' he asks.

I shake my head. I go past the posters, the cutesy Cuzzy Bro Cock pulling on his raincoat and the signs: SO MANY MEN, SO LITTLE TIME. Through the Stygian gloom of the television lounge to take one last look at the shower room.

The room is small and octagonal. The showers are silver stalks and each shower nozzle is like a metallic rose. One bar of soap. Three Rough Boys sharing the soap. Looking up at me, questioning, inviting. To the left of the shower room is the corridor leading to the cubicles and bunk room beyond. And there is the door to the steam room itself.

Who knows who will come through the door? Someone youthful, bringing hope. Someone strong, someone handsome, someone pliant, someone shining, someone succulent.

Someone.

Anyone.

The shower room is like a crossroad. And suddenly I see my reflection shooting off the glistening octagonal walls like a steel honeycomb. The uneven planes make my face sphinx-like, shimmering and remote.

What is it that walks on four legs in the morning, two legs in the heat of the noonday sun and three legs in the evening?

There they are. The two eternal boatmen, looking up at me. And, already, they know.

'Oh, we shall miss you,' Fat Forty And A Fairy sighs. 'The displays you've given us. A legend in your own lifetime. My God, the exhibitions —'

'Ride 'em cowboy,' Always A Bridesmaid remembers.

'Toss you for him,' Fat Forty And A Fairy continues.

'Swinging in the rain,' they say together.

They are a Laurel and Hardy duo, tapdancing on my memories. They laugh and laugh.

'You'll tell the others I said goodbye?' I ask.

They nod and give me benediction. Then:

'Now go, David. Now, before it's too late. And don't look back. Don't. Look. Back —'

Out, out, out.

Someone is coming up the stairway. Unsure. Smiling. I step past him. He looks so familiar. He could be me. If I ever saw myself I wouldn't recognise myself.

The hatch opens behind me. The Spaniard always knows —

I hear the stranger say, 'I rang earlier —'

Don't look back.

Later. Ringing Chris.

His sleepy voice answers the telephone. He is still on tour at a small town out the back of beyond.

'Hello?'

Get the words out. I have decided that I want to give this relationship with him the best shot.

'I love you, Chris.'

He pauses. 'Do you know what time it is? Three o'clock in the bloody morning! Are you ill? Drunk? Has the apartment burnt down? Are the girls all right?'

'I just telephoned to say I love you.'

There is a long pause. Then Chris gives a delicious, contented sigh.

'Well, it's about *time*.'

Click.

56

A WEEK LATER. Tonight is the Hero Party, the annual celebration of gay culture. Chris is back from his tour and is appearing in the huge spectacular that will close the show. He is secretive about his role and has not allowed me to go to the rehearsals.

The overseas terminal has been turned into a huge dance floor for the party. At one end a staircase has been built for the show. Four thousand gay men and lesbians have come to party and affirm the heroism of being gay. In street wear, carnival costume, leather wear, fantasy dresses, jock straps, tee-shirts and jeans, or hardly anything at all, they pack the overseas terminal with their sass, sexiness, outrageousness and bravado. Above, searchlights are slicing the sky like the 20th Century Fox logo. Inside the venue, lasers twist and refract, bend and warp into surreal rainbows of light.

Among the crowd are familiar faces and friends: Wet Dream Walking, Born To Boogie, The Bald One, Italian Stallion, Bright Eyes with a boyfriend, Left Dress. Gay men, lesbians and supporters.

Go well, Bright Eyes.

Suddenly the dance music stops. The show begins. And there, standing at the topmost tier, is The Noble Savage, back briefly in the city, with his group of proud Maori and Polynesian gay men and women. They are calling in the way of their people, the women sending out a proud cry above where we stand and cheer, the men gesticulating in a war dance, moving down and chanting:

Make way, we are a new tribe. We are coming through.

Then a hush. Dry ice starts to billow from the ceiling. The

lasers begin to focus on one place amid the cloud. They twist and glitter there, where a trapeze descends. Standing on the trapeze is a beautiful angel.

He is a gorgeous young man with huge feathered wings, wearing only a diamante jockstrap. At his appearance, the crowd roars with ecstasy. Chris, arms outstretched.

Suddenly the trapeze disintegrates in a shower of glitter.

Someone screams.

But the angel is still there, suspended on invisible wire. To the haunting music of Enigma, he begins to execute slow choreographed acrobatics, his white wings folding and unfolding as he twists and tumbles and circles in muscular beauty.

Everyone begins to reach up for him. He is anything we want him to be. He is everything we want him to be. He is whatever we wish ourselves to become.

Chris, a radiant angel, an icon of hope.

At the Hero Party I am among my kind and this is where I want to be. All these brave gay men and lesbian women, all seeking a brave new world. But that world is not waiting for us. This, too, I have learnt since the divorce. Nothing is *waiting* for us. We have to go out and claim a space and build it.

That is the way when the phoenix is born.

57

I CANNOT STOP the habit. I have come away from the party to drive up a moonlit street to The House On The Hill. Something wicked might come this way. Something evil, something harmful with jagged teeth. Something bearing a red apple or poisoned needle to put my princesses to sleep.

There is a light in the bedroom I shared with Annabelle. Barry's car is in the drive.

Annabelle is right of course. This has got to stop. This driving across the city to watch the house where my little princesses live. Watching from the darkened street, guarding them while they dream, just in case.

I must let that Ship of Lost Dreams go, watch the sails unfurl with moonlight, and bid God speed as it sets its course to that second star on the right. They must go their way and I must go mine.

Suddenly, a pencil of light. In the girls' bedroom Miranda is awake, shining her torch. Her bedside light snaps on and there she is, framed in the window, looking down at me.

I step out of the car. I look up. Miranda turns away and I know that she is waking Rebecca. Then they are both there. Watching. I lift a finger to my lips: Sssssh, don't wake Mummy. They nod. Then, slowly I point at myself.

I.

Pressing my heart with both hands.

Love.

Pointing at them, opening my arms to them.

You.

I blow a kiss. Miranda watches it coming, reaches for it and catches it. She blows a kiss back, one which I have to reach very high for but, once caught, I safely tuck it into my pocket.

Then Rebecca is talking to Miranda who is starting to look tearful, rubbing her eyes with her little fist. Rebecca hugs her sister and, trying not to make too much noise, lifts the window slightly open.

'Please, Daddy, go home.'

Miranda is still shaking her head.

'Wait, Daddy, wait.'

She disappears. When she comes back to the window her tears have dried and she is grinning. In her hand she has that silly, stupid wand, and she is waving it like mad.

Waving, waving, waving.

I step back into the car.

The night tides are swelling. The sails on the Ship of Dreams snap and bell into fullness, making it a shining fairy galleon spun of dreams and laughter tossed on stormy seas. All that is needed is Tinkerbell to sprinkle fairy dust so that it can fly, someone to weigh anchor, a strong hand and —

And Rebecca and Miranda have come aboard. Rebecca has Miranda by the hand. She takes a deep breath and says:

Daddy has his life. Mummy has hers.

I'm frightened, Becca, frightened.

Don't be afraid, darling, because you and I still have each other. We will always have each other.

Then:

Come, Miranda.

When I look back their little ship has already weighed anchor, already on course for the stars. Two brave little girls are at the helm.

Oh Rebecca, you must hold Miranda *very* tight. And, my darlings, among all those millions of stars you could get lost, so listen:

It's the second star from the right. Can you see it now? That's the one, yes! So hold the wheel on course now. Hold steady.

But, once you've reached that star there's still such a long way

to go and it is so dark out there. So listen to Daddy:
  You must go straight on till morning, darlings.
  Straight on till morning.

Author's Note

THIS IS THE second version of *Nights in the Gardens of Spain*. It was written between 27 September and 6 November 1993, while I was the Katherine Mansfield Fellow in Menton, France. My thanks are due to the Katherine Mansfield Trust, the Electricity Corporation of New Zealand, the New Zealand France Association and all those friends who supported me with love, in particular Leni Spencer, Terry Goldie, Te Whanau Pani Thompson, Murray Grimsdale and Stephen Acott, who were with me in Menton during this period. Professor Albert Wendt and the English Department of the University of Auckland granted leave to enable me to take up the Fellowship. Jane Parkin edited the manuscript. Linda Pears checked for accuracy.

The original, more explicit and ruthless version of *Nights in the Gardens of Spain* was written in November–December 1991. It postdates an earlier manuscript called *A Walk in the Sun*, on a similar theme, which I destroyed in 1984, but for which the notes still exist; I may yet return to it. The first version of *Nights* is held in the Literary Archives, Library, Victoria University of Wellington, New Zealand, where all my papers are held under an agreement sponsored by INL Limited. My thanks to Vincent O'Sullivan of the English Department, Vic Elliott, VUW librarian, and Mike Robson of the *Evening Post* for making this possible. There are strict reading conditions.